Fair Trade

MILLIE PEREZ

For those who need a gentle reminder:
You don't have to sacrifice your softness to be strong.

Luisa

AUTHOR'S NOTE

Hello lovely readers and welcome back to the world of the New York Monarchs.

This is the second book in an interconnected series, and I am so excited and cannot wait for you to dive into these new characters. I have included aspects of my personal journey with Polycystic Ovary Syndrome (PCOS) and concerns about fertility with our lead character, Luisa. I know that many of us with PCOS have very different experiences, but I hope that I have handled these discussions with the care that they deserve. And I hope a few of you feel seen, too.

If you can't get enough of Nick and Luisa or the New York Monarchs, I've added a special treat at the end of the book. A sneak peek of the next couple that come after Fair Trade, which I'm super excited about!

Below are some content warnings. Please take them into account before reading this story to ensure an enjoyable experience.

Happy Reading!

xo,
Millie

CONTENT WARNINGS

Mention of death of a parent (off page)

Discussions about a parental figure with depression

Discussions about PCOS

Brief mention about a parents' experience with secondary infertility

Open door spice with explicit sex scenes

LUISA

WHAT. HAVE. I. DONE?

I take a deep breath and try to fool myself into believing that it's normal to hear my heart beating out of my chest.

Stupid, stupid, stupid.

I punctuate each word by slapping my hands against the marble countertop of the immaculate half bathroom I'm currently hiding in.

Like a coward.

Stalling seems to be the only play left for me. So I do whatever I can to keep myself distracted from what's waiting for me behind the locked door.

The steady sounds of a growing crowd that have kept my racing heart company have come to a halt, and suddenly, all I can hear is *him*.

Shit, shit, shit.

I'm running out of time to come up with an escape plan. And honestly, it's futile, since there is no running from what I've done.

My ambition has blitzed my sense of reason, because surely there was another way out of this predicament without having to take such drastic measures.

His voice booms louder, yet my mind still struggles to comprehend how I got here.

Here, as in, hiding in a billionaire's bathroom at *my* wedding reception.

Facing the inevitable, I finally allow myself to look into the mirror that's been taunting me since the hair and makeup glam squad released me from their prickly fingers.

But instead of a blushing bride, I'm met with the reflection of a woman who is clearly unhinged.

Certifiable.

In need of the nearest padded room.

Because no woman in her right mind would sign a marriage certificate, lawfully binding herself to a man she can barely stand being in the same room with.

I mean, sure. I had my reasons for signing on the dotted line. But as I stare at my fitted white pantsuit, because like hell was I wearing an actual wedding dress to this sham, I can't seem to figure out how I ended up married to the man who has been the bane of my existence for the past six months.

A man who has managed to get under my skin and take up residence in my mind. Specifically, the murderous part of my brain that wonders if twenty-five-to-life is really worth it.

The man who is the current owner of the New York Monarchs. The team I manage. Which technically makes him my boss.

Donned "hottest Black billionaire" by any magazine that has a decent spot on New York newsstands.

And last, my friend's older brother, who must have been adopted, because there is no way that our sweet Daisy and that man share DNA.

The egocentric, conceited, and—it pains me to say—devastatingly handsome Nick Stonehaven.

As if my thoughts summoned him, I hear two hard knocks and realize that my spiral session has officially come to an end. I unlock the door and brace myself for his arrogant smile. Instead, I am taken aback by the white tuxedo jacket perfectly tailored to his broad shoulders and muscular biceps. The look is completed with a black dress shirt with pearly buttons in the same color. As well as his coordinating black pants and shiny shoes.

When our gazes lock, I am momentarily stunned to be met with warm eyes. They search mine before doing a quick sweep of my look, from head to toe. But clearly, I must have been imagining it, because that smug smile that I've become so acquainted with makes a swift return.

With more confidence than any one human should ever hope to possess, he leans in and kisses my cheek.

There's no one watching us, and the deal clearly states that we only need to be affectionate in public. I move to lean back and remind him of this fact when he gently grabs my hand and threads our fingers together.

His touch brings back a flurry of memories. To a brief time when things were much simpler. When I was just a woman at a bar, and he was meant to be forever a stranger. A fond memory at most.

He must be a mind reader, as well as my personal shit disturber, because he simply smiles as he leans in and whispers in my ear. "C'mon now. It's showtime, *wife*."

Chapter One

LUISA

Six months ago

I should go home.

The day has been long enough as it is. But I can't seem to peel myself off my barstool while aimlessly stirring my untouched dirty martini.

I thought a stiff cocktail would make me feel as though I was just a normal New Yorker having an overpriced drink at a fancy hotel bar instead of someone who'd left her boss's wake.

God, I can't believe he's dead.

Arthur Stonehaven, owner of the New York Monarchs and the man who single-handedly changed my life by offering me a dream job as general manager of a New York major league baseball team, passed away in his home in the UK. His granddaughter, Daisy, asked that his friends stateside come together to memorialize him today.

It feels odd to grieve for a person I'd barely known. Even weirder when it was made quite evident that Daisy herself hardly knew the man she was honoring. It wasn't the ideal way to finally meet her in person, seeing her standing in front of a small crowd, alone, attempting to come up with nice words for her estranged grandfather.

I don't know why I thought jumping in would be a good idea. Not like I had much more to add to the already awkward welcome speech turned eulogy. But my less than graceful ramblings got the attention off her, and the grateful look in Daisy's eyes was well worth it.

After, she mentioned she might be able to get me a meeting with the new team owner on Monday, and I'd take any chance I could get to make a good first impression on my new boss.

But tonight, it's not about work. Tonight is about treating myself. I've spent my whole life aspiring to be half as successful as I am now, and I need a second to myself before my life becomes unrecognizable.

The fact that I'm even allowed the luxury to mope over a thirty-dollar cocktail is an achievement in itself. Waltzing into the glitzy hotel I only ever dared to look at from the street corner while growing up in the city was never part of the plan tonight. But walking straight up to the hotel lounge, picking a stool in the center of the bar, and ordering a drink without even looking at the price made it feel like I was finally living in the New York City that only blond, white women on TV and movies experience.

Not Dominican girls from Harlem.

Though, if I'm honest, the overall vibe so far has been a bit lacking. The soft jazz playing on a loop is putting me to sleep more easily than my melatonin can. The actual bar is smaller than I anticipated for a hotel so grand. And the company in this place is nothing like the neighborhood spots I've always frequented.

I won't run into anyone I know here. Which is a bit alluring on my last night of living a somewhat normal life. But it is weird that there will be no sudden appearance of a random cousin, blood related or otherwise, or any of the ladies who blow dry my hair on 125th Street, and I certainly won't be bumping into any of the usual guys I date.

The guys I *dated*, because I've just signed a million-dollar deal to become the first female general manager in the MLB, and my new schedule, which includes traveling with the team, will assure that there will be zero time for dating.

Not like my love life was thriving *before* Arthur made me an offer no one in their right mind would turn down, one that ensures I'm about to be thrust into the spotlight.

Our season is about to start, and there is no chance I'll allow anything to stand in the way of my focus.

Unfortunately, that memo has yet to be sent to the men at this bar. I try to look completely enthralled by the three olives in my drink while expertly avoiding the eye contact of the man a few stools to my right who's been trying to get my attention all night. I'm surprised he's still trying after I turned two of his friends away.

He moves in my periphery, but one can hope that he's making his way to the exit.

"Hey, I'm sorry to interrupt—"

Ugh, bachelor number three is up to bat, I guess.

"—but I wanted to ask if I could buy you a drink." He slips into the space between me and the next barstool over as he leans a forearm on the bar and offers an overly cocky grin that I'm sure has served him well in the past.

One day I'm the coach for the women's softball team at the local community college, and the next I'm wondering if my *Hannah Montana* cover has already been blown.

Did he read my GM announcement in the paper last week? Or see the *Sports Illustrated* cover I posed for in a hot pink pantsuit? Is he a Monarchs fan? Or perhaps a plain run-of-the-mill finance bro?

I don't know why I even bother asking myself these questions. Even if he were the man of my dreams, handwritten by the creators of my favorite rom-com movies, it still wouldn't matter.

Because as soon as I signed my seven-figure contract, I became married to my job, and happily so.

Although I'll have to figure out what I'm going to do about sex.

Because I'll be damned if I accidentally force myself into a vow of celibacy before my thirtieth birthday.

Because I love sex.

I really do. I just don't love the men I have to deal with in order to get an orgasm that isn't delivered by a sex toy.

My ex-boyfriends never understood that I liked it rough in the bedroom. Ignored me when I asked for dirty talk, instead whispering sweet nothings as if I were a delicate flower. But there's nothing fragile about me.

Because when it comes to sex, I want to be railed. Give it as good as I get and ride them like it's my first *and* last rodeo. Instead, I'd end up on my back like a starfish, watching them get overexerted by missionary.

I quickly learned that I'd have to get myself off once they were about to come... before even attempting to make sure I got there first.

And somehow, even after my less than stellar experiences, I still loved dick. But I haven't found the right one. The one attached to a man who will speak the filthiest words in my ear while pushing me to my breaking point.

If only it were that easy.

I've only had sex with men I dated, too chickenshit to entertain the idea of a one-night stand.

But now, as I look toward the exit that opens up to the fancy hotel lobby, I can't help but picture going upstairs with a stranger and getting exactly what I want without all the pretenses. Being well and truly fucked without having to endure the mutual half-assed attempts to meet up for drinks or dinner later in the week when we'd both rather to skip to the part where we're naked and sated.

The more I think about it, the more I believe this might be exactly what I need. So I decide to give the generically attractive man before me a long perusal, reevaluating him under a different lens.

A clearing of a throat reminds me that I have yet to respond to bachelor number three.

"As you can see, I already have a drink." I smile softly as I point to my full martini.

"Ah, yeah, but it seems like a crime for a woman like you to be sitting alone at a bar." His eyes drop to my conservative cleavage, eyes straining as if he can somehow conjure x-ray vision.

I suppress an eye roll at his lack of discretion.

You're trying to get laid, not swept off your feet, I quickly remind myself.

Before I can respond, he continues. "You know what?" He knocks on the bar once and waves down the bartender, who is currently drying a wine glass. "Bring us something fruity, like a sangria," He winks at me. "And a tequila, neat."

The bartender and I share a look, as if saying *can you believe this guy?*

I immediately decide that I like her and will be leaving her a hefty tip.

It takes superhuman strength to control my facial expressions now. Because not only do I loathe when a man orders on my behalf without consulting me first, but I absolutely hate the fact that this man thought ordering me a sugary drink was the way to go.

One, because he didn't clock that I was already drinking hard liquor, so he clearly hasn't taken a moment to think of what *I* would actually like to drink. If he pays no attention to detail, how can I trust him to read my body while we're having sex?

Second, I prefer to *eat* sugary snacks, not drink them in my alcohol, since I have polycystic ovary syndrome. Unlike my cousins, my PCOS is mild for the most part, but put me in a room with a carb, and it'll try and find a way to sweet talk itself onto my hips.

But you would have to pry Dominican birthday cake out of my cold, dead hands if you think I would ever give that up.

And third, it's abundantly clear that he believes I would enjoy a "girly" drink because, well, I'm a woman.

That might not strike some as a big deal, but as a woman who is currently entering an extremely male-dominated field, yeah, I'm going to have feelings about that.

Orgasms, Luisa. There's still a good chance he might know how to find a clit.

Maybe. Possibly. I think to myself as the bartender places the sangria in front of us and pulls out a short glass for the tequila.

I muster up the fake smile I reserve for the older white men who love to call me *little lady* and don't miss the opportunity to point out how I'm usually the only woman in the room, and ask, "So, do I get a name, or are you only here to offer drink suggestions?"

He leans in as the glass of tequila is gently placed next to the sangria. "The name's Tucker." He leans even closer, whispering the next part. "And you are Luisa Álvarez, a real ball buster." He grins. "I mean, to enter the big boys' club over at the Monarchs..." He whistles low. "I can only imagine the things you can do." His tongue swipes the top row of his expensive veneers as the poorly veiled insinuation settles into my bones.

Won't be the first or last time someone accuses you of sleeping your way to the top, girl, so buckle the fuck up.

I lean back, reaching for our drinks. He follows my lead, only to stop short as he sees me grab the tequila. Confusion mars his face as I take a long, sensual sip of the smooth drink, never breaking eye contact. "Well, Tucker, you got one thing right." I pierce him with the same icy glare only a woman constantly questioned and harassed while working in the sports industry could master. "You can *only* imagine the things I can do. And if you don't walk away in the next five seconds, you'll get to see first-hand how much of a *ball buster* I can be."

He falters for a moment, looking for a way to backpedal, I'm sure, but I don't give him the chance.

I make eye contact with the bartender as I say, "Put his fruity drink on my tab." She grins in my direction and nods before sending him a dry look.

Slack-jawed, he stares at me. The turn of events might be too much for his peanut brain, because he hasn't moved a muscle. I roll my eyes—*ah, that feels good*—and straighten in my stool as I face the bar. He shakes his head, probably trying to bounce his two brain cells together to form a sentence, but I'm over this interaction.

Good thing I always leave my vibrator charged.

I lift the tasty tequila to my lips as I lock eyes with him for what I hope will be the last time ever. "Hey, Tucker?"

"Ah, um, yeah?" He blinks.

"Get fucked." I nod my head toward the exit and take another sip, keeping all my focus on my drink while ignoring the low mutters of "sorry" and "but you didn't need to be such a bitch."

Again, nothing I haven't heard before.

The bartender—Jess, according to her name tag—stops in front of me and laughs. "Damn, that was satisfying to watch. Can you stay for the rest of my shift and do that a few more times, please?" she pleads, batting her eyelashes.

I tilt my head from side to side. "Tempting, but it's probably not a good idea to loiter at a hotel bar." I wiggle the glass in my hand. "A few more of these, and I might turn this fine establishment into a titty bar."

A choking cough breaks out at the other side of the bar. We both look at the man who was most likely eavesdropping on us and didn't see my boob joke coming.

Whoops.

When he lifts his gaze and gives us a soft "My apologies," I almost forget to breathe.

Jesucristo.

That man is the embodiment of sex on a stick without the weird porno vibes. And did I detect an accent? Because accents make you 15 percent hotter. I don't make the rules. *Actually, yes. I just did.*

Short, black hair, upkept by a neat fade. With an expertly trimmed, barely there beard framing his chiseled face. His glass of amber liquid seems five sizes too small in his large hands. Decadent brown skin that seems kissed by the Caribbean sun shining over my loved ones in the Dominican Republic or a nearby island.

He must be older than me, but I'm guessing not by much.

Muscles pushing his well-tailored suit to its limits.

And even though he's sitting, there is no question this man is well over six feet. Something a woman like me can appreciate, since I'm five nine and apparently a giant compared to all the petite women in my family.

I shake my head, reminding myself that I am officially off this ludicrous merry-go-round of entertaining cocky men for the night, and tear my gaze away from the man I'm sure is the star of many wet dreams.

Maybe he's an actor or something?

"Jess, I'm going to call it a night. Can I get the bill when you get a minute?" I ask as I try to keep my eyes from veering back to the gorgeous stranger.

Jess smirks while taking an innocent tone. "It would bring me no greater pleasure than to comp your drinks for the night, but unfortunately, your tab has already been taken care of."

I raise a confused brow, and she nods at our sexy eavesdropper.

I inwardly groan as I scold my rising libido.

No. We do not need to accept free drinks from sexy strangers, I quickly remind myself.

I begrudgingly look in his direction, for the essential reason of letting him know that I can pay for my own drinks, only to find his amused gaze already on me.

I open my mouth to speak, but he lifts his hand and beats me to it.

"You don't have to show me your tits," he says with a straight face.

I'm momentarily stunned into silence.

What in the ever-loving fuck? "Excuse me?" I ask incredulously.

He smirks, then sighs dramatically. "Well, now that you've given away the fact that all it takes is a few tequilas to set those puppies free, I guess the mystery is gone." He attempts to hide his grin behind his drink before taking a sip.

Wait. Is he...?

"You—You're fucking with me. I think?" I let out a dry laugh.

He rolls his eyes playfully. "Lady, I'm not fucking you either. God, what ever happened to the art of dinner and a movie?"

A zap of energy runs up my spine at his cheeky banter. Something I never see enough of lately with city boys. And now I'm certain I've picked up a slight British accent, which is doing my panties no favors.

I point at myself. "No. No, you see. You've got this all wrong. I'm not fucking *you*. Which is why there is no need for you to pay for my drinks. I've got it handled." I drain what's left of my drink to drive home my point.

He shakes his head slightly. "Well, you see, that's where you're mistaken." He pauses, and I gesture for him to carry on. "I believe in fair compensation, and for the last two hours, you have been my main source of entertainment. Billing those three drinks to my room is the least that I can do." He shrugs.

"Entertainment? Care to elaborate?"

His tongue runs over his bottom lip, and I forcefully refrain from biting my own. "At first, I truly felt sorry that you couldn't be left in peace to just stare at your martini, which, for the record, is a very sad sight to see, but I digress."

Do not laugh. Do not laugh. Don't you dare fucking laugh, girl.

He continues, "But little did I know that you were more than capable of not only holding your own but actually bringing them down a peg in the process. Truly a work of art. I got drinks and a show, although the experience would have been better had you enunciated your words more." He fake scolds.

"You don't say." I tilt my head, face serious, feigning that I'm taking his silly critique into consideration.

"Solid eight out of ten. Although the 'get fucked' was brilliantly delivered. I'll bump up your score to ten for that line alone." He points his drink in my direction, then elegantly tips back the rest of it like I did moments ago.

I couldn't hold back my goofy smile if I tried, and his teasing eyes take on a softer look for a moment before Jess interrupts us. "Are you guys gonna keep eye fucking each other from across my bar, or is one of you switching seats?"

I keep my eyes locked on his. "Sorry, Jess, but I'm fine right where I am. Besides, I've been told I need to learn how to *enunciate* my words better. Why not work on my voice projection while I'm at it?" I taunt.

This time it's his smile that's unrestrained. And damn it, it has my heart fluttering out of my chest.

He makes a fuss about standing, and like I assumed, the man towers over everyone at the bar. He grabs his empty glass and makes his way toward me as if his steps weigh on him tremendously. Then he makes a show of pulling the barstool next to me away before he takes a seat. "Guess one of us has to be the mature one." He sneaks a quick wink at Jess while not so subtly nodding his head toward me.

"Yeah. Uh-huh," I say. I twirl the empty glass in my hands, wishing I still had some of my drink left so I'd have something to busy myself with.

We stare at each other unapologetically, not rushing to fill the silence with small talk. I would never be so brazen as to check someone out too obviously, but given that the three duds who approached me tonight all struck out, and given that I have no intention of taking this little banter further than saying good night in ten minutes, I allow myself to indulge.

I'm new at this having a bank account that isn't dangerously close to overdrafting thing, so I wouldn't be able to name his watch if my life depended on it, but I know it looks expensive. He most definitely has a tailor, and the suit is probably Italian. This knowledge is strictly from the mafia romance novels I read.

This close, I can smell his cologne, and I swear it's doing things to me. I wish I knew what scents like sandalwood or bergamot smelled like, because maybe then I could describe what this sexy as fuck man smells like and explain the number it's doing on my pheromones.

I shift in my seat so I can cross my legs and hopefully smother my horniness with the strength of my thighs.

His eyes immediately lock on the motion, and he has the gall to smirk, as if he knows exactly what I'm doing.

I eye him suspiciously as he waves Jess over. "I'd like to order for us."

Jess and I both make no attempts to hide our groans, and I swear I hear her mumble, "And to think he was doing so well."

Oddly, our reactions seem to please him as he says, "Could you bring us two waters, please? And absolutely no fruit in hers." He hooks his thumb over his shoulder at me. "Not even a lemon. Wouldn't want to tempt her to use it as a weapon and squeeze it in my eye as revenge for the male population failing so pitifully."

Jess laughs before she walks off, but my amusement turns into sober curiosity.

How does he know I hate the idea of fruity drinks? Is he really that perceptive, or was it a wild guess? Am I reading too much into a freaking glass of water, or am I missing something else completely?

There has to be an angle here. In this day and age, when getting a man to text you back seems like a herculean effort, no guy is this smooth.

"For the love of God, I'm not a piece of meat, you know. A little discretion while ogling would be the polite thing to do. At the very least ask if this is my good side." He huffs, barely containing the smile playing on his lips.

I clear my throat. "Not ogling. Studying." I pause. "Like a rare form of fungus."

He snorts, eyes widening at my statement, and his own reaction, it seems. "I beg your pardon?"

"You know, some people think fungus and picture the ointment their uncle has to apply between his toes, while others think of truffles and pay top dollar for it. The eye of the beholder and all that jazz, I suppose."

"Do I even want to know which category I land in?"

Jess places two waters in front of us, then quickly adds a tiny umbrella to his. She winks at me before hurrying away.

I raise my glass. "Don't worry, you seem like the bougie kind."

He shakes his head while eyeing my raised glass. "You know it's bad luck to toast with water, right?"

I bite my bottom lip while narrowing my eyes at him. "Don't tell me you believe in bad omens." I nod at his glass, and he slowly lifts it. "It's okay if you're a little superstitious. I'll make sure to keep eye contact as we toast. Even though you have zero intentions of sleeping with me, it would be a shame to condemn you to seven years of bad sex. I'm not a monster, after all," I tease.

He tips his glass, eyes locked on mine. "And what should we toast to…"

I hesitate, because this is the moment where I should tell him my name. But the last time I tried to exchange pleasantries with a man, it ended with me telling him to get fucked, so I'm not exactly inclined to have my most exciting night out in months be tainted by talking about Luisa Álvarez, New York Monarchs' GM.

So I shake my head instead. "No names."

His eyebrows almost hit his hairline. "Pardon?"

"I'm trying to reclaim that mystery, remember? No names needed to toast, last I checked."

He seems genuinely unsettled by my statement. So much so that I almost say to hell with it and give him my first name. "And I suppose you don't want to know my name either?" His words spill out slowly, as if assessing them as they leave his lips.

I nod, and he searches my face tentatively, as if hoping he can decipher my intentions.

After a moment, he must find what he's looking for, because he leans in closer and whispers, "I'd like to renegotiate the terms after this toast, but for now, I accept." He clinks his glass against mine. "To us—"

"To us."

"For doing a spectacular job of pretending we don't want to rip each other's clothes off."

A small gasp leaves my lips as he reaches under my seat and drags it closer to his. "Chin-chin, or get fucked, love."

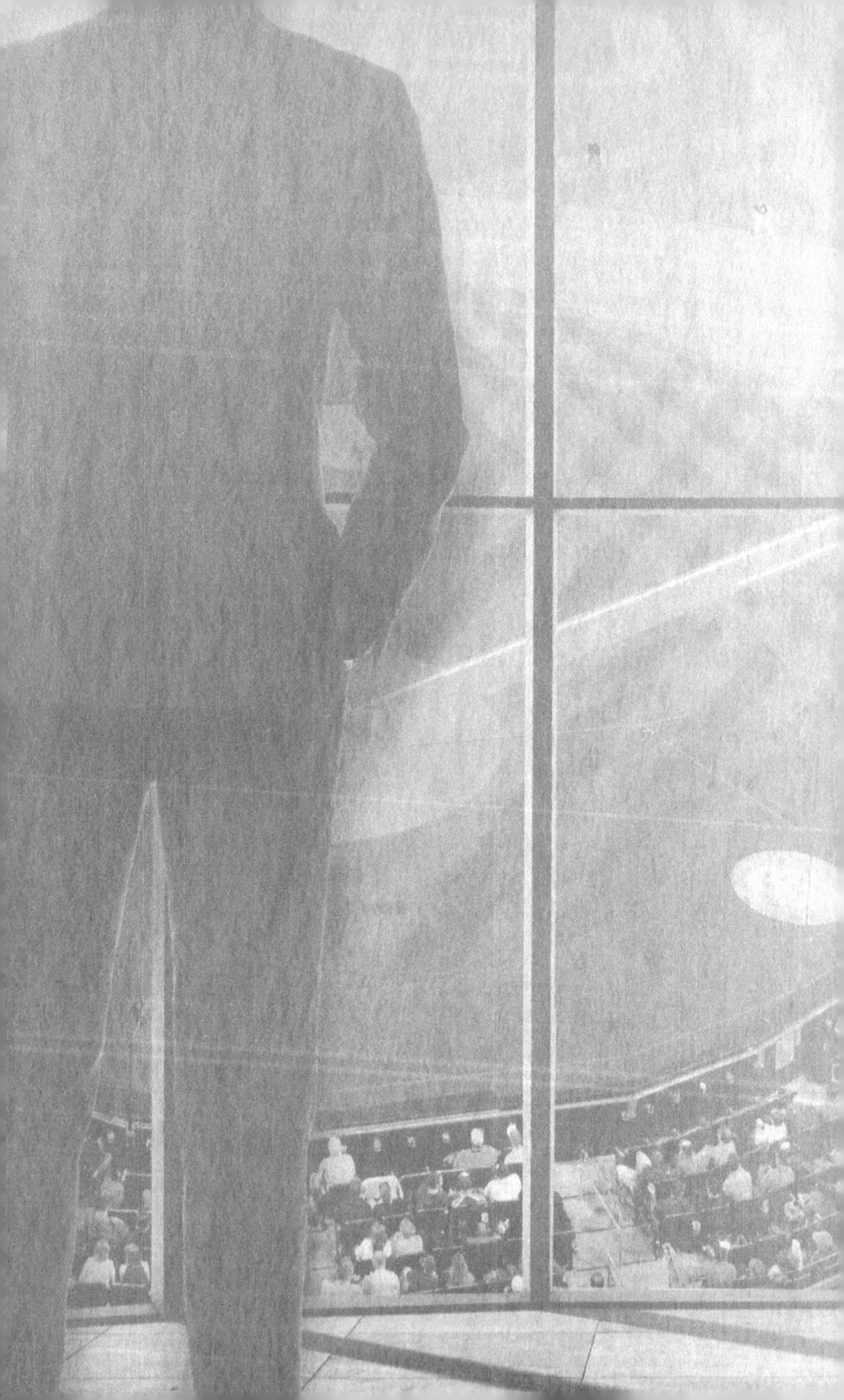

CHAPTER TWO

NICK

I NEED TO KNOW her name.

This woman has captivated me since the moment she sat her fine ass down at the bar.

At first, she seemed sad.

Something I could empathize with, given the shitstorm I've currently found myself in. My life may have taken an unexpected turn, but I'm sure it's nothing compared to living life in the shoes of a young woman sitting alone at a bar. Unable to just exist without having to put up with overly eager men looking to get their dicks wet.

Yet one by one, she dismissed those pathetic excuses for men while keeping her head held high. To say I was impressed by her finesse would be an understatement.

Something I've learned quickly about this spitfire is that she exudes power. She doesn't shy away from eye contact and she gives as good as she takes.

I wonder if she can take all of me. No, I'm sure she can.

I shake away my dirty thoughts. Although it's pointless, given that I left her momentarily stunned when I showed my hand and let her know with perfect clarity that I would, in fact, love nothing more than to bring her up to my room and have my depraved way with her.

I'm amused that my admission has surprised her. Beyond enjoying the verbal sparring we've easily slipped into, the woman is drop-dead gorgeous.

Small mercies must be the reason I spotted her before she knew of my presence. It allowed me an embarrassing amount of time to wipe the proverbial drool off my face and lift my jaw off the bar top.

Her big brown eyes are feathered by long lashes. Full lips that send every sinful thought rushing to the forefront of my brain. Lush brown skin that I'm itching to kiss every delectable inch of and long wavy black hair cascading down her back, stopping right above her ass. The same ass my eyes locked on to like a heat-seeking missile when she walked past me to take her seat.

She's dressed modestly, but even the respectable neckline does nothing to hide the full breasts I'm sure would feel heavenly in my calloused hands.

"Are you having dirty thoughts about me right now?" She finally speaks, and from her tone, I can tell she has regained her footing.

"Yes."

Her jaw drops. "Oh, wow. Not even going to deny it?"

I shake my head. "I don't lie. It's a waste of time, and I don't make a habit of being inefficient."

She faces me as she crosses her arms over her chest. "The first thing that came out of your mouth was something about not having sex with me. Have I already caught you in a lie?" She clicks her tongue.

My lips twitch. "Actually, the first thing I said was 'You don't have to show me your tits.'" She raises an unamused brow and I chuckle. "When I said I wasn't fucking you, that was to ease the sting of having to deal with so many incompetent men in one night. I thought I was being a good Samaritan by taking myself off the table. For your sake, of course."

"Oh, so is this some charity dick you're offering? Can you claim it as a tax write-off or…"

The laugh that bursts out of me is so unexpected, I have to place a hand over my chest to make sure it's real.

I didn't know I was capable of it, given the wringer I've been put through, but it seems this woman might be exactly what I need tonight.

I regain my composure and lower my voice. "Give me your name."

She smiles as she takes a sip of water. "No."

"No?"

"No names," she confirms.

Apprehension begins to build within my mind. This woman must be too good to be true. And it wouldn't be the first time I've been targeted because of who I am. "What game are you playing at?"

She doesn't miss a beat. "No game," she assures. Then she raises her index finger and points at me. "But I do feel like it's my responsibility to ask whether you're a serial killer."

I give her a flat look. "I sincerely hope that asking straight-up isn't your complete vetting process."

"Oh, of course not. I seamlessly weave questions about any childhood fascination with fire or harming small animals into the conversation. Usually before appetizers arrive. Gives me a good idea of whether I should stick around for dessert." She winks, and I roll my eyes at the absurdity of this conversation. And the absurdity of how much fun I'm having. So much fun, in fact, that I almost forget that I'm in a constant state of arousal being this close to her.

"Quite the exciting dating life. Never know if you're going to meet Mr. Right, or Mr. I-just-landed-my-own-dateline-episode," I deadpan.

She throws her head back in laughter. The sight has my own lips twitching, wanting to join in on her unabashed joy. But my focus is pulled elsewhere when her hand lands on my forearm.

I stiffen momentarily at the electricity that buzzes through our point of contact. How is that even possible when there's a suit jacket and dress shirt between her skin and mine?

She must notice my change in demeanor and mistake it for discomfort, because she frowns. So I put my free hand on top of hers before she tries to pull away.

And there it is again. That unexplainable jolt that makes my body awaken with painful awareness.

She looks down at our hands, then back up at me before she blurts, "I don't date."

"Unless it's a potential serial killer, I presume?" She shakes her head. "No, as in I don't have an exciting dating life... because I don't date." She straightens, taking her hand with her, and for a second, I have to bite back an absurd demand for her to give it back. "I don't have time to date. So I don't even bother," she clarifies.

I take a gulp of water. That statement has me needing to cool down. "So that enlightening chat you were having with that loser moments ago... that was you looking to make a new friend?" I eye her skeptically.

She pauses for longer than she has throughout our whole conversation, but I don't dare make a move to rush her.

She leans on the bar, mimicking my stance, not breaking eye contact when she says, "I was considering having sex with him."

Fucking hell.

I try.

For the love of God, I try to keep my face impassive.

I didn't get to where I am in business by not having a good poker face. But I'm unable to hold the heavy breath in my chest as her words play on a loop in my mind.

She's perfect.

She doesn't date, and she's only looking for a good time. This is my dream scenario.

Yet why is it that instead of turning up the charm, I find myself irritated that she was actually considering giving that asshat the time of the day?

"You could do better," I gruff.

"I'm aware," she shoots back immediately. Instead of taking offense to my lackluster response, she toys with the rim of her glass as she gives me the look of a predator that likes to play with her food before striking. "And I don't owe you an explanation. But that scrunched-up face you're making is going to give you a few extra wrinkles, and I'll be damned if I'm the reason you leave tonight looking a little less pretty."

"Did you just call me pre—"

"I came here because I was looking for a moment to myself. To decompress. Yet when the opportunity for a different kind of stress reliever presented itself, I took it into consideration." I go to interrupt, but she lifts a hand, stopping me. "Again, I don't owe you this, but in case you were wondering, I am a twenty-nine-year-old woman who can decide to do whatever she wants with her body. If that means fucking a loser who ordered me a fruity cocktail, then it's my prerogative. And if it's sending him on his way to fuck his fist tonight?" She shrugs nonchalantly. "Well, that's my call too. Are you going to try to judge me for it as if you don't move the same way?"

Jesus Christ.

I don't know whether I've just been told off or coddled, and the feeling has me speaking recklessly. "Judge you? Woman, I'm more likely to declare my undying love for you than cast judgment." She eyes me warily, so I continue. "But then I would run into the possibility of being told to fuck my fist tonight, and between you and me—" I lean a little closer. "I have much more interesting ideas about how to use my hands tonight."

She studies me fiercely, giving nothing away, and for a moment I fear she's going to see how desperate I am for her.

My life has been a series of calculated risks. I didn't get to where I am by playing it safe. And if I spend one more second pussy-footing around this woman, I'm going to live to regret it.

"Name," I demand, using the authoritative voice I usually reserve for the boardroom.

At my hardened tone, something flips in her. If I weren't so fixated on her every move, I might have missed the subtle moan she tried to keep from escaping her lips. But it's too late.

And I'm ready to chase her as far as she wants me to.

If her hardening nipples against her thin dress are any indication, she might want to be caught sooner rather than later.

But instead of giving me the name I'm so desperate to hear, she shakes her head slowly, eyes filled with lustful mischief, making my hands itch to touch her bare skin and teach her a lesson. "Nope."

I groan as I plead, "Are you going to make me beg?"

Her eyes darken as she leans closer, bravely sliding her hands up my thighs. I suck in a harsh breath but don't dare break eye contact until her face stops just a hairsbreadth from my ear. "Now, now. Don't start putting any kinky ideas in my head. Because the thought of you on your knees begging might just be the thing that breaks me."

Fuck. Me.

Did I find a woman with a mouth as dirty as mine?

Impossible. But I'll gladly take whatever she's got for me.

"Careful. Don't start something you can't finish," I taunt, hoping to spur her on.

Instead, she almost makes me fall flat on my ass when she cocks her head to the side. "And here I thought a man like you would make it your personal mission to make sure I would *finish*." She sighs. "How very disappointing to hear."

I'm crazed.

I keep fisting my hands and releasing them, hoping to keep them to myself while in public. Something that I may not be able to do if she keeps teasing me like this. So I decide to make her aware of the tightrope we're currently walking.

I pointedly look at where her hands continue to rest on my thighs. She looks down and her grip on my thighs tightens the moment she sees the bulge straining in my pants.

"Keep playing this game, and I'll have no choice but to bend you over the bar and give you the spanking you're asking for."

A whispered "fuck" escapes her lips as her hands squeeze my thighs once more. But I'm not letting up. If she thought she could throw me off with her sexual innuendos before, she's in for a rude awakening. Or, at the very least, a very sexy one.

"Tell me, love. If I were to slip my hand up your dress right now and slide my fingers over your pussy, how wet would you be, hmm?" Her eyes widen before she bites her bottom lip again. "Because the way you're holding yourself back from outright grabbing my cock in public, I'd guess you're fucking drenched."

I place a single finger on her bare knee and trail it up her skin until I reach the hemline of her dress. Her breaths start to come out in short spurts, and I momentarily wonder if I could get away with getting her off right here at the bar.

But that would mean I'd have to share the sounds she makes when she comes with the rest of the bastards here, and for some godforsaken reason, I'm feeling a bit too possessive to allow that to happen.

"Sweetheart, I need you to keep breathing so you can tell me how close I am to the truth." She shifts oh so subtly, but again I miss nothing when it comes to her. I tsk. "It pains me that you're trying to find some friction to ease the ache when I'm literally *right here*."

She glares at me. "Don't be so smug about it. It's a biological reaction."

"Which part? Your pussy begging to be played with or your hands inching up even closer to my cock."

She seems shocked to find that her hands have, in fact, traveled higher, and the jolt my cock makes at her nearness has the zipper of my trousers fighting for its life.

"Oh—I..." I place my hand over one of hers and let my other caress her cheek before settling on her chin, angling her face closer to mine.

I speak the words into her lips, featherlight touches too soft to be considered a kiss. "I'm flattered that you trust me, a perfect stranger, to be this close to you. I tell no lies when I say I'm honored to be allowed the privilege to taste your sweet breath on my lips. But please don't test the final tethers of my restraint, because I promise you, I am no saint."

She sucks in a breath, and me along with it. My lips drag across hers for no more than a few seconds. Yet it feels like the most erotic thing I've done in ages.

"Give. Me. Your. Name." I stare at her lust-filled gaze, which I'm sure mirrors my own.

I swear she's about to give it to me. Victory already tastes as sweet as the brief touch of her lips.

Until she tortures me with "No. Names." I feel my sanity slipping right as she says, "But there is one thing I need you to tell me."

"Anything. Name it." I'll tell her my fucking bank account number at this rate.

My house in the Hamptons?

My private jet?

Fuck. Anything, and it's hers at this point.

But what she asks for instead?

Well, that might be the most satisfying request I've ever heard.

"Give me your room number."

Chapter Three

LUISA

WE BARELY MAKE IT to the room in one piece.

After my mystery man dropped five hundred-dollar bills as a tip for Jess, we were off in a blur of giggles and heated looks.

He held my hand firmly in his as we strode across the lobby and planted his hand on my lower back as we entered the elevator. I was sure he was going to pounce on me as soon as the doors closed, but a group of tourists entered at the last moment, prompting him to place his hand on my stomach, pressing my back into his front.

Whether it was to make sure I didn't make a run for it or to torture my ass with the feel of his hardened cock, I'm not sure.

The doors opened on a random floor and the crowd exited, unaware of how close they'd been to watching a show more exciting than anything on Broadway.

His firm hold tightened on my front when we were alone, and the heady silence was almost enough to make me beg for an elevator quickie.

Luckily, the doors opened to the top floor, and he silently led me to the double doors of his room, murmuring "almost there" in my ear, as if he could read my prior thoughts.

I walk into the room and immediately admire the gorgeous suite we've stepped into. There's a dining table set for eight people, an impressive living room with seating for a small crowd in front of a massive fireplace and floor-to-ceiling windows that overlook Central Park.

But before I know it, all I can see is him.

He crowds me into one of the front doors, his eyes turned into dark coals. He steps into me, one of his thighs between mine, his hardness pressing into my stomach.

I swallow audibly as I try to even out my breathing.

Shit. This is really happening. I'm actually going to have sex with a stranger. And not just any stranger, but one who looks like he's about to ruin me for all future men. I thought I would be more nervous, but I don't really have time to overthink anything since all my mind can focus on is seeing this man naked as soon as possible.

He props one arm on the door above me and leans down so his eyes are level with mine.

"This is the time where you tell me what I want to hear." His voice is a gravelly whisper, and I wonder if he can make me come on command with it.

It has me hypnotized, so lost in him that I don't even try to filter my next words. "I'm all clear and I'm on birth control, but it doesn't mean I'm going to let you fuck me raw."

He tenses above me, then a low growl vibrates from his chest as he brings his body flush against mine. "I meant your fucking name, but now... fuck."

His lips crash against mine, and I almost buckle at the sensation. He shifts his stance so I'm practically straddling his thigh for support. His hand finds purchase on the back of my neck, and he angles us to his liking.

The feeling of being consumed has me opening for him, and he doesn't hesitate for a second as his tongue slips against mine in a silent promise of what's to come.

I don't attempt to suppress my wanton moans, causing his grip to tighten, dominating every one of my senses.

I rock back and forth, my hands clutching his shirt in a death grip as the pressure builds deep inside me.

Yes, this is exactly what I need.

He tilts my head, breaking our kiss as he chuckles darkly. "Oh, sweetheart, as much as I love the feel of your hot cunt rubbing on my leg, getting you off is my job." He takes a step back and slowly removes his suit jacket. Then he folds it over the back of a nearby chair. He continues speaking calmly, as if we're talking about the weather. "Besides, the first time you come tonight will be on my cock."

I sag against the door in a huff. God. The mouth on this man.

He unbuttons his shirt unhurriedly, and if it wasn't for the massive tent in his pants, I would assume he wasn't as affected as I am.

Once the shirt is off and carelessly tossed onto the ground, I have a front-row seat to the show that is his sculpted body. If he didn't look so comfortable in a suit, I would guess he was an athlete of some sort, given that these muscles take time and maintenance to get to this level of perfection.

I continue to watch as his hands nimbly unlatch his belt, open the button of his pants, and pull down the zipper in a smooth, practiced dance.

I'm so enraptured by the way he moves that I'm slightly startled when he speaks. "If you're partial to a bed, I suggest you get moving." My eyebrows lift in surprise. "Because once I'm naked, I'm fucking you right where you stand."

I'm frozen in place, replaying his words in my head. He can't be serious.

The whipping noise his belt makes as it's removed from his pants tells me he is, and my body goes into flight mode. I haul ass toward what I hope is the bedroom and am immediately relieved when I'm greeted by a massive California king.

I can faintly hear more ruffling of clothes and quickly decide I'm not going to get fucked in the dress I wore to a wake.

I bring down the side zipper and easily wiggle out of my black dress, thanking God I had the foresight to wear matching black underwear. It's not fancy lingerie, but the panties are lace and the bra does wonders for my sizable breasts.

I sit on the edge of the bed and bend down to unbuckle the clasp on my heel.

I don't even hear him enter the room before I hear him speak. "Time's up."

My head snaps up to see him standing before me in nothing but tight black boxer briefs, with multiple condom wrappers in his hand.

He slowly stalks toward me, and I use that time to remember who I am and what I like.

Tonight, I am not his plaything.

He is mine.

He doesn't know my name, and we'll never see each other again, so I decide to be bold.

I lean back on my elbows, giving him his first sight of me in my underwear. My size eight body is nowhere near as chiseled as his, but I do work out multiple times a week, and I know I have certain assets in my favor.

His eyes rove over me, and he seems pleased at the position I've taken.

He moves to climb over me when I lift my foot and press it square in the middle of his chest, stealing the breath right out of him.

His shock is quickly replaced by amusement as he drops the condoms on the bed and circles his hands on my ankle. Without needing direction, he undoes the clasp, removes my heel, and unceremoniously tosses it over his shoulder. I bite down on my smile.

He starts massaging the arch of my foot, and *damn*. If he's this good with his hands, I'm going to be in for one hell of a night.

I slip my foot out of his grasp and place my other heeled shoe on his chest. A bit harder than last time.

He shakes his head and lets out a short chuckle. One that threatens that I'll pay for the move.

I sure hope so.

Once my heels are tossed in different directions, he stands before me, his thinly covered cock mere inches from my face. I can tell his restraint is on its last thread, so, of course, I push him further.

"Someone doesn't know how to follow their own directions, it seems." My arms go behind my back, and I unclasp my bra. I hold the cups against my chest as I slide each arm out of the straps. "You said you were going to fuck me right where I stood once you were naked." I nod to his underwear, noting the small wet spot near the tip of his dick.

"You planning on fucking me through that material? Because naked looks a little more like this." I grab the middle of my bra and toss it.

The golden eyes I first admired at the bar now seem like dark pools of amber as he stares at my chest. His hand darts forward, and I think he's finally going to unravel, but his hand cups my face instead.

For a moment I panic. It seems far too gentle for a situation like this. Way too intimate. I'm about to make another snarky remark when his thumb brushes along my lower lip. Softly at first, but then with more pressure. So much so that I find myself opening my mouth to make room.

He slips his thumb in, and I suck. He slips it in deeper, pulling down and forcing my mouth to pop open. It's a lewd gesture, the way he watches me with such dominance. "Keep running that mouth and I'll have no choice but to fuck your face until you're choking on my cock."

Wetness pools between my thighs and my body hums in excitement. I've never been this turned on in my life. I can't wait a second longer to have this man.

I pull back and bite the tip of his thumb.

He smiles wickedly, and fuck me, it's the sexiest look he's given me thus far.

"All right, smart-mouth, enough bark. Now take out my cock."

I don't hesitate. I lean forward and give him my best doe-eyed look as my hands pull down on his underwear. By the time I've gotten it halfway down his thighs, I feel his cock bump against my cheek. I don't miss the flash of unbridled lust in his eyes as I take him in for the first time.

He's massive. I knew that already. But as I wrap my hands around his hardness, I realize how truly fucked I will be by the end of the night, because as I stack both hands around him and stroke, I know this is going to be a tight fit.

And this is exactly what I wanted. An ache that lasts throughout the weekend, reminding me of the delicious stretch he's about to give me.

I lock my eyes on his as I lean forward and lick the drop of precum from his tip. His façade briefly cracks.

He closes his eyes and reinforces before shaking his head. "After. I need to be inside you. Now."

He maneuvers around me fast, picking me up bridal style, only to toss me in the middle of the bed.

An embarrassing squeak escapes my lips. "I am not the kind of woman you can throw around in bed. I'm not exactly petite."

He crawls on the bed toward me. "I can, and I just did." He gently smacks the inside of my knee. "Open."

"Say please." I smirk.

He raises up on his knees and lets his hands roam over my stomach and up to my breasts. He weighs them in his palms, letting his thumbs brush over the pebbled peaks. My head lolls to the side as I hum pleasantly. That is, until he pinches them both. Hard. "Now."

My legs drop open on either side of him instantly.

Just when I think I'm a step ahead, he turns the tables. I'm trying to keep my wits, but I'm quickly slipping. "P-panties off," I mutter. He shakes his head, hands playing with my nipples. "I said off."

He raises a bemused brow. "As you wish."

It takes me a moment to realize what's happening. Only when he rips the second lace string of my thong do I recognize the fact that he tore my underwear clean off me.

He shrugs unapologetically. "You said 'off.'"

My head plunks back on the bed as he continues to shift below me. I can't believe this man. And he hasn't even tou—

"Ohmygod, w-what—"

He lifts his tongue off my clit as his eyes connect with mine. "See? At a time like this, when I have my face buried in your pussy, don't you think it would be a good idea to know my name? Because if you keep calling me God, you're going to give me a complex." His tongue swipes against my center once more.

"You're the devil," I breathe. The sound is followed by a humorless chuckle. "I'll call you Lucifer. How does that sound?"

I only have a second to feel a faint breeze before he slaps my needy center.

I moan, my body bowing off the bed, as he sucks on my clit mercilessly. "Music to my ears, *Angel*." He straightens. "But now I really do have to fuck you, and you need to tell me now if you want it slow—"

"Don't you fucking dare." I threaten.

He grins as he sheaths himself with a condom, then runs the tip of his cock up and down my wetness. He's lining himself up, about to sink into me, when the realization hits me.

He's about to fuck me missionary style.

Oh, fuck that.

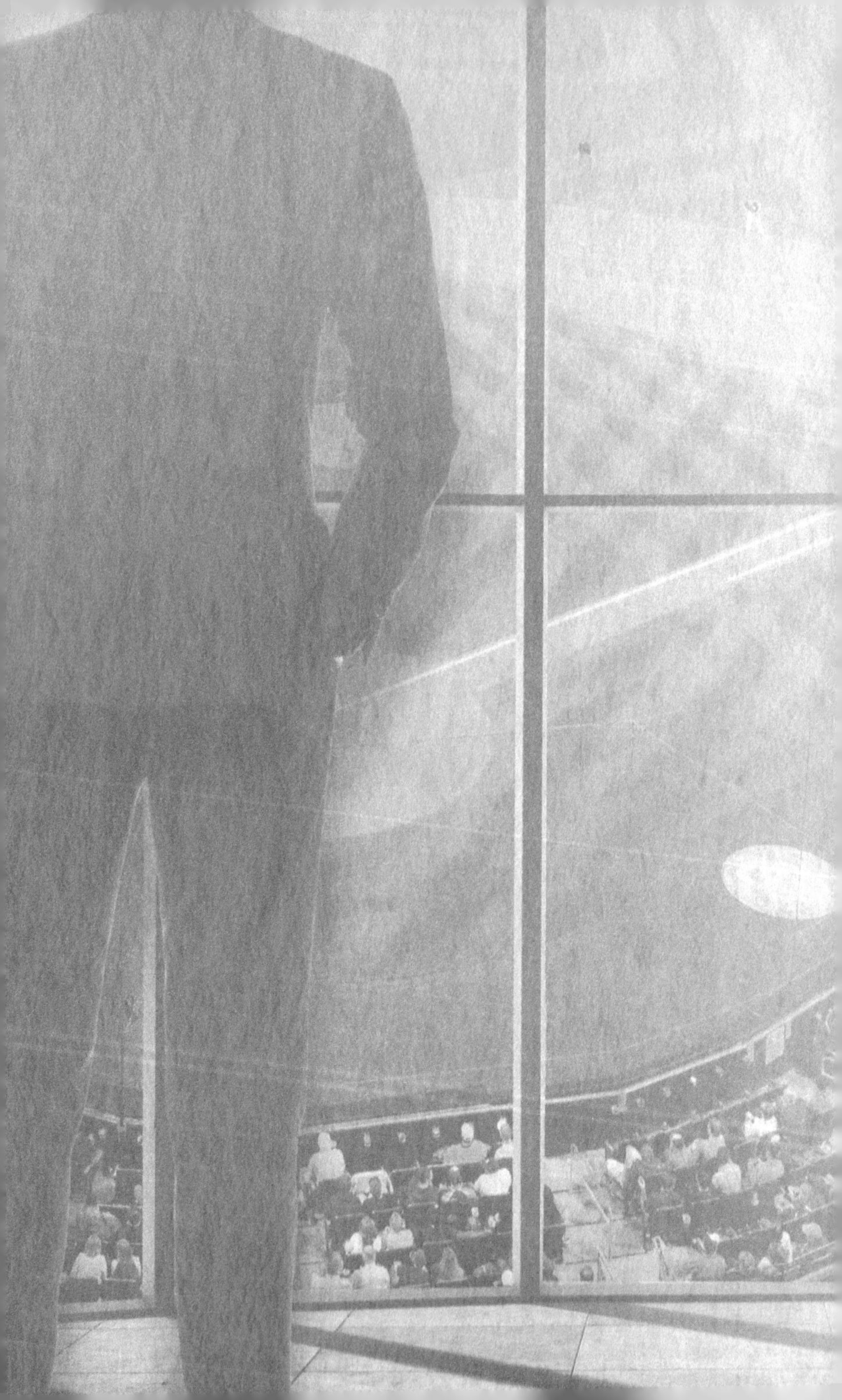

Chapter Four

NICK

This pussy has magical powers.

There's no other explanation for why I continue to tease us both by running the tip of my cock through her slit.

I shake my head.

Enough of this. I should be inside her already. I notch my tip at her entrance, but before I thrust in, I'm suddenly shoved.

Landing on my side, I look up to see her getting up. "What the—"

"Sorry, Lucifer, but if you think you're fucking me missionary, you've got another thing coming."

I'm starting to think that she-devil is a more appropriate name for her as she straddles my hips with a grin stretching across her face.

Her tits sway as she lines me up with her center. My hands hold her hips in place when what she's planning finally hits me. "Stop." She freezes, and I see some of her confidence dissipate. I can't have that happening. "You sure you don't want to ease into it before you ride me?" I can't decipher the look on her face, but thus far, she's preferred me being dominant and direct, so I continue with that. "I have plans for the entire night that consist of you deep throating me and me fucking you from behind. Don't want you to lose all your stamina in the first round," I goad.

And it seems to work.

She grips my cock tightly. I almost blow my load in her hand, but I can't give her the satisfaction after what I said.

She lines herself up again and slowly, painfully so, sinks onto me. We moan in unison at the relief of finally being connected. I keep my hands on her waist to support her slow descent. She makes it halfway before she stops, focusing on her breathing.

"You got this, Angel." I lift her up slightly and bring her back down an extra inch.

She rests her hands on my chest for leverage, and the new angle has me clenching my teeth. She starts rocking back and forth, her face etched in determination and ecstasy.

I move a hand away from her hip and let it travel down until my thumb lightly brushes her clit. She gasps and her eyes fly up to mine.

"That feel good?" I press down and start rubbing tight circles as I thrust up slightly, meeting her halfway. She mewls and claws at my chest. I want to make a kitten joke, but I'm far too gone for any humor now. "Look how well your pussy is taking me. Look how deep you've already gone as I play with your needy little clit."

She clenches around my length and I internally curse in every language I know.

She gets impossibly wetter by the second, and on my next thrust up, she takes all of me. Triumph and pleasure broadcast on her beautiful face.

She begins to really ride me, and I know exactly when she finds the spot she likes because she lifts her hands off my chest and starts playing with her nipples.

Never thought I could get jealous of the woman I was actively fucking, yet here I am. I reach up and take over for her, and she leans back with her hands on the bed. This view will forever be ingrained in my mind.

I'm certain she's about to come.

But if there's one thing I know for sure about this woman, it's that she's going to take every opportunity to surprise me.

Because in the next moment, she lifts herself up high enough for my cock to slip out of her. I don't have the mental capacity to question it, and luckily, I don't have to.

She quickly turns around, straddles me again, and throws a wink my way before dropping back down on my cock. "Thought you'd enjoy the view from behind."

Fucking hell.

Instead of riding me like before, she leans forward on her forearms and bounces on my cock. Correction, I'm pretty sure she's twerking on it. And this view? Fucking lethal.

I knew her ass would be delectable, but this has me feeling like my heart is about to give out. And I'll be damned if I don't make her come in the next five minutes.

She's already in the perfect position, so I grab her hips and halt her impressive performance. She looks back, confused, sweat glistening on her skin, as I get on my knees.

I slip out of her as I shimmy us higher up on the bed.

"What are you—"

I sink back into her without warning. "Brace yourself against the headboard, Angel. No more playing around."

"Oh, that's so... deep."

"I said... hold on." I grit as I really start to pound into her.

Her hands hurry to find purchase on the headboard as she tips her head back and releases a sultry gasp.

I reach around her and rub her clit again. Her pussy clenches around me so tightly I roar in satisfaction.

"Oh God. I'm... I'm..."

She starts to flutter around me, and I know it's time.

I don't let up on her clit as I lean over her and fuck her into the bed. Her hands slip from the headboard and desperately grab on to a nearby pillow.

"Come for me, Angel."

She screams as she does, and her pussy's grip on my cock sends me into a frenzy. I fuck her deeper throughout her orgasm, finally triggering my own release.

I collapse on top of her. She grunts and wiggles her ass, knowing full well that I'm still inside her.

Slowing my breaths, I aim for a nonchalant tone. "All right. Don't be so needy. We'll go again after you've had a water break. Give me five."

Her head turns so she can eye me, laughing as she says, "You really are Lucifer, aren't you?"

"Whatever you say, Angel."

It's ironic really.

She called me the devil the moment I felt like I walked into heaven.

CHAPTER FIVE

LUISA

I SIGH INTO MY pillow, no longer able to ignore my small bladder.

Damn. When did I buy new pillows?

Feels like I'm sleeping on a cloud.

Wait. Where are my pajamas? And is there a hand on my ass?

I'm naked. And I'm not in my bed—

Last night's events start replaying in my mind. Every sordid and delicious detail.

Jesus, that man's dick is so powerful he almost erased my memories, *Men in Black* style.

The room is still dark, but it feels like I've slept in. Shit. I don't know all the rules about one-night stands, but I'm pretty sure you're not supposed to have a sleepover once the deed is done.

I look over and can faintly make out Lucifer's features. His face resting on his pillow, his bare chest slowly rising and falling.

I almost snort.

Lucifer.

This man knows what every inch of my body looks and feels like, and I don't even know his real name.

Last night far exceeded my expectations. After we both came the first time, we hopped into the shower only to get a lot filthier before we got clean.

He asked me to stay for room service, stating that he wouldn't be a gentleman if he let me leave without replenishing my electrolytes.

Or at least that's what I think he said. His voice was muffled, given his head was buried between my thighs.

After splitting a burger, pizza, and fries, he demanded I sleep off my food coma with a short nap with him. He promised he would wake me up and accompany me home in a cab. I waved off his offer to ride along but had no fight left in me to turn down a little shut-eye.

An hour later he woke me as he promised… with his hand between my legs and his cock ready and sheathed, waiting at my entrance. I hooked my leg over his without thought and let him slowly fuck me from behind.

After that round, I must have passed out immediately after we came, because I don't remember getting up and using the bathroom after. Which is a big no-no, because this girl right here is not looking to get a UTI.

But now I'm anchored in place by his large hand on my bare ass, and I need to get out of here before I make it awkward.

I slowly lift his wrist and gently place it on the bed. I breathe a sigh of relief that he's still asleep and quietly wiggle myself out of bed.

When my feet touch the floor, soft lighting illuminates under the nightstand, ensuring I won't bump into anything and make a fool out of myself.

I wince as I feel the soreness between my thighs. This man carries himself like an athlete or a CEO, yet here I was, riding him like a damn cowboy.

I have to cover my mouth to avoid giggling. Damn, I think I'm funny after getting laid.

I can't believe I'm doing the walk of shame. Is it weird that I feel kind of giddy? Like I've checked off some kind of rite of passage?

And to think I could have been having all this great sex instead of spending a fortune on sex toys.

Okay Luisa, focus. And stop getting distracted as you stand buck naked in a dark hotel room with a sexy stranger.

I go to move but am caught off guard when I realize that my phone is on the nightstand next to me, plugged in and fully charged. The sweet gesture takes me aback for a moment. That is, until I notice my small purse right next to it.

My phone... it was inside my purse. And so was my ID.

Fuck. Did he go through my bag to see who I was?

All he'd have to do is open my wallet and see my New York State ID on the clear plastic side.

Shit. Shit. Shit.

I grab my stuff and make my way through the room, trying to collect my discarded items. I know my panties are shredded somewhere in here, but those are a lost cause, so I'm going to have to go commando.

I get dressed in the living room area and make a plan to pee in the lobby bathroom, where I'll fix my hair and makeup.

I'm in the clear, ready to take off, but something doesn't feel right.

I know I'm new to this, but it feels wrong leaving without a trace.

I'm Latina. It's ingrained in me to never show up anywhere empty-handed and never leave without saying goodbye to your host multiple times. Even if it takes almost an hour to actually get out the door.

I look around the room, and my eyes snag on some stationery.

How do I write a "thanks for the great sex" note?

I don't want to be cringey, and I'm not giving him my phone number when it's obvious that this was a one-night thing. I refuse to come off as the clingy girl who can't differentiate between casual sex and dating.

I'm sure he'll wake up in a few hours, feeling satisfied, and go on about his day, business as usual. So I don't need to overthink it.

I land on the dumbest idea, but I decide to do it anyway. I draw two small angel wings.

Huh. Not too shabby.

I rip the paper off the pad and place it on the entry table.

But instead of dropping the pen, I linger.

C'mon, Luisa. Don't be so sentimental. This isn't a rom-com, just a hookup.

And yet... it doesn't stop me from being a little reckless.

Because between the two little angel wings, I finally give him what he's been asking for all along.

I write down my name.

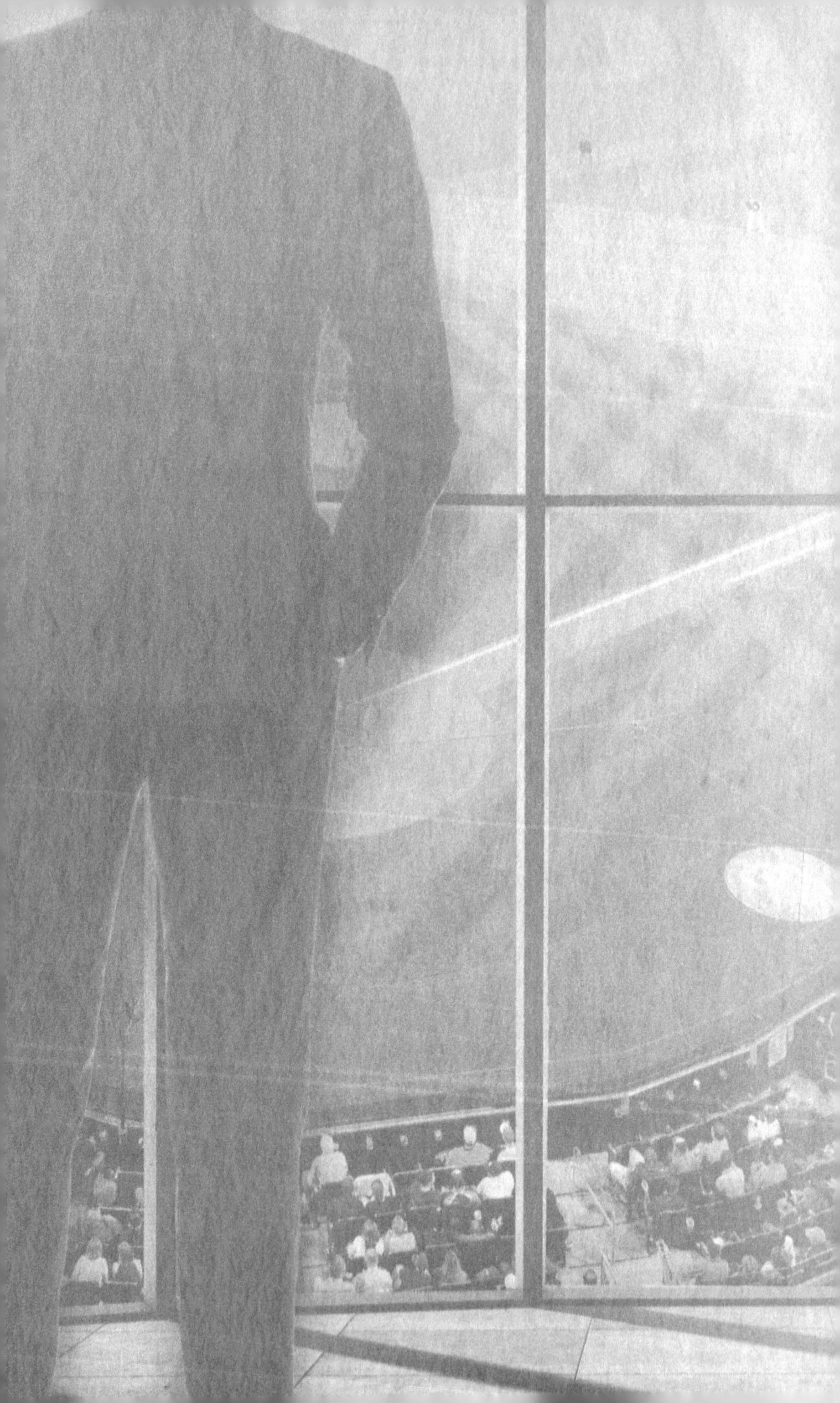

NICK

She's gone and I'm losing my mind.

We're not done here. Not by a long shot.

But it's going to be all right.

Because my Angel left me her name.

I'll play the role of the nice guy and give her the weekend to come down from our high.

But come Monday morning, I'm coming for my Luisa.

LUISA

It's Monday morning and I'm freaking out.

Daisy texted me that the new team owner will be available to have a quick fifteen-minute coffee break with us in an hour, so I need to get to Monarch Stadium before his tour of the facilities ends.

It's a bit unconventional to be meeting my new boss this way. There's usually some form of a soft handover when a team gets transferred to a new owner. But since Arthur passed away and apparently left the entire organization to a family member in his will, we're playing by different rules today.

I want to make a good impression, since the rest of my career will hinge on how well we work together. Even though it's my call who we trade, hire, and fire, it's still their team, and therefore they can veto me and have final say.

I decide to pull out all the stops with my wardrobe. I pull out a cropped black dress pants and blazer, removing the staples and tags from the dry-cleaner, and choose a soft pink button-down to go with it.

I don't have time to try on ten pairs of heels, so I go with the pair I left by the front door on Friday night.

A small tremor runs down my back.

It's been two days since my wild night, and I can still feel his presence between my legs.

I wonder what he thought when he saw my note.

Probably not much, since he most likely already saw my name when he snooped through my bag.

Ugh, not this again. We got places to be and people to meet, woman.

I stop by the mirror by my front door and double-check that my makeup is subtle and professional. I grab a scrunchie off the entry table and start twisting my long hair and securing it into a low bun. I pull a few wisps around my face loose and consider myself ready to go.

I grab my oversized purse that has a folder with my résumé and other documents regarding my work in the sports industry. It seems silly since I already have the job, but I still feel like I have to prove to yet another person why I should keep it.

Deep breaths. It's all going to be fine.

Besides, what's the worst that could happen?

Gridlock traffic.

I'm going to be late.

In a rookie move, I decided to take a taxi instead of the subway. I wanted to arrive looking refreshed, and lately, there's been a guy at my nearest train station who loves to run after people while peeing, and today was not the day to test my luck.

Only in New York.

But I failed to remember how long it would take me to get here with traffic, which is how I find myself running the last two blocks and zooming past security while waving my staff lanyard.

I feel my phone vibrate in my hand, but I don't look down until I'm in the elevator, heading for the executive offices.

DAISY:

> Hey, my brother needs to leave in five.
> Are you here yet?

Wait. What?

Her *brother*?

Sweet baby girl, Daisy. Could she not have mentioned that her own *brother* would be the new team owner?

I was thinking it would be an older relative, someone closer to Arthur's age. And now I have to meet with someone who's young enough to be Daisy's sibling, and she's in her mid-twenties?

That's fine. We're fine. No need to panic.

He is my peer. He's probably laid back. He'll understand that shit happens and Manhattan traffic is insane. I'll still apologize profusely and hopefully salvage my image in the span of five minutes.

Aw, that's actually really sweet. If he's good to his family, he'll be good to the Monarchs.

I'm rounding the corner, my heels the only noise on this floor, since opening day is Friday and we have no scheduled meetings, just this surprise one.

As I approach the office, I catch Daisy's laugh. For some reason it settles me hearing her be so carefree. I really like Daisy, and if her brother is half as decent as she is, this might turn out to be an amazing working relationship for me.

I'm already smiling as I reach for the office door, not bothering to knock since she knows I'm rushing in and they seem to be at ease.

My phone vibrates once more as I push the door open.

I quickly read Daisy's text before entering.

Yeah, he's a real saint!

I chuckle softly as I walk in and catch Daisy waving enthusiastically at me with her phone in hand.

Her brother has his back to me, so I give her a little wave as I stride toward them.

I barely have a chance to glance his way before Daisy starts introducing us.

"And this, my dear brother, is your new secret weapon. Álvarez here has procured the best team the MLB has ever seen, and I wouldn't be surprised if she takes us all the way to the World Series during our very first season."

I drop my head slightly, blushing at Daisy's glowing remarks.

"That's exactly what I want to hear."

Time slows, and for a moment I wonder if I'm still in my bed dreaming.

This can't be real.

I must be imagining things.

That voice. I've heard it before.

Last Friday, while he was buried deep inside me.

My head whips up as he turns toward me, and we both freeze the moment our eyes meet.

"Angel," he mouths to himself.

It's... it's him. He's here. He's...Oh God.

He's my new boss!

Daisy is looking between the two of us, her smile morphing into confusion.

I don't need her asking any questions, and I don't know what else to say as his eyes search mine for answers I don't have.

So I stick my hand out and force the words out of my mouth. "Hi. Um, it's nice to meet you. I'm—"

"Álvarez." He pauses. "*Luisa* Álvarez."

Nope. I can't do this.

I can't hear my name on his lips as his eyes bore into mine.

This is a mistake. A massive, colossal mistake.

I don't know what I'm doing when I start to pull my arm back, but it seems he's not having any of that when his arm darts out and both his hands clasp mine in a firm grip.

He raises a brow, and I realize what I'm supposed to say next. "And you're Stonehaven...Uh—"

"Nicholas Stonehaven. My name is *Nick*, Luisa." He squeezes my hand, and I feel it all the way between my legs. Especially when his eyes linger on my shoes for a moment.

My devil has a name, and it's Nick.

No. Not my devil. My *boss*.

As in the person holding my career in his hands. His very strong, large, and talented hands.

His gaze seers my skin, like he can read the dirty thoughts running through my mind.

"You can let go of her, Nick. Don't make it weird." Daisy's strained laugh has me whipping my hand out of his grip before he can tighten it. "Sorry about that. Luisa. My brother can be intense sometimes."

"Thanks for the glowing review, sis."

"Anytime." She faces me. "And to think you were anxious about meeting him. I promised you'd get along great with the new owner."

His entire demeanor changes at the drop of a hat.

Eyes that were moments ago heating my skin have now turned cold.

He straightens, and the rigid movement makes him look like he's made of stone.

But his voice? Might as well belong to a completely different human. "So you knew who I was," he states instead of questioning.

Daisy's phone rings, and she excuses herself. I want to tell her to stay, or that I'll leave. Because I'm still trying to wrap my head around the last few minutes.

The office door clicks shut and Nick takes a sizable step forward. "So you knew who I was," he repeats, eyes lasered in on mine like a human lie detector.

"No! I didn't know who you were. I didn't know the owner was Daisy's brother either. I didn't even know Daisy had a brother!" My voice rises as the accusations start to become clearer.

His laugh is sinister, worthy of the name I gave him while we were in the throes of passion. "Oh, now that's rich." He shakes his head while looking down, fixing his cufflinks. "I must say, it's been a long time since someone's duped me like that. Gotta hand it to ya. You really had me fooled."

"I'm sorry. Are you really—"

"Oh, good. You're starting with an apology," he clips.

I put my hand up between us, my mind struggling to decide whether to defuse the situation with my new boss or curse him out six ways till Sunday.

"Look, I'm going to need you to simmer down for a second and listen like a damn adult." His eyebrows rise, but he allows me to continue. "We had sex last weekend."

"And here I thought you were about to tell me something I didn't know."

"Wow. You're a real gem, aren't you?" I mutter.

"You know I'm worth way more than a gem, so at least make your analogies accurate."

"Honestly, if my job weren't on the line, you wouldn't even be worth the headache." He huffs as I tread on. "What I was trying to say is that, yes, we had sex. Like two consenting, *mature* adults. And if you recall, I didn't even want to know your name."

"Because you already knew it!" His voice booms, his eyes quickly darting to the office door, probably looking for any signs of Daisy. He takes a deep breath and lowers his voice. "You knew who I was and seduced me, and for what? Job security? To ensure that if I tried to fire you, you'd threaten a lawsuit? Or best case, see how much money you could squeeze out of me?" He shakes his head, lost in thought. "Just tell me if you took photos of me while I slept, and we'll deal with this privately. I'll even keep the lawyers out of it."

My jaw drops, and it takes everything in me to keep the tears rimming my eyes from falling.

The fucking nerve of this man.

This isn't the first time someone has accused me of sleeping my way to the top. But it is the first time someone's accused me of having sex to not only keep a job but to blackmail someone for it.

One by one, every sweet and sensual memory of my time with Nick turns to ash.

There's a reason there's a risk with sleeping with strangers, the main one being you have no idea how much of an asshole they can really be when the offer of sex is no longer on the table.

But he is my boss, and by the sounds of it, he seems like he wouldn't dare fire me in case I resorted to criminal activity.

For all I care, he can take every single hundred-dollar bill to his name and shove it up his ass.

I take two steps forward, his scent now intoxicating for a different reason.

I look him square in the eye and don't mince my words. "I know this might be a bit outside of your depth of understanding, but my value resides in places other than my vagina. I'm not going to waste my breath trying to convince you that I didn't know who you were, because clearly, you are extremely stubborn and quite full of yourself. So I'll say this instead." I point at his face, not caring how rude I'm coming across. "You may not believe me, but you will respect me. I worked my ass off getting this team together while having men more qualified than you questioning me at every turn." I take a deep breath. "And to put your wallet at ease, I have no reason to use you, nor do I have any interest in it. The last thing I want is to tell the world I wasted a single night with the most egotistical man alive," I heave.

I should leave. I should go while I've left him momentarily speechless.

But I've never really made it a habit of doing what I'm supposed to, so why start now?

"And the real kicker? Is that between the two of us, you were the one who knew who I was. Or am I supposed to believe you went through my purse to pull out my phone without chancing a glance at my ID? For a man with so much to protect, you think you'd be a little more careful, no?"

"I did no such thing. I wanted to make sure your phone was charged so I could... it doesn't matter. You're completely off, and if—"

"I wrote down my name. First name only, but surely a—what was it again? That's right—a *billionaire* would have the resources to find out who I was. I'm sure you have a guy for that kind of stuff, right?" My voice drips with condescension.

He opens his mouth like he was about to say something but promptly shuts it firmly.

"Yeah, just what I thought. But no worries, *boss*. I'm sure we can find a way to work together without butting heads. As long as you don't accuse me of being a trifling, conniving whore, it should be smooth sailing."

I turn and make my way to the door without another glance in his direction.

My hand touches the handle when he speaks.

"Luisa." His voice sounds pained, but you'd need to actually have a heart to have feelings. I turn my head just enough to make eye contact. "You really expect me to believe you didn't know who I was?"

His eyes seem a fraction softer, but his tone remains the same glacial temperature.

I turn the handle and speak over my shoulder.

"You know what? You're right, Nick. I always knew you were the devil."

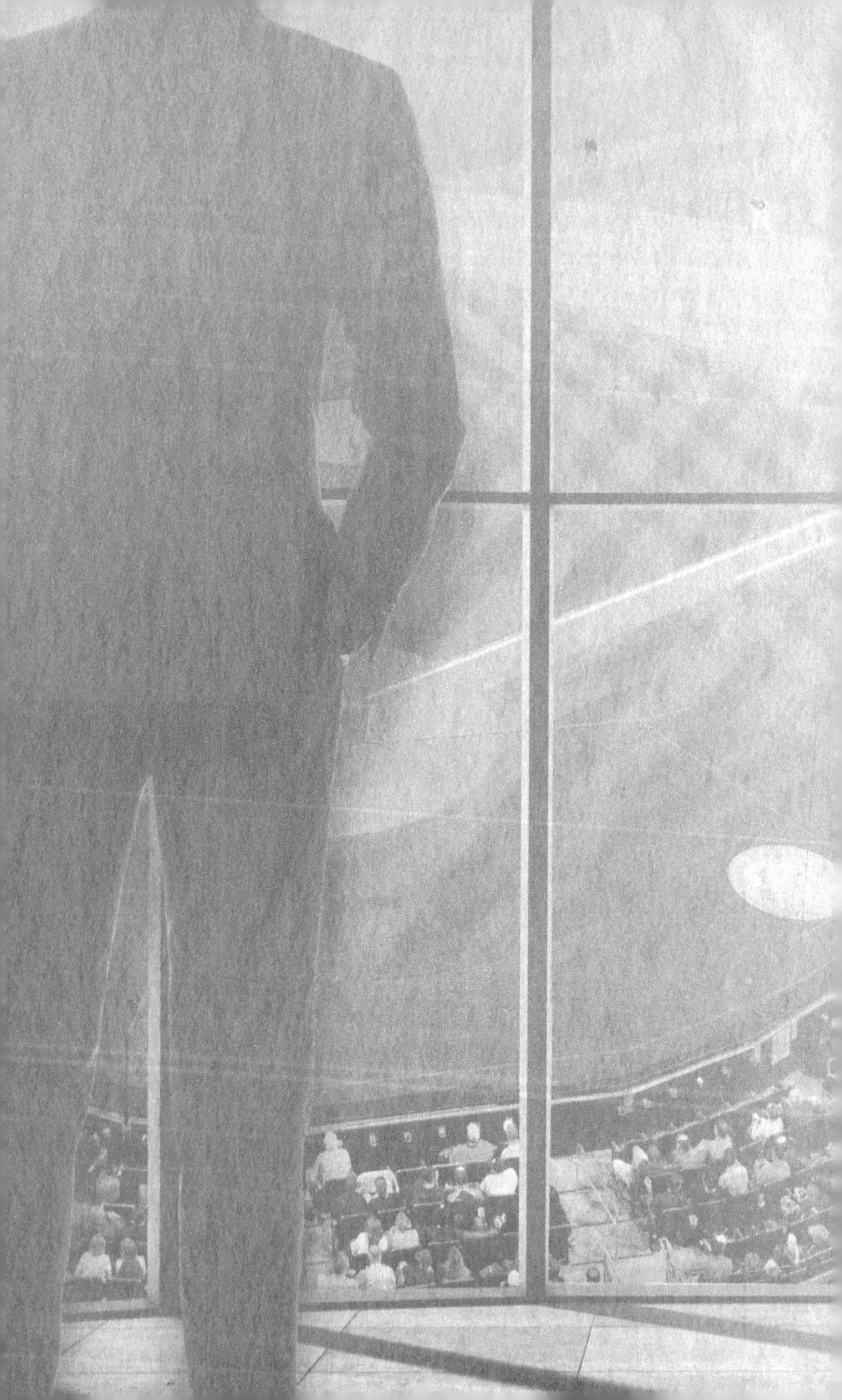

CHAPTER EIGHT

NICK

IT ONLY TOOK ME twenty-four hours to process the cold, hard truth.

I fucked up.

Like Luisa suspected, I did have a guy who could look into people. And from the report staring back at me from my laptop screen, she was telling the truth.

My guy is known to bend the law and sometimes search in places that some might consider illegal, but I've never claimed to always play by the rules.

She never googled my name. Instead, she searched for "New Monarch team owner" and was directed to the article I had published with no real answers, in order to keep my cover concealed until I was ready to step into the unwanted spotlight.

Her texts with Daisy also confirmed that she didn't know about Daisy having a brother.

She didn't know about me at all.

Truth be told, the report is overkill. Because the second she looked me straight in the eyes and told me I was the devil, I knew.

She was telling the truth.

And I fucked up.

Chapter Nine

LUISA

That smug son of a bitch.

I spent the rest of the week cursing his name with every Spanish swear word I could recall. And when I ran out, I made some up to keep the momentum going.

I thought I had heard it all. Thought I had thick skin.

But I'm tired of being strong. Tired of having to defend myself solely because I dared to shatter the glass ceiling.

And I hate to admit that my dream job of being a general manager has soured due to my interactions with Nick.

No, not Nick.

Ese pendejo doesn't get to be called any name that could humanize him.

I could almost laugh at how spot-on I was when I called him the devil.

Almost, but not quite.

I spent all of last night and this morning curled up on my couch, ordering takeout and yelling at my TV. Watching a marathon of cheesy romantic comedies from the 90s and 2000s. It's my favorite pastime, and something I only ever do alone. Although I spent the evening picking them apart and grumbling about how they're incredibly unrealistic.

Growing up, I was a tomboy. I loved baseball, and, honestly, any other sport I could sneak my way into.

So, of course, someone who enjoys any athletic activity couldn't possibly be layered enough to also like romance. Or the color pink. Or daydream about her future wedding.

Because young girls are only ever allowed to slip into one category.

Sadly, I'm finding that it isn't much different once you enter womanhood.

Women are expected to be everything at the same time, while also being shamed for it.

From my cousins who are already moms, I've heard some of the most vile and judgmental shit. Most coming for other mothers.

You want to be a stay-at-home mom? People will say "Don't you like making your own money? Are you really letting all your previous work aspirations go to waste just to sit home with a baby? What would you even do all day?"

If you decide to be a working mom, you'll hear "But who will raise the baby? Is being a girl boss more important than being a mother? Why even have kids if you're not going to be around to raise them?"

I'm not immune to the commentary reserved for women about to turn thirty, with no romantic prospect in sight. I get the well-intended "Oh, you'll meet someone when you least expect it. Put yourself out there; I'm sure there are still single men in the city looking for love at your age." Or the not so nice "Nobody likes alpha women, Luisa. You need to let the man lead and start being more submissive to your men if you want them to stick around."

That last one was said by a family friend who my mother no longer brings around.

My fucking rockstar of a mother who has gone through hell and back and still continues to fight for the ones she loves on a daily basis.

Crazy how I didn't always feel this way growing up.

In fact, for a large chunk of my teenage years, I resented my mother. I was too young to understand the demons she battled, because none of my other tías suffered from depression. None of my friends had moms who stayed in bed most days, missing school recitals and birthday parties.

Just me.

For the longest time, I blamed myself.

Clearly, I was the reason she felt this way. I was a child and didn't understand that my mother's infertility journey triggered her depression. All my mind could focus on was "She's not happy because she can't have another baby. Because I'm not good enough. I'm not enough, period."

I could get myself ready for school by the time I was in fourth grade. Made sure I had all my clothes washed and ready the night before. My homework was always done before I made myself ramen noodles or rice with eggs.

My dad was a true savior, always trying to pick up the slack where my mother couldn't. Taking me to baseball games, daddy/daughter school dances, and throwing the best holiday parties in our cramped apartment in Spanish Harlem with all of our loved ones. But even he couldn't do it all, having to work long hours to support our family.

My mother would make appearances every now and then, a strained smile in place. Because it seemed like the cultural expectation of her being present and hosting family get-togethers was stronger than the grip her depression had on her.

We later found out that she had something called secondary infertility. It's a condition where someone who's previously been pregnant can no longer conceive for some unknown reason.

I've researched this condition numerous times, and the one flashing acronym that pops up among the rest, the one that always makes my stomach drop, is PCOS. The same condition I have. One that is hereditary and, apparently, shared by many women, especially women of color.

It's why I try not to think too hard about motherhood.

Why bother yearning for something that may never happen for me?

Not like I can grieve something I've never had. Right?

Besides, I have a lot to be grateful for.

Before I entered high school, my mother finally went to therapy, and shortly after that, she got on medication that would help with her depression.

It wasn't an instant fix, but with time, I got my mom back.

The newer, stronger version of her.

We've since gone to therapy as a family, and her guilt about not being present in my life for a few years was gut-wrenching.

It felt like she had been taken from me for a while, and when she returned, we had to learn who we were to one another again.

But I'm older now. I understand the disease better, and I can confidently say that my mother has always loved me deeply.

That the disease was the reason she could not show up for me during moments I needed her the most.

Yet even after many sessions of therapy of my own, I still can't seem to convince my brain that the lessons I learned during that time aren't true.

I can't convince my brain that I am enough.

That the people who love me will stay.

And that only I can determine what I deserve.

I knew the email was coming.

The all-staff meeting to introduce the new team owner that came from HR.

What I wasn't expecting was the direct email that came from Nick shortly after.

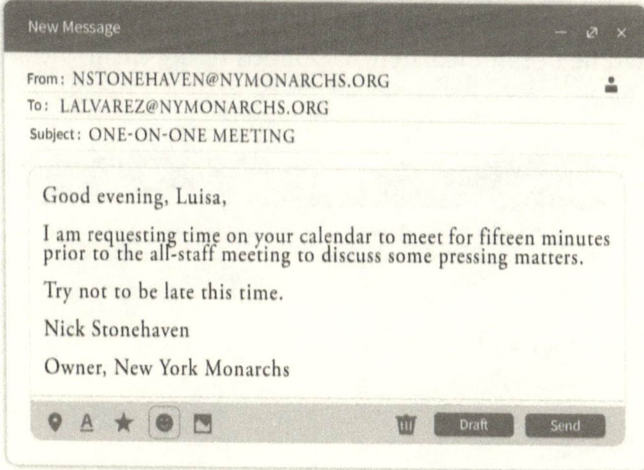

New Message

From: NSTONEHAVEN@NYMONARCHS.ORG
To: LALVAREZ@NYMONARCHS.ORG
Subject: ONE-ON-ONE MEETING

Good evening, Luisa,

I am requesting time on your calendar to meet for fifteen minutes prior to the all-staff meeting to discuss some pressing matters.

Try not to be late this time.

Nick Stonehaven

Owner, New York Monarchs

Draft   Send

It takes everything in me not to reply with a bunch of middle finger emojis. Instead, I ignore the rage bait and show him that one of us is capable of remaining professional.

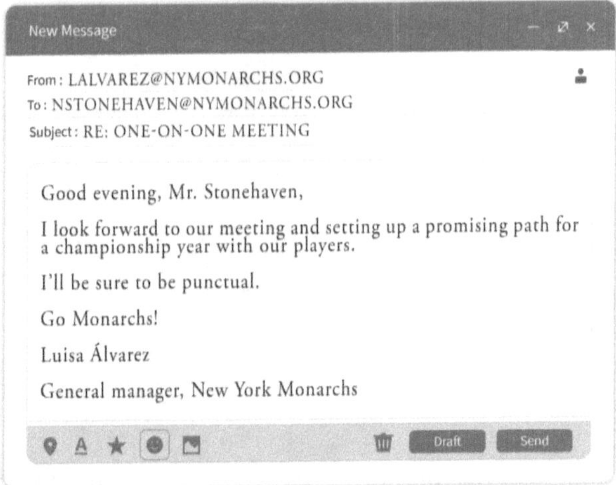

There.

I did it. I managed to respond to my new boss in a positive, professional manner.

And it could have remained that way.

Had he not immediately responded to my email with only two words.

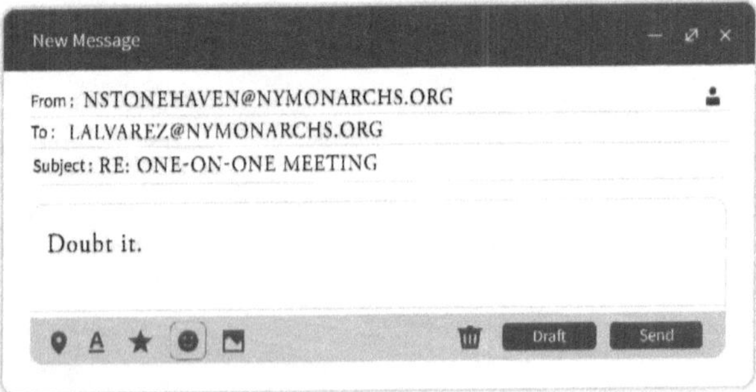

Seems like we're playing it his way then.
Good thing I know exactly what my next move will be.

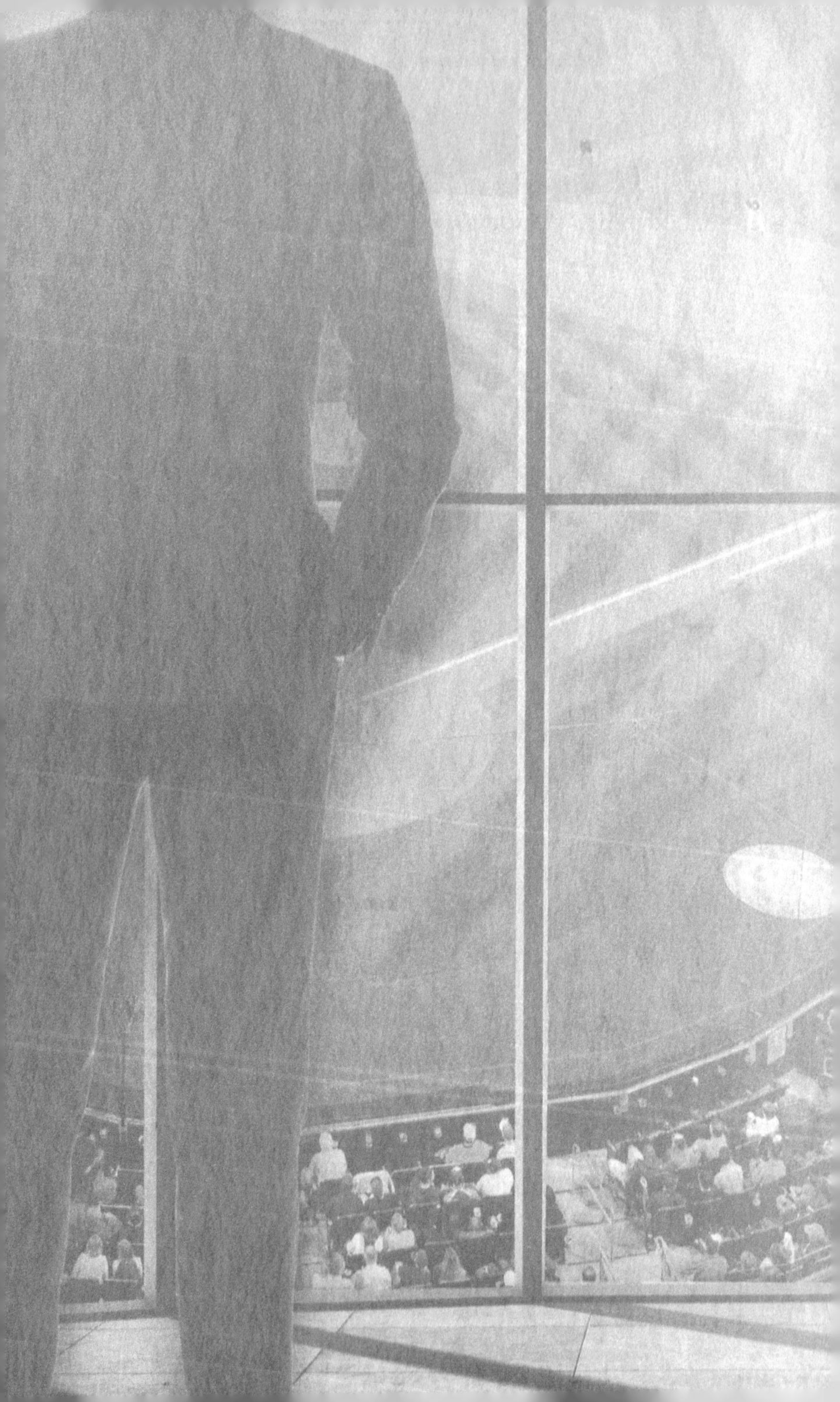

Chapter Ten

NICK

I'm being a dick.

I know I am. But I can't help it. Something about being wrong about her makes me feel uncomfortable in my own skin.

Running Stonehaven Media is simple.

The empire I created has me living the dream. Last year, I secured the biggest deal of the century, acquiring the world's most famous publications as my own. Afterward, I decided to ditch the States and move back to London for the first time in over twenty years.

Thinking it might feel more like home than my mansion in the burbs did.

But I was met with a lot of the same.

Gold diggers? Opportunists? Fathers who lack human decency?

I knew how to handle the lot of them.

All a walk in the park.

But Luisa is proving to be different from what I was expecting.

And I hate being caught off guard.

I smiled as I shot off that email yesterday, expecting a snarky response to my jab about her prior tardiness when we first met.

So imagine my disappointment when she was... pleasant.

Again, proving me wrong.

I also hate being wrong.

Which is why I sent off that asshole response before I could stop myself. I instantly regretted it, and I knew I would have to apologize to her in person today.

That was the plan when I invited her to this meeting, but a little gremlin in my mind took over momentarily, sending me down that immature spiral.

But I'm not immature.

This isn't like me at all.

I respect those who work for me, especially women.

It's how my mother raised me.

And if she were around today to see how I've been conducting myself lately, she'd be gravely disappointed.

And would probably whack the back of my head with a chancleta.

Only a handful of people know that I was raised by a Dominican single mother. One who was brilliant and destined to be one of the greatest barristers the UK had ever seen while also being the best mother to me and my little sister.

Unfortunately, she never saw Daisy grow past her first year, and at the age of eleven, I made a promise to be there for my sister in every way humanly possible.

We were sent to a boarding school in Connecticut shortly after my mother's death, and I have remained stateside for the most part for these last two decades.

I was the only kid with a funny accent. And for years I tried to speak like an American. Adapt to their mannerisms and sayings. I learned to code-switch and tamp down my English ways when I found it to be beneficial. But my accent never really went away, and I'm glad it didn't, because it's a part of me I never want to forget. Like when I used to make fun of my mother's English due to her heavy Dominican accent. Hearing her try to pronounce her vowels correctly will forever remain some of my fondest memories.

Memories I clung to in order to survive the cruel and colorless world that was left for me once her existence was no longer.

Navigating being motherless while also being my baby sister's only family, her protector, is a childhood experience I don't wish upon anyone.

Skipping lunches with friends so I could play with her at the daycare side of the school. Convincing our nannies to speak to us in their native Spanish, even though they were explicitly told not to do so, in hopes that we could feel closer to our late mother. And sharing lonely holidays together, me promising to make something of myself so we'd never have to spend another Thanksgiving home alone.

Luckily, Daisy has grown into a beautiful and kind woman. Someone who wouldn't hesitate to give the shirt off her back to someone in need.

A woman who, at times, can be too trusting.

Which is why I'm fiercely protective of her.

Because my mother would have been.

I am many things, but being immature is most definitely not one of them.

Emotionally stunted? Now that I could make a case for if I call and schedule an appointment with my therapist again.

It's been a few years, but I'm sure she's expecting my call any day now.

I walk down the hall that leads to my new office.

I want to get settled and have a cup of coffee before my meeting with Luisa in order to get my head right.

But those plans are out the window the second I turn the corner and spot Luisa standing by my assistant's desk, laughing. She's dressed in a bright pink blazer, matching dress pants, a fitted black top, and those "fuck me" heels she wore the night she was mine.

Dammit. There it is again. My heart hammering in my chest the second I lay eyes on her.

I thought the other day was a fluke. The shock of seeing the mysterious woman I had a one-night stand with, who ran out on me when I was just getting started with her.

Ridiculous thought, really, since I don't make a habit of bedding a woman twice. I've made that mistake before and have found leaked articles about personal information carelessly shared by yours truly during post-sex pillow talk.

I tell myself that I'm hung up on the chase. That it's been a while since I've spent the night in a woman's company, and she came along at the right time.

But I'm not stupid.

I can smell an excuse from a mile away, and I currently reek of them.

It's just an attraction. A crush at best. Most likely my body's natural reaction to being near the woman who gave me the best sex of my life.

So yeah, I'll cut my racing heart some slack and maybe skip my coffee this morning. I'm sure it'll do the trick.

"Good morning. I see you've made introductions already."

My assistant, Marla, squeals. I've never heard a sixty-year-old woman squeal, but I guess meeting Luisa will do that to the best of us. "She's such a doll, Nick. And funny! Did you know she was funny? She has me tearing up, and it isn't even eight thirty."

Luisa is leaning on the desk, looking much too relaxed for my liking. As if she's the one in control.

Fuck. Is she?

She makes a show of looking down at her watch and sighing dramatically. "Cutting it close there, boss."

I'm ten minutes early to our meeting, but clearly, she was even earlier, making me feel like I'm running late.

I move past her and open my office door. "That just means we have more time for our meeting. Lucky us." I gesture for her to step inside my office. "Hold my calls, Marla."

She chuckles. "No one even has this number yet, Nick."

God. Am I being awkward? I feel like I'm trying to play it cool but can't be sure if it's actually working.

Luisa snickers as she walks past me.

Yep. The cool shtick is not fooling anyone. I shake my head and make my way toward my desk. It's actually my first time sitting here. When I visited earlier in the week, it still felt like it was my grandfather's office. I asked Marla to hire a designer to redecorate and get rid of all the furniture. But his energy still lingers. As if he enjoys watching me play along with his ridiculous requests.

A part of me thought that there'd be a long, handwritten explanation for his absence in my life. Or, at the very least, his reasonings for gifting me this team.

But there was none of that. Just more terms and conditions.

It's no bother to me. For all I care, he and my father were the same breed of men, and nothing I aspire to be.

Yet he gave me this team with impossible expectations. Ones I have to abide by in order to recover what I've lost, the one thing his trust is keeping over my head.

I'm brought back to the present when Luisa takes a seat across from me, crossing her legs slowly. I'm sure she's just getting comfortable, but I can't help but feel like she's already fucking with me. I move my mouse to wake up my computer in an attempt to look like I'm at ease but quickly abandon that plan once I realize it's protected with a password that I have yet to be given.

"Need a minute?" Luisa asks sweetly.

Oh yeah, she's definitely fucking with me.

"Actually, no. Let's get right to it." I point at the two of us. "Is this going to be a problem moving forward? I know we didn't end on the best of terms when we last saw one another, but I'm hoping we can put our differences aside for the sake of our working relationship."

She nods emphatically. "Of course. Accusing someone of extortion is an honest mistake. In your world, I assume. Not mine." I open my mouth to interrupt, but she carries on, feigning seriousness. "But moving forward, I'll be sure to keep our communication open and honest to prevent any potential misunderstandings."

I sigh deeply. "Luisa, look. I owe you an apology." She looks me over cautiously as I speak. "I jumped to a conclusion much too quickly and hurt you in the process, and for that, I am sorry."

She narrows her eyes slightly. "Thank you for the apology. That's very... big of you."

Try as I might, I can't hold back the smirk that overtakes my face.

Yes, Angel. You know very well how big I am.

She realizes a moment too late how that sounded, and I can see her reinforcing those walls she put up the moment she walked out on me a few days ago.

She picks up her oversized bag and hikes it over her shoulder. "Like I was saying, it's all water under the bridge. In fact..." She moves closer to my desk while pulling out a couple of bulky printouts. Wait, are those magazines? "I got you a gift for your first day on the job."

Thump. Thump. Thump.

Vanity Fair. GQ. The New Yorker.

Each magazine lands on my desk with a deafening thump.

The kicker? I quickly recognize that Stonehaven Media owns all of these publications.

"If that's all, I'll be heading to the all-staff meeting. Good luck."

I'm stuck staring at the images of her on every cover, only pulling my focus away when she's stepping through the doorway.

"Hold on, Luisa..."

"Oh, don't worry. I even signed them for you, boss. See you around." The look of satisfaction on her face has me diving into the first magazine, pawing my way through the pages to her article to see what she wrote.

I have to reread it a few times to let it finally sink in.

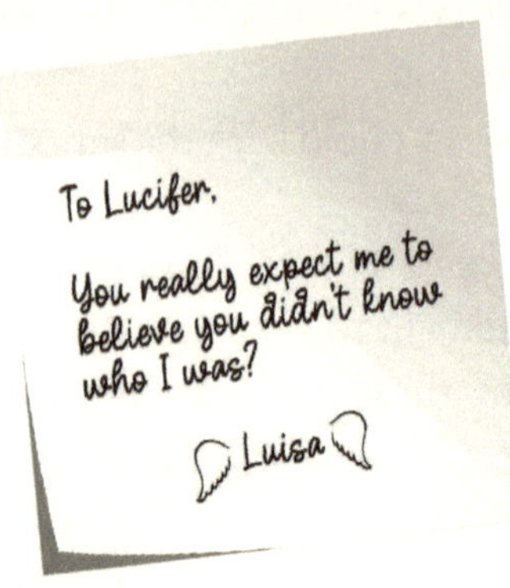

Check fucking mate.

I roughly run a palm over my face, processing what occurred.

She wrote the last words I said to her here in this very office earlier this week. Right before she called me the devil.

The woman is brilliant, I'll give her that.

I should feel ashamed. Beg for forgiveness. Maybe even quit.

But I'm not going to do that.

Because Luisa just declared war.

Not with what she wrote.

But by drawing the little angel wings beside her name like she did the morning after we fucked.

An illicit thought flashes through my mind, leaving as quickly as it arrived, making me equal parts furious and aroused.

I think I just lost my first fight with my future wife.

CHAPTER ELEVEN

LUISA

I shouldn't have done that.

Doesn't mean it didn't feel good.

Especially while watching him try to avoid eye contact with me as he spoke to the front office staff.

Meanwhile I relaxed back in my chair, hands clasped over my stomach, looking like I didn't have a care in the world.

It gave me a good vantage point. Allowed me to see how the women from other departments reacted to Nick, and it was clear that they were hanging on his every word.

I pushed down the stupid feelings of possessiveness that surged inside me. Because Nick was mine in the same way that yearly taxes were. Something you have to bear and play nicely with in order to not end up in prison.

But as I head into one of the smaller conference rooms, preparing to meet with my three assistant general managers and pitching coach Luke Weston, I start to feel my nerves creeping up.

Could I do this job on paper? Yes. In my sleep.

But stepping out and doing it now that the season has begun? It feels like a much different ball game.

Thank God Daisy has coordinated our schedules so we can have daily lunches and coffee breaks to help me release some of the tension I carry.

Walking down the hallways with a bunch of old, rich white men in suits will do that to a girl.

Lucky me, the person I'm meeting with now is nothing like that.

Luke arrives first, which is how I planned it, since I need to run something by him before the AGMs arrive. I probably should have allotted more time for this conversation, but I figured the element of surprise might work to my advantage.

It also gives me less time to chicken out.

The fact that Luke Weston has come out of hiding and is gracing the Monarchs with his presence is nothing short of a miracle.

He left his professional baseball career behind at the top of his game—after winning the World Series for his team.

The tragedy that followed shortly after was to blame, and I honestly wouldn't have been surprised if he decided to never walk back into the limelight.

Which is why I was shocked when Arthur told me that Weston had signed on to be our pitching coach. I have no idea how he managed that, but once I discovered he was on staff, I wanted to see if I could make my first big professional team shuffle of the season.

"Álvarez." He nods as he takes the seat next to mine.

I'm here in a professional manner, but I'd be a bald-faced liar if I said that Luke Weston wasn't an attractive man. At the height of his career, he looked more like a Hollywood movie star than a starting pitcher of the Texas Stars. But now, after years away, he's taken on a new look.

His boy-next-door vibe has been switched out for wilderness hunk. I wouldn't be surprised if his workout routine included splitting wood with an axe or carrying logs over his shoulder while he builds a cabin with his bare hands.

His glacial blue eyes have a way of pulling you in. And his unkempt beard and wavy brown hair keep you intrigued about the man behind the scruff.

But his obvious beauty truly does nothing for me. Seems like I've been cursed to be aroused solely by men who rule the underworld.

"Luke, I've told you to call me Luisa a million times." I smile.

His lips twitch slightly. "Sorry, ma'am."

I raise an unamused brow. "Oh, I'll report you to HR if you ever call me ma'am again. I'm younger than you. That keeps me safely out of ma'am territory."

He shakes his head, ignoring my banter. "Did I get the meeting time wrong?" He looks around the room, reminding me that it's time to make him an offer I pray he won't refuse.

"Actually, I wanted to chat with you before the rest of the guys arrived." He nods slowly. "You see, when you were hired, I had no idea you'd be interested in working in the industry, much less on the field."

His shoulders straighten slightly. "I wasn't."

Oh, right. I forgot how little Luke likes to talk. I'm going to have to do it for the both of us.

"Look, Luke, I'm going to give it to you straight—"

"You're firing me."

"What? No! Of course not. Shit. Am I doing this wrong? Let me start over." I take a deep breath as Luke's unwavering stare threatens to unnerve me. "I want to offer you a promotion. To manager. I think you being a pitching coach is great, but I believe that managing the coaches on the field and being in full control of our game would be an even better use of your skill set."

He's already shaking his head. "I can be a coach, but manager? Too much media attention, and I'm no one's puppet."

I put my hands up in a placating manner. "Yes, I already thought about this, but look at what's already happening. Ever since you arrived at spring training, the reporters have been all over you. Unfortunately, this industry comes with media vultures. Trust me, I know." His eyes soften slightly. I'm sure he's seen some of the media chatter questioning if I was a PR hire or actually qualified to do this job. "But we have no control over their interest in you or me. And they are not the reason we're in this field. We do it because we love the game and we know how to make our team better."

He sighs as he shifts back in his seat. It might as well scream "I'm considering it," so I continue.

"Look, you'll still technically be a coach. Like the mega coach. Main coach in charge. Head honcho—"

"Álvarez, I know what a manager is."

"Right. Exactly. So you know that you'd be in charge of who plays, what strategies we should make mid-game, and how to direct the other coaches to best position their players. You were always a cerebral player on the field. You saw things that most couldn't. No one could have predicted your former team would win the World Series 4-0, and yet they got it done. Because of you." I point at his chest.

His hand rubs his beard, and I force myself to stay silent and let him process what I'm offering.

If he agrees, he'll be the youngest manager in the history of major league baseball at the age of thirty-one. This will open the floodgates to media attention, and he will be expected to do more interviews.

His face will be synonymous with the New York Monarchs like Joe Torre was for the Yankees.

After a minute of silence, he asks, "What about DiSorbo?"

DiSorbo is our current manager and, frankly, someone who should not be allowed in front of a mic because the mouth on that man will get us fined after every game. "DiSorbo is out. I can get an interim pitching coach while you establish yourself as manager."

His brows rise. "You're ruthless, Álvarez."

I lean forward, steepling my hands on the desk. "So, what do you say, Skipper?"

His face scrunches, and for a moment I think I've blown it.

"If anyone dares call me Skipper, they're getting benched for the entire season. I may be the new manager, but I will not take on the manager pet name when I'm in the dugout or elsewhere. I'll always go by Coach."

Did he—did he accept the job? Did I actually get this done during the week after opening day?

I don't dare breathe. "So do we have a deal, *Coach*?"

He matches my posture over the desk as he replies. "Looks like we do, *Luisa*."

Thank God I have a big office with actual walls instead of frosted glass. If not, I wouldn't have the liberty of dancing barefoot in my office, celebrating the win I had with Coach Weston today.

The official announcement went live an hour ago, and the sports outlets have run wild with the news.

I was sure to set up Coach's first interview for next week, giving the media frenzy a few days to simmer down so they don't hound him too badly, although it'll be a miracle if they get more than yes or no answers from him.

I'm so caught up in the moment, shaking my ass to my Rihanna playlist, that I don't notice the massive form leaning against my open office doorframe until I turn around and let out a very unimpressive squeak.

Nick doesn't try to hide his amusement one bit. "Oh, don't mind me. I was looking to debrief with my GM about a major change in staffing that was announced to the media before we had a chance to discuss it in detail. But by all means, continue dancing to 'Bitch Better Have My Money.'" He waves me on.

I slap my cell phone screen a few times to pause the song, my go-to when thinking about trades and potential deals, and catch my breath while staring at my office intruder.

"Have you heard of knocking?"

The side of his mouth kicks up slightly. "I did."

"Oh. Well, I didn't hear you."

He gives me a look that screams "Obviously."

I shake my head. "I did give you a heads-up, to be fair."

"Ah, yes." He pulls out his phone and reads. "Promoting Luke Weston to manager. DiSorbo is fired. Figuring out interim pitching coach now. Let me know if you have any questions. Luisa."

I wave at his phone, my gesture communicating "Well, there you go."

He straightens and closes the door after fully stepping into my office. Being enclosed in here now makes my office feel a whole lot smaller than it was moments ago.

"You see, Luisa. That's just not going to work for me." He walks up to my desk and starts picking up the small frames and knickknacks I have displayed across it. He smirks down at the picture I have of me sitting on my dad's lap while at a baseball game, my two front teeth missing. "Cute."

I snatch the frame out of his hand and place it face down on my desk. "I'm sorry, Mr. Stonehaven, but you're going to have to be a bit more detailed about what doesn't work for you."

He makes a noise in the back of his throat. "Mr. Stonehaven. How... formal." He makes his way around my desk, and I have to focus on keeping my breaths even and my expression unbothered. "I do think we're past the formality, given our... familiarity, dare I say?" He stops when we're standing toe to toe, with my head tilted up to keep eye contact.

I don't know what his play is here, but if he thinks he can undermine my authority by reminding me of our tumble in the sheets, he has something else coming to him. "Sorry, I'm not sure of what you're getting at. Because it would be beneath you to not only backpedal on an apology that seemed genuine but also speak of matters that are outside of the scope of our professional positions. Don't you think, Mr. Stonehaven?"

The fucker has the audacity to full-on grin in my face. And for a weak moment, I consider either slapping or kissing it off his face.

"My apologies, Luisa, but I was referring to the fact that you are now one of my sister's closest friends. You're all she talks about lately, while leaving me in the dust. I'm still waiting for an invite to one of your lunch dates, by the way." He fake pouts. "So I'm not exactly sure what you were alluding to." He places his hands in his pockets, and the smooth motion makes me want to throttle him. He chuckles before his voice turns playful. "I can feel the violence vibrating off your skin, Luisa. Do we need to have an HR training on interpersonal conflicts?"

I cross my arms under my chest, accidentally lifting my breasts in the process. His eyes drift down for a split second, long enough for me to notice that he looked, and now I'm the one sporting a grin. "No need. I have no problem keeping my hands to myself, *sir*."

I think I hear a faint growl before he takes a large step back, running one of his hands down his navy silk tie. "Splendid. But I didn't come here to discuss HR matters."

I rest my ass on the desk. "Then why did you *come, sir*?" I taunt again. And now I swear he's the one who wants to have his hands around my neck. The visual, shockingly, feels much more appealing than I'd ever admit.

"Cut the shit, Angel—I mean Luisa." I stiffen at his slip of the tongue. It now feels like it's been decades since he called me that in bed. "You can't make unilateral decisions about the hierarchy of the team I own and not include me in the decision-making process." I stand to defend myself, but he powers on. "I'm not here to stifle your authority. I've caught up quickly on what your role is here in the organization, and I respect it. But as the team owner and the person in charge of running the business, I would expect the same respect to be given in return."

I deflate slightly, because he's right.

I ran everything by Arthur when it came to signing on the players. Because while who we hire is up to me, he was still my boss and needed to be in the loop with the finances to make sure that we were abiding by our spending pot and budget. Giving Coach Weston a promotion also meant tripling his pay, which is most definitely something I would have discussed with my boss had he not been... Nick.

If I'm going to preach about being taken seriously in my role as GM, I'm also going to have to wear my big girl panties and do the things that a responsible GM would do. Which includes maintaining open communication with my team owner.

I nod. "You're right." He gives me a look of disbelief, and I roll my eyes. "I'm woman enough to admit when I'm wrong. And in this instance, I should have kept you abreast of my intentions. It won't happen again."

"Hmm, nice apology." He looks lost in thought for a moment. "Although I could have done without the word 'abreast.'"

I snort and cover my nose immediately, embarrassed by the noise that came out of my face.

His face lights up as he moves toward the door. "Look at us. Getting along. Looks like hell has frozen over."

It takes a second, but once I get the devil reference, I scowl. "Let's not get too ahead of ourselves."

He grabs the doorknob and begins to close it behind himself before he stops abruptly, his face morphing into one of stern professionalism while his eyes blaze with heat.

"Oh, and Luisa?"

I grit my teeth, "Yes?"

"Call me sir again and see what happens."

The door clicks shut a second before I crumple into my chair.

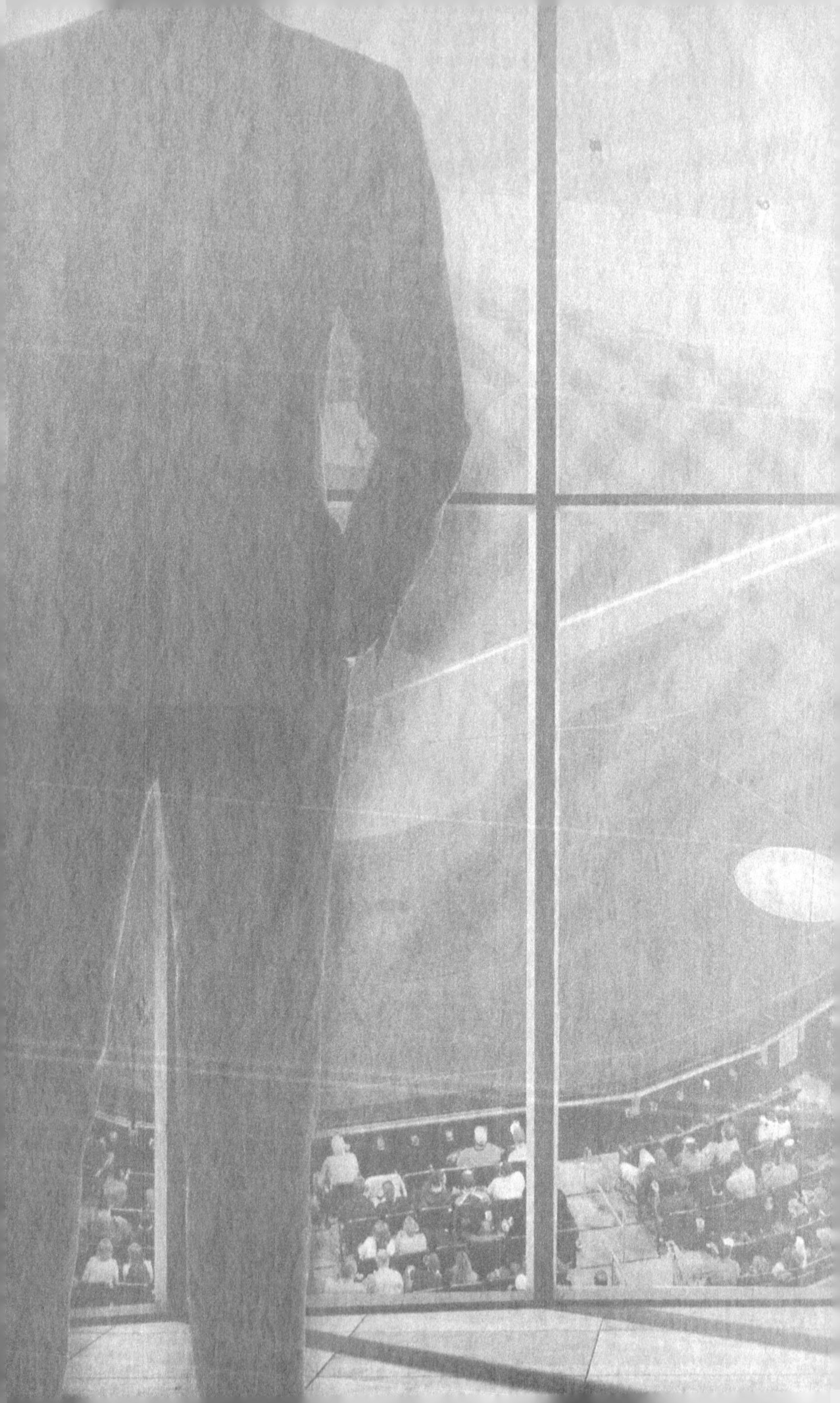

Chapter Twelve

NICK

I MAY HAVE WON that round, but at what cost?

Aside from the raging hard-on I had to hide with an open stadium map pamphlet.

She's embedding herself under my skin.

Making a home where she's not welcome.

As much as I love to spark the fire in her, I know it's a fruitless game to play.

Because I'm meant to be alone. As I've always been.

And once I've completed the terms of my grandfather's will, I'll be gone, and the days of pushing Luisa Álvarez's buttons will be a faint memory.

Or so I tell myself.

Every night when I dream of her.

CHAPTER THIRTEEN

LUISA

I'VE DONE A SPECTACULAR job of ignoring my new boss.

I mean, I've emailed him an unhealthy number of times in the last two weeks in regard to the deals I have in the pipeline, but aside from that, I've been able to steer clear of the angel of darkness.

That is, until I walk into a meeting I scheduled with my assistant general managers and find him sitting at the head of the conference table.

I swallow a shocked gasp and move to the seat beside him as if this was planned ahead of time, nodding in his direction without making eye contact. I ignore his displeased "and good morning to you, too," and as he types at a furious pace on his laptop, I keep my eyes trained on the door.

I need to be on my A game today.

The rest of the team files in, and I remember why I was dreading this meeting long before I realized Nick would be chaperoning it.

Mark Webber, James Ashton, and Richard Pembroke walk in, offering their hearty hellos, while I try to remind my nether regions that I'm here to inform my team of some unpopular shakeups, not to ogle Nick, who looks incredible in a gray suit.

"Good morning, gentlemen. Thanks for coming. I've provided some coffee and tea on the table by the entrance, and please help yourselves to the pastries."

Mark and James make a beeline for the muffins while Richard takes the seat across from me. He forgoes any refreshments, instead opting to lean back in his chair, studying me.

He's closer to Arthur's age, having been the general manager of another team for almost forty years. I don't know why he agreed to come out of retirement to be an AGM here, but the way he's looking at me now makes me feel like I'm an inconsequential steppingstone on his path to taking back my office.

I try for small talk. "No coffee for you this morning, Richard?"

He offers a practiced smile, one that comes after many years of being in front of the camera as the general manager of one of the biggest baseball teams on the West Coast. "Finished my second cup before the sun was up, kid."

Nick's loud typing stops abruptly, and it takes everything in me to act like I don't notice. Just how I'm acting like Richard calling me "kid" when I'm his boss isn't unprofessional or downright inappropriate.

Richard turns toward Nick, offering him a much more sincere smile. "Didn't know you'd be sitting in on the meeting today, Nick. Something big happening that I don't know about?" He looks in my direction, as if I'm his lowly intern who has somehow mixed up his calendar.

Nick speaks, pulling Richard's attention away from me. "It's Mr. Stonehaven. And you are?"

My eyes almost bug out of my face.

I may be wishing I had a voodoo doll of Richard, but that doesn't take away from the fact that this man's name is synonymous with baseball stardom since the team he previously managed has the most consecutive World Series wins in the last decade.

Richard's cheeks redden as he pitifully attempts to play Nick's words off as a joke. "Oh, c'mon. I know you inherited the team from your grandfather, but a good businessman would never enter a meeting not knowing the name of everyone around the table, am I right?"

Nick doesn't miss a beat. "Only the ones worth knowing." His eyes quickly flash toward me before he looks down and closes his laptop. "Luisa, when you're ready."

"Right." I stand a bit too quickly, sending my chair rolling behind me. I quickly wrangle it back and push it into place. I catch Nick's confused stare and follow it down to my feet. I'm wearing flat Mary Janes. The shoes I often opt for, rather than my usual power heels, when I'm meeting with my AGMs.

I ignore Nick's potential disapproval and make my way toward the presentation I have set up on the screen at the other end of the conference table. It truly isn't necessary for what I have to say, but I feel more comfortable having the numbers and proof behind me as I make my case for the changes I have in mind.

James and Mark take their seats next to Richard and settle in with their array of morning snacks.

"So," I begin nervously. Fuck. Why am I nervous? I practiced this last night. I know the information like the back of my hand. This isn't a spelling bee; it's baseball. It's in my blood. I need to start acting like it. And I will, the second my backbone decides to come back to me after taking an apparent coffee break.

"Oh, Luisa, before you begin." Nick stops my panic spiral. "I know this space isn't massive, but if you could please be sure to project your voice. And while you're at it... remember to *enunciate* your words."

I suck in a shocked breath.

He didn't.

He wouldn't.

But as he leans back and steeples his hands over what I know to be a set of rock-hard abs, eyeing me expectantly, I realize he did.

He's taunting me with the conversation we had that first night at the bar.

Here. Now. At work.

Right as I'm about to present to my subordinates. All of whom are older and much more experienced than me. I push down on the insecurity that had me overpreparing for this meeting in the first place and focus on the smug asshole sitting at the other end of the table.

The recklessness of his actions has me seeing red. I straighten as I feel my eyes turn to slits in his direction. I tap on the touch screen more forcefully than necessary as I begin. "I'll try my best, Mr. Stonehaven. But in any case, you're free to switch seats if that suits you." I pause as he bites down on a slight smile. "And I know you're new to the sports world, so when you see the letters M-L-B on the presentation, know that it stands for Major League Baseball." I nod patronizingly.

The satisfied grin that overtakes his face has no place in the boardroom, and yet it's the one thing I must have needed to get my head on straight before I dove into my presentation.

By the end of the meeting, everyone, including Richard, is on board with the idea that we need to find a new shortstop, given that our player is currently hiding an injury from us. Clearly our rookie doesn't understand that his strength and conditioning coaches don't miss a thing, and neither do I.

They all file out of the room as I start to gather my things.

I'm riding a high so powerful I don't even care that Nick has made no attempts to move from his seat as he stares me down.

"Impressive work, Luisa."

"I know." I don't try to downplay how good I'm feeling.

He chuckles to himself. "Although I do have a few questions."

I grab my purse and hoist it over my shoulder. "Okay, so a shortstop is the baseball player who is positioned—"

He rolls his eyes as he interrupts. "I know what a... never mind. Care to explain why you let that Richard guy call you a kid?"

I smirk. "Oh, so you do know his name."

"Answer the question."

I shake my head. "He's old-school. Probably still has a hard time wrapping his head around the fact that his new boss not only holds his prior job title but is a woman less than half his age."

He nods thoughtfully. "Understood. Now tell me why the fuck any of that should be your problem."

My jaw drops slightly and he tsks.

"Wouldn't do that while you're alone with me, Angel." I stiffen and my mouth snaps shut. "And you're welcome, by the way. Seems like any time I reference the night that shall not be mentioned, you somehow are able to refocus your wrath toward me and hone it into your work. Something we can discuss during your quarterly review, so no need to dive into all that now."

"Are you—you did that on purpose?" I seethe.

He waves my rage away like it's something he's become accustomed to. "And the shoes. Can I get an answer on where the hell those came from and why you aren't wearing your usual dagger-like heels?" He rubs his chest absentmindedly, and I think back to when I shoved my heeled foot into it. "I have my suspicions, but I'd like to hear directly from you."

I cross my arms over my chest as I lean on the table. "Humor me."

He waves his hand up and down my body. "It makes you look shorter, at least shorter than the men who attended this meeting." He studies my face as he continues. "Maybe in an attempt to seem, what? Less threatening? Docile, even?" He huffs out a dry laugh. "Good luck with that, by the way. Everyone saw how you stared me down, the damn owner of this team, without breaking a sweat. So I don't think that shtick is fooling anyone, sweetheart."

"Enough with the names." And with perceiving me way too clearly.

He puts his hands up as he nods. "My apologies. You're right. We are in our workplace. Must keep up professional attitudes and all that." He pauses. "But you never stopped wearing heels around me. Care to at least answer that?"

I must be coming down from the adrenaline rush. There is no other way to explain why I decide to answer him with the truth. "I think it's safe to say that we both know you're not like most men who work here."

"I'm not like most men. Period."

"Ah, yes. The ego stroke that you most definitely did not need." I push my shoulder past him as I make my way to the door.

"One last thing, Luisa."

I stop and don't know whether to groan or smile at how hard he's working to keep me in this room. I turn to face him. "Final question, and then I must get back to work, Mr. Stonehaven." I sigh, acting like it's a hardship to be in his presence.

He ignores my use of his last name as his eyes turn serious. "Next time someone is sitting in your seat, you tell them to get the fuck out. Don't you dare let anyone question your rightful place or be afraid to put them in theirs." Confused, I look over at the table. He points to the seat he occupied at the head of the table. "Including me."

He grabs his things as I stay rooted in place, only stopping momentarily by my side before he heads out. "Especially me."

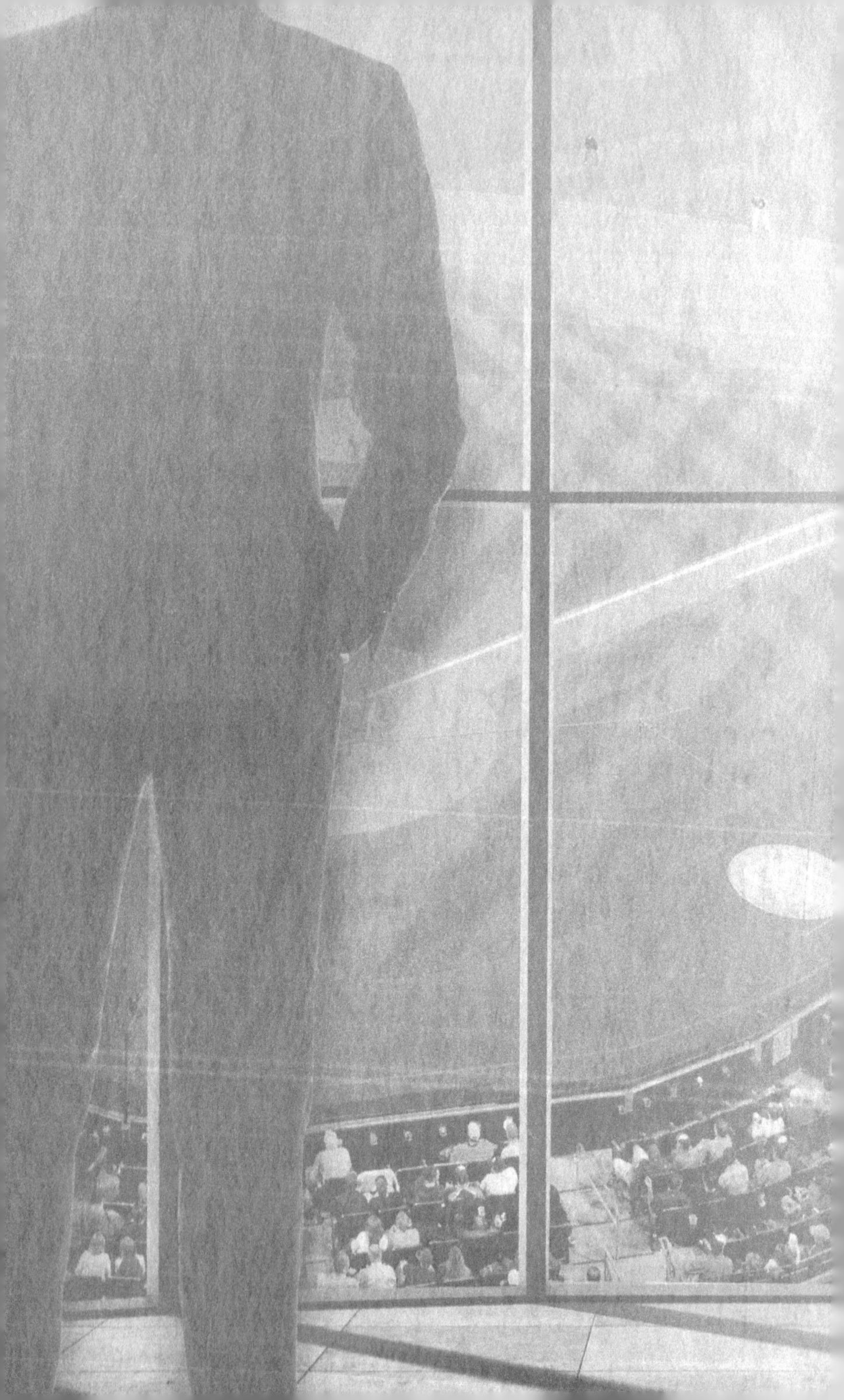

NICK

It's another lonely night, and I'm bored out of my mind in my new home that feels more like a TV show set.

I purchased this lovely brownstone when I realized a move to New York City would no longer be avoidable. I was hoping an actual home in the Upper West Side instead of a downtown apartment in a skyscraper would help bring in some warmth into my surroundings, given that the spaces I usually reside in tend to feel cold and sterile.

Maybe I overcorrected by buying a home clearly meant for a family that decorates for the holidays and share meals with their parents instead of communicating via their attorneys.

But there was something about this space that made me feel like I had some semblance of control of my future, even as my dead grandfather pulled the strings from beyond the grave.

This was not supposed to happen.

I was not supposed to lose.

And yet, the look in my father's eyes when he realized he had once again managed to break through my fortified armor and hurt me in the only way he knew how, proved how stupid I had been to make a bet with something that was not solely mine to risk in the first place.

And now I'm paying the price.

Alone in some sitcom house that's only missing the chorus of laughter and applause from the hidden audience.

At this point in the night, I've given up on trying to watch TV or read a book. My mind seems much too loud to allow it.

So I resign myself to taking up residence in my office instead. It's well after midnight in the UK, but if I fire off a few emails now, my team abroad can tackle their tasks while I'm sleeping here on the East Coast.

I'm usually most comfortable in a tailored suit while tending to business, but here in my home office, you will never catch me in one. Instead, I opt for dark sweatpants and don't even bother with a shirt.

I pour myself a glass of red wine from my bar cart, a cheap Cabernet Sauvignon that used to be my mother's favorite, and settle into my chair.

A few emails in, I start to grow frustrated with my lack of focus. I can usually run my media company in my sleep. That's exactly how it goes since moving back to the states, yet I find myself growing bored with the same song and dance.

I created Stonehaven Media with my bare hands. Many think that I got help from my father, who comes from old money, but quite frankly, those people would be dead wrong.

In order to ask for help from your father, you would first have to know he existed. Which would be hard to do, since I grew up thinking my dad was either a deadbeat or dead. My mother raised me on her own, struggled with every dirty penny to make sure I was well taken care of as she climbed her way toward being a respected barrister.

I knew my mother was brilliant. I could see it with my own two eyes as she studied cases at the dinner table while I worked on my schoolwork. Her work ethic was only matched by her devotion to being an amazing parent to me.

After asking about the whereabouts of my father as a young boy and my mother giving vague, roundabout answers, I learned not to ask anymore. And honestly? It didn't matter, because she was more than enough to fulfill every role in my life.

My mother and I were a team. A well-oiled machine when it came to our routines. Until she dropped a bombshell on me.

She was pregnant.

The kicker?

My dad, the man who was a ghost for all I knew, was the father of the baby girl on the way.

Things were never truly the same after that conversation.

I was angry and confused. Understandable for anyone to be, but for a ten-year-old boy whose mother was the sun he orbited? It was downright devastating.

To know that she lied, even if by omission by keeping details about my father a secret, cut deeply.

That she would dare go back, even for a night, to a man who had no qualms about abandoning his family and would continue to live his life in luxury while we were always on the fringes of financial ruin.

A man who had the gall to walk into my life with a stuffed animal and a balloon as if I were a toddler and not a preadolescent, brimming with rage at the unfairness of it all.

"Things will be different. We're finally going to be a family now, mijo." My mother would say, sometimes, I believe, more for herself than for me.

Because as my mother's belly grew rounder, we saw less and less of my father.

Calls went unanswered and visits became nonexistent.

He never even bothered to visit my mother in the hospital when she gave birth to Daisy.

The baby I was also angry with for infiltrating my life and forcing me to share my mother, my only family.

But the second they placed my little sister in my arms, wailing softly moments after she was born, I knew I had it all wrong.

Because my little sister was not the enemy; she was our saving grace.

It feels foolish to say, but the longer I held her, the more I could feel my anger quickly leaving my body. No longer furious with my mother and her choice of procreation partner, but grateful that she had given me another person I could now call my family.

After my mother passed, the most my father did for us was pay for boarding school here in the States. Mostly because the cat was out of the bag that he had two illegitimate children, and apparently that's what cold-blooded rich people do when they want a problem solved. They make it go away. Daisy was only a year old, but I begged for him to keep us together. She was the only family I had left.

It was me and her from there on out. She was the last piece of my mother here on this earth, and I vowed from a young age that I would always protect her, that no harm would ever come to her.

Yet here I am, tangled in a clusterfuck with my sperm donor because I dared to gamble something that rightfully belonged to both Daisy and me, and he had managed to beat me at my own game.

And my grandfather, in a pitiful attempt to make amends with me for turning a blind eye when he knew damn well of my existence, offered to play peacemaker for my father and me.

He was legally in possession of what I needed to get back.

I was hoping his will would state that he was gracefully returning it to me in one piece, but in true Arthur Stonehaven fashion, everything seemed to be a game for him. There were two ways for me to resolve this matter according to his will. One I'm currently taking seriously by actually putting in the work as owner of a damn baseball team.

The other option would be much quicker, but I'd much sooner flush my billions down the toilet than entertain the preposterous idea.

With that in mind, I pull up my New York Monarchs inbox and skip over every email Marla has flagged for me until I land on an unread email from Luisa.

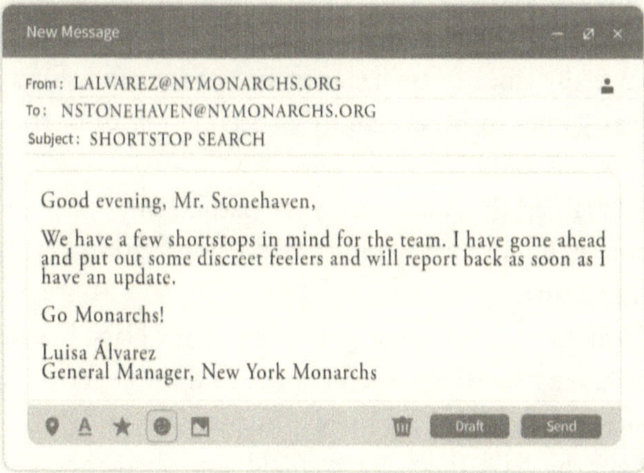

Ah, Luisa. Just what I needed.

I don't think. I let my fingers fly as I respond to her email.

As I press Send, I feel the faintest bit of a smile on my face and realize it's probably the closest I've come to that expression since I last saw her.

I roll my eyes at my absurd thought as I gleefully reread my response.

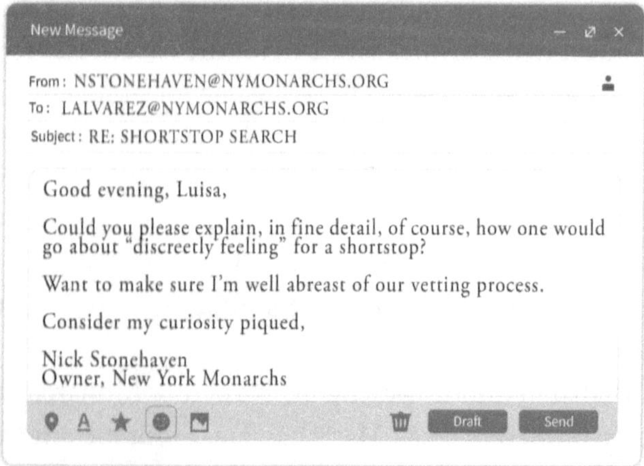

New Message — ⤢ ✕

From: NSTONEHAVEN@NYMONARCHS.ORG
To: LALVAREZ@NYMONARCHS.ORG
Subject: RE: SHORTSTOP SEARCH

Good evening, Luisa,

Could you please explain, in fine detail, of course, how one would go about "discreetly feeling" for a shortstop?

Want to make sure I'm well abreast of our vetting process.

Consider my curiosity piqued,

Nick Stonehaven
Owner, New York Monarchs

Childish? Perhaps.

Entertaining? Absolutely.

Especially since Luisa has been out of the office for a string of away games in Miami and I've been left with nothing but actual work to do.

I've drained the rest of my glass, pathetically ready to call it a night, when my laptop pings with a notification.

From Luisa.

Thank God there was no wine left in my glass, because the embarrassing speed at which I clicked on my keyboard would have left my desk looking like a crime scene.

I right the glass, then set it at a safe distance from myself and open her response.

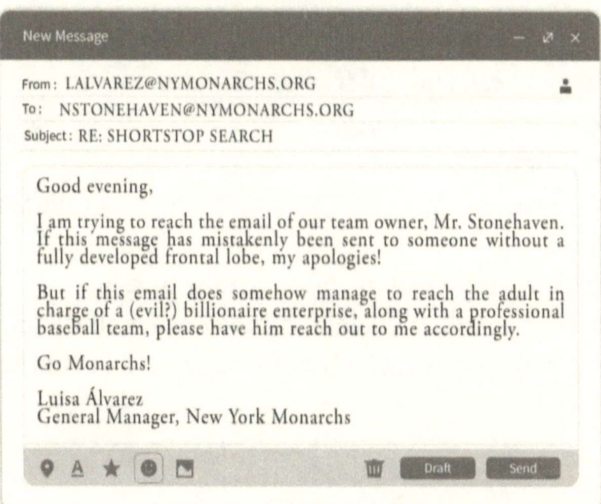

It takes me five solid minutes to stop laughing and get my breathing under control. I know based on the time I received the email.

I should stop.

I've indulged for the night and gotten my fix. I really shouldn't push the boundary, but then again...

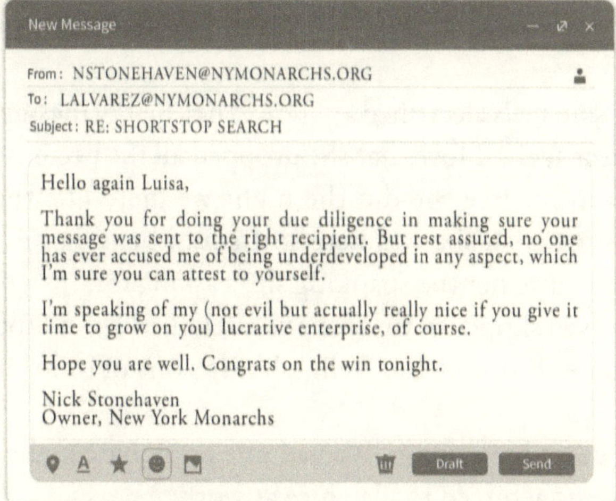

There. Not so bad. Still cheeky while reeling it in at the end.

I can go ahead and call it a—

Ding.

Surely not.

This quickly? Was she waiting by her phone for my response?

The thought pleases me more than it should.

I quickly open her email and can see that all the niceties are long gone. I smile widely before I can even read the first word.

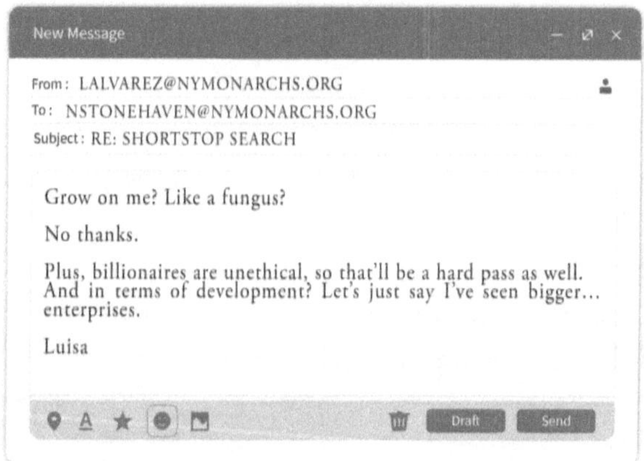

My skin feels electrified as I reread her snarky message over and over again. I love that she dropped all the pretenses and spoke to me like she did the night we met. The thought makes me wish she was here so I could bend her over my desk and give her the spanking she's asking for.

She even slipped in that fungus reference I wasn't too keen on before. But now I'm feeling like it's one of our things.

No.

We don't have *things*. We had one passionate night of sex and are now forced to play nice at work.

But then again, I am the boss, so how nice do I actually have to be when it comes to my naughty angel?

I respond like I have nothing to lose.

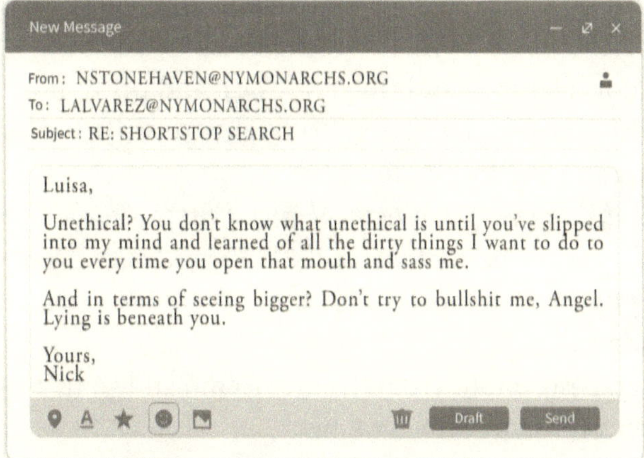

After I hit Send, the part that sticks out to me the most is how I signed off on the email.

Yours.

I've never done that before and don't know what possessed me to do it now.

Must be the cheap, sentimental wine.

I send a quick message to Marla and tell her to make sure any email correspondences between Luisa and I remain confidential and are not screened by a third party.

I usually do this with my company when I'm sending encrypted emails containing sensitive information, so it's not an uncommon request coming from me.

I close the laptop and force myself out of my office.

She isn't going to respond to that tonight. Or at all. Knowing Luisa, she's cursing me out as she stares at her screen.

Would love to see the look on her face, though.

I enter my room and go straight to my ensuite bathroom. I drop my sweatpants, along with my underwear, and stand in the shower, turning it on with high pressure before the cascading water has a second to warm. I'm telling myself it's not a cold shower. Just a quick refresh before bed.

I don't let my hands linger. I wash and rinse and am out of there before I allow my thoughts to drift back to my smart and snarky employee.

God, I try hard not to think about the forbidden aspect of it all, because surely that would be my undoing.

I put on a fresh pair of boxers and slip into bed without incident.

I grab my phone from the nightstand and go to plug it in when a thought occurs to me.

I never set up my Monarchs email to my push notifications.

It didn't seem necessary before, but now I wonder.

Before I can give it too much thought, I log into it and turn on my notifications.

Must be divine intervention. Or the universe's cruel joke.

Because staring back at me is Luisa's response.

Short and to the point.

I smile as I shut off the screen and rest the phone against my chest.

Jokes on her, though. Because in my dreams is exactly where I'll find her tonight.

CHAPTER FIFTEEN

LUISA

I'M BACK AT THE office, and my head is on a swivel.

I haven't heard anything from Nick in the last few days, which is only adding to my paranoia. After he sent those not safe for work emails, he went radio silent.

I should be glad and shake it off. But instead, he feels like the bogeyman. Like he's about to jump out from every corner I turn.

"Morning, Luisa!" Daisy chirps.

"Ay, coño." I curse as I slap my hand across my heaving chest.

Daisy startles as she looks around us. "Um, is everything okay?"

I nod repeatedly as I try to get my breathing under control. "Sorry about that. I'm a bit jumpy today." I raise my empty to-go cup. "Must be all the caffeine," I lie.

Daisy smiles gently. "Maybe you could swap it out for decaffeinated tea. I can bring you some from home if you'd like. Maybe something more calming to start your mornings? I have a couple of blends you could try out, and if you don't like those, I'm sure I can head to a tea shop and find something," she says eagerly.

I'm not a tea drinker. I actually can't stand the taste of it, but I'd sooner kick a puppy than turn down a nice offer from sweet

Daisy. "That is so kind of you to offer. Thank you so much." I give her arm a squeeze right as the phone in her hand lights up and her fiancé's name flashes on the screen.

Her smile dims a fraction before she settles it back into place. She lifts her phone as she raises her finger at me. "Hold on a sec! I need to take this and then we should be all good for lunch. I'll be quick. Promise," she finishes as she steps into her office and closes the door.

I've noticed her do that before. Shy away from speaking about her relationship or directing the conversation to me when I ask too many nosey questions, especially since she walks around with a rock the size of a golf ball on her ring finger.

But just like she's learned to accept that I'll never give her a straight answer as to why her brother and I aren't the best of friends, I've learned to respect her boundaries and allow her to keep her relationship to herself. For now.

I'm still staring at her door when a deep voice almost has me shooting out of my heels. "Hey, Luisa."

"¡La puta madre!" I gasp before I cover my mouth in embarrassment.

Coach Weston's eyes widen. "Did you call my mother a slut?" He scratches his bearded chin while taking in my current state. "Are you all right?"

"Yes. No. I'm sorry. I did not mean to call your mother a—it was a figure of speech."

He tilts his head slightly. "You do know I'm fluent in Spanish, right? Easy to pick it up when you play in a sport where more than half your teammates are native Spanish speakers."

"Yes. Well, please rest assured that I was not trying to disrespect your mother. I was startled, that's all." I force a chuckle. "You know, in a moment of panic, your body goes into either fight or flight or slut-shaming the universe mode."

He nods, and in true Coach fashion, changes the subject abruptly. "I'm back from a three-hour lunch with the team's PR team. Tell me again why I need to attend more press conferences than any other manager in the league right now?"

"Well, for one, you refuse to call yourself a manager. Therefore, you have the media swooning over you as the 'bad boy of baseball who will only answer to Coach.'"

He groans. "Had I known it'd be such a topic of discussion, I probably would have changed my mind."

"No, you wouldn't have." His mouth twitches slightly as I continue. "Also, you're the youngest manager in MLB history, a former player who ended his career on a World Series win and—" I stop abruptly, but it's too late.

Coach stiffens, then sighs deeply. "And my personal stuff."

I won't insult him with a lie, so I nod instead.

He blows out a breath. "I figured. But I thought—never mind. I'm done for the day, so I'm heading home."

Luke isn't a touchy-feely guy, so I offer my fist for him to tap his as our way of saying goodbye.

Before he turns to leave, Daisy comes bounding toward us with a broad smile. "Hi, Luke! Nice to see you again."

He clears his throat. Multiple times. "Hi there, Daisy. How's, uh, it going?"

Daisy smiles softly as she nods. "Really well. I still don't know exactly what my job here is supposed to be, since my brother basically roped me into the Monarchs family. But I've been toying with an idea lately that I want to run by a few people. I want to know whether it's worth mentioning to the social media team or not."

My phone pings with a notification as Coach struggles to string a simple sentence together.

Interesting.

Can't wait for you to get here! Let me know when you're close so I can start on the tostones.

Shit, that's right. I promised my mom I would come over for lunch since I've been out of town and insanely busy since the season started.

I feel terrible about ditching Daisy last minute, but it truly has been forever since I've seen my mom, and that is a Dominican cardinal sin.

"Hey, so please don't hate me." Daisy eyes me warily. "But I totally forgot that I'm supposed to be meeting my mom for lunch today. I'm so sorry."

"Oh." Daisy places her hand over her chest. "Of course. Don't worry about me. I'm not even that hungry." She laughs, but her poker face needs some work. "I can grab something quickly from the vending machine. It's no big deal. Go see your mama."

For a moment I swear I see sadness in her eyes.

But it can't be because I'm canceling lunch. We've both had times where we had to call off our lunches last minute when our schedules have shifted throughout the day.

I quickly run through what I said and wonder if she's ever told me anything about her mom or her parents, but I'm coming up blank.

Before I can invite her to come with me—my mother certainly wouldn't mind—Luke cuts in. "I could eat." Daisy and I turn toward him, sporting different looks. Daisy's is filled with hope, while mine settles on confusion, given he had a long lunch. "And never let me hear you say you're considering eating out of a vending machine when we literally have a cafeteria that feeds some of the best athletes in the world."

He waves her over as he begins to walk away. Daisy looks back and forth between me and Luke's retreating back. "Okay, guess I'm heading to the cafeteria. Have a great lunch with your mama. Remember to give her a big squeeze when you see her." She turns and gets in step with Luke.

Huh. Now that I think about it, I'm not sure if Daisy has ever mentioned her mother to me, which is odd, given how much I've told her about mine.

I'm stuck on the thought when I hear Coach's echoed words as he leads Daisy to lunch. "I want to hear all about this idea you've got for the social media team."

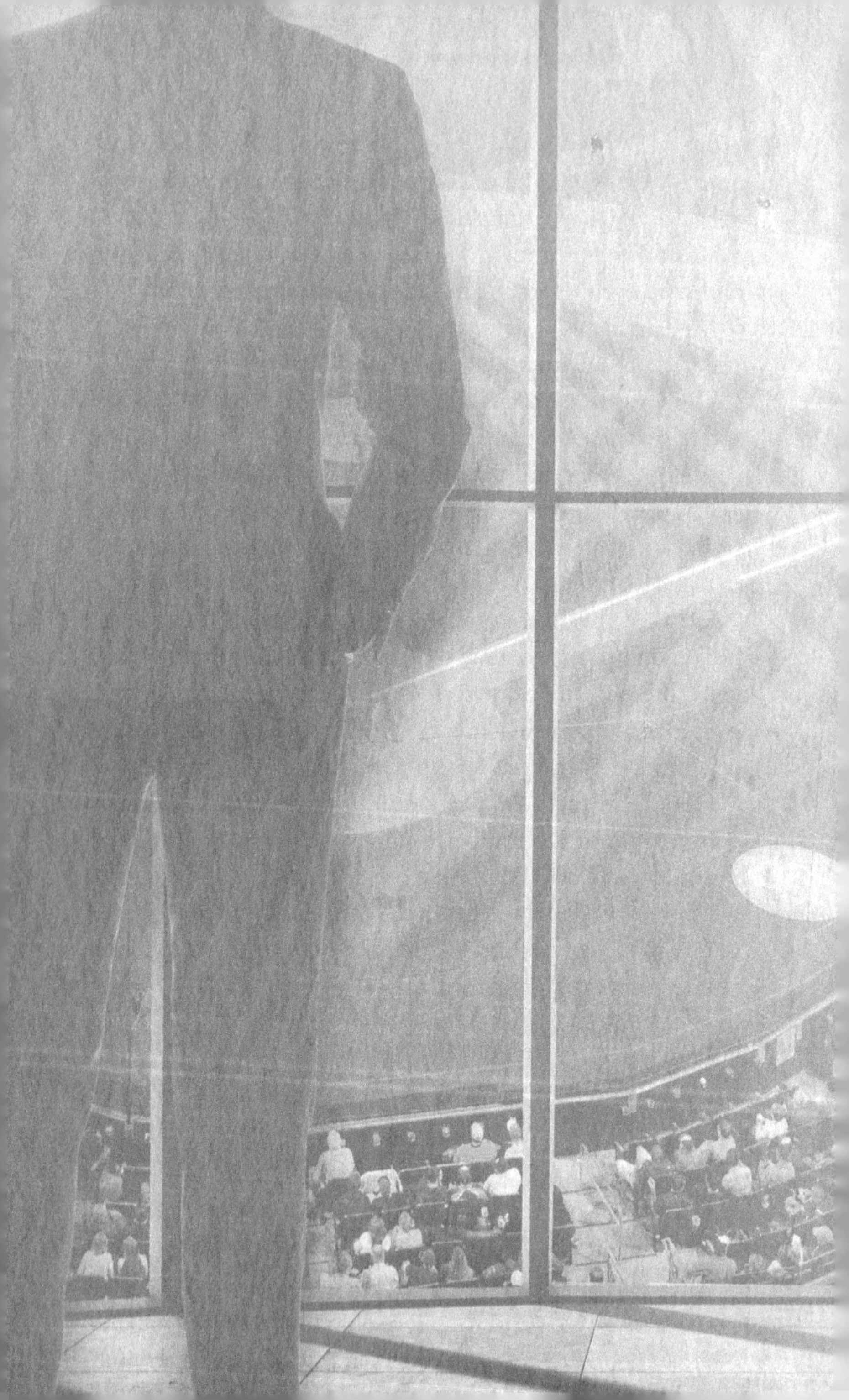

Chapter Sixteen

NICK

I'VE BEEN A GOOD boy.

Or so I tell myself as I wait for the special delivery to arrive at the Monarchs clubhouse.

We've been on a winning streak lately, and tonight is looking to be no different.

Our starting pitcher, Mateo Martinez, has been striking out almost every batter that's stepped up to the plate.

Guess he was worth the seven-hundred-million-dollar contract after all.

I've only stepped into the clubhouse once. It was on opening day, and only to give a "go get 'em team" speech. Because I've never really been inclined to make any other visits to spaces that hold air thick with body odor and sweaty athletes.

But today I'm making an exception.

It's been almost a month since I've laid eyes on Luisa, and that comes to an end now.

During her travels with the team and my attempts to keep physical distance from her here at the office, I've learned a few more aspects of the baseball culture.

There was one in particular that caught my attention. It seemed juvenile and silly at the time, but then again, I live for shit like this.

I can feel the stadium vibrate above me. The crowd is going absolutely mental over an out caught by our new shortstop, Samuel Juan, signaling the end of the ninth inning and making the Monarchs win official.

I watch on the screens around the room as the players topple over one another in celebration. The camera pans to the dugout, and I spot Luisa, smiling as she pats Coach Weston's back in congratulations.

I haven't spent much time with Luke, and the little I've heard alludes to the fact that he's a bit of a recluse. But now I'm wondering if maybe that was a mistake on my part. Luisa and Luke travel with the team and have most definitely spent a considerable amount of time together so far this season.

I wonder if he's Luisa's ty—

Enough.

I didn't come here to act like a jealous fool.

I'm not sure exactly what you would call the relationship Luisa and I have, given that we only communicate via email.

But those messages have become more and more consistent. I find myself emailing her multiple times a day, never having to wait more than half an hour for a response.

We've both ditched the signatures and work-related pretenses and have somehow fallen into becoming pen pals.

It usually starts with me asking her a barrage of questions, none of which have to do with her actual job. And she responds with the quick wit and snark that I've begun to crave.

So much so that I have taken things a step further in my teasing and have arranged for a special surprise in hopes that Luisa will engage in that new baseball tradition I have recently grown quite fond of.

The team slowly filters in, along with the coaching staff. They don't seem to notice me standing in the middle of the room, as they're all filled to the brim with excitement, high on their win.

The players head to where their belongings are stored and start pulling out various bottles of champagne.

Luisa walks in last, alongside my sister.

My heart softens for a moment when I see them together. My sister would never admit to it, but I know she struggles to make long-lasting connections. The friends in her life are shallow, social connections at best, and her relationship with her brainless fiancé is a whole other mess.

The fact that Luisa is a close confidant to someone as tender-hearted as my sister further proves that there is more to that woman than I know. Which is maddening for reasons I won't allow myself to dig into.

But tonight, we are all here for some fun.

And, hopefully, at Luisa's expense.

Daisy spots me first, as cafeteria staff start wheeling in tables full of red refreshments.

"Nick! What are you doing here?" my sister asks excitedly.

Luisa's head snaps in my direction, and I take in her white suit with blood red heels. Her eyes narrow in suspicion as I openly stare at her beauty.

Oh, just you wait, sweetheart.

I wrap my sister in a hug and lift her off her feet, like I did when we were kids.

She pinches my side as she squeals. "Put me down right now. We are at work, Nick," she scolds between a fit of laughter.

It's nice to hear her this way. Even though she plasters on those fake as fuck smiles day in and day out, I know my sister better than I know myself. And I know that something is up with her. I have a feeling my father is involved in this somehow.

"If I have to." I place her down next to me, then look up to greet Luisa. She's giving me a quizzical look. As if she cannot reconcile the person she spent the night with and the man standing before her. "Hello there, Luisa. Congrats on the win tonight." The cheering around us hasn't subsided, but I swear I can hear her thoughts from where I stand.

"What are you doing here?" she asks, straight to the point.

I make a show of looking around the clubhouse. "You know, oddly enough, last I checked, I owned this place. Can you believe it?" I scratch my chin as I feign astonishment.

Her eyes scan up and down my body, and I don't miss the momentary appreciation in them before she shuts that shit down. "What are you up to, Stonehaven?"

I don't attempt to hide my predatory smile as I wave at the coaching staff to get their attention. Quickly, they garner the attention of the rowdy players. I'm tall enough that I don't need to hop on a chair to get their eyes on me, so I begin right where I stand. "Congratulations on the win, guys. You were amazing out there." The cheering continues for a few seconds before they settle again. "You have been performing at a level that has far exceeded anyone's expectations, given that it is your first year playing as a team, but I know this is only the beginning."

Cheers erupt again as the team catcher, Anthony Torres, yells, "¡Así es! We're riding this straight into the World Series, baby!"

I wave my hand to settle them once more. I need to wrap this up before they go completely off leash on me. "I know there is a tradition for big games like these, where you seat a player or manager in one of the carts and wheel them into the shower while they're doused in champagne."

The players start shaking bottles in preparation and shoving the new shortstop into a cart.

I raise my hand. "I was wondering if you'd be open to a suggestion. You guys dominate the field, but there's a certain someone who has been dominating behind the scenes and went above and beyond to get our newest teammate here traded in what I've been told to be quite an impressive deal."

"Álvarez!" Chants start to break out as another cart is brought out. She glares in my direction as the players start to circle around her.

"No way. This outfit is new."

"I'll buy you a new one." The words spill from my lips before I even register what I'm saying.

The dare hangs between us. Someone rolls a cart my way, and I aim it in Luisa's direction, raising a challenging brow.

She slowly removes her white blazer, and the noise level reaches an alarming high. She keeps her eyes locked on mine and removes her heels. In this moment I'm glad there's a cart blocking the view of the bulge in my pants. She walks toward me and smacks the heels against my chest. "Hold these for me, would you?"

I grunt a response, since she's activated the caveman mode in my brain. She seats herself in the cart as delicately as possible, but eventually slumps in until her cute little feet are pointing up and out of the cart and she uses her arms to stay somewhat upright.

"Okay, let's get this over with, you overgrown children." She huffs as the team claps with excitement.

"Oh, I forgot to mention one thing. Since this is Luisa's first go at this rite of passage, I thought we'd do something more original than bottles of champagne."

Everyone looks on in anticipation as Luisa mutters under her breath, "What are you up to, Lucifer?"

"Everyone, please help yourself to those small buckets of sangria I had brought in. They have extra fruit in them. *Luisa's favorite.*"

Luisa turns in an impressive exorcist-style manner as I toss her shoes to a laughing Daisy and start to wheel her into the showers myself.

This wasn't part of my plan. I was supposed to look on from a safe and dry distance. But over my dead body will anyone else be in charge of leading this experience for her.

"Nicholas León Stonehaven, you absolutely did not plan all of this in that tiny peanut brain of yours," Luisa rants.

I tuck a piece of hair that's slipped from her ponytail behind her ear. "Angel, you know my middle name? I'm touched." Her cheeks pinken slightly, and for a moment I want to force everyone out of the clubhouse so I can explore this further.

But before I know it, everything I've put into motion starts coming at us fast. Mateo Martinez hands me a bucket as he smiles. "Something tells me you want to be the one who does the honors."

"Martinez, you're officially on my shit list," Luisa barks as she rushes to put her arms around her head, as if that will help the onslaught that's about to come her way.

He winces and moves back to a safer distance.

I stop momentarily, thinking maybe I've taken our bantering too far. I duck down to ask if she's really okay with this. What I find is a massive grin on her face and her body trembling with what I hope is excitement. I speak directly into her ear, "You ready, Angel?"

She looks up at me, and the sight of pure joy reflected in her gaze has me staggering back a step. I'm used to her bark and bite. But the vulnerable split-second look of unbridled happiness aimed my way?

Well, that might be the thing that makes a man like me feel good and holy.

Might even make me vow to make her smile again.

"Do your worst, Lucifer."

I shake my head as I lift the bucket high above her head. "Ready boys?" I shout, and the team crowds around the two carts. Samuel and Luisa let out war cries as I yell, "Let's get 'em!"

My bucket is the first to hit Luisa, and her shriek is high and loud. Before long, the whole shower area is doused in red sangria, leaving my Italian suit wrecked. Not that I give a shit.

I scan the massive shower and note the smiles on everyone's faces, the camaraderie shared among this team, the euphoria that comes with doing something as absurd as dumping perfectly good alcohol on their boss in a form of celebration. I spot Daisy at the mouth of the shower, recording this all on her phone. As I watch, a rogue bucket is tossed her way, and Coach Weston places his hands on her arms to move her out of the splash zone.

Once the flying flashes of red come to a stop, I look down at Luisa. She smiles up at me. She looks adorable, her lashes wet and clumped together, her bright white outfit now a ruby red color.

"I look like a wet rat, don't I?" she asks as she shakes her arms out.

I'm not thinking straight as I wrap her wet ponytail around my fist and start to wring the liquid out of it. She sucks in a shocked breath. "More like Carrie, but it suits you."

She slaps my hand away from her hair but surprises me when she clutches my forearm. "Use your Neanderthal strength for good and lift me out of here. My ass feels like it's sitting in swamp water."

My hands dip to her waist and pull her out immediately. I wait until I know she has her feet firmly planted on the shower floor, then check to make sure there's nothing she can slip on. "Hands off the merchandise, Luci." The smirk on her face has her looking downright devilish, and it has nothing to do with the fact that she's covered in red.

"And here I thought you weren't a fan of pet names."

"You're like a fungus, Stonehaven. Remember?"

"Yes, but last I recalled, I'm the fancy kind."

She plucks her wet shirt away from her body and I can see that she was wearing a white lace bra underneath. Her nipples are visibly hard. "You owe me a new outfit," she mumbles absentmindedly.

"And apparently some white lingerie. Is that what you always wear to work, or is tonight a special occasion?" My voice hardens at the thought of another man unwrapping Luisa at the end of the night as I lie in my bed like a fool dreaming about her. "Someone throw me a towel," I bark at no one in particular.

Ace Middlebrooks, our third baseman and resident ladies' man, stops in front of me with two towels. When I go to grab them, he momentarily moves them out of my reach. "One is for Álvarez to cover up with and the other is for her hair." He hands one to her, and she secures it around her body quickly. Then she grabs the other one offered.

"Thanks, Middlebrooks. Who knew you could be such a gentleman?" Luisa smiles as she delicately wraps the towel around her wet locks.

Ace puts a finger against his lips. "Shh, it'll be our little secret." He backs away and joins his teammates, who are now enjoying the unsprayed bottles of champagne. I stare at his retreating form and wonder if being playful with his GM is reason enough to get him kicked off the team.

"Huh, interesting," Luisa says, breaking me from my running thoughts. "Never thought I'd say green looks good on you."

I look down at my black suit and white shirt that are now resembling a deep blush color. "Did we accidentally waterboard you or something? Because there is most definitely no green on my body right now."

She rocks back and forth on her bare feet. "*Sure*, if you say so."

It clicks a second later. "I wasn't envious, or jealous, or whatever else it is that you've conjured in your mind."

She places her hand on her chest. "I wouldn't dream of it, Stonehaven. Remember size 36DD when you go shopping for my white lingerie. The one I only wear for 'special occasions,' and, of course, the kind you'll never actually see worn on my body because we"—she points between the two of us—"are nothing more than work colleagues. Correct?"

She's taunting me. I know the game she's playing. I shouldn't take the bait. But it's no surprise that when it comes to Luisa Álvarez, my sense of control is weak at best. But I'll be damned if I roll over and show her my belly. I lean down low, using the cover of the noisy clubhouse to keep our conversation private. "Incorrect. I am your boss, not your colleague. Just because I know what your sweet pussy tastes like and how tight you feel when you come around my cock does not mean you are going to pull me around by the collar and walk me around like a lovesick puppy here at our workplace. I'll get you a new suit. Hell, I'll buy you a lingerie store. But think twice before you try to taunt me with the memory of your tits, because two can play that game."

Her eyes are wide as saucers as she takes in shallow breaths. I wipe a drop of sangria from her cheek with the pad of my thumb, but the rosy color remains.

This wasn't part of the plan. But I find myself telling her anyway. "I have a charity event to attend this weekend. Come with me."

She stares at me for what feels like an eternity before she starts to shake her head. "What? No. Are you insane?"

"Clinically," I deadpan.

She tightens her hold on her already secured towel. "How do you think it's going to go over when I show up to a fancy event with you, arm in arm, huh? The internet is going to go crazy with conspiracies of how I got this job, and the most common ones will involve accusations that I slept with you."

"You did sleep with me."

"Shh." She slaps my bicep. "Not to get the job. And that was before I knew who you were. Or do you still think I'm a conniving liar? If so, we have other hurdles to climb before we can even—"

"I believe you."

She nods, eyes bouncing between mine. "Good. Right. Well, that's great and all, but I'm finally starting to get some respect thrown my way with this new trade and winning streak we're on, so I'd be an idiot to throw it all away by being arm candy."

I look her up and down. "You do look good in red."

"Stonehaven."

"Nick. My name is Nick, Luisa. I thought we'd established this already." I lean in even closer. As much as I love anything that comes from her lips, I'm waiting with bated breath to hear her call me Nick one more time.

She takes a step back, and I can practically see her placing the bricks up one by one around her. "I'm sorry. I can't."

"To what part?"

"All of it," she whispers as she stares down at her bare feet.

I look away as I try to reel in my frustration. I can be mad all I want, but I'll never let Luisa feel an ounce directed her way.

"Got it. But just a heads-up: I have to take a date to these types of things." I peel off my wet suit jacket as I speak. "There will be photos in the press."

She tries to keep her eyes trained away from the wet shirt pressed against my chest and fails spectacularly. "Real mature, Stonehaven. Do you think you're rubbing something in my face by telling me that?"

I shake my head. "I'm telling you exactly how these things go. And by these things, I mean me making public outings. I will be accompanied by a date. If not, women will badger me to no end." She scoffs, but I carry on. "At the end of the night, I will have my date dropped off at her apartment and I will go back to my place. Alone." I start to unbutton my shirt, uncaring that my team is about to see me shirtless. They see much more in these showers anyway.

"Why are you telling me all of this? We're not... a thing. You're free to bang as many supermodels as you want. You don't owe me anything."

I wonder if the words taste bitter on her tongue since her face scrunches up as she speaks.

"I suppose I could, but I won't. And I'm telling you all this for the same reason that no other man should ever see the obscene amount of lingerie I'm about to purchase and have delivered to your apartment."

"Which is?"

"I may be the devil, Luisa, but I am *your* devil. And don't you forget it."

CHAPTER SEVENTEEN

LUISA

She's fucking stunning.

And she's everything I'll never be.

Petite. Blond. And rail thin.

Fashion designer Marie Jensen hangs on to the crook of Nick's arm as if a gust of wind will blow her into oblivion. Her short red dress seems a bit out of place for the charity gala they're attending.

The adoring puppy dog eyes she aims in his direction are also a bit much, if you ask me.

It's stupid, really. I should be used to this by now. It's been over a month since Nick informed me that he would be seen in public with a date on his arm. I guess my silly brain didn't anticipate that he'd go out so often.

Marie is woman number twelve. Not that I'm keeping count or anything.

I zoom in on the latest paparazzi shots, trying to see if his face shows any sign of having a good time. But like in every other photo, Nick's face looks stoic and closed off.

Unlike the cheeky bastard I know him to be.

"Is it part of your job to stalk your boss, or is that something you like to do in your spare time?" my mother asks as she swats me with a tea towel on her way to the stove.

"I wasn't stalking. Just making sure he wasn't doing anything that might reflect poorly on the Monarchs," I respond, a bit too quickly.

"Ha. You think I was born yesterday?" She places a hand on her hip as she stirs the carne guisada on the stove.

"Who was born yesterday, Clarissa?" Tía Gloria asks.

My mother points her lips in my direction. "Esta. Looking at photos of her boss like it's her homework."

"Are we talking about that papi chulo billionaire Luisa refuses to introduce us to?" Tía Marisol chimes in, topping off her sister's wine.

I point my finger in their direction. "And that is one of the many reasons I never will. Papi chulo? Really?"

Tía Gloria chuckles to herself. "Luisa, we may be married and a touch too old for that man, but we still have eyes, you know."

I mouth exaggeratedly, "A touch."

They start to cackle among themselves as I shake my head. "You three are like the Dominican Sanderson sisters. But instead of cauldrons and spells, you have calderos and chisme." I walk away, leaving them in a fit of laughter.

I fight off a smirk, because as outrageous as they can be when they're together, I wouldn't take a minute of their teasing for granted.

For a while—when my mother was in the pits of her depression—the magic between the three of them was gone, but they never gave up on her.

It makes me a little sad that I'll never have a sibling to share moments like that with, but I never fester on the thought, not wanting to give the very reason my mother struggled so much with her mental health another ounce of my energy.

Instead, I walk into the living room and take in the expected sight.

My father, along with my two uncles, playing dominoes.

My father catches my eye and raises his glass of Brugal rum in my direction. "Mija! Get over here. We need a fourth. Playing these two pendejos gets old after a while." My dad winks as he takes a sip of his drink.

"Pendeja tu madre," Tío Marcos says as he mocks a backhanded slap to my father.

"¡Que en paz descanse!" the women in the kitchen shout.

"Can we stop talking about people's deceased mothers and focus on the game?" I tease as I slide into the empty seat.

"As long as you don't cheat," Tío Ernesto grumbles.

"My daughter and I never cheat. You're just a sore loser," my dad defends.

"Yeah, yeah, yeah. It's pretty clear you guys have the winning genes. No need to rub it in," Tío Marcos groans.

My father and I share a secret smile as he smacks the dominoes on the table. My uncles make a show of shuffling the pieces around the table before we quickly make a grab for the tiles we'll line in front of ourselves.

My father lifts the bottle of rum in offering, and I shake my head, opting for the bottle of Presidente beer my Tío Ernesto offers.

The bottle is *vestida de novia*. Which means the beer is so cold, there is a layer of ice around the bottle. It makes it look white. Therefore, resembling a bride dressed in white. This is the proper way to drink a Dominican beer, and I love how my family keeps up with traditions even though they are so far from home.

"All right, tell us. Is that Stonehaven guy behaving himself, or do we need to pay him a visit?" Tío Marcos asks while cracking his knuckles.

I give him a dubious look. "You're a part of the little league staff at your grandson's school, not the mob. What are you going to threaten him with, a plastic bat?"

"That's pee-wee baseball. C'mon, Luisa. You should know the difference," he teases.

"I don't know," Tío Ernesto chimes in. "Something tells me you shouldn't trust the guy. He comes out of nowhere and has all that money." He shakes his head once. "Something ain't right."

For reasons unbeknownst to me, I find myself feeling the need to defend Nick. "He's harmless." I shrug, aiming for nonchalance.

When three pairs of eyes stare back at me expectantly, I continue. "Seriously. I mean, yeah, he's playing catch-up when it comes to learning about the sport, but he has the business acumen to get things done. And sure, maybe he could ditch the suit every once in a while and spend more time with the players, but he is busy balancing being the owner of a brand-new baseball team with running his own media conglomerate-corporation thingy. I'm sure it doesn't leave much space on the calendar for free time. Unless you count all those dates he's—"

Why am I still talking?

"I don't know. But it seems to me like you've got plenty to say about the man," my dad says with a raised brow.

"I said that part out loud too, didn't I?" I stare down at my dominoes as if they hold all of life's answers.

"Uh-huh," my uncles reply in unison.

"Cuidado mija. That's all I'm going to say." I open my mouth to tell my dad there's nothing to worry about, but he continues. "I know you're more than capable of holding your own. Trust me, I know. I raised you that way. And sometimes it even bites me in the ass." I roll my eyes as he smiles softly. "But be careful. That man is powerful, and I'd hate for him to take advantage of you in any way. Especially after you worked so hard to get to where you are."

I sigh deeply. "You don't have to worry. We only communicate unless we absolutely have to. It's all strictly business. I promise."

We all focus back on the game, and I try to ignore the biggest lie I've ever fed my father.

I'm tucked in bed, watching *The Real Housewives of Salt Lake City* on my laptop, when an email notification pops up.

Like clockwork.

Ever since Nick started having these public dates, he's been emailing me stupid little debriefs.

And I hate how I've become dependent on them.

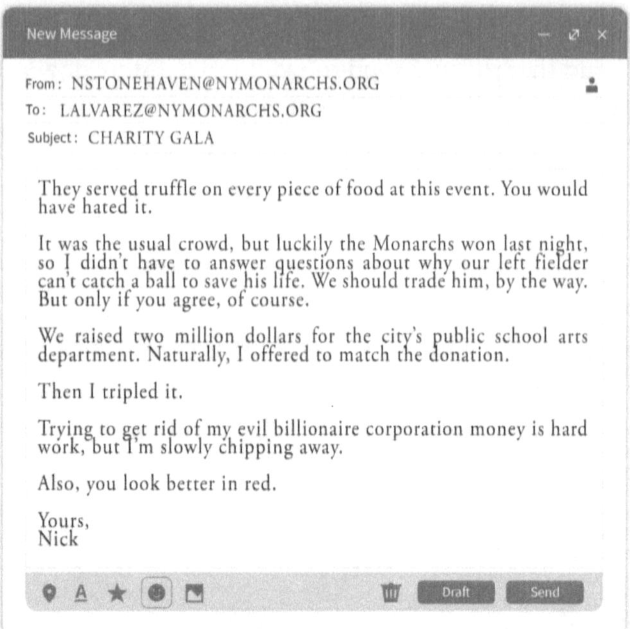

The last sentence before he signs off is always something along those lines.

She was less entertaining than watching paint dry.

Watching her walk in heels was similar to witnessing a baby giraffe's first steps.

I swear this one tried to steal my wallet.

That last one was my favorite.

Until this current email.

He usually sticks to pointing out silly flaws in his dates. But this last line is the first time he specifically mentions me.

And the emails aren't only coming after his dates.

Nope. Because Nicholas doesn't do anything on a small scale.

The barrage of emails are endless ramblings of a man who seriously needs a group chat to pester. But instead, he's got me.

So far, I've learned that he has trouble sleeping since he is managing businesses in two time zones, he has regular Sunday dinners with Daisy in which he cooks, and he's a big baby when he gets a cold.

The rest of the information is nonsensical, yet I've stored every detail away in a tiny box in my brain.

Try as I might to ignore him, I find myself responding to each and every one of his musings and even giving him unimportant details of my life.

I love to cook but don't bother, since my mother never taught me to cook portion sizes for less than six people, even though we were a family of three. I think I want to get a pet at some point but would need my parents to watch it when I'm on the road with the team. And I prefer heels over flats unless I'm on my period. Then it's my black running sneakers for comfort and to match my mood.

I still cringe at that last one. I sent it after having two glasses of wine while I was on my period a few weeks ago. I'm grateful that he has never brought it up.

When he started sending me these date debriefs, my go-to response was something like "I don't care." Or the more savvy "Don't you have a woman in your bed waiting to fake an orgasm?"

He responded to that last one with an attachment.

A photo of a massive bed that I can only assume is his. It had a cushioned leather headboard and expensive-looking sheets. Yet what immediately caught my attention was the massive Bernese Mountain dog in the middle of his bed. The email stated, "The only one allowed to warm my bed."

And that's when I learned that Nick had a dog. A gorgeous, goofy-faced furball. The kind of dog you can spoon while rubbing their belly.

Not exactly the hounds of hell I would have picked for a man like Nick, but again, he seems to be full of surprises.

But I'm not naïve. Because even if he isn't sleeping with all his dates, it doesn't mean that he's not sleeping with someone else.

A man like that wouldn't know the first thing about celibacy.

Not that it matters. Because as much as I feel this push and pull between Nick and me, nothing will ever come of it.

He is my boss.

I am the first female general manager in Major League Baseball. I have little girls who look up to me and more than a few grown men waiting to see me fail.

I refuse to become a cliché.

A woman who made it to the top, only to have the validity of her accomplishments questioned because she's now sleeping with a powerful man.

Not sleeping. Slept.

Past tense.

I've held out strong these past few months, not giving into my unbridled desire to have his hands all over me again.

Although I spend half the time I'm in Nick's presence planning my true crime documentary interview answers, because the way he pushes my buttons while I'm leading my meetings makes me think that life behind bars isn't as bad as they make it out to be.

And while I'd never admit it to another living soul, his relentless questioning has made me better at my job. Sometimes I need to slow down and look at things through a different lens. I've realized I sometimes rev myself up before a meeting in anticipation of someone trying to go against me, and in doing so, I miss opportunities for collaboration.

I've spent so long clawing my way to the top that I fear I may always be waiting for the other shoe to drop. Someone to walk in and announce, "Sorry, but the jig is up!"

I live my life under the pressure of knowing that every move I make is being dissected by camera crews, journalists, and fans around the world.

But Nick is always there. And the sparring we do in these meetings tends to keep me focused and grounded. Nick is someone I'm not afraid of going head to head with. Which is how he's become the only person in my life with the ability to challenge me in a way that doesn't feel threatening.

Maybe it's because I know that he slept with a night light until he was nine or that lately he's been on the hunt for the best Dominican food in the city.

All because of these damn emails.

I've managed to say things that I'd never to say to his face, only to continue our bickering like business as usual the following day at work. And our touches are subtle but laced with reined-in violence.

Like when he pulled out my chair at the head of the conference table, only to push it in a bit too deeply, causing my breasts to momentarily rest on the table as I leaned forward. Or when I walked around the table, dropping off materials in front of my seated staff, only to lean over Nick a tad longer, enticing him with the view of my cleavage right before I sank the heel of my stiletto into his shiny black shoe. Hard.

The muffled grunt as he bit his fist put me in the best mood that lasted the rest of the workday.

But these emails? This is the only place I allow myself to be a little reckless. Where I don't feel like I have a million eyes on me. Where I am allowed to be myself.

Which is why I hit Reply, not fully thinking through what I'm about to type.

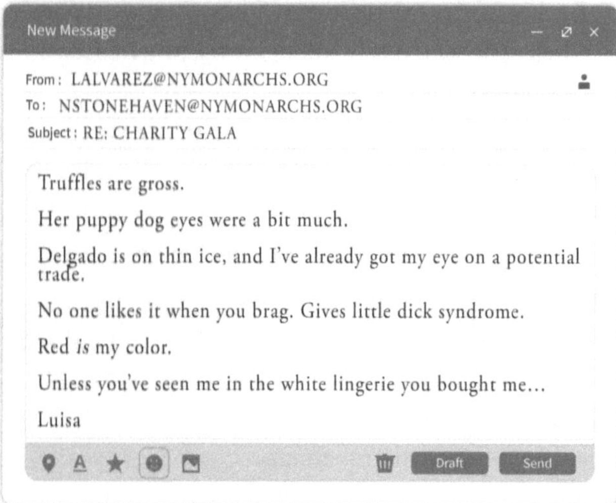

I let out a low, evil laugh.

Nick wasn't lying when he said he would replace my damaged clothes and underwear.

After I was drenched in sangria by Nick and my entire team, I had to toss every single piece of clothing in the trash.

But when I got to my apartment later that night, I had ten new sets of suit pants and jackets.

Prada. YSL. Celine. Chanel.

All in my size.

I was surprised to find a few pairs of designer heels that fit perfectly.

And when I opened the last package, I discovered an insane amount of lingerie. And not the super skimpy stuff that would dig into my skin. The box was full of beautiful lace bras I can wear under a dress shirt for a night out if I'm feeling daring.

I emailed him immediately after.

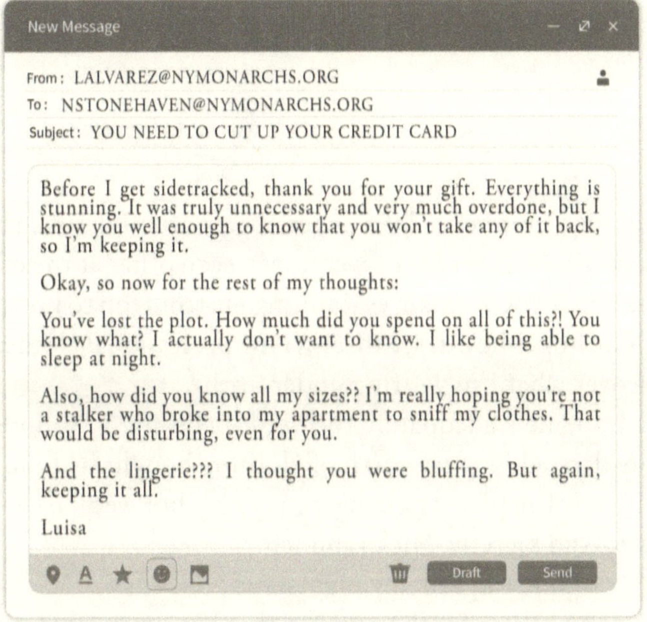

From: LALVAREZ@NYMONARCHS.ORG
To: NSTONEHAVEN@NYMONARCHS.ORG
Subject: YOU NEED TO CUT UP YOUR CREDIT CARD

Before I get sidetracked, thank you for your gift. Everything is stunning. It was truly unnecessary and very much overdone, but I know you well enough to know that you won't take any of it back, so I'm keeping it.

Okay, so now for the rest of my thoughts:

You've lost the plot. How much did you spend on all of this?! You know what? I actually don't want to know. I like being able to sleep at night.

Also, how did you know all my sizes?? I'm really hoping you're not a stalker who broke into my apartment to sniff my clothes. That would be disturbing, even for you.

And the lingerie??? I thought you were bluffing. But again, keeping it all.

Luisa

His response had been immediate.

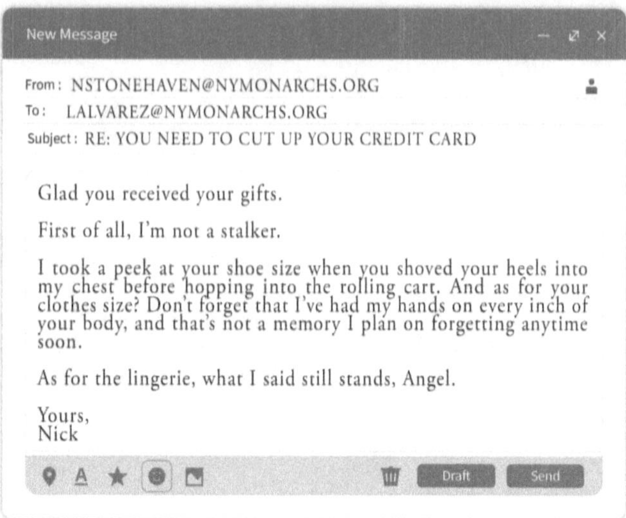

I haven't referenced the lingerie again after I thanked him via email. But every time we've seen each other at the office since then, I sense his eyes scanning me from top to bottom, as if he hopes he can see through my professional clothes to discover what I'm wearing underneath.

I hope he's adequately tortured, believing I am indeed fully dressed in every stitch of clothing bought by him.

I know I'm playing a dangerous game, but we all have our vices. And secretly, Nick is mine.

My phone rings on my nightstand.

I don't recognize the number that has a few more digits than a local number should. I hope no one has gotten a hold of my private number, because it'd be a real bitch to change it and update every online shopping account I have linked to it.

I answer the call but don't speak, in case it's a rowdy fan or a wrong number calling.

"Luisa Marie Álvarez. What. The. *Fuck*. Was. That?"

I bolt up in bed and look around my room, as if a growly Nick Stonehaven is about to barge into my home.

"How did you get my number?" I ask stupidly. The man has more than enough resources to find my number, including my personnel file.

But up until this moment, we've never spoken on the phone or even texted, keeping it strictly to email.

"Luisa," he warns, his voice dropping an octave.

"Lucifer," I say innocently, my brain catching up on why he's probably calling.

"I'm going to be very clear here, so listen closely," he starts.

I immediately clamp my thighs together at his demanding tone.

"I've been on my best behavior here. Truthfully, I could be considered a monk at this point. I've respected your wishes. I've treated you with nothing but respect in front of our staff and have even let your bratty ways slide when you try to push my buttons."

"I'd hardly call you a saint, Luci. Last week you pulled my hair when—"

"If you think you can mention wearing a piece of lingerie, one I've handpicked for you, and expect me to not crash through every door to get a good look for myself, then you're dangerously unaware of the frail tether of restraint I'm holding on to."

I gasp, and he releases a sinister chuckle.

"Yes, Angel. Now you're getting it."

"That's not—We're not, uh."

"Trust me, I'm painfully aware." I hear him groan faintly, as if he's pulled the phone away from his face momentarily.

"But just because I've shown I can be on my best behavior, that doesn't mean you can taunt me mercilessly."

I shake my head even though he can't see me. "No, I didn't. I was only stating the facts. Maybe I can concede that it was a bit of a tease, but nothing more than usual," I venture.

"Save your excuses for another time, Luisa. Because we are going to get to the bottom of this, once and for all. I expect you in my office tomorrow at eight a.m., and we're going to have a long overdue conversation."

His voice brooks no room for argument.

"Okay. Sure. Fine. I'll be there."

He hums in agreement, the rumble causing goose bumps to rise along my skin.

"Oh, and Luisa? Please be careful when you call for the devil." His tone is laced with amusement and warning all at once. "Because he just might show up."

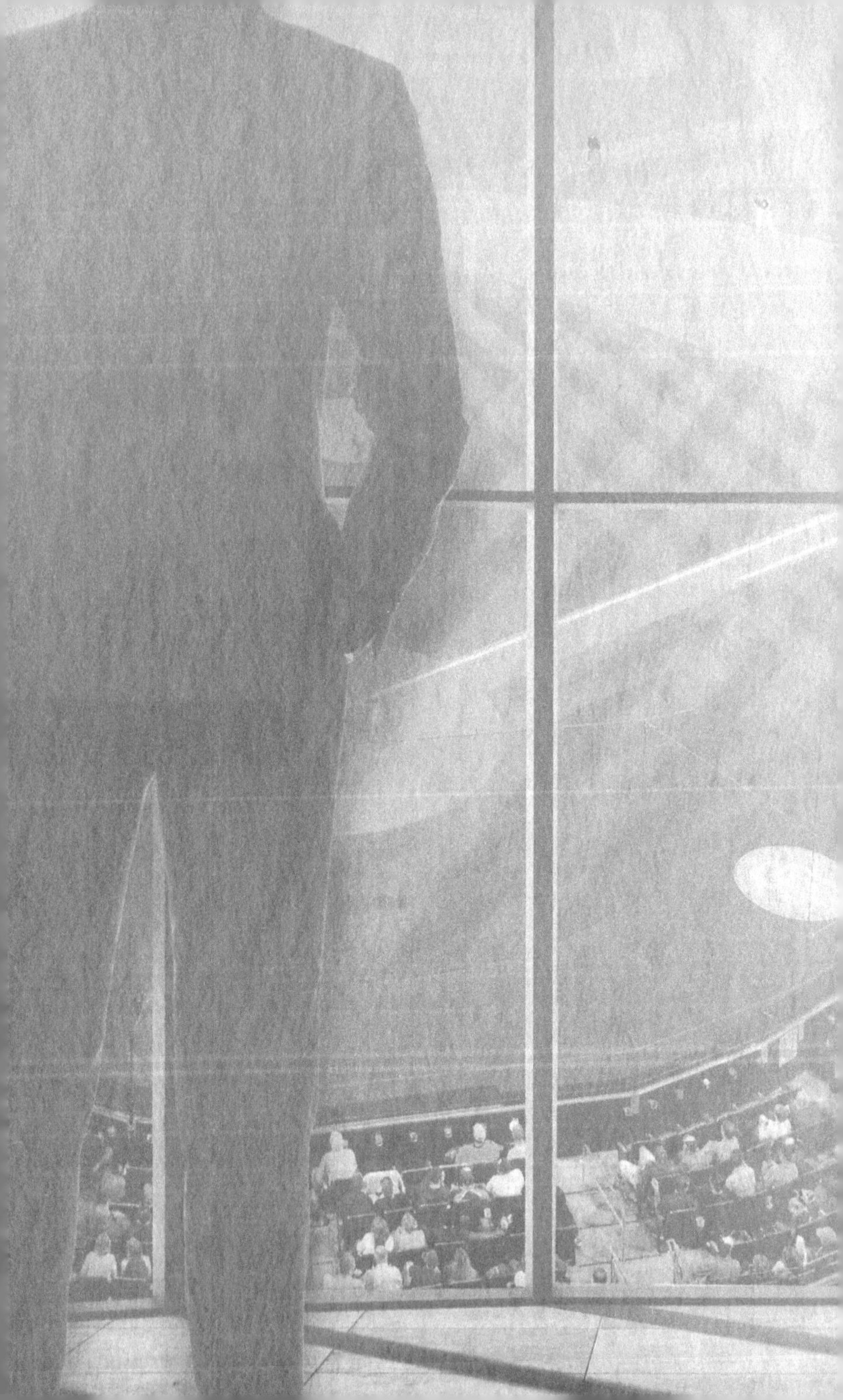

Chapter Eighteen

NICK

I'VE OFFICIALLY REACHED MY breaking point.

Luisa and I have danced around the obvious long enough, and today, that comes to an end.

I want her. In a bone-deep way that I've never yearned for another woman.

Seeing her command the conference room and dreaming about her are no longer cutting it.

And having to spend hours with women who don't hold a candle to my Angel's beauty is downright torturous.

When I learned of the financial mess my grandfather left when he threw money like a madman at the players and staff, I quickly realized I was about to put in some major schmoozing to make deals that would help finance the Monarchs for the rest of the season.

Apparently, it's frowned upon to write a check yourself.

Instead, I've shaken hands and kissed the cheeks of the right people and am now about ready to announce Monarchs Live. A streaming channel where viewers will be able to get early access content on our players, watch games, and get behind-the-scenes interviews and announcements before they go out to the general public. Other major teams have similar platforms, and this allows us to have a separate flow of revenue.

One we don't have to share with the other MLB teams as part of the spending pot, which will allow us to perform at the level we're at without getting fined for overspending.

Half of business is getting into the mindset, and no one ever wants to hand over cold, hard cash to a single man who could potentially steal their wife out from under them. The mental game is as important as the business itself. Early on, I learned from a mentor that it is crucial to always arrive with a date on your arm. Someone who can entertain the spouses of the investors I need to deal with and, in the process, make me seem like less of a threat.

Marla chose the women strategically. Women who were influential but still working toward their desired level of recognition. I get the bullshit date I need for appearance's sake, and they get the publicity and internet chatter they crave.

In the past I had no problem mixing business with pleasure, but ever since I laid eyes on Luisa Álvarez, my body only answers to her.

I end each date with a side hug, then usher them into a private car that will deliver them safely to their homes, unable to even consider giving them a platonic kiss on the cheek, since it feels like a betrayal toward Luisa.

Utterly ridiculous.

And today, it's coming to a stop.

I asked Luisa to meet in my office before Marla is scheduled to arrive, because if things go how I hope they will, I want no one within earshot of my office.

Two strong knocks rap on my door before it flies open and Luisa barges in as if she owns the place.

Almost as if she knows that she owns *me*.

She's dressed in a red suit, like she's ready for battle. Her white top is open a button too low to be considered work appropriate, but it clearly communicates what she wanted when she got dressed this morning, since I can see the beginning of her lacy white bra from where I stand.

"Okay, Stonehaven. I'm here, but make it quick. I've got things to do." She drops her oversized bag in the chair meant for her and strides around my desk, not stopping until she's standing right before me.

I try to keep my hands in my pockets but quickly lose the battle when I look down into her top and can see the tips of her hardened nipples through her sheer lace bra.

She moves fast, but not quick enough.

I have her back pinned to the glass wall overlooking Monarch stadium, one hand placed against the glass by her face and the other keeping her chin tipped up toward me. "Date me," I demand.

Her eyes widen briefly before she schools her features into perfect indifference. "Very funny, Stonehaven. Now tell me what you called me in for before I knee you in the crown jewels."

I ignore her quip and repeat, "Date. Me."

She tries to shake her head, but my firm grip keeps her in place. "You can't be serious."

"I don't like to repeat myself, Luisa. But for you, I will. Date me." I soften my tone.

Many emotions flutter through her honey-colored eyes before landing on skepticism. "So that's it? You're going to bulldoze through all the formalities and, what? Demand I date you? Because that sure as hell wasn't asking."

My lips twitch, but I force myself to stay on task. "Demanding opens up space for negotiation."

She scoffs, but I see the fire in her eyes. The spark that ignites when we do what we do best. When we battle for dominance like we did the night I fucked her so deeply she stole my sanity.

"Say yes," I push, leaning in closer, our breaths mingling.

"You know we can't," she offers weakly, but I came prepared for this.

I start to move slowly, giving her the time and space to push me off if she wants to. But her curious eyes let me move without disruption as I lean down and kiss that spot beneath her ear that drove her wild the night we met. "I told you I came prepared to negotiate."

She sighs softly. "I'm pretty sure this isn't standard practice, Stonehaven."

I move up and kiss her temple, inhaling deeply as the rattling in my brain seems to settle at her nearness. "We can keep it a secret. Only go out to places we won't be seen, so nobody would have to know." I feel her stiffen beneath me and move back slightly to read her face. Hurt mars her expression momentarily, but I act quickly to wipe it away. "Let me be very clear here: I have no issue with sending out a companywide email, along with a press statement, informing everyone that we are exclusively dating. You are not and will never be my dirty little secret. We play by your rules here, Luisa. Public or private, it's all the same to me as long as you say yes."

She softens slightly at my words but still attempts to shake her head. "It's just... I—I can't. I'll be crucified in the—"

"Quickly. Answer me this. If public scrutiny weren't an issue. If we were just two people who met at the bar and shared a life-altering night. Followed by months of explosive chemistry with a dash of violence—on your end, of course—would you *want* to date me?"

I might be ashamed of the pleading tone my voice has taken at a later time, but right now my eyes are locked on Luisa's, begging her to answer me honestly and put me out of my misery.

I see it then.

Her shoulders sag and her eyes look tortured. They start to water, but she quickly tries to bat them dry. A rogue tear runs down her cheek as she opens her mouth to answer, but nothing comes out.

My thumb catches the tear, wiping it away as I rest my forehead against hers. "Don't worry, Angel. You don't have to say anything. I already have my answer."

We stay like that, synchronized breaths having the conversation our voices can't. She's the first to pull away, and I let her.

I brace for it. The moment where she builds back her walls right before my eyes.

But it doesn't come.

Instead, she places her hand on my cheek, and I fight the urge to nuzzle into her palm.

She seems to contemplate what to do next, her eyes searching mine—for what, I'm not sure.

She must find it, because in the next moment, she lifts up on her toes and softly brings her lips to mine.

I don't hesitate. I slide my hand behind the base of her neck and angle her up to me. The kiss is slow and unrushed. I'm about to demand more when my body stills, seeming to have realized what this was before my brain could.

A goodbye kiss.

Luisa's lips leave mine as she takes a step back, leaving her hand on my cheek for a moment before I lose that too.

Don't say it. Please don't say it.

"I'm so sorry, Nick."

She places a hand over her lips before she turns away, gathers her purse, and walks out the door.

I wait one minute—a solid sixty seconds—before I bend down and send all the contents of my desk toppling to the ground with a roar.

Eyes unfocused, I take in the sight of contracts, electronics, and pens falling haphazardly around me.

I pant as I try to reel in the scorching pain in the middle of my chest. The space where Luisa's been residing, against my better judgment.

I bet on myself, and I lost.

Again.

But this time, I lost *her*.

I force my breaths to even out and start getting to work on cleaning up my mess. It doesn't take me long, but as I replay our kiss for what feels like the millionth time, the mind-bending pain returns with a vengeance when I realize I missed the most fatal blow of all.

She finally called me Nick.

CHAPTER NINETEEN

LUISA

I CAN FIX THIS.

Maybe.

Sorta.

Fuck.

Goddamn it, Nick. Why did you have to mess this all up?

We were perfectly fine, dancing on the edge of a knife blade, teetering past what was appropriate for a boss/employee relationship.

And then I went ahead and kissed him. Right before I said I was sorry and walked out on him.

It was probably always going to end this way, but why did it have to be now?

This doesn't feel over.

It can't be.

But Nick was vulnerable enough to ask for what he wanted, so maybe it's time I did the same.

Something that I've learned I need to work on is slowing down while under pressure. That's something *he* taught me. Yet when he had his body pressed against mine, I couldn't think, couldn't trust my own judgment, and ran to my first instinct.

To protect my image.

It sounds callous now that I've had a day to reflect on everything, and I think Nick and I need another conversation to really talk things through. Preferably one where we're not touching each other. That way my brain cells can be present.

"Good morning, Marla. Is he in?" I point at Nick's closed door.

Marla looks between the door and me, as if a wild animal might escape its confines. "Maybe you should stop by later? The boss seems to be in a bit of a mood."

"Oh." I drop into the extra seat by Marla's desk, guilt consuming me.

I hear a door swoosh open and a sudden energy shift.

"No need. I'm here now. What do you need, Ms. Álvarez?" Nick stands before his open office door, more imposing than ever. Gone are the flickers of mischief in his eyes or the slight upturn at the corners of his lips.

As well as my name, apparently.

"Uh. Hi, Ni—Stonehaven. I wanted to know if you had a minute. To talk." I clear my throat, feeling awkward.

Nick looks down at his watch and gives me a slight shake of his head. "I'm afraid I don't have a minute to spare." He looks at Marla. "Call my pilot and have my plane ready to go within the hour, please. I'd like to be in London before midnight."

"London?" I ask, my voice coming out dangerously close to a shrill.

"Yes. I have an actual company to run besides this side gig, in case you've forgotten. And I have pressing matters that need my undivided attention," he offers cooly.

"Noted. When will you be back? You know, in case I have to discuss business matters with you?"

"What other matters besides business would we need to discuss, Ms. Álvarez?" The second time he refuses to say my name stings even more. "If anything needs my immediate attention, be sure to email Marla. She'll keep me informed and up to date on anything urgent."

"Oh." My voice cracks as I rock back on my heels.

His eyes meet mine, and for a brief moment, I can see him.

The Nick who laid his heart on the line yesterday.

The man who begged me to jump into the deep end, because he was right there to catch me.

The same one I kissed right before I walked away and acted as if I couldn't hear his agony as I slumped against his office door.

His face softens, and I swear I can almost see the white flag being waved in his eyes.

His shoulders slump on an exhale, and I wonder, if I just stare at him long enough, whether I can wear him down. For a few minutes to make my case. I haven't got the first clue what it is, but it sure as hell isn't indulging in this alphahole gimmick he's putting on to save face.

He shakes his head, as if he can read my mind and is telling me to let it go.

Let him go.

I shake mine right back at him. Because now that I'm faced with the reality of Nick really leaving, I'm not sure if the idea of being ridiculed in the media was reason enough to let myself run away from the one thing I can't stop thinking about.

I want Nick.

I open my mouth, the truth on my lips.

Nick watches me intently, almost as if he's waiting with bated breath to hear what I should have said yesterday.

But then I realize that Marla is watching us with poorly veiled curiosity, causing me to hesitate. The slight delay seems to be the final nail in the coffin of Nick's resolve.

He rubs his hand roughly over his short beard, and I remember how delicious it felt while my nails lightly scratched alongside his jaw while we kissed.

He faces Marla, his voice turned gentle and low but not low enough that I can't hear his next words.

"Don't forget: I'm bringing Delilah with me. I know it's last minute, but please make sure all arrangements are made for her to join me. Spare no expense. I want her to be comfortable on the flight."

His brown eyes raise to meet mine, and his bravado turns into pity. My stomach takes a nosedive as he shakes his head one last time before walking back into his office without so much as a backward glance.

I bite down on the inside of my cheek and force myself to focus on the physical pain instead of the punch to the gut he just delivered.

He's taking a woman to London with him.

Someone he's clearly familiar with.

All this time, I ate up the bullshit that he wasn't sleeping with any of his dates. In reality, he probably was, while also banging this Delilah woman on the side.

A tidal wave of regret, disbelief, and repulsion pummels through my body.

How could I be so stupid?

He clearly was only in it for the chase, and once I turned him down, he was onto the next.

I leave without saying goodbye to Marla, not trusting my voice not to crack.

My heels click loudly on the tiled floor. I itch to take them off and chuck them into the nearest trash can, since I'm wearing one of the pairs that Nick bought me.

I place a hand on my stomach as I continue to walk swiftly back to my office, holding back the sudden urge to barf.

I literally paraded around the offices like his personal little Barbie doll, dressed in the clothes he bought me.

I make it to my office and slam the door shut, rattling the hinges.

I take a seat at my desk and force a handful of deep breaths into my lungs.

I'm okay. He's just a man. And men are trash. We already know this.

I open up my email and stagger back slightly at his name staring back at me.

So many emails.

I ignore all of our past correspondence and instead shoot off an alarming amount of meeting requests with my team and agents across the country.

It's time for me to remember who I am and why I'm here.

I'm going to make a name for myself.

And I'm going to do it in *spite* of the men who try to stand in my way.

Because this is what I was meant to do with my life.

Because people are counting on me.

Because I'm going to make my family proud.

And, most importantly, because Nicholas Stonehaven can get fucked.

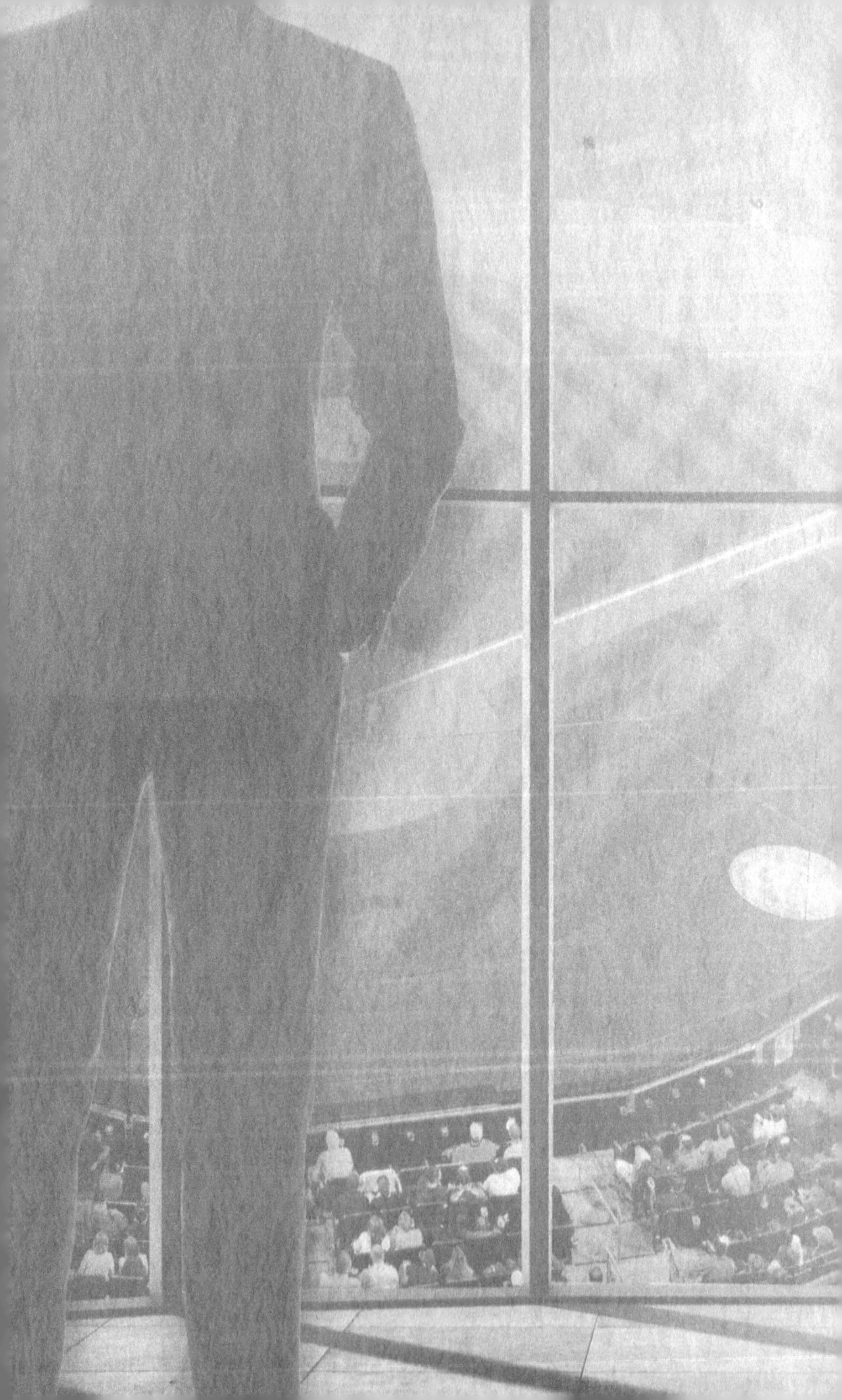

NICK

I NEED HER TO hate me.

I keep repeating the thought in my mind.

It's for the best. She needs her anger to keep her company when I can't.

She won't allow herself to date me, and I'm not going to make her life difficult by making her feel guilty about her choice.

When I saw her standing outside my office, with that look of hope in her eyes, I knew I would be submitting us both to a world of pain if I didn't nip this in the bud.

I knew what she'd come to say. Hell, she probably needed the day to process her feelings around dating me instead of murdering me.

But I knew how things would ultimately play out.

She would give in. I would fall in love with her and try my damndest to make her stay. But time would pass, articles would be written, and she would grow resentful until, eventually, she left me.

She would always be remembered as the woman who slept with her boss, while I would walk away unscathed. The media never holds men to the same diabolical standard they do women, and I'll never let that happen to Luisa.

Therefore, I need her to hate me.

Because if she doesn't and she comes at me once more with that look in her eye, I'll crumble and welcome the inevitable pain.

I run my hand through my hair as I look around the airplane.

The flight attendant is making me a stiff drink as the pilots prepare for takeoff.

I look over at the only lady who can bear to be in my presence when I'm in this dark of a mood. "Get over here, Delilah."

I pat my lap, and she comes willingly, her pretty eyes shining bright.

"That's my good girl," I say, as she wags her tail and her tongue lolls out the side of her mouth.

I'm an asshole to the highest degree for not clarifying to Luisa that Delilah is my beloved pup who always travels with me.

But there was no reason to.

Because in the end, I need her to hate me.

At least half as much as I hate myself.

CHAPTER TWENTY-ONE

LUISA

They say time heals all wounds.

I say not seeing your boss's arrogant mug for a month does the trick.

Yep. This office has been Nick-free ever since he decided to hightail it outta here with his flavor of the week.

And during that time, I've relished our team's incredible season.

I've visited some of the most iconic baseball fields while on the road. It's not lost on me how lucky I am to not only do what I love but also get to travel across the country on the team's jet and stay at nice hotels.

Money was tight growing up. My family was lucky if we scrounged up enough cash to fly down to the Dominican Republic every couple of years to see family. Even then, we would crash with a relative to save on accommodations.

Now, I FaceTime my parents and show them where I've landed and what I've been up to. And if they finally agree to it, I'll fly them out for an away game so they can experience a Monarchs game in enemy territory.

It probably would have happened sooner, but they refuse to take any more help than I'm already giving them. Because the second I signed my contract, I took over paying their rent and bills.

I think every first-generation kid's dream is to retire their parents. It's a way of saying thank you for all the sacrifices they've made.

Unfortunately, New York is one pricey place to retire, and my parents aren't ready to leave the city and head south to the Caribbean to sip on rum and Cokes on the beach quite yet, so this is the best I could come up with.

Life honestly has never been better.

Until this morning when I finally got my period after more than two months.

I should have known last night when I was overly emotional during an episode of *Summer House* that something was awry. Yet when I woke up, curled into the fetal position, I knew even before my eyes fluttered open that I was in for a hell of a day.

I hate that I sometimes feel at war with my body. Treating it like an unpredictable adversary instead of a supposed temple.

But this isn't my first rodeo.

So I walked to my closet and pulled out the knee-length dress that would be my saving grace. It flows away from my body, hiding the bloat that had already formed and is short enough to keep me comfortable in this July heat. And it's black, meaning it's the best choice in case of a worst-case scenario.

I paired it with a structured maroon blazer and my comfiest black running sneakers.

I knew exactly how this day would go, and I was starting to dread it.

I had an important meeting lined up that couldn't be rescheduled, so I was going to have to load myself up on caffeine and snack often if I wanted to survive.

I start to carefully orchestrate my day in my head as I weave through the executive offices.

I wish I was still in bed.

The cramping has begun, and I haven't even made it to my desk yet.

I could take a sick day. Maybe even work from home. But I'm too stubborn to let my PCOS win.

And paranoia—that someone would find out why I called out—would forever haunt me.

The moment I was hired, the internet trolls were commenting on all the things I could do wrong. And that was before I set foot in the stadium. I ignored most of the chatter, but the idea that I wouldn't be a good GM because I'd be a moody bitch who'd miss a week of work every month simply because I had a uterus struck a little too close to home.

Don't piss her off during that time of the month or you'll get traded, boys!

Can we schedule the games around her cycle so we can make sure our players win all our home games?

Can't wait to see how the trades go when she's on maternity leave.

That last one cut even deeper.

To suffer this unpredictable limbo every couple of months and not know whether my body will ever let me carry my own child is cruel beyond measure.

For me, it isn't the pain, unpredictable timetables, weight fluctuations, or even the stray hairs that need to be plucked from a random part of my body that makes me hate having PCOS.

It's the mental gymnastics it puts me through while it holds the keys to my future tightly in its clutches.

You've got the dream job and the paycheck that helps provide for your family, so suck it up.

I let out a sigh of relief at the sight of my office door.

A couple more steps, and I'll be able to pop pain meds and be good as new. Or as good as the first day of my period can be. Which is never great.

I dig into my purse as I open my door, hoping I didn't forget to pack the extra strength pills, when a deep voice pulls me from my thoughts.

"There you are, Luisa," he says, looking awfully too comfortable as he sits in my chair.

My mind goes blank as it tries to reconcile the vision in front of me.

He smirks as his eyes rake over my body slowly, burning me up inch by inch. But when he reaches my comfy shoes, all playfulness is swiftly replaced by a menacing scowl.

"Get the hell out of my chair, Lucifer."

And just like that, the devil is back in town.

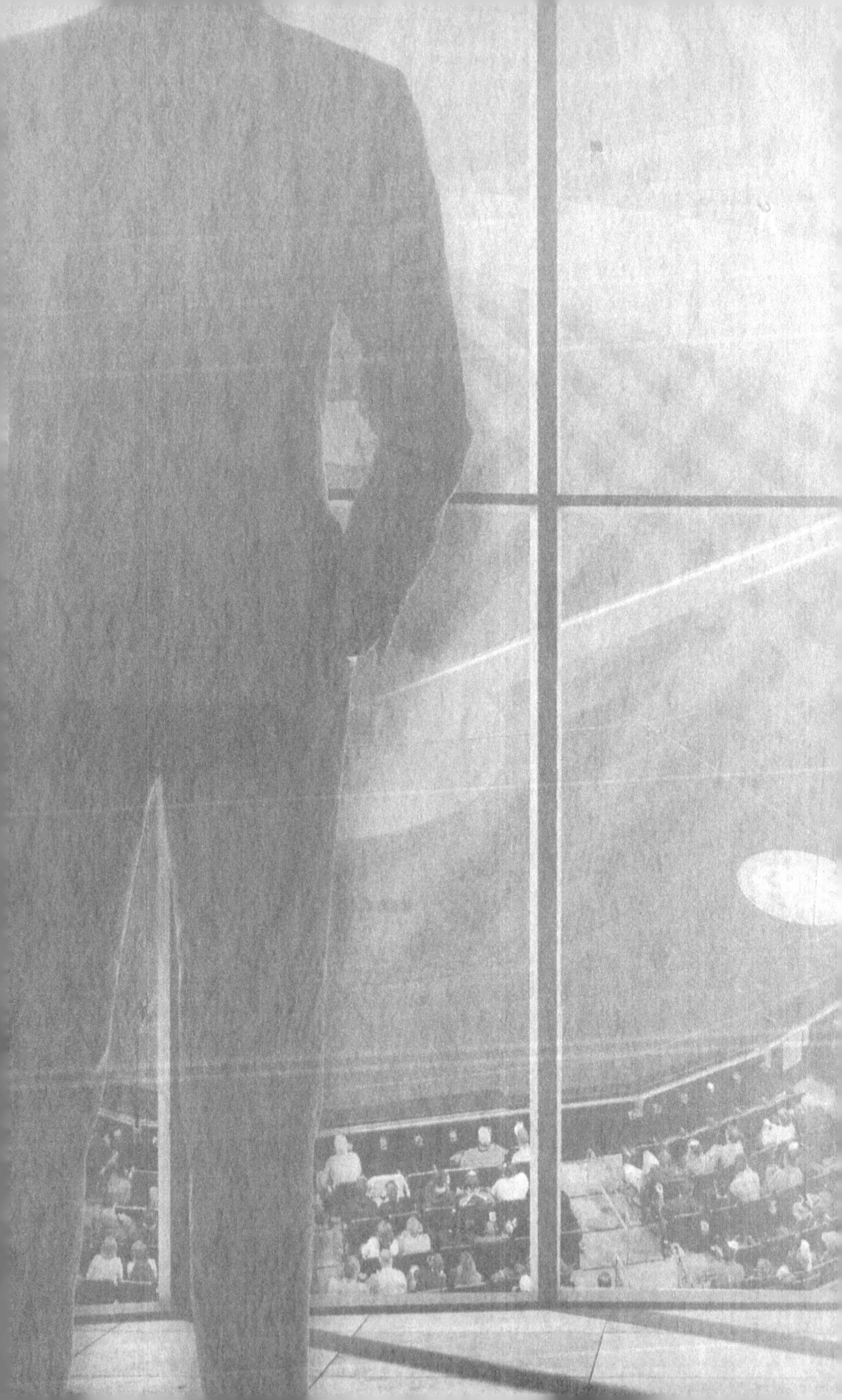

CHAPTER TWENTY-TWO

NICK

I RAISE A BROW at Luisa's tone.

I wasn't expecting a warm welcome, but this isn't exactly what I envisioned either.

I lasted a measly three days before I succumbed and emailed Luisa directly. I kept it professional, not wanting to stir the pot too soon.

She responded by cc'ing Marla and her entire team, asking them to take the lead on a simple question that she could have answered with a few words.

But I've made my bed and had to lie in it.

Alone. Unless you count Delilah, but she's known to be quite the bed hog, so I regularly send her down to her massive custom-made dog bed before I'm able to actually fall asleep.

Which has been a rare occurrence. And when I do drift off, my dreams of Luisa have been replaced with nightmares. Ones with her dressed in white, marrying someone whose face I can't see and, therefore, can't punch.

I had my reasons for leaving. I must have. Though I can't remember a single one worthy of keeping me away for so long.

Daisy certainly hasn't been any help, frequently posting pictures with Luisa while at away games, smiling from ear to ear.

I've tried to discreetly ask my sweet sister about Luisa, but that led to a surprising response. One that included "Get your head out of your ass and fix whatever you did to my friend."

So here I am, back with my tail between my legs, trying to figure out how to erase the past month from Luisa's memory and somehow ease my way back into her good graces.

That is, until I spot her footwear.

She's wearing black sneakers, something she only dons when she's on her period. A fact I've read time and time again since I spent an outrageous amount of time rereading our old emails.

Which is why I know she probably feels like crap and should be at home resting.

"Go home." My words come out harsher than expected. I can't help but be irrationally upset with Luisa's cycle. I want her home, with a heating pad and a plethora of snacks at her disposal.

And if I dared dream a bit too hard, that home would be with me.

She places her hands on her hips, a fighting stance in her book. "Excuse me? This is my office, and *that* is my chair. You have five seconds to get the fuck out of it."

A smile blooms on my face without permission.

Ah, how I've missed her.

"And before you go running off to HR, remember that it was you who told me that's exactly what I should say to anyone who dared take my rightful place." She tilts her head, eyes studying me. "Or was that all bullshit too?"

My scowl is back in full force.

I told myself I wouldn't engage in any arguments with Luisa since I am, in fact, trying to rebuild some of what we lost. But it seems like I'm going to have to set the record straight on everything that's been playing on her mind since I left.

"I've never lied to you, Luisa. Not once. But I have—"

"Oh, spare me," she interrupts. "I'm not doing this song and dance with you any longer, Stonehaven. If you don't mind, we can go back to doing business as usual, so feel free to hop back on your jet and fly your ass to—"

"Knock, knock. Am I interrupting something?" Daisy asks as she stands by Luisa's open office door with a look of concern on her face.

Perfect timing.

Luisa takes a deep breath, fortifying herself it seems, before she plasters on a polite smile and turns Daisy's way.

I angle myself so I don't miss the moment she sees my dog happily wagging her tail by my sister's side.

She doesn't attempt to hide her surprise, and for a moment, she forgets that she loathes me and drops down to her knees and squeals, "You brought your doggie to work today?" My pup wastes no time, smothering Luisa in sloppy kisses. I have to bite back my insane jealousy.

Daisy gives me a "what the fuck?" look as her eyes bounce between Luisa and me.

I shrug, as if to say, "It's how we are." And she shakes her head with a slight eye roll.

I take this opportunity to clear up a misunderstanding that's been weighing on me. "Luisa, please take my dog out on a proper date before you take her to second base." I tease as I stand and walk their way.

Luisa rears back, as if realizing that I've seen her smile and giggle for the last thirty seconds, leaving her vulnerable to my banter.

"Oh, she's a girl dog? I thought—" She stops before she says something in front of Daisy that will most likely lead to more questions. Like how she already knew I had a dog.

Daisy leans down to pat her furry niece's imposing side. "Oh yeah. She's a big girl, but still a puppy at heart. Aren't you, my sweet little Delilah?"

Luisa's hands on my dog still as her head whips up toward Daisy. "Wh-what did you say her name was?" Her voice comes out scratchy, as if she's attempting to swallow a tough pill.

I squat down next to Luisa, giving the excited ball of fluff a gentle pat. "Her name is Delilah. My dog goes wherever I go, which includes my travels to London." I attempt to make eye contact, but her gaze seems unfocused, as if she's replaying the last time she heard that name. The same moment I've come to regret each night as my fingers itch to send her an email.

She stands suddenly. Wobbling a bit while blinking rapidly.

I shoot up quickly. "Easy there. You okay? Need to take a seat?" I ask worriedly.

She takes a deep breath. "No, I'm fine. Just need a minute."

"Why don't I get you a water? Or maybe a juice. Something with sugar?"

"I don't trust you not to poison it," she mutters.

"Why would I use poison when I can think of much more creative ways to make you docile?" I grin.

Daisy groans loudly from the doorway. "Why are you guys so weird all the time? Is it some gross sexual tension that needs tending to?"

"No!"

"Perhaps."

Luisa and I speak at the same time. She scowls in my direction. "The only tension here is the one forming a headache as we speak. So if you guys don't mind, I have actual work to do." She straightens her blazer as she continues to look down at my dancing pup.

"All right, Daisy. You heard the woman. Out we go."

"You don't have to tell me twice." She's out and down the hallway at an impressive speed.

I lower my voice in case anyone passes by. "I'm going to have something sent up to your office for you to eat and drink, so tell me now if you have any preferences. If not, I'll order everything off the daily menu."

She shakes her head as she pets my dog lovingly. "Out, Stonehaven."

I nod in acquiesce. "As you wish." I tap my leg twice, a signal for Delilah to come. Instead, she stays put, making sweet puppy dog eyes at Luisa.

Trust me, my girl, I know.

Luisa smirks. "Actually, there is one thing—"

"Name it."

"The dog stays."

Delilah barks in what seems like agreement. And if that wasn't enough to convince me, the speed in which her tail is wagging might send her flying.

I sigh exaggeratedly. "You know, there is a joke somewhere here about me liking bad bitches, but I'm much too evolved to actually—"

"*Goodbye,*" Luisa singsongs. "Nuggets, fries, and a chocolate milkshake, if you must. And make it snappy." She slams the door in my face, and I release a hearty laugh as I rest my forehead against the wood, happiness like no other consuming me.

Because she slammed the door with the biggest smile on her face.

CHAPTER TWENTY-THREE

LUISA

I'M ENJOYING THE LAST sips of my milkshake when I get a companywide email informing all employees to work from home today and tomorrow. Other than a command to wrap up whatever we're working on and be out of the building in the next thirty minutes, there wasn't much information.

I start to pack up my things when I get another email notification.

I freeze when I see his name in my inbox.

I saw the man in the flesh earlier, but we've always been different people when we write to one another, and I can't let myself fall down that rabbit hole again.

I consider ignoring the email, but I don't think straight-up ignoring my boss is going to help me either, so I click it open.

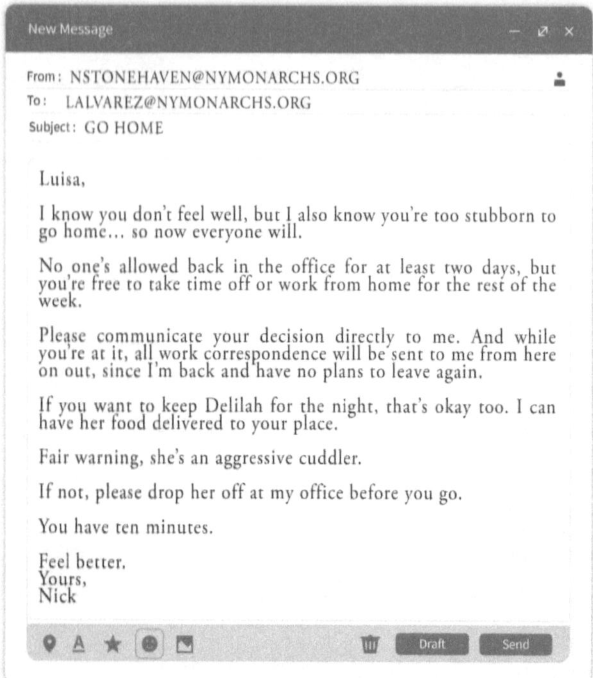

I stare at my screen, unblinking.

Did he...? No. He did not. Could not.

I sigh deeply.

But of course he did. Because he's Nicholas Stonehaven.

"Your dad is insane." Delilah places her sweet face on my lap, requesting more head scratches. "And I guess you both love attention." I chuckle as I pet her soft head.

I hear three rapid knocks before my door opens. I brace myself to rip Nick a new one for not waiting to be invited inside, but clamp my mouth shut when I realize it's Richard.

We've been getting along... for the most part.

But he still calls me "kid" every now and then and doesn't try to hide his annoyance at answering to me.

I don't know why I haven't addressed the issue head-on. Maybe because I was raised to respect my elders or because I don't want to develop a reputation of being problematic in the workplace. But neither of those reasons excuses the disrespect Richard has displayed, and I think it's time I pulled back on the reins.

"There better be a fire in the stadium or a mass evacuation happening. Otherwise, what other reason would there be to barge into my office, Richard?" I pin him with a questioning brow.

His face turns bright red with embarrassment, which he attempts to tamp down on by nodding once as he clears his throat. "Right. I, uh, thought I heard you say to come in. Sorry, but I read the email that we have to leave the premises, and we have that important call with Jake Bryant's agent later today. You have any idea what's going on? This is all so last-minute. Why didn't they alert us of this before we came into work today?"

"I don't have an answer for you on that," I lie, because like hell am I going to tell him that our boss is sending us all home because he wants me to take it easy while I'm on my period. "But we'll still have the phone call with Bryant's team. The call link will remain the same. It was never a video conference, so we'll carry on as scheduled, from our own homes."

He nods thoughtfully, looking around my office until his eyes land on Delilah and his face scrunches. "You brought your pet into work today?" he asks, judgment lacing his tone.

I straighten in my chair. "No. She isn't my pet. She's—"

"She's mine," Nick's voice booms from the doorway, causing Richard to jolt as he turns to meet his icy glare.

I panic for a moment before I realize that Nick was referring to his dog.

I think.

Although being claimed by Nick doesn't feel all that terrible.

Keep it together, woman. One day back, and you're already losing all of your senses.

"Oh, I didn't realize we had a pet-friendly workplace." Richard fake laughs, turning his question my way. "Any reason why you're pet-sitting for the boss?" Condescension drips from his lips.

I can see the moment Nick is about to lash out with his words, but I raise my hand as I speak. "In case you've forgotten, Richard, we're all supposed to be packing to leave for the rest of the day. I suggest you get to it and prepare for our call."

He almost seems miffed I didn't take the bait. Assuming that I'd react like a "fiery Latina" as the media has, at times, reduced me to.

But in true Richard fashion, he doesn't seem to know when to quit. "About that." He turns back to Nick. "Care to explain the sudden need for us to leave?" He places his hands in his pockets, giving Nick a mildly disapproving look.

Nick mirrors his stance as he takes a step closer, towering over him. "No." Richard fumbles for the right words, but Nick deems them unnecessary. "Unless you need assistance leaving the facility, please make your exit. You have five minutes." He opens my office door wider and waves for him to step out.

Richard seems truly baffled by the gesture but, probably thinking better than to go toe to toe with Nick, leaves quickly.

Nick closes the door harder than necessary, then turns my way.

"I had it handled." I cross my arms over my chest. Delilah whines due to the loss of her head scratches, so I drop my arms back down to give her what she wants while accidentally triggering the voice I only use while speaking to adorable pups. "Okay, fine. One more minute, and then I gotta get outta here because your daddy is Mr. Crazy Pants. Yes, he is. So, so crazy. He should get his noggin checked for head trauma." She yips happily. "I agree. You should put holes in all his fancy suits, but make sure to start with his shoes. I love stepping on them every chance I get," I coo into her blissed-out face.

I wait a few seconds, expecting Nick to chime in. When silence greets me, I look up, only to wish I hadn't.

I thought I'd seen every version of this man. Every sexy and infuriating feature. I was ready to act like the last month hadn't happened. To jump back into a bickering relationship with my boss that would go nowhere.

But the look of absolute adoration as he stares down at me with his dog has me rethinking it all at lightning speed.

The worst part? I like that look. Way too much to deny that I could fall for this man if I'm not careful.

I cursed his mere existence after I thought he had played me for a fool, and yet today, with a few interactions and a couple of cuddles with his dog, I feel myself ready to melt into a puddle for him.

I was so enraptured by our game of cat and mouse that I didn't realize how far I had fallen into his trap.

Even if this last month was all a big misunderstanding, it doesn't change a thing.

He's still my boss.

Objectively an asshole but, one could argue, with good intentions.

And, unfortunately, the only man that has ever held the power to set my world on fire with a simple touch.

I need to set better boundaries around Nick, and I need him to be on board, because my pitiful willpower can only take so much.

"I don't think I want to know what's running through that head of yours, Angel," he whispers softly.

I squeeze my eyes shut and push down my desire to hear him call me Angel while tangled up in bed.

"Nick—"

"I'm sorry, I—wait. Did you just call me Nick?" he asks cautiously.

"That is your name, is it not?"

"You never call me Nick." He eyes me warily.

"This," I point between the two of us, "is a dysfunctional—yet enjoyable, at times—*working* relationship. That's something we both seem to forget every now and then. But this merry-go-round stops here. It's safer to keep things professional. At least as professional as you and I are capable of being."

His hand rubs against his clenched jaw. "I know it was fucked what I did, letting you believe—"

"Yes, it was. But it doesn't matter. We're both here for the same reason, and that's to make this the best team the MLB has ever seen. And I personally can't do that when I don't know what version of my *boss* I'm going to get."

I stand and grab hold of Delilah's leash, bringing it up and placing it in Nick's hand. His brief touch has me taking a step back and playing off how affected I am by the brush of his fingers.

He chuckles darkly as he shakes his head. "Of course. As you wish, Luisa." All traces of vulnerability are locked up tightly behind his impeccable suit when he hits me with that arrogant smirk. "Business as usual is what you can expect from me." He pulls on Delilah's leash softly, and this time, she goes with him without any protest.

It's ridiculous how sad that makes me.

"Enjoy working from home this week, but when we get back, I need a full analysis of the state of our players and any trades you have in mind. Because make no mistake, Luisa, I expect this team to make it all the way to the World Series, and I'm counting on you to make that happen."

I match his smirk and meet his arrogance head-on.

Now this is a version of Nick I can handle. There is nothing I love more than cutting a man at his knees and proving what I'm made of.

I give Delilah a little wave as I grab my bag and phone and meet Nick by my open door.

"As you wish, boss."

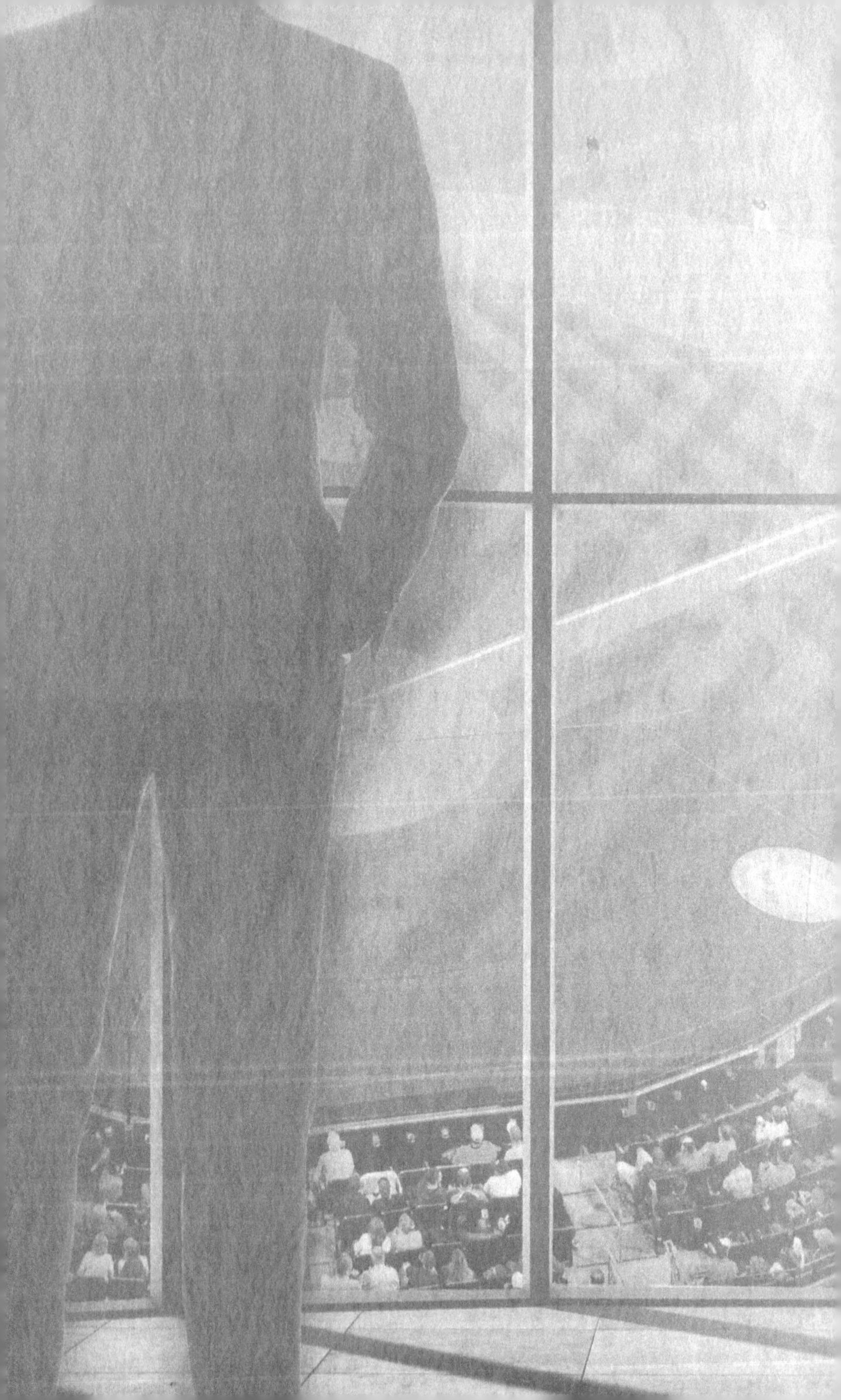

CHAPTER TWENTY-FOUR

NICK

THAT LITTLE BRAT.

She has managed to do exactly as I asked, helping craft the perfect team as we head into the playoffs.

She's also managed to keep me at arm's length for the past few weeks, which I can respect, since one of us should possess some semblance of self-control.

Time is flying, and we're only a few games away from qualifying for the World Series. Everything is going according to plan.

And yet, last night, I almost caved.

The whole team, along with their family and friends, were celebrating after we hosted a charity game for hurricane relief in the Caribbean.

I saw all the players pair up with their women, and I somehow found myself holding up two glasses of scotch from my personal stash in my office and was on my way to hand one to Luisa.

I ran into Mateo Martinez, our starting pitcher, on my way to her. I tried to keep up a friendly conversation, but my eyes kept drifting to my Angel, who was ripping up the dance floor with my sister and the rest of their newly formed girl gang.

It was then that Mateo realized who I couldn't keep my eyes off.

I've always kept my cards close to the vest. It's helped tremendously in building my empire. Steering my competitors in the wrong direction, never allowing them to predict my next power move.

But when it comes to Luisa, those carefully honed skills are long gone.

I ended up giving Mateo the glass intended for her and sequestered myself in my office until I knew the party was over and she was gone.

Now I'm back in my home office, looking over contracts that seem to blur right before my eyes the more I try to read through them.

I need to keep my head on straight.

I am so close to achieving my ultimate goal.

Soon, the team will make it to their first World Series game, and I'll be off the hook.

I can walk away with my asset and hand off the team to someone who actually knows the sport.

Wipe my hands clean of this mess and focus solely on Stonehaven Media.

Keep true to the plan I formed in my mind the moment my grandfather's will was read to me over six months ago.

I try to run through the details again, but like every time I do, I get a stabbing pain in my chest at the thought of walking away from the team that has slowly started to feel like family.

An office that has begun to feel like home.

And a woman who, no matter what, will never belong to me yet still feels like mine.

My Angel.

But the clock is ticking, and I'm running out of time.

It's game night.

The game night.

We're in the second inning, and it feels like I'm about to crawl out of my skin.

I've been on the phone with my attorney all day, making sure he has all the paperwork ready for the transfer of assets. He's thorough, so he has contracts drawn up for any potential misstep.

Mateo Martinez is playing one hell of a game, ensuring an easy win tonight, so I don't bother keeping a close eye on the field below me.

Luisa and Daisy walk into my office arm and arm with wide smiles on their faces.

Any other day, I would allow myself to daydream about the possibility of Luisa and me. Together somehow. But in this moment, it's as clear as ever that that future will never come.

"Hey, big bro. Why the long face? We're about to make baseball history."

"Shh!" Luisa elbows Daisy. "Don't jinx us."

Daisy rolls her eyes. "What is it with everyone being superstitious today? I'm sure I saw at least five odd rituals happening as I passed by the clubhouse to wish Coach good luck."

"Trust me, it's taken some teams decades to dig themselves out of the curses they found themselves under." Luisa shudders.

"Ladies, while I do appreciate the visit, now is not the best time."

They both tilt their heads in the same direction, and I can't help but find it adorable.

"Everything okay, Nick?" my sister asks.

Damn, I feel like shit. Daisy has really seemed to find herself while working for the Monarchs. And soon I'll have to tell her I'm selling it off. I make a mental note to ensure she maintains her position when I'm gone.

"All's well. Would prefer some solitude tonight, is all."

Luisa narrows her eyes. "No such luck, boss. Tonight is a big game. Win or lose, we're going to need you down there on the field to cheer on the team."

I fear I won't be able to look any one of my players in the eye by the end of tonight, but I nod anyway, because I can't bring myself to say that out loud.

"All right. We'll go and leave you to brood over your kingdom alone," Daisy teases as she pulls Luisa closer to the wall of windows behind my desk. "But first let me take a quick picture of the team from up here. You have the best view of the stadium." Daisy pulls out her phone and snaps pictures as Luisa stands next to me, her eyes assessing.

"What's going on, Nick?" she asks low enough for Daisy not to hear.

God, I'm going to miss the sound of my name on her lips.

But Daisy's loud gasp pulls our attention to the field.

I don't understand what's happening.

Why are all the players running onto the field?

"Oh my gosh. They're fighting!" Daisy yells.

"Did Martinez throw that first punch?" Luisa asks, dazed.

"He definitely threw the second and third one. Oh God, now everyone's getting in on it!" Daisy shrieks.

"Where is security? How has this gotten out of hand so quickly?" I shout to no one in particular.

"Do you really think security can pull back dozens of amped-up professional athletes? Give it a minute. It'll die down. In the meantime, I need to get my ass down there and rip Martinez a new one." She's gone before I can ask any other stupid questions, with Daisy hot on her heels.

I stare back at the rowdy crowd and unruly baseball players.

What the fuck just happened?

Monarchs lost.

They fucking lost.

I waited down by the dugout, hoping for a miracle. But once that final home run was hit by the opposing team, I stormed off, knocking over one of those huge Gatorade coolers on my way out.

I was on the warpath.

I called my lawyer and told him to look for any loopholes in the will. Figure out if there was any room for negotiations, anything.

I was screaming at the top of my lungs, not caring who heard or saw me.

But it was all in vain.

Because I knew.

It was all over.

And I had lost yet again.

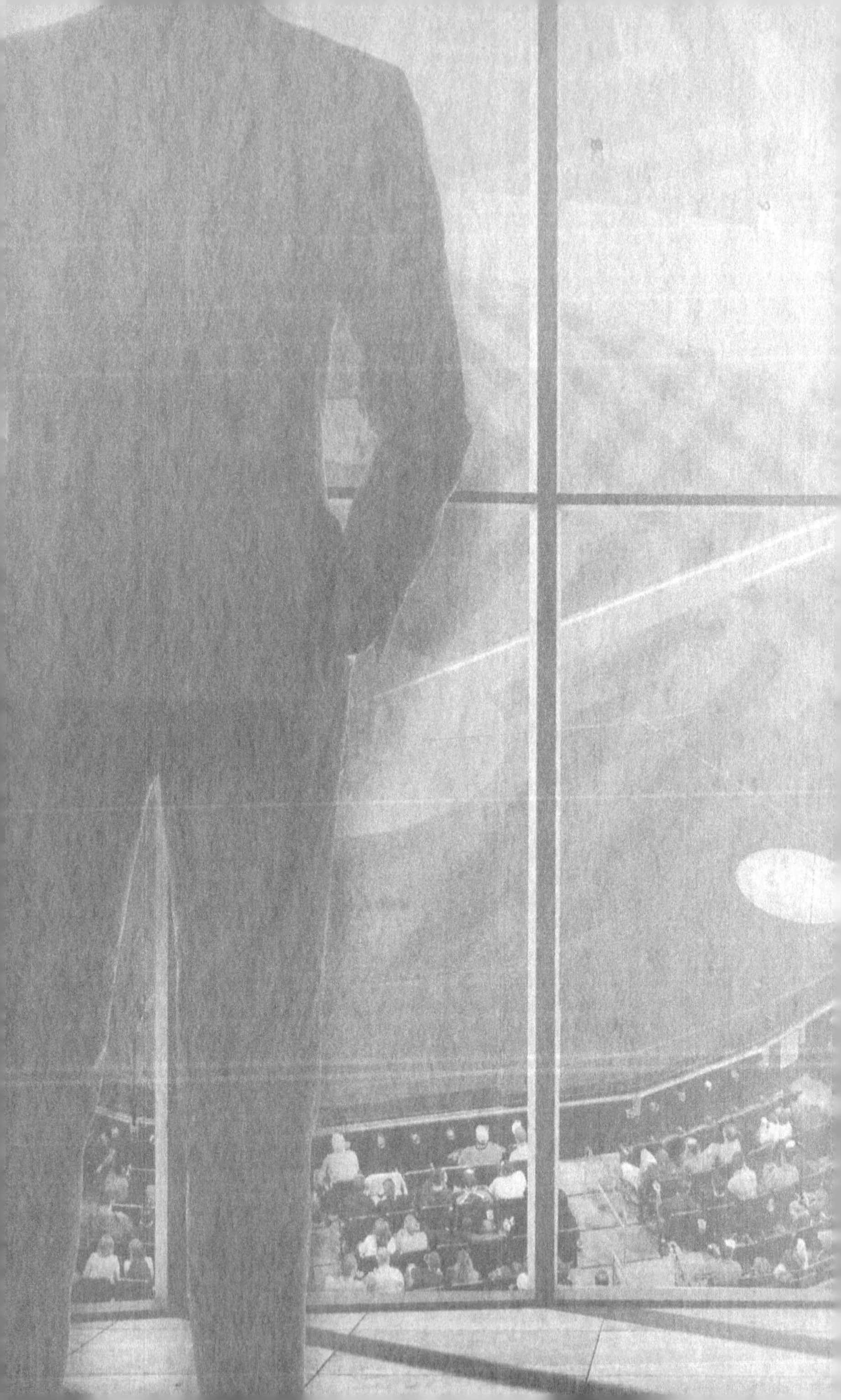

CHAPTER TWENTY-FIVE

NICK

I STORM INTO MY office, tugging off my tie as I do.

I was stupid. For a moment, I believed this team could win and I would walk away clean, having accomplished one of the proposed terms of my dead grandfather's will and getting back what I so carelessly lost.

Fuck. I was so fucking close.

I'm granted only a moment of serenity before Luisa bursts through my office door, having no problem bulldozing in here, since it seems to be the only way she knows how to enter my workspace.

"What the hell is wrong with you? Stepping out on the team as they were handed their loss? For what? So you can drink your expensive booze and sulk in silence?"

"Silence, in my office? I would never dream of such a delight," I snark as I get up to pour myself a glass of the alcohol Luisa helpfully reminded me of. Even though my guest wasn't invited and can currently be described as hostile at best, my manners ensure that I pour her a glass as well.

Looks like we both need it.

We're both itching for a fight. I'm usually enthralled by her fire, willing to sit back and see how far she'll let herself burn.

But with the way my life has taken a turn, I find myself not wanting to back down as she continues to berate me.

"Those men down there have put their blood, sweat, and tears into this game. Their families deal with not having a family member for most of the year. Did you know that baseball has the longest season of all professional sports?"

I eye her over my glass as she continues to spew sports facts that have no hope of being retained.

In my defense, the way her chest heaves as she tries to prove her point makes it quite hard to pay attention.

While I've thoroughly enjoyed this season, with Luisa ready to rip me a new one at every turn, it seems our perverse form of foreplay has abruptly come to an end.

Because it's all coming to an end.

As in the New York Monarchs.

All because I didn't satisfy the terms of the will that haunt me daily.

"Love, hate to interrupt, but your breath is being wasted."

"Love? You think 'cause you own this team, you can avoid HR complaints? We promised to keep things professional from now on, and if you think—"

"It's over, Luisa. All of it. The New York Monarchs played their first and final season as a team. And there's nothing we can do about it. So yes, scurry off to HR, and while you're there, let them know that a severance package is coming their way."

Her face drops. And so does her body—into the chair in front of my desk.

Feels like she's docile enough to allow me to slide the glass in front of her without the risk of having it boomerang back to my head.

She takes it without a fuss and throws half of it back in one go.

Rookie mistake.

But to my surprise, she doesn't flinch. Nor does she have an exaggerated coughing fit.

The woman is a whiskey drinker. Another thing to add to the list of reasons why she intrigues me so much.

But not even the slit in her fitted skirt can get a rise out of me at a time like this.

"Explain," she says warily.

I stand and close the doors that Luisa so unhelpfully left open.

Instead of walking back to my chair, I move to stand in front of my desk, forcing Luisa to sit back or sit face to face with my crotch.

I cross my arms and pin her with an unyielding stare as I start. "What I'm about to tell you cannot leave this office, understood?"

She nods.

"Use your words. We both know you know how to cut me with them," I push.

"Yes, understood," she grits out.

I smile condescendingly. "Good. I'd usually have someone sign an NDA, but if there is anyone else who has as much to lose if this goes public, it's you."

"Get to the point. Explain what kind of rich man's mess I need to clean up. Go on, I know it's coming. What is it?

Found yourself in a sex scandal? No, too boring for a guy like you. Has to do with money. Maybe a little embezzling or money laundering? What's your poison, Stonehaven?" She pushes back, and my God, now is not the time to admire the woman.

"Trust me, Luisa. If I had a poison, it would be you. Since I can't seem to stop myself from drowning in it." I pause as I watch her take a smaller sip this time, her eyes never leaving mine. "Very well. I'll save you the sob story and get to the point. My father and I have never gotten along. A few years back, after I made my money—and became a true thorn in my father's side, by the way—he bet he could acquire a company quicker and more efficiently than I could."

"You said this story would be quick, but all I'm hearing is that you have daddy issues. If the next sentence out of your mouth is close to 'I'm self-made, but I took a one-million-dollar loan from my dad to do it,' I'm out of here."

"Retract your claws unless you plan on leaving marks down my back, Luisa." Her jaw drops slightly, and I take it as my cue to continue. "I was foolish, and in my haste, I didn't do my due diligence. What I put up for the bet wasn't fully mine to give. And to ensure my father wouldn't play dirty, I made sure to move that asset into my grandfather's name, another man I no longer had a relationship with, although he seemed like the lesser evil at the time. Needless to say, I had no idea my father was sleeping with the wife of the CEO of the very company we were vying for and therefore had insider information. The asset has remained in my grandfather's name since then. Once he passed, I went to the reading of his will to see if he would give it back. First, he gave me this team, which

I had no interest in keeping and was planning on immediately selling off. But then the asset was offered back, but only as long as I accomplished at least one of the two proposed terms."

She waves me on. "Well, what are they?"

"One, I keep the team and lead them to a World Series game in their first season. He didn't require the team to win the World Series, only make it. Something they would have accomplished had they won tonight."

I can see the wheels start turning in her pretty little head, and I know she's connecting the dots as to why I was so furious earlier.

Not my brightest moment, but we all have flaws, don't we?

"This team can't be over." She stands abruptly, not bothering to step back and leave appropriate space between us. "This is my first season as a general manager. Hell, I'm the first woman general manager ever. If this team goes down the drain, so does my career." She digs her hands into her high ponytail, and my hand twitches to let her hair down once and for all. "It'll fuck my career and that of any other woman who's working her ass off to get a respectable position in the sports industry. Me going down is a clear message that I've failed and that there is no space for women in professional sports." She shakes her head, her spine straightening, resolve in her voice. "No. Not an option. What was the second term?"

Well, this one's the real kicker.

"I get married."

"*Excuse me?*"

"For a year, I have to be a married man. With no public scandals and no claims of infidelity made against me."

She huffs out a laugh. "Perfect. Call up one of your brainless bimbos and give them an offer they can't refuse. Have them sign an NDA, and you're golden."

I take a sip of my drink as she paces back and forth. "You see, that's where things get dicey. Because I thought about it immediately after I heard the will. But I'm not allowed to have a prenup. Meaning, that once our one year is up, if my bride decided to take half of my net worth, she'd be well within her rights to do so. And I'm sorry to say that I'm not keen on giving away five billion dollars to a, what did you call it? Ah, yes, a brainless bimbo."

Her eyes widen. "You're worth five billion dollars?"

"No, that's the half I'd have to part with. Please keep up, Angel."

Her mouth snaps shut as her mind spins, her eyes looking like the slot machines in Vegas, spinning to land on the winning solution.

She goes rigid, and for a moment, I worry that she's going to pass out.

"What is it?" I ask.

"I'll do it."

"And what exactly are you offering to do, Luisa? You don't leave a man with a mind like mine to go off and assume."

She comes to stand in front of me, face stoic as she says, "I'll do it. I'll marry you."

I roll my eyes. "Yeah, that five billion sounded nice enough to sweeten the deal, I bet."

She scoffs. "Is it a stupid amount of money? Yes. Should there even be a singular human walking around earth with that kind of cash at their disposal? No. But that's not what I'm after." She takes a step closer, and I drop my arms. "This might look a little different from your point of view with all the zeros in your bank account, but I am self-made too. I have worked tirelessly to carve a path not only for myself, but for the women coming up behind me. So believe me when I say I'll marry you, and when the clock runs out on our sham marriage, I'll happily walk away without a cent of your money, because I'd get to keep what I brought into it."

"Hmm, and what's that?"

"My integrity."

Silence.

We stare at each other for what feels like an eternity.

I'm well versed in reading people, and Luisa isn't bullshitting me.

This is stupid.

A much too rash decision.

I can clearly hear my accountant screaming in my ear to reconsider.

But it doesn't stop me from goading her. "I retrieve my lost asset and keep my money, and you keep your position not only on this team, but as the beacon of light for all women everywhere."

She glares at me, and I smile.

"Oh, and that integrity. Let's not forget that."

"So, Stonehaven. What do you say? We getting married or what?" She holds out her hand as if to shake on a simple deal.

I take it and quickly pull her into my chest. Her soft gasp does something to me, and I make a mental note to make sure I get to hear it again.

"I recover my asset, and you keep your job. Sounds like a fair trade to me."

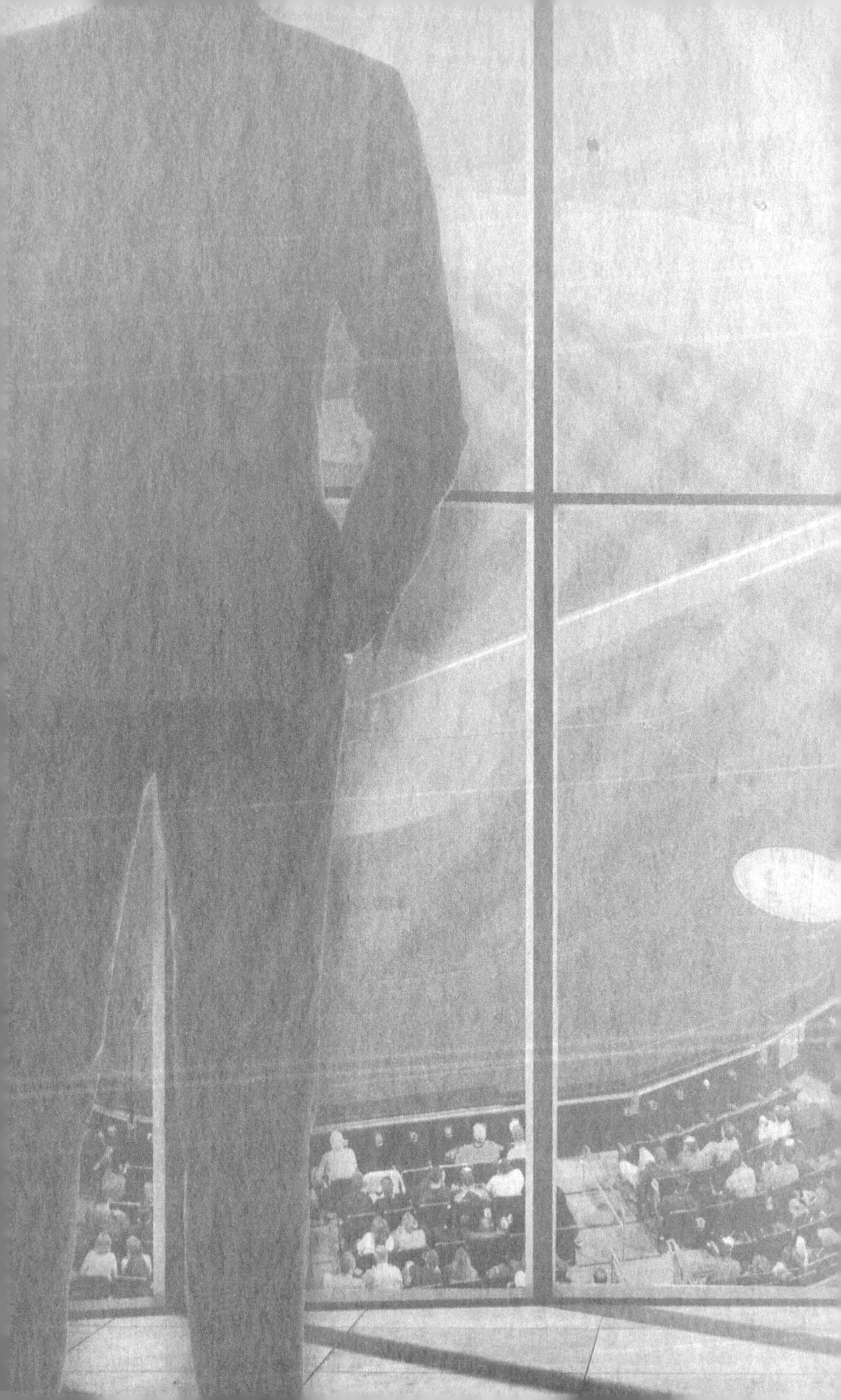

CHAPTER TWENTY-SIX

NICK

Present

I MARRIED LUISA FUCKING Álvarez.

Or is it Stonehaven now? The thought sends a zap of electricity down my spine as we enter her apartment.

We just left my attorney's office. The place that will now be forever known as the spot where I married my Angel.

Not the most romantic setting, but it got the job done.

I can't believe we actually did it.

I'm stuck somewhere between disbelief and wonder.

My new missus, on the other hand, seems much more annoyed by her new relationship status, mumbling under her breath words that sounded like "cleaning up after rich men's messes."

And to be fair, she's not wrong. A part of me feels unbearably guilty for pulling Luisa into this farce of a marriage. Yet the other part of me, the one that's been secretly pining for this woman for the better part of a year, feels like it can howl at the moon at any moment.

She's mine for the next year, and I don't plan on wasting a single second.

"I've come up with a plan. One that helps cover our bases, so to speak." I interrupt her hasty packing. She'll be moving into my place tomorrow morning and seems to want to get a jump on the preparations now, at almost midnight.

"Oh, are we doing baseball puns now?" She aggressively stuffs a few pairs of socks into a duffel bag.

I walk around her bedroom, taking in every detail of the place she calls home. "I think that in order for us to make this marriage believable, we need to focus on three key areas. Manhattan society, our baseball world, and the toughest out of the three: our friends."

"You mean *my* friends. You have Daisy by default, but I'm also claiming her in this marriage." She moves to her closet and pulls out a few jackets.

I ignore her quip. "We need to be seen out and about, at charity functions or newsworthy events. Introducing you on my arm for the first time sends a clear message that I am now a married man and am smitten with my wife."

"Who's gonna tell all your old supermodel dates they're off the payroll?"

"Second..." I ignore her snarky remark and secretly hope I detected a hint of jealousy. "We need to be the face of the Monarchs organization. We need to show that we are a team and dispel any potential murmurs of inappropriate behaviors."

"I've yet to see you act appropriately even once. Guess we're doomed."

"And last, we can't hide in our home for the rest of the year. We still need to live our lives and have fun, meaning that we need to spend time with our friends, and they need to believe that we're the real deal. I don't think any of them would tattle on us, but I don't want to put anyone in a position where they feel like they have to lie for us."

She stops moving for the first time tonight and nods. "I hate the idea of burdening anyone I love with our secret. It's our mess, and we will handle it accordingly."

"Which means we're going to have to be convincing. We have to prove to the world that we are so in love that we ran off and got hitched. So this," my pointer finger swings back and forth at the two of us, "needs work."

She scoffs, "Oh yeah? And why do I get the sense that I'll be the one doing all the work?"

"Well, I am the one that's easier to get along with."

"I literally call you the devil."

"Further proves my point that I'm the nice one."

She rolls her eyes. "So what? We have to be friends now?"

"Oh, honey, we are well and far beyond that." I raise my hand with the silver wedding band. "No, I fear it's going to take drastic measures in order for this to work."

She raises a suspicious brow. "Oh? And what's that?"

"It's simple, really." I shrug. "You're going to fall in love with me."

LUISA

My flying heel barely misses Nick as he ducks.

"Woman, are you mad? What the hell was that for?"

"I didn't have a chancleta nearby, so a flying Louboutin will have to do."

"I'm scared to ask any follow-up questions, but it seems to be pertinent that I understand why the flying *fuck* I almost got a stiletto to the eye!" He points at his face.

"Because, Lucifer, you're a self-centered, narcissistic, arrogant—"

"Angel, I hope you know those words all mean the same thing. If we're going to fight, at least save us some time."

I release an animalistic screech. "That right there." I point at him. "You think I could so easily fall in love with someone like you? As if you could snap your fingers and I'd be writing hearts around your name?"

"Of course not." He runs a hand down his tie. "I'd much prefer for you to scream my name while—"

"Stop." I raise my hands. "Just stop talking. Nothing good happens when you do." I pace back and forth. "I don't know how the thought weaseled its way into your brain, but I suggest you swiftly remove it. Because I, Luisa Álvarez, will not be falling in love with you. Ever. So we're going to have to work on our acting skills and rely on them to get us by for the next year.”

"Fine."

"Great."

"Splendid."

"Great."

"You already said that."

"Shut up."

"Aw, c’mon, look at us. I think we just survived our first fight as husband and wife. What do you say we celebrate by getting naked?” He winks.

And for the second time tonight, a shoe flies through the air, but this time, it hits its mark.

Chapter Twenty-Eight

LUISA

I married Nicholas fucking Stonehaven.

Those words play on a loop in my head as I look down at the glittering wedding band covered in diamonds on my left ring finger.

The party is over, and the last of the guests have left Nick's home.

Our home for the next year.

Explaining this to my parents was the toughest part. I asked them to arrive before anyone else, because they deserved a heads-up before the news became the biggest media story in the country.

My mother was shocked, but she immediately burst into happy tears, pulling Nick into a fierce hug as she mumbled nonsensical plans for our future. My father, on the other hand, was silent. He'd be happy for me if he was sure this was what I truly wanted, accelerated timeline be damned. So I put on an Oscar-worthy performance to ensure that he knew I was okay, and, in fact, not being held hostage by a billionaire.

It seemed to have worked when he accepted Nick's handshake. But then he said, "One. You get one strike with me, and you've already used it by not asking for her hand in marriage. Tread lightly if you expect to remain welcome in this family."

"Understood." Nick bowed his head in an unexpected sign of respect. "And trust me, I will go about things the right way from here on out. I'm sorry our excitement got the better of us and we ran off to get hitched without any of Luisa's family. Believe me when I say from here on out, you will all be included in everything we do." He made a sweeping motion around the grand living room we're currently all standing in. "Consider this place your home. Please don't hesitate to ask for anything. I truly want to do right by your daughter, and that includes having her family at ease with her decision to marry me. I am well aware that I married up."

My mother's eyes had widened right before she slapped my father's arm. "You heard the man. We're family! Wait until my sisters check this place out. And that kitchen. Dios mío. We are going to have the best holiday parties here. I can feel it."

"Wait. Hold on, Mami. Nick was being polite offering his—"

"Angel." Nick stopped me with a gentle hand on my lower back, and I'm surprised at how easily I leaned into his touch. "This is no longer my home. It's ours. We've discussed this." He places a soft kiss on the top of my head, and I feel myself sinking further.

"Ay, Javier. Look at them! They're so in love. My little girl is married." My mother started to weep softly, and my father moved in to rub her back.

"Javier, I would love to give you a tour of our place. I haven't really had the chance to do much with it since I've left most of the work to the interior designer. But there is a game room on the floor below that opens up to the patio. I have multiple TVs, gaming consoles, and a pool table. And I had a domino table delivered this morning in hopes that—"

"Hold it right there." My dad lifted a hand. "You're telling me you got a gaming room with TVs so I can watch the game while I play dominoes?" My father's eyes bored into my new husband's as Nick slowly nodded. A loud clap and laugh from my father startled us all. "Pero mijo, why didn't you lead with that? I could have saved you a few gray hairs." He playfully pointed at Nick's trim beard. "Yep, right around there. I could see a few coming in right before my eyes," my dad teased and I swear Nick deflated beside me. To the point where I found myself mirroring his stance and placing a hand on his back to make sure he stayed upright.

After that, he gave them a quick tour that passed in a blur, and then I had to get ready to announce to the entire Monarchs family that their team owner and general manager had gotten married.

We were able to fend off our friends by promising to give them the full story at a later time—a fake one we'd have to rehearse in order to keep straight. My friend Isabella, Mateo Martinez's girlfriend, gave me a look like she was onto me. Daisy seemed happy but slightly bummed that she was kept in the dark about our whirlwind romance. And everyone else got drunk on Nick's dime.

I'm exhausted, and all I want to do now is climb into my bed and forget about the media shitstorm that's about to hit us.

"And where do you think you're going, my blushing bride?" Nick chimes from down the hallway that leads up to the master bedroom.

"I spotted some bedrooms this way during the tour earlier, so I'm going to claim one and settle my stuff into it later in the week. When I find the time and energy. So good night, Stonehaven," I say as I take off my heels and wiggle my toes on the smooth wooden floors.

Nick tsks as he closes the distance between us. "You clearly didn't pay attention on the tour, since our bedroom is that way." He tips his head, gesturing behind him.

I lift my hands to my face and start to rub my temples. "Nick, I don't have the energy for this. If you really think we're about to consummate this marriage, you're clearly more deranged than I gave you credit for."

"Is your mind always in the gutter? I was merely pointing out the fact that your belongings have already been stored and sorted in our room. There is no need to run off like a bandit in the night. Besides, we've already been well acquainted with one another. Seeing your unicorn jammies shouldn't be any more intimate than what we've already done." He smiles salaciously.

What the hell?

I blow past a chuckling Nick and enter his palatial master bedroom, heading straight into the walk-in closet that is twice the size of my one-bedroom apartment.

There, along one side of the wall, are all my work suits and tailored shirts. It only takes up about a quarter of the space available, but that's for sure everything I had hanging in my closet this morning.

I start to pull open drawers and find the rest of my comfy clothes. Leggings, sweaters, underwear, even the lingerie Nick bought me. All of it's there. Including a set of unicorn pajamas I bought for my cousin's five-year-old's birthday party sleepover. They're fleece, and I only wear them during the winter when I need the extra warmth.

But if Nick knows about these jammies, the ones that were in my bottom drawer, then he must have seen... oh God.

I spin and almost run into Nick's solid, bare chest. He's removed his dress shirt, shoes, and socks and is currently standing in only his slacks, expensive-looking watch, and his silver wedding band.

Holy shit, my husband is hot.

Fake. Fake husband, I remind myself, forcing my mind back to the task at hand.

"Where is the rest of my stuff? You couldn't possibly have gotten..." I clear my throat a few times. "Everything."

Nick moves closer to me, his steps silent on the plush closet carpet as a wicked smile plays on his lips. "Oh, dear wife, I most definitely got... *everything*."

My face heats up at the insinuation, because that means he most definitely saw my collection of sex toys.

His eyes gleam with unrestrained mischief. "Oh, no need for that. We're a very sex positive household, aren't we, Angel?" He licks his bottom lip, and for a second I almost allow myself to lean forward and bite it. "But no need to worry. I handled the delivery of your special toys myself. Even washed and stored them in your nightstand. At least as many as I could fit. I had to organize them by size, charging capabilities, and—"

"Okay, that's enough." I interrupt, knowing my cheeks must be as red as a tomato. "And I don't know when you had the time to do all of this," I wave around the closet, "but I'm not sleeping with you. Like actually sleeping. There are more than enough rooms in this house for me to claim one as my own."

His head is already shaking before I finish my sentence. "Sorry, but that's not how this is going to work."

"Oh?" I raise a threatening brow as I place my hands on my hips.

"What is rule number one about our little arrangement?"

"No one can find out." I repeat the words his attorney drilled into us right before we signed our marriage license.

"Exactly. So what do you think would happen if one of our housekeepers or maintenance staff were to notice that the loved-up newlyweds were actually sleeping in different bedrooms, hmm? It would raise questions. Questions we can't afford at a time where our focus is to spin the story of how we fell in love *before* we started working together and how our relationship was never inappropriate."

Dammit. Our team publicist almost had a coronary when we told her we had eloped last night. And I know every important media outlet is working on overdrive, waiting for any juicy detail to offer the world besides the carefully written wedding announcement Stonehaven Media put out a few hours ago.

I know better than anyone how easy it is for stories to leak and have the full wrath of social media come at you at a moment's notice. Isabella had a rough brush with it once, and Nick recently played a hand in making sure the tabloids wouldn't speak ill of her again.

He protected her and Mateo's now public relationship.

Which means he would do the same for us, and it seemed like I was going to have to play by these ridiculous rules.

"Fine," I say through gritted teeth. He flashes a satisfactory smile, so I continue. "But first, repeat *my* rules back to me."

His scowl automatically brings a smile to my face.

"We're adults, Luisa. Surely we don't have to—"

"Mr. Stonehaven, are you going back on your word?"

His hands fist at his sides and he slowly works to unfurl them. "Of course not."

"So let me hear them." I wave him on.

"All right, let's see." He sighs as he rubs his large hand over his mouth, his wedding band playing a quick round of peek-a-boo with me. "Ah, yes. I'm only allowed to touch you in public, and only for the purpose of solidifying the validity of our relationship. Kissing is okay, as long as it's a quick peck and not overly indulgent." He rolls his eyes, and I work to hold back my laughter. "After the year of marriage is up, you have full control of the media narrative as to the reason for our separation. Something along the lines of: we are better suited as friends and that there is no scandal to speak of. And I'm pretty sure I've captured it all."

"Nick," I warn.

"Luisa."

"You're conveniently leaving out a big rule."

"Have I? It has been a long day. I don't know if you recall, but I got married less than twenty-four hours ago—"

"Stonehaven."

"Fine. No sex. It's off the table, as explicitly expressed by your wishes."

"You know that would complicate things. We already know it wouldn't be a one-time thing."

"Again, I'm failing to see the problem with that," he mutters.

I sigh, because there's no way to explain that if I have sex with him again, I'm going to be in deep shit. Because I've already caught myself falling for this infuriating man. The man who is now my *husband*. Add in earth-shattering sex, and I'm a goner. But this marriage will only last a year. It's in the contract I signed. And once Nick walks out of my life and I move out of his home, I will have to go on. And it doesn't feel smart to add walking away from a broken heart and mind-blowing sex at the same time.

So, instead, I've inadvertently signed us up to a year of celibacy.

I haven't had sex since the night we met, so it's not like I have a roster of men to clear. But I doubt Nick is holding on to the same record as me, and I have to push down the ugly green monster that threatens to choke me with jealousy.

"You promised," I say instead.

Nick surprises me by gently grabbing my left hand and lifting it between us, the sparkly diamonds on my ring shining under the closet lights.

"And I never break my promises." He squeezes my hand. "Look, I know this is a lot. It is for me too, believe it or not. I know our relationship has been anything but conventional, but I need you to know that no matter what, you can count on me. I may be your husband in name only, but I vow right here and now to be your person.

"You have a shitty day at work? You come to me. See a funny meme that is meant to be insulting toward the entire male population, you send it my way." His thumb brushes over my ring. "If you feel like you need a minute to catch your breath because life can get overwhelming, turn around and you'll find me standing there, ready to hold you up until you feel steady on your own two feet again."

My eyes instantly start to water, and I have to swallow roughly and pray my voice doesn't betray me. "You promise?" I ask shakily.

He lifts my hand and presses a soft kiss over my ring. "I vow."

I let out a ragged breath, not used to seeing this side of Nick. If I thought withholding sex from our arrangement was going to help salvage the future tattered pieces of my heart, I may have gravely underestimated his capabilities.

"Okay, I guess now is a good time for me to hear your rules." I softly remove my hand from his gentle hold.

I'm certain he's not going to answer when he simply smiles and turns to leave.

But when he eyes me over his shoulder and opens his mouth to speak, I have to strain my ears to make sure I heard him right.

Yet there was no mistaking what he said.

"Wife, when it comes to you, I have none."

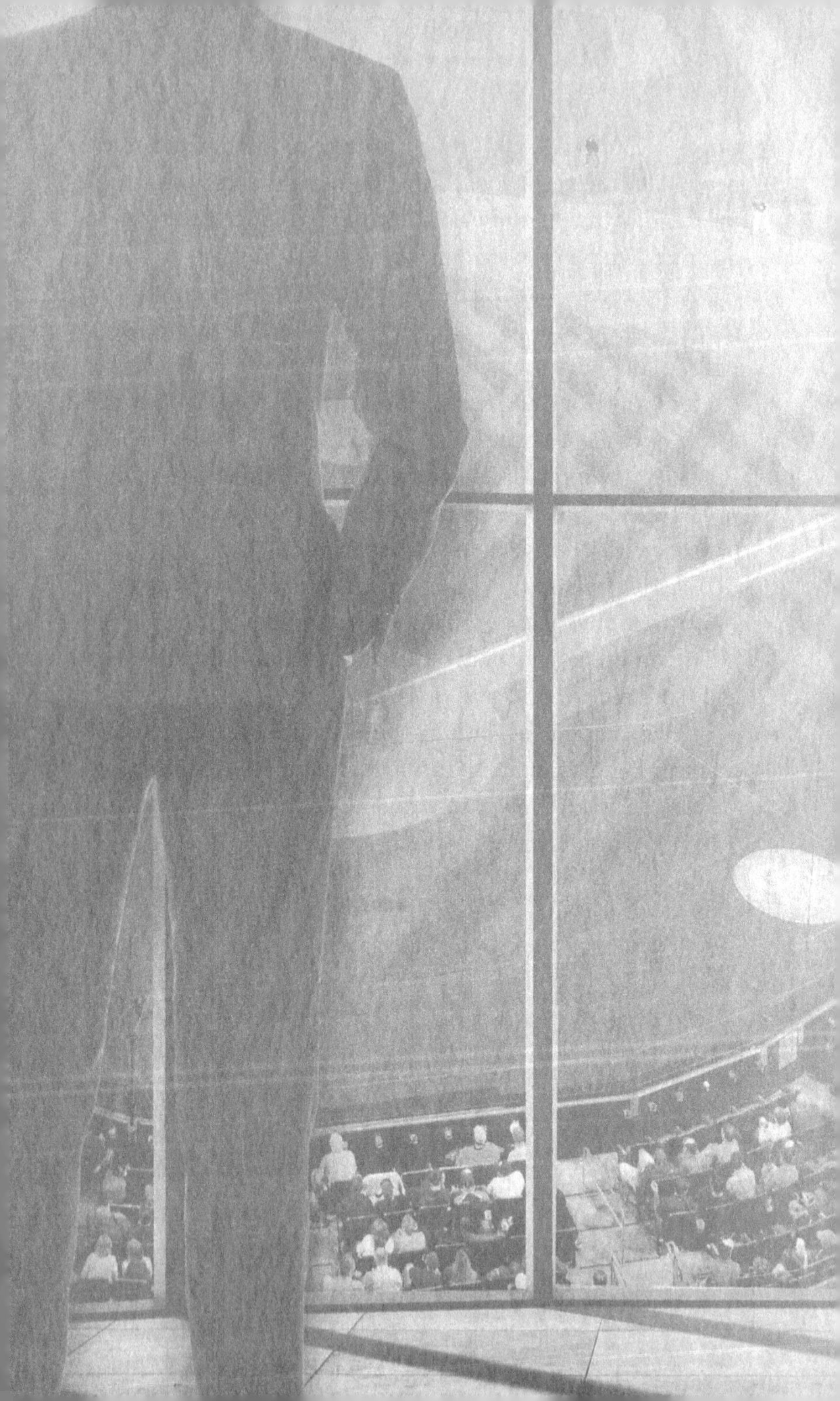

CHAPTER TWENTY-NINE

NICK

I'VE BEEN HIDING IN my office for the last hour.

Luisa is showering in our bathroom, and the thought of her naked and wet was enough to send me running to another floor. I quickly stepped into a guest room and took the coldest and quickest shower known to man. After I changed into gray sweatpants—*yes, I wore them on purpose*—I banished myself to my office.

But now I'm walking back upstairs, ready to sleep in the same bed as Luisa.

My Angel.

My wife.

The thrill that hits me every time I remind myself that we're now married hasn't dissipated. If anything, it cements the feeling that Luisa is exactly where she's supposed to be.

By my side and in my bed.

I know she has a no-sex rule, and I will respect her wishes.

But I'm no fool. I know the need runs both ways. I may have promised not to lay a finger on her, but that doesn't mean I won't make her want me to.

So sue me for throwing on a pair of gray sweatpants and hoping that all those magazine articles that Luisa graces the covers of were right about the mighty powers of this comfortable garment.

Anticipation builds in my chest as I reach our room. I can see that Luisa is already in bed, between tousled sheets.

I catch the moment she spots me, and I swear she glares at my outfit of choice.

Good. I can work with that.

I'm itching to get closer to her when movement in the center of my bed catches me off guard.

Luisa smirks triumphantly, and I worry what the hell my wife has gotten up to. "No need for a pillow barrier. Especially since we have this—" She flips down the covers to reveal Delilah's goofy smile. "She can be our mediator, and I'm sure she'll keep you at bay if you get any naughty ideas." She smiles fully now, and all thoughts of lust are replaced by a warm feeling in my chest.

This woman... she's more.

She's everything.

And that smile. God, it makes me feel like a better man. Makes me want to act like one too.

I decide to play into her silly game. "Ah, I see how this is going to go. My girls have teamed up to plot against me, is that right?" I scratch under Delilah's jaw, and she leans into my hand.

Luisa bites her lip pensively, and I force myself to keep things PG for tonight. Especially since it's late and in the aftermath of recent events, my body is begging for sleep.

Luisa's phone lights up with a reminder that says "BC." She catches me staring and answers the question floating in my mind. "It's my birth control reminder. But I took it before I got into bed."

"Interesting." I rub alongside my jaw in an attempt to hide my grin.

Luisa rolls her eyes, clearly not impressed with my knee-jerk reaction. "Don't get any ideas, Loverboy. I've been on birth control since I was in high school to help regulate my periods because I have PCOS. And I don't know why I'm even telling you this. Good night." She turns off her bedside lamp, and I immediately turn it back on. I swear I hear her mutter something about this being the worst sleepover ever.

"Is PCOS the reason you have tough periods? Is there a medication you can take for that?"

"Ugh, stupid me for answering those emails while enjoying a little pinot noir." She pulls the covers over her face, and, of course, I pull them back down.

"C'mon, tell me. Is there something I can do to help?"

"You really want to know? You don't think it's gross to talk about these... lady things? Most guys I've dated have preferred to steer clear of the topic of my period altogether."

"It'd suit you well to never mention any of your exes while you lie in our bed with my ring on your finger." Her eyes widen, and if I'm not mistaken, flash with heat at the sudden edge in my tone. "And please don't insult me by comparing a man to boys who are afraid of knowing and worshipping a woman's body. So yes, I really want to know. And heads-up: tomorrow I'll probably research the topic on my own and call up a few specialists to see what else we can do to help you feel better."

She shakes her head. "No, you really don't need to do all of that. My new doctor is great, and while PCOS does make my periods irregular, this current birth control I'm on has me on somewhat of a set schedule, even though it's still not perfect. I do have a bit of an iron deficiency that I need to keep an eye on, but I take iron pills for that. And if I eat a low glycemic index diet, the worst of the symptoms are manageable. That doesn't mean I don't indulge in sweets and comfort food when I'm feeling crummy; it's just something I need to be mindful of."

She continues. "I actually like working out, and weightlifting is great for PCOS. Honestly, it's not that bad, I swear. It could be worse. I'm lucky that the pain is never excruciating. That can happen sometimes; I know it does with some of my cousins who have PCOS and endometriosis. It's not a walk in the park, but I make sure to stay on top of it so it doesn't interrupt my work or daily life." She shrugs one shoulder.

I nod, taking it all in. I'm still calling the specialist first thing in the morning. And researching the type of meals I should be cooking for her. Or having sent to her office since I know she has a habit of skipping lunch when she's in back-to-back meetings.

"Okay, I've given you more than enough information on my uterus, so can I go to sleep now? Jeez, marrying you is exhausting." She smiles slightly as she drops her arms on the bedding, causing Delilah to bark and wiggle her tail with a rhythmic thump.

I'm actually surprised that Luisa shared as much as she did without much pushback, so I concede and make my way over to my side of the bed.

The trek over makes me feel like I'll actually be sleeping a bit farther than I hoped from my Angel, but there is no point pouting about it now.

I slide into the bed, pulling the covers over myself, right as Delilah becomes Luisa's little spoon. Her paws rest on the left side of my body.

"Looking comfy over there, Stonehaven." I can hear the smile in Luisa's tone as I close my eyes.

"Sweet dreams, Mrs. Stonehaven." I place my hands over my stomach, but don't hide my grin.

I hear a soft intake of breath and smile wider.

Mrs. Stonehaven. I like the sound of that. I'll have to make sure my attorney files the appropriate paperwork to have her name changed. But knowing Luisa, she'd sooner call herself the devil's mistress than Mrs. Stonehaven. Whitewashing herself while losing the name she helped build for herself? There's no way.

And to be honest, aside from the pride I have over what I've created with Stonehaven Media, I'm not too fond of the name that connects me with my father's side of the family.

Hell, by the way she has me whipped, I might be calling myself Mr. Álvarez by the end of the week.

The pleasant thought helps lull me into a peaceful slumber.

For only a second, since Delilah decides that now is the time to get the zoomies and keeps scratching me with her sharp nails.

"Delilah, no. Stop it. Right now—"

With a hard double kick, I'm sent rolling off the bed and onto the carpeted bedroom floor.

I can hear Luisa's gasp a second before her head pops over my side of the bed and she spots me lying helplessly on the ground. Delilah's head pops up next to hers, looking a little too innocent for my liking.

"You okay?" she asks, giggling.

"Peachy."

"Aw. Well, look on the bright side, hubby. You got that romp in the sheets you were jonesing for after all."

My laughter echoes around the bedroom and is quickly joined by Luisa's cackles and Delilah's barks.

And I realize in this moment that this house now feels like a home.

CHAPTER THIRTY

LUISA

AFTER DELILAH PUT HER fighting paws away, we all fell into a deep slumber.

I was certain I'd spend the night tossing and turning, but the pure exhaustion of the day, combined with Delilah's sweet snores, was enough to put me in an instant coma.

I woke up to sweet doggy kisses and a hot, shirtless husband brushing his teeth on the other side of the open bathroom door, watching us.

That's a view I could definitely get used to.

By the time I made it down to the kitchen in search of some food, I was almost in need of using one of my special toys. But the thought of Nick handling and washing them almost sent me into a spiral I need coffee for.

The kitchen is open and airy, with a large curved window looking out over the patio. And even though this place is huge, even for Manhattan standards, the kitchen still manages to feel homey. Touches of wood everywhere, with pockets of yellow and green mixed into the backsplash and tea towels, coexist peacefully among the double ovens, six burner stove, and touch screen gadgets.

I trail my fingers over the smooth countertops in search of my caffeine fix, Delilah's prancing steps right at my side.

The coffee machine is built into the wall. Because of course it is.

I'm about to start tinkering with it when a clear coffee mug is placed under the espresso machine in front of me.

I feel the heat from Nick's bare chest at my back and force myself to stand straight. He presses a few buttons, and the machine comes to life. Loudly.

I turn in place. "I had it all figured out," I fib.

His mouth twitches. "Of course you did." His arms move around me, setting another mug in place and pressing more buttons. I'm sure this task would be much easier if he just asked me to move out of the way.

I'm just about to duck under his arms when he speaks again. "Okay, first things first: how do you take your coffee?"

"I'm a café con leche kinda girl. One sugar packet if I have time to sit down and savor it. No sugar if I need to wake up and get down to business."

He places a hand on my hip and moves us over a step. I turn to see what he's doing—and to escape his intoxicating natural scent.

There are two chic coffee mugs in front of me, both half filled with espresso.

I didn't notice that he'd already steamed milk, and it's in a stainless-steel milk frothing pitcher.

He picks it up and says, "Tell me when." He starts to pour the milk into a mug, and when it turns the perfect shade of pale brown, I tell him to stop.

He studies it dutifully, then nods. "I don't have sugar packets, but I can buy some for the house. If I don't have any packets, how many small spoonfuls would be enough?" He scoops sugar into a dainty spoon and holds it over my coffee, waiting for my response.

"I'm sure one would be fine." My voice has suddenly turned shy at all the attention placed on my coffee preferences. Somehow this is starting to feel more intimate than sharing a bed.

I can feel Nick studying my face from above me. "All right, then. Two it is."

I don't have time to hold in the quick laugh that escapes from my chest. I don't dare look up at him, but I can sense that he's smiling by the satisfied hum as he stirs the sugar in my cup.

"All right. Time to put my skills to the test. Have a sip, and please, be brutally honest."

I grab hold of the warm mug and take a small sip, followed by a much larger one, and moan. "Good God, that is some good coffee. Damn you rich people for having access to the good stuff."

His chest rumbles with restrained laughter behind me. "You better watch your mouth, talking around rich people." His voice drops to a stage whisper. "You're one of us now."

My stomach drops at the thought.

To the outside world, I became a billionaire through marriage. I made a verbal agreement with Nick that I wouldn't touch his money when we went our separate ways, but it seems like I'll be enjoying a bit of the high life until the jig is up.

"All right, it's your turn. Put your coffee down before you burn your tongue, you little gremlin." He attempts to pry the delicious goodness from my hands, and I have a deep desire to hiss at him.

I eventually concede. "My turn for what?"

He nods at the other espresso cup. "To learn how your husband takes his coffee. This is something we should know about each other."

Oh. Is that what this is? Marriage 101 homework? I guess that makes sense, since we need to convince the world that we're a real couple. I'm sure there will be a lot more information for us to learn about one another.

Yet why do I feel a sudden pit of disappointment?

I blow out a quick breath and get my head on straight. I know Nick is watching me intently—it seems like he always is lately—but I don't pay him any mind and continue with this little exercise. I make a show of cracking my knuckles and bouncing my shoulders. In a teasing tone, I ask, "All right, Lucifer, how do you take your coffee? I would assume black, like the souls of those you've condemn—"

"Luisa," Nick chides from behind me.

"What?" I look up to meet his serious gaze.

"I'm going to let this slide, just this once, because I know you haven't had breakfast or finished your coffee. But this." He taps my forehead twice. "Letting your thoughts run wild without clueing me in to what's got you changing up on me at the flip of a switch? It's not going to work. We need to be open and honest with each other at all times if we want to survive the next year."

I inwardly groan. Why must this man be so perceptive?

I bite my lip, feeling embarrassed by what I'm about to say. But I do so anyway, because he's right. "It's no big deal. It's just... I don't know. I thought you were asking how I liked my coffee because you were being, I dunno, you? I didn't realize we were doing marriage bootcamp. Maybe I need a heads-up when we're doing this kind of husband and wife study session."

Nick's intense gaze doesn't leave mine, even seconds after I've stopped speaking. I'm about to start rambling, because I'd rather that than the awkward silence I've created, when he opens his mouth. "You prefer plátano maduros over tostones because you can reheat the leftovers the next day and throw them into your scrambled eggs, but you'd never claim that in front of your family because tostones are the clear winner among them."

My mouth drops. How did he—

The emails.

Shit. We've never discussed in person the things we've written to one another. Mostly because they were nonsensical chatter. But as I look into Nick's determined eyes, I'm starting to wonder if it was more than that.

"You like wearing heels every day because your cousins were allowed to wear them at fifteen, but your parents only let you start wearing them right before your eighteenth birthday, and you made it your personal mission to make up for all that lost time. On busy days at work, you forget to eat lunch, so on your way home, you order takeout from your favorite Thai restaurant and make a little game of beating the delivery guy to your apartment. There have been a few times he's beat you there, and he's now in on the little game.

"You like the color pink and wear it often because it reminds the old geezers at work that their boss does, indeed, have a vagina—these are your words—not mine. And you have a deep love for all reality shows produced by Bravo. The Housewives from Potomac, Salt Lake City, and Miami are having top-tier seasons, according to your expertise."

"Put it on my gravestone, I guess," I mumble as I look down at my hands.

His fingers tip my chin up, and I have no choice but to make eye contact again.

"If I need to know something about you that I don't already know, for the purpose of our arrangement, I will ask you that directly."

I nod, words failing me.

"But if you thought that making your morning coffee was some kind of exercise, something I wouldn't naturally want to know, then…" He trails off.

"Then what?"

He leans closer, my heart picking up at lightning speed, "Then clearly, wife of mine, you haven't been paying attention."

My mind whirls, and I'm trying to figure out what he means when the doorbell rings.

"Right on time," he says more to himself than me as he makes his way to the front door.

I take a moment to collect myself, then turn back to the untouched coffee belonging to Nick.

I need something to do with my hands, so I pick up the steamed milk and add a dash. I forgo the sugar—because who are we kidding? That man probably hasn't had anything sweet in a decade—and start to stir mindlessly.

By the time Nick walks back into the kitchen, I'm sure I've stirred all the heat out of his coffee.

"Special delivery," he says with a pleased look on his face while lifting a small package.

I don't have time to come up with a snarky remark or a penis joke before he's standing in front of me with a black velvet ring box in his hand.

"Wh-what is this?" I point to the box as if there is a tiny cobra waiting inside, ready to strike at me. "I already have a wedding band," I say, almost babbling.

Nick's assured smile only kicks up a notch at my clear confusion.

"Okay, to be clear, this part is for optics." He nods slightly, giving me a moment to recognize that we are now speaking about our arrangement. "I would have gotten you this at the same time as your wedding band, but this specific ring wasn't ready in time."

I'm about to protest because, truly, my wedding band is more than enough.

And when I'm alone, all I do is stare at how pretty it is and think of how I wish it were my real wedding band for life.

But then he opens the box.

My gasp is so loud, Delilah nudges my leg with her nose as I lean onto the kitchen counter for support.

"No. Nick! What? How?" My eyes must be popping out of my head as Nick grins.

"I'm hoping your Pinterest board from three years ago still holds true and that this is the ring you had pinned as your 'dream ring.' Of course, the one you had was a respectable three carats, but there is nothing respectable about the man you married, so I had to go ahead and settle for seven," he announces proudly.

The sparkling cushion-cut ring stares back at me.

"Please, Angel, close your mouth before my mind thinks up ways for you to thank me."

I snap my mouth shut and find the strength to slap his hard chest. He catches my hand and keeps it in place, then slowly slips the ring on my finger until it reaches my wedding band.

"Never seen anything more perfect," Nick says, all traces of his teasing tone gone as his thumb sweeps across my knuckles.

I look up to see him staring at me instead of the ring, and my heart kicks up for the second time this morning.

"Luisa, I know this is anything but conventional. Our arrangement, the way we met, our working relationship. Everything about us seems to be at odds with what the world deems as normal. But frankly, I wouldn't change a single thing if it meant having you standing in our home, sharing morning coffee, with my ring on your finger."

"Nick," my voice begs. For what, I'm not sure.

He smiles almost sadly. "Oh, none of that. I'm a big boy." He wags his eyebrows, and I muster a giggle. "You're worthy of the real thing. A real marriage, a real proposal. And I feel like I've robbed you of that. So... please don't make a fuss about accepting this engagement ring. It holds all the guilt I feel for not being the man you deserve. For being the lucky bastard who gets to call you mine for what I know will be the best year of my life."

I don't think twice. I can't form any coherent thoughts around this man anyway. I throw my arms around his neck and pull him into a hug. His arms wrap around me instantly and pull me even closer.

"Buy a woman a diamond, and she breaks her own no-touching rule," he jokes as he speaks into my hair.

"Shut up. Hugs are on the approved touching list as of right now."

"Unlimited hugs?"

"Stop negotiating, Stonehaven. Keep hugging me back before you do something that makes me call you an asshole in my head."

"There's still room in that pretty little head of yours to curse me? I figured your endless berating would get it all out."

"What I've given you can hardly be called berating, and if you think that was bad, buckle up, buddy."

"Noted."

"Why is your chest so warm when your nipples are so hard?"

"And the moment is now over. Thanks for that, Angel." A laughing Nick pulls away.

I smile as I shrug. "Fine by me. Besides, it's time you test the coffee I made for you." He quirks a brow. "Okay, the coffee you made but I helped perfect," I defend.

He rubs his hands together. "Tell me, wife, what concoction have you come up with?"

"I still think you drink your coffee black since you only drink from the best coffee beans in the world. But then I thought maybe you added a bit of milk so that it wouldn't be too strong?" My voice lifts at the end of the statement, making it sound more like a question. I'm suddenly and ridiculously anxious over a silly cup of coffee.

Nick's smile doesn't waver as he picks up the mug and takes a generous sip. "Well done. You nailed it, Angel."

I unexpectedly preen at his praise and take great pleasure in watching him enjoy his coffee.

We spend the rest of the morning cooking breakfast, making each other second cups of coffee, and planning our next public outing while Delilah lounges by our feet.

I take my first real breath in days when I realize that this might work out after all.

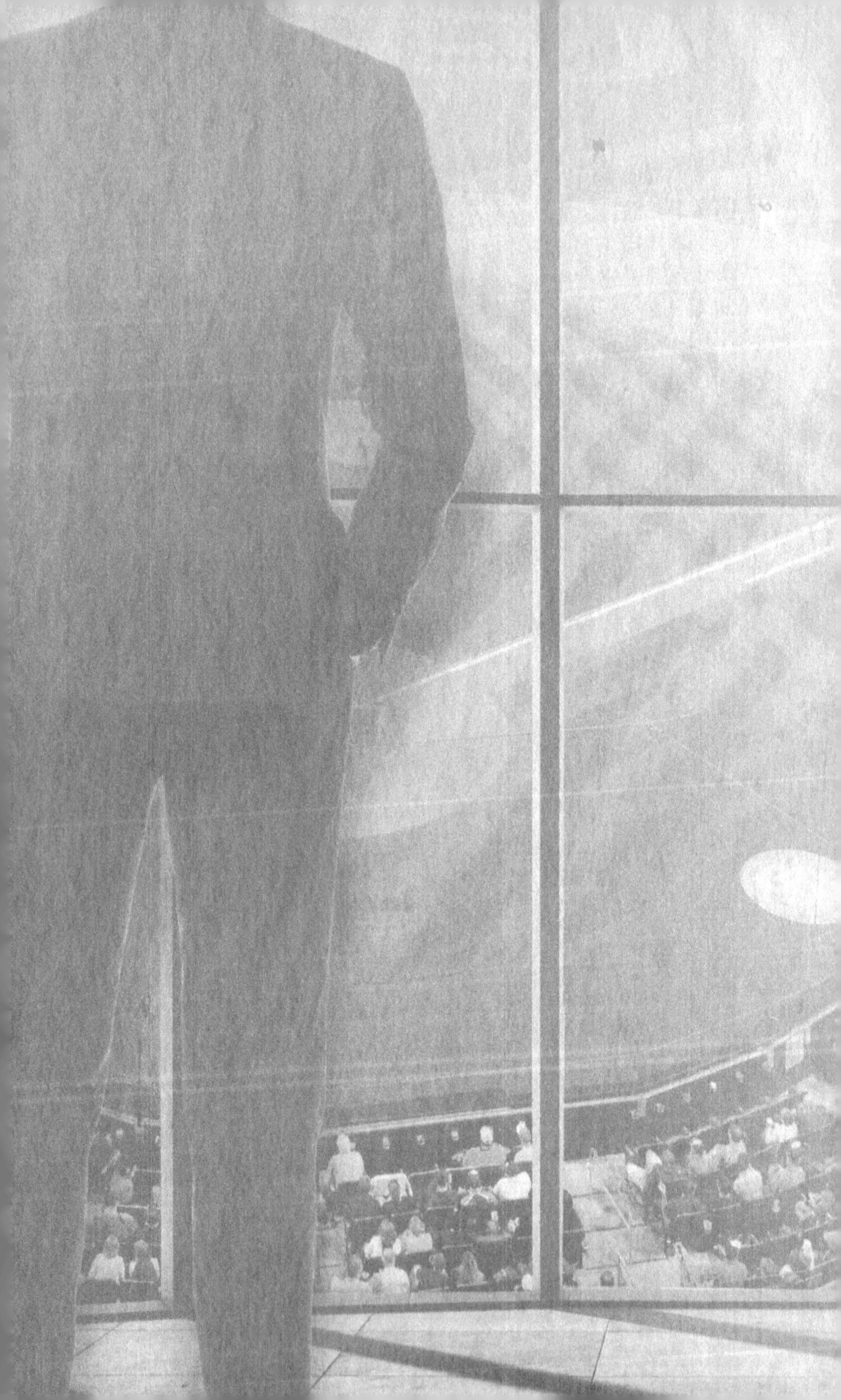

NICK

I'm lactose intolerant.

As Luisa predicted, I usually take my coffee black.

But I'll deal with the repercussions, because from now on, I'll take my coffee with a dash of milk.

Just how my wife makes it.

LUISA

Two weeks have passed, and we have slipped into our new normal.

Nick wakes up way before I do to touch base with his team in London while I try to soak up every second I can in our insanely comfortable bed.

Delilah has remained a permanent fixture between us as we sleep, although I have nudged her lower toward our feet throughout the night because the girl does love to make a tangled mess of the sheets.

I've fended off questions from my staff with the well-practiced answers Nick and I have come up with.

Even used the same lines to placate our friends. When they pried for more, Nick simply added that I couldn't live another day not married to the man who gave me the best sex of my life, which had Daisy fake dry-heaving and the rest of the gang backing off. Except Isabella. I swear she could see right through it all, but she went along with it.

But we've held off the press long enough, and tonight we are on our way to our first public outing as husband and wife.

We knew we'd be under a microscope tonight, so Nick suggested we make our grand reveal at a charity for the local children's hospital, hoping that the extra eyeballs on us would bring extra attention to the cause.

I'm fidgeting in my seat as our driver pulls up in front of the hotel hosting the event.

Nick slips his warm, comforting hand in mine and squeezes lightly. "You're going to do great. We'll be there two hours, tops. Then I'll have you back home in time to watch your TV shows."

I smile at the memory of Nick walking behind the couch as I watched an episode of *Southern Charm*. After he quit acting like he wasn't watching intently as the cast fought while watching a polo race, Nick asked if I'd ever been to Charleston and if I'd like to visit sometime soon. "Don't you mean *our* shows, dear?"

He rolls his eyes but doesn't hide the faint smile playing on his lips.

"You're a gateway drug, Angel. Next, I'll be buying the network's stock."

I'm too busy laughing to realize we've stopped and that there are already cameras aimed at the tinted windows of our vehicle. The nerves come back in full force, but they are no match for my new husband.

"Stay here. I'll exit first, wave to the cameras, and try to get the initial barrage of flashes out of the way. Place your clutch by the opening of the slit in your dress to make sure no one sees anything they're not supposed to as you step out." His words turn more growly as he speaks. "Have I mentioned how fucking beautiful you look tonight?"

I look down at my red satin dress and smile. "You have. You also said I looked sexy and downright sinful, and you swore you'll be responsible for the deaths of the men who dare look my way tonight. Did I miss anything?" I smirk.

"Yeah, the part where I said I wasn't joking," he grumbles as he steps out of the car to the sound of my laughter.

He's at my door in a flash, opening it an inch, mouthing, "You ready?"

When I nod, my focus is solely on him and not the media zoo surrounding us.

He opens my door wide but steps in before a camera can catch a glimpse, giving me a second to adjust myself in my strapless dress, then take his offered hand and step out of the vehicle. When I come up to my full height, the top of my head hitting below Nick's chin, I hear the crowd go wild.

Nick keeps a firm hold of my hand as we make our way to the red carpet.

People shout our names as we take our spot, lean into one another, and finally pose for the cameras.

The flashes are disorienting, and if it weren't for the string of inappropriate jokes Nick whispers in my ear, I don't think I could keep the smile on my face.

"Luisa Stonehaven, over here to your right!" a photographer shouts.

"Hmm, you hear that, Luisa Stonehaven?" Nick says with more satisfaction than any man in a fake marriage should possess.

I'd be lying if I said I didn't like the way that sounded.

And although I know this marriage isn't real, it is for all the women who have followed my journey and look up to me. It might seem silly to think, much less shout, but I want my name to really fit me. To fit the woman I've created and hope to continue to become. So I let the world know. "Actually, it's Luisa Álvarez-Stonehaven." Nick looks down with an amused look on his face, and I shrug. "I'm hyphenating."

He nearly blinds me with his smile before he turns and faces the flashing lights. "You heard the lady. She's an Álvarez-Stonehaven, so address her as such." He teases the crowd before he whispers in my ear. "It suits you quite nicely, if I do say so myself."

I pinch him discreetly under his suit jacket, and he does the same to my hip.

My smile is no longer forced.

"Now?" he questions quietly.

My stomach clenches. We planned this. A kiss on the red carpet. The official seal of our deal for the masses.

I was fine with it in theory, but now, having him so close to my lips, I fear this kiss won't feel very fake for me.

"Mm-hmm," I hum, keeping my smile in place for the cameras.

Nick's eyes sweep my face. "You sure? We don't have to if you're—"

My hand slides up his chest, trailing up until my fingers reach his neck. "Oh, c'mon. Don't tell me the devil is afraid of a little—"

His lips meet mine in a bruising kiss. The noise around us reaches a new high, but I can't make out a single sound over the pounding in my chest and the moan on his lips.

I don't know where I find the mental capacity to pull back and playfully tap him on the chest for getting carried away in public. He catches on quickly and fakes wiping the edges of his mouth like the cat that got the cream.

"Good save, wife. We might have landed on the front pages tomorrow for a completely different reason if you hadn't kept me on a tight leash," he says, low enough for only me to hear.

I ignore him and wave at the cameras one more time before I give Nick's hand three quick squeezes. He recognizes our signal immediately and offers one last smile before we walk off the carpet and into a much quieter reception area.

I release a deep breath. "Step one, complete. Now all that's left to do is schmooze and avoid truffles at all costs." I accept a glass of champagne from a passing waiter and turn back to Nick.

The heat in his eyes is burning up every inch of my skin as he slowly takes his fill.

"Lucifer," I warn lightly.

"No, you see, I think you've got this all wrong. Because you, in that dress, with that... that fucking slit that goes so high and would make it so easy to slip my hand in and—" He stops abruptly and releases a frustrated groan. "God dammit, woman. Why is every inch of your body meant to test and tease me?"

I take a small sip of the delicious bubbly as I move in closer to him.

When I rest my free hand on his chest, he grits his teeth. "Rules. Give them to me now. What am I allowed to do tonight? Can I kiss you?"

"Yes, when we—"

"Thank fuck." His hands smoothly slide along my hips until he's pinned my body against his and his mouth is firmly on mine. He takes full advantage of my surprised gasp and slips his tongue past my lips, demanding more.

I moan softly and join his fight for dominance.

Fuck, my husband can kiss.

His hand lowers to my ass and he gives it a hard squeeze, and I find myself lifting my hips in response, looking for friction to help with the sudden ache between my legs.

Somewhere in the back of my muddled brain, I remember that we're in public, and the headline printed about us tomorrow morning shouldn't include the term dry-humping.

I move to pull back, but a hand lands at the nape of my neck, keeping me in place. I smile against his lips.

"And where do you think you're going?"

His mouth has turned feral, and his hard length pressed against my core informs me that I'm going to have to be the one who saves us from tearing our clothes off.

I swipe my tongue along his full bottom lip once before I lean in and bite it. Hard.

"Ouch, bloody hell. What was that for?" His finger wipes along his lip and comes back with a tiny speck of blood. It was barely a scratch.

I shrug as I wipe around the edges of my lipstick. "Eat the rich, they say." His jaw drops and he releases a dry laugh. "And what I was going to say before you pounced on me is that, yes, we can kiss when we're in front of other people. But it should be more appropriate, like a simple peck. Not something they'd have to pay a monthly subscription fee to see." My head nods at the clear hard-on in his dress pants, and he curses.

I hand him my glass of champagne. "Here, cool off. And maybe you should go to the bathroom before someone—"

"Yeah." He shakes his head, as if his good sense has arrived. "Meet me by our table. Let me... wait this out for a bit."

"Sounds like a plan, Mr. Stonehaven."

"Yeah, yeah. Tease all you want." He goes to walk past me but stops when we're shoulder to shoulder. "But you try and bite me like that again, and you better watch that ass, *Mrs. Álvarez-Stonehaven*. Because I'm coming for you, rules be damned."

I feel like my cheeks are brighter than my dress as I move among the elegantly clad crowd.

I spot air kisses and exaggerated laughter as I focus on finding my table.

I'm glad that no one tries to stop me on my quest, given I've caught more than a few waves and nods in my direction. It seems like some may be biding their time until I have my groom on my arm in order to approach and congratulate us.

But that's fine, because this part of the night doesn't stress me out as much.

I've gone to more than my fair share of events since I became the GM of the most popular team in the country. Most of them weren't connected to the sports world, so I don't feel intimidated by the glamour and hoopla of it all.

If anything, it feels like being a spectator stepping onto the set of *Gossip Girl*. None of this is real, but it's fun to watch.

I think I've spotted our table when a man steps into my line of vision. I want to scowl because I really want to sit and give my wobbling knees a break after that scorching kiss, but I came here to play nice, so I plaster on a pleasant smile as the older gentleman reaches for my hand.

Suddenly, I realize there is something familiar about him. Like my brain is yelling, trying to tell me who he is before I have to ask.

Is he a part of the board? A member of the Monarchs organization?

No, that's not ringing any bells.

I don't want to seem rude, so I place my hand in his when I say, "Luisa Álvarez... Stonehaven." I almost trip up. "Nice to meet you."

I'm surprised when he takes my hand and brings it up to his lips. "The pleasure is all mine." He places a smarmy kiss on my hand, and I force myself to keep the smile on my face, promising myself I'll wash my hands as soon as this interaction is over.

The atmosphere changes suddenly.

Voices around us seem to come to a halt.

I can feel him before he utters a single word. But I wasn't prepared for the pure venom that comes out of Nick's mouth. "Get your fucking hands off my wife."

The man's eyes gleam with a level of evil I thought was only reserved for horror movies. I'm no longer concerned about prying eyes and pull my hand back as Nick's arm wraps around my waist and he tugs me back to stand slightly behind him.

I can see Nick's chest heaving beneath his expensive suit, and I place a tentative hand on his back, not understanding what's caused his visceral reaction.

I don't have to wonder for long, since the man before me answers that question with one simple sentence.

"Aw, c'mon, son. I was just saying hello to my new daughter-in-law."

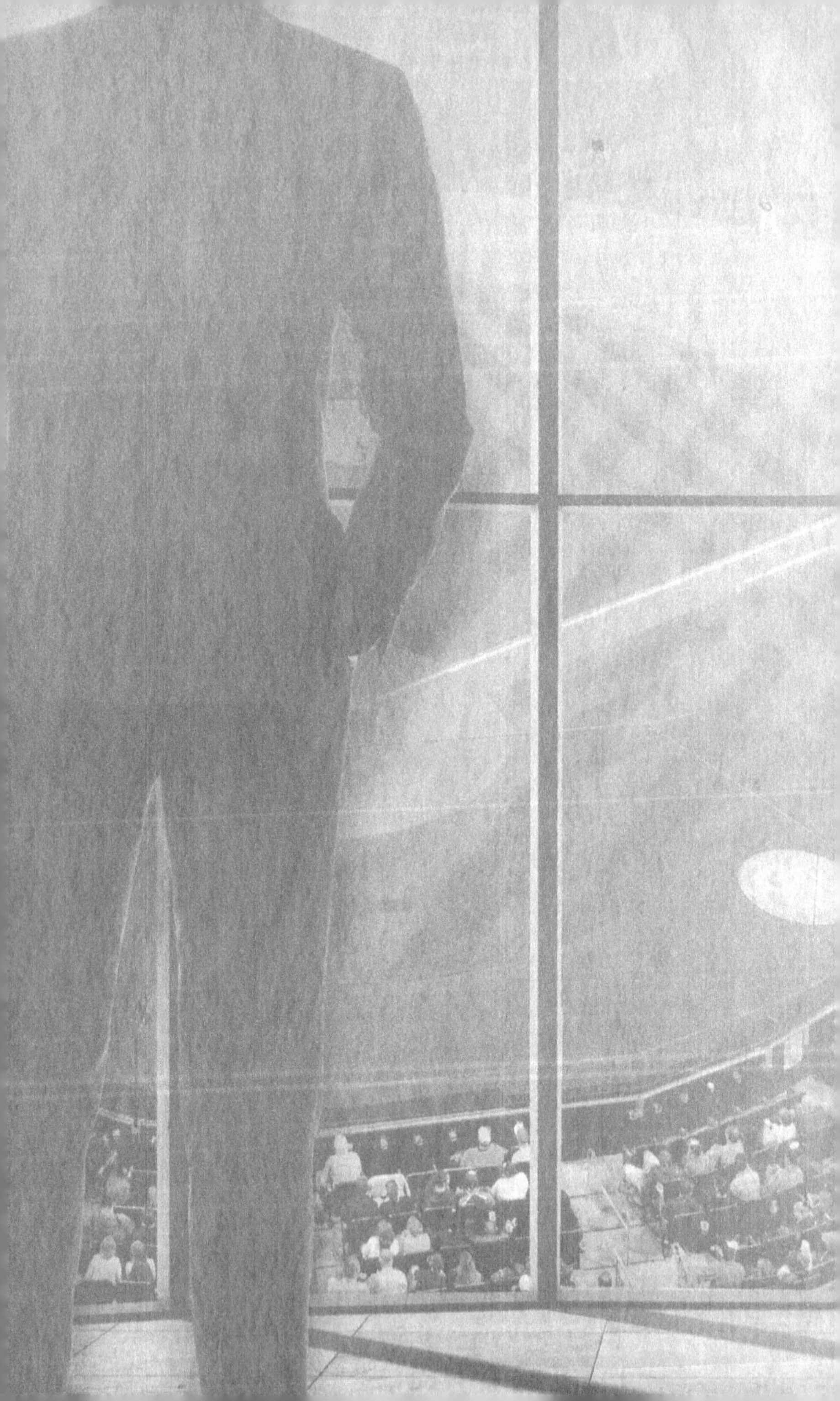

Chapter Thirty-Three

NICK

I'm going to break his hand.

No. I'm going to break his hand *and* every finger that dared touch my beautiful wife.

I make no attempt to hide my ire.

"Oh, calm down. I was merely trying to welcome her into the family. She does carry our family name now, does she not?" He looks around me to Luisa. "My name is George Stonehaven, in case my boy has failed to fill you in."

I move to block his view of her. "You do not speak to her, am I clear? Do not even look in her direction if you want to leave tonight on your own two feet."

I feel her soft touch, and it helps ground me. My Angel rubs calming circles on my back, and it recedes a bit of the red covering my vision.

My father chides, "Oh, Nicholas, always one for the theatrics. Has any of the boarding school education I paid for not taught you how to act while out in society?"

I'm about to rip his head off with my bare hands when Luisa slips in front of me and places her hands on my cheeks, forcing me to look down at her.

My nostrils flare as I struggle to regulate my breathing, but I concede to my wife.

"That's it, big guy. Focus on me, yeah?"

My shoulders drop marginally as her fingers scratch along my beard. My thoughts duel between wanting to fight and fuck.

"You trust me?" she whispers.

I don't know what she has planned, but I nod.

Because I do trust her.

"This might be hard, but you're going to let me handle this. Okay, husband?"

My body comes alive every time she teases me with my new title, but the way she says it now has me wanting to wrap her in my arms and leave this party in the dust.

"I don't want you talking to him," I argue.

"Well, tough shit. Because I got all dressed up tonight, and I'll be damned if I have to go home before I even get the chance to send a picture of my dress to the girls' group chat."

I feel my lip wanting to lift, but I can't manage it.

She raises up on her tiptoes and whispers in my ear. "My panties are already ruined, and it's all your fault. Don't let the rest of the outfit go to waste, Nick."

I'm almost winded by her statement. Too stunned in the moment to act before she spins around and faces my father.

Fuck, my wife fights dirty.

"Okay, pal. This is how it's going to go." Her business persona has been activated.

"Pal? Who do you think you're—"

"Don't care," Luisa talks over him. "What I do care about is you keeping your distance from us. If Nick wants a relationship with you, he'll seek it out himself. No need to ambush him at a charity function. Did they not teach that at *your* expensive boarding school?"

Luisa steps closer to him, and my hand clenches with the need to pull her back from that vermin.

"I don't know what my son has told you, but he has a debt that has yet to be settled. As soon as my attorneys figure out the holdup on my father's will, he will be banging at my office door, begging for a meeting."

"Nicholas Stonehaven begs for no one." Her words crack through the room like a whip, and my father's face drops into a scowl.

"You've been married for all of fifteen minutes, and you think you know him? You expect me to believe that you married him for love and not his money?"

Luisa must have eyes in the back of her head because she raises her hand, stopping me from plowing into the poor excuse for a man.

Instead, she leans forward and plucks the pocket square out of my father's suit jacket. I don't miss his slight flinch as she does.

"Ah, yes. Apparently my husband is *loaded*." She uses the small piece of fabric to wipe at her engagement ring, shining it until it sparkles under the lights. "And if you haven't noticed, he decided to marry a Dominican woman who didn't go to a fancy boarding school in Connecticut. But I promise you, Harlem public schools taught me how to act right. And, more importantly, how to handle bullies who are all bark and no bite. So let this be a lesson to you." She balls up the pocket square and shoves it back into its small opening. "Fuck with me and mine, and you'll find your balls in the same pocket as your tacky Gucci square." She taps over the spot where she placed the wrinkled fabric and turns toward me. "Walk me to the bathroom, please? I need to wash my hands."

Pride like I've never felt before fills my chest as my wife walks past me, hips swaying. "You coming or what, Stonehaven?"

I don't even have to think twice.

"Anywhere with you."

CHAPTER THIRTY-FOUR

LUISA

MIAMI WINS THE WORLD Series.

The office is getting settled into the offseason. Many people think that this period would count as my downtime. And those people would be dead wrong.

The offseason is when my team and I need to hustle and regroup so we can come back stronger and ready for spring training.

The trading deadline for free agency is January fifteenth, which means my ass will be working through the holidays. Something I don't mind doing, since I need the distraction from my home life.

The one where I go toe to toe with Nick's dad and not so subtly threaten to cut off his cojones. I'm surprised I haven't been hit with a lawsuit. Though I'm sure Nick and his team of attorneys would have no problem tackling anything his father throws our way.

After our little showdown last week, Nick clearly needed some alone time to cool down.

Even though I have taken up the role of that man's personal peace disturber, I respected his space and made sure to keep my teasing to a minimum.

I've even been wearing more conservative pajamas to bed, hoping not to stoke the fires burning inside us.

Because the kiss on the night of the charity event will be seared into my brain for the rest of time. I've had to resort to sneaking into random guest bedrooms with one of my special toys to get myself off before bed since I don't trust myself to lie next to that man with all the tension that builds in my body after spending the whole day with him.

But as the days go on, even my strongest contender isn't doing enough for me. I blame the stupid hunk of a man I'm currently not having sex with for that.

Because I know how it feels to be taken by him in every position possible, and it's only with the thoughts of our first night together that I can reach my release.

Maybe one more time wouldn't be so bad.

The thought has crossed my mind more than once. Okay, more like a million times, if I'm honest. And maybe I would have succumbed to the feeling a few weeks ago.

But after facing off with his father, I find myself questioning more than my increased sexual desires.

Because the moment I saw the way George Stonehaven looked at Nick, I felt an indescribable surge of protectiveness within me. The feral need to defend a man who clearly needs defending from no one.

What's more confusing is that I felt like it was my rightful place to do so. As if I were a real wife, protecting her husband.

But there was nothing fake about the way I wanted to inflict real violence on that man or how quickly I wanted to get Nick's mind off his sorry excuse of a dad and focused back on me.

When I pulled him onto that dance floor, I could still feel his chest heaving with unstrained fury, his eyes unseeing.

But when my hands drifted up and tickled the tiny hairs on the nape of his neck, I felt his shoulders drop. When I placed his hands low on my hips, his frown disappeared. And when I leaned up on my toes and sealed my lips to his in front of event photographers, I felt him come back to life.

And now I'm drowning myself in an unhealthy amount of work and depleting my vibrators of battery to keep myself from doing something I might not be able to come back from.

Luckily, the best distraction has come in the form of the World Baseball Classic games, now to be hosted at Monarchs Stadium.

The series was scheduled to be played in Puerto Rico, but with the current hurricane season devastation, the organization thought it best to streamline aid and resources to the island and have the game played elsewhere.

And since we recently had a spectacular turnout during the charity game we hosted for the same cause, it was a no-brainer to offer to host.

And this truly couldn't come at a better time, because not only do I need time away from my infuriatingly hot fake husband, but I also get the opportunity to meet the players that are currently on my radar for the next season and see up close how well they are playing.

The teams are split into players who are born in or descendants of the Dominican Republic, Puerto Rico, Cuba, Mexico, and Japan.

I have my eye on at least one player from each team and am looking forward to seeing how our own Monarch players perform now that the season is over.

I'm sure Mateo Martinez will be putting on quite the family-friendly show, given that the last time he was on the field, he was pummeling Isabella's douchey ex into the ground.

Not our proudest moment as a team, but what can I say? We're a protective bunch.

As if my thoughts have summoned him, number thirty-five knocks on my open door, wearing a wide smile. "Hey, you got a minute?"

I wave for him to enter, and he closes the door behind him. "And to what do I owe the pleasure, Martinez? Have my friend and your daughter finally kicked you out of the house so they can make their sprinkle cakes in peace? Or is it pancakes for dinner night?"

His eyes soften at the mention of Isabella and his daughter Anna. "Actually, that's kinda why I'm here." He leans forward and rubs his hands together. "I'm proposing to Isa, and I need your help."

I shoot out of my seat and let out a happy shriek. "Yes! I'm so excited. Anything you need. Do you have a plan? Want me to take her out to get a manicure? What about the ring? Do you need—"

"Okay, boss. Slow down." He chuckles as he stands.

I round my desk and give him a big hug. I don't make it a habit of being this close to my players, but I've gotten to know Mateo better since he started dating Isabella, and he now feels more like family.

"I need you to rally the troops and have them waiting at my place. *If* she says yes, I want to have a small party with our friends and family." He smiles to himself. "I know she would spend the rest of the night FaceTiming you guys anyway, so I figured she'd like for all of us to celebrate together."

I nod repeatedly, laughing hysterically when I realize a tear is running down my cheek. "Oh God. Now I'm crying at work. I should fine you for this, Martinez." Our combined laughter only causes more tears to form, and before I know it, I'm a weepy mess.

A soft knock sounds on my door before Nick strides in with a reusable bag in hand. Most likely another home-cooked meal for me, since he's been supplying me with lunch since we got married. I know he passes it off as if it's nothing, leftovers of his meals, but I'm no dummy. Because every meal he's delivered consists of protein, healthy fats, and complex carbs. A PCOS friendly diet.

He usually strolls in and tries to keep the focus off the nice gesture, but one look at my tear-stricken face, and his relaxed stance turns lethal.

"What happened?" He drops the bag and is already pulling me away from Mateo before I'm able to speak.

"Calm down, I'm fine." I hiccup as I wipe away my tears. The sight seems to anger Nick further and he makes to move toward Mateo. I hold him back by his arm and give him a strong tug back toward me. "Husband," I singsong, but Nick isn't having it.

He points at Mateo without breaking eye contact with me. "He made you cry."

I realize that we have an audience, and Mateo's amused chuckle is only making matters worse.

Before Nick lunges at my star player, I slip my arms around his neck and lift to give him a kiss on his cheek in hopes of defusing the situation.

We haven't really shown any PDA in front of our friends, and I use the weak excuse to place another kiss on his opposite cheek.

Nick blinks a few times, most likely taken aback by my sudden show of affection, then dives down to place a kiss worthy of alerting HR on my lips. I allow myself to indulge for a few moments—I'm only human after all—then slowly push back from Nick's intoxicating touch. "Mateo's asking Isabella to marry him. He's asked me to help out. That's why I was crying."

He lifts a large hand and cradles my face, swiping away a fresh tear. His voice drops to a whisper. "These are your happy tears?" I bite my lip and nod. "Good." A soft kiss lands on my cheek, where the tear was wiped seconds ago.

"Wait till I tell Isabella about this. She's going to ask me to replay this scenario a million times over." He chuckles. "She's going to be so pissed she missed out on your little make-out session. My woman has been trying to find a way to casually invite you guys to a double date. But if I'm being honest, I'm pretty sure she was going to use the opportunity to interrogate you, Nick. Glad I have enough material to hold her over for a week or so."

Nick finally makes eye contact with Mateo, but not before tucking me into his side. "We'd love to double date, and I welcome a good ole interrogation." Nick looks between the two of us, gauging the room before he offers, "Actually, how about I do you one better? In honor of your upcoming nuptials, I'll host a joint bachelor and bachelorette party." He stares down at me, as if I should know the next words that are coming out of his mouth. Unfortunately, my telepathy skills have yet to kick in, so I'm in the dark and he continues. "Actually, if you don't mind, maybe Luisa and I will join in the festivities, since we eloped and never had the opportunity to celebrate beforehand." He quirks a brow at me. "What do you say?"

"Of course," I answer, catching on that this is part of our arrangement, where we need to convince our friends that we're madly in love. The kiss we shared earlier should set off the group chat once Mateo talks to Isabella, and the rest we can take care of once we're out celebrating as a group. "Sounds like a fun night out. Maybe we should also celebrate Daisy and her fiancé that night as well. A triple bachelor and bachelorette party?"

Nick and Mateo share the same unimpressed look. "I'm pretty easy-going. I'm fine with whatever you all decide." He looks at Nick. "But with all due respect, that guy is a tool."

"What did he do now?" Nick all but growls, his brotherly instincts flaring to life.

I feel myself tense up as well. I've come to see Daisy more like a little sister, and even though I've only met Daisy's fiancé in passing, it was more than enough to firmly place him at the top of my shit list. He even had Nick beat.

Mateo shakes his head. "Nothing crazy. Seemed a bit passive aggressive when we chatted during the charity game a while back. And from what Isa tells me, it seems like he treats Daisy more like a prop than a priority." He sighs as he looks around the room. "I've only known Daisy for a short period of time, but even I know that she has a heart of gold. Any man who doesn't kiss the ground she walks on isn't worthy of her time." His eyes bounce between Nick and me, a small smile playing on his lips. "But I guess Nick and I are the same in that regard. When we found the right woman for us, there was no turning back."

Nick's hold on me tightens as his gaze lands on mine. "You have no idea how right you are."

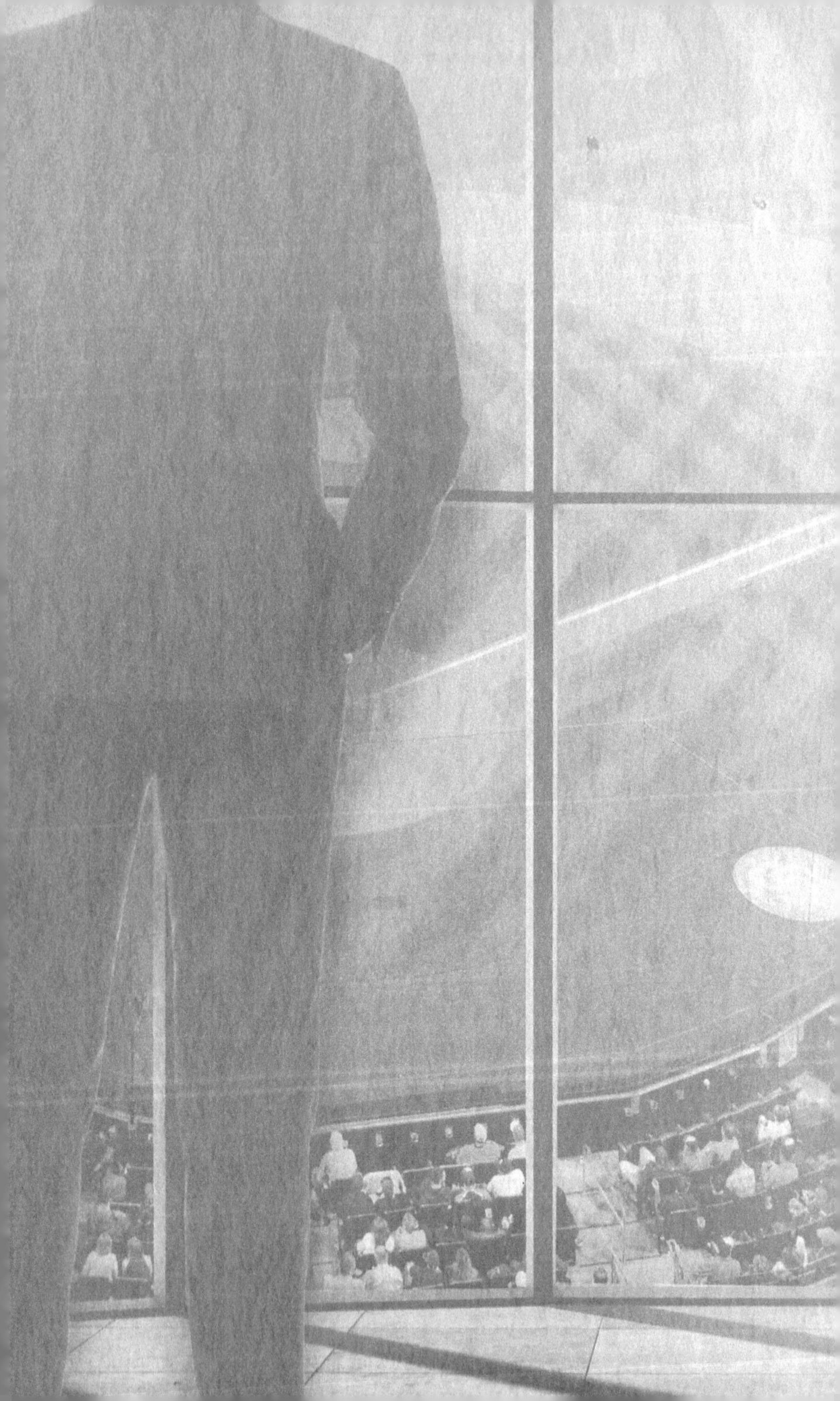

CHAPTER THIRTY-FIVE

NICK

I'VE BEEN ON EDGE since the charity gala that almost turned into a crime scene.

I'm usually able to keep my emotions locked up tight around my sperm donor, but seeing his hands on Luisa made me see red.

And his mention of my grandfather's will added fuel to the fire.

But then again, he could have just been schmoozing with the 1 percent of high society that his old money can't seem to buy him a ticket into.

But it's better to play it safe, especially since I now have Luisa. The fact that he's in the city sniffing around could be a cause for concern. I'll reach out to one of my guys and have him start looking into him to see if there's anything I should keep my eye on.

He sure as hell isn't here to see his daughter, since Daisy always gives me a heads-up when our dear old dad has decided that he's due for a photo op with his kid and future son-in-law, who is a New York senator, currently in the running to be our new governor.

I don't know how my father was able to influence Daisy in that situation, but the closer my sister gets to walking down the aisle with a man who has the emotional intelligence of a gnat, the more my mind races, running through ways I can help get her out of this engagement.

I know I'm hardly the person to come to for romantic advice, but I know my sister, and I know she's not in love with that man, at least not anymore.

For the life of me, I can't understand why she doesn't walk away. She has the means to do so. I set up a trust fund that made her an overnight billionaire when she was twenty-one. Walking away shouldn't be hard. It's not like it's something our father hasn't taught us to do time and time again.

"Hey, you ready?" Luisa asks as she straightens her blazer for the hundredth time.

I tug on her hand, forcing her to leave the poor garment alone. "Are you?"

I'm supposed to be focusing on the press conference I'm about to sit in on where we'll discuss the World Baseball Classic games. Although it's no secret that what the journalists are really aiming for during the Q&A is information about Luisa and me.

We've sat with the PR team and have gone over our vague yet playful answers repeatedly. We'll give an inch but make sure to circle back all conversations to the games.

She rolls her eyes. "Yeah, let's get this over with. It's always the same song and dance with these guys, trying to get a reaction out of me. It won't work, but it's annoying to sit through."

"What do you mean?"

Someone from the PR team waves for our attention. "Okay, they're ready for you."

Luisa slips by me without answering, and my hand twitches with the desire to touch her.

We've been doing a lot of that lately. Touching.

But it's only when there's an audience. And if I'm being honest, I'm getting kind of sick of it.

I hate how I can see the desire in her eyes clear as day, yet the moment we pull away, she scans the room nervously, aware of the attention set on us, and retreats to a place in her mind where I can't reach her.

I don't want to keep playing this game, but I know it's far too soon to broach the conversation, so I'll have to keep biding my time.

I enter the room reserved for the media and take my seat at the table lined with microphones next to Luisa.

Pleasantries are quickly exchanged before the reporters get right to it. "Mr. Stonehaven, how would you compare running a media empire to running a Major League Baseball team?"

I've been asked this question countless times, and I'm well aware it's a throwaway question meant to lower my guard for when they ask what they really want to know.

I give them the same tongue-in-cheek answer I always do and keep it moving along.

"Hey there, Luisa," a fresh-faced journalist starts. I'm not too pleased with his unwarranted sense of familiarity with my wife, but it's too early to start biting people's heads off when I'm supposed to be selling the image of domesticated bliss.

"Hi, Jake." Luisa nods.

"So, the season ended abruptly after the team showed signs of getting an easy ride to the World Series. What do you plan on doing differently next season to make sure the Monarchs play their very first championship game?"

The stupidity of the question has me answering before I can stop myself. "My wife didn't exactly throw that right hook that left us without our star pitcher last I checked."

Luisa smiles uncomfortably as she not so softly pats my hand over the table. "Such a funny guy, this one." She forces a chuckle. "But to answer your question, Jake, this team has managed to exceed every expectation from our point of view. Coming onto the scene for one of the most competitive years in the league is no small feat. And we've had some great wins and some tough losses, but I expect to see some amazing baseball from my guys next season. A few of them put on quite the show during the Dominican Republic versus Puerto Rico game last night, wouldn't you say?" She flashes a saccharine smile, and my cock twitches.

God, there's nothing I love more than this woman exerting her authority over everyone, including me.

Jake nods, though you can tell Luisa didn't give him the sound bite he was looking for.

An older man with ruddy cheeks jumps in before Jake has the chance to ask a follow-up question. "Luisa." He flips through a small notepad, and in that moment, I recognize that no one would dare call me by my first name without me explicitly stating that they could. I mistook that veiled disrespect for a sense of familiarity earlier. It's so small, I'm not sure they realize they're doing it.

I move closer to the mic to rectify it immediately. "That's Mrs. Álvarez-Stonehaven." My voice comes out harsher than intended, so I give a subtle shrug to lessen the tension in the room. "She's hyphenating."

Luisa sends a glare my way as the room erupts into low chuckles and the reporter carries on with his question. "My apologies. Mrs. Álvarez-Stonehaven, as the first female GM, do you think you've got an edge when it comes to acquiring new players, since you're able to give a woman's touch and tap into the more sensitive side of the negotiation process?"

What kind of fucking question is that?

I almost shout my thoughts as Luisa speaks.

"Thanks for the question, Tom. But to be clear, there is no touching when we're negotiating, more like consuming an alarming amount of caffeine while sitting in on multiple speakerphone conversations at once," she jokes, clearly using humor to deflect from the sexist question. And just as I think she's about to let it slide for the sake of keeping the peace, my wife continues. "But let's back up a bit to the part about me being the first female GM." She pauses and looks around. "Don't know if you've heard about that fun fact." The room erupts into laughter as she charms them all with her wit. "I'm honored to hold the title, but to be frank, the answer is much more boring than you'd expect. My AGMs and I work hard to make sure that we are putting the best players in our stadiums for our fans to enjoy. There is a mutual respect in the role we play within this organization, and the fact that I'm a woman has very little to do with it, aside from selling magazines. Is that why you asked the question, Tom? Are you angling for me to sign your copy of GQ? All you had to do was ask." She winks at the old man, and I swear I see hearts in his eyes.

Luisa would have bitten my head off if I made a comment like that, and rightfully so. But it seems that my dear wife is no stranger to these types of questions, and the realization has me fisting a hand under the table.

"Last question, over here!" A guy similar to Tom waves.

Damn, why aren't there more women in this media room? Maybe if there were, Luisa wouldn't have to answer some of these stupid questions.

I make a mental note to remodel how we do press conferences from here on out as the man starts.

"Dan, here, and I guess I'll be the one to address the elephant in the room." The tension in the air raises slightly. Here it comes, the moment Luisa and I have prepared for. The question everyone wants to know. Something that has to do with our marriage or how we manage to work together in the same organization. "You know, I had the perfect question lined up, but this morning, before I left my house, my wife begged me to ask her question instead. Now, I know bypassing what my paper wants me to find out and instead listening to my wife may be unconventional, but as a happily married man of almost thirty-five years, it was an easy decision." He smiles, as if recalling the vision of his wife, and somehow, I find myself smiling along with him. "So, the question from Mrs. Betsy Wallace is... Was it love at first sight?"

The room goes quiet, and I look over to Luisa.

Her mouth opens and closes a few times, as if she's hoping that the words she didn't prepare for will magically fall out.

I find myself answering instead.

"No."

Her head whips toward me, her expression slightly alarmed as the crowd starts to murmur lowly.

"Love at first sight would imply that I fell for her that night." I keep talking, my eyes trained on Luisa's big, beautiful brown ones. "But if I'm being honest with you, I haven't stopped falling since the moment I laid eyes on my wife. And I hope I never do."

Luisa sucks in a sharp breath as her eyes bounce between mine.

"Although, if I had to pinpoint a singular moment, it might have been when she decided to call me the devil." Gasps and laughter fill the room as Luisa's eyes widen, only to immediately narrow.

I break eye contact with Luisa so I can sweep the room to see their reactions.

Dan scribbles intelligibly on his own notepad. "Mrs. Álvarez-Stonehaven calls you the devil?" he asks while barely holding in his own laughter.

He addressed her appropriately, so I decide then and there that Dan can stay once I restructure the media room attendees.

"Yes, and to be fair, I can be. Especially when it comes to my wife. So I'd tread lightly when you consider how to address her, and I suggest you rework your questions into something worthy of her time." I sound like a ticked-off professor strongly suggesting his students not slack off while studying for a final.

"Okay, that's all the time we have for today," the head of PR announces as she waves for us to stand. We take a quick photo by the Monarchs team logo before we walk off into a hallway, away from prying eyes and ears.

Luisa's forced smile stays on her face. "My office. Now."

I keep stride with her, only slowing when I can't help myself and need another peek of that black flowy skirt that softly molds around her ass that's kept me semi hard all morning.

We make it to her office, and she shuts the door with more force than necessary.

Ah, my little Angel looks so tough, thinking she's got me locked up in her domain.

When in reality, she has no idea that my patience has run out and so has her time.

And I've got her right where I want her.

CHAPTER THIRTY-SIX

LUISA

THAT WAS RECKLESS.

We had a plan. Keep everything vague and family friendly.

We'd play the role of the newlyweds, playing coy.

Until Nick took a sledgehammer to the carefully crafted plan by revealing that I call him the devil.

It won't take long before they pin that nickname to something sexual, and then the articles will steer away from our wholesome image to something more sensual.

Something kinkier. Something... like the look of desire Nick has on his face as he prowls toward me.

"Lucifer," I warn.

He doesn't stop until he rounds my desk and pins my ass to it. "Angel," he all but growls.

The look in his eye and the tone of his voice have me clenching my thighs together.

His wicked smile is my only warning before he has me sitting on my desk. And before I can register what's happening, he's stepping between my open legs.

"What are you doing?" I ask, my voice coming out breathier than expected.

"I'm having a long overdue conversation with my wife. You?" His hands land on my waist, and I flatten my lips to keep a moan from escaping.

"What you did out there. What you s-said." I shake my head. "What were you thinking?" I say more firmly, grasping at straws to find my train of thought as Nick's warmth consumes me.

"Hmm, good question. Thank you for asking." His chest rumbles against mine as he leans closer and places a kiss under my ear.

"Nick—"

"I love hearing my name on your lips." He nips my ear. "But you asked me a question, and it's rude to interrupt." His hands travel down to my thighs as he spreads them further.

"I was thinking that it's quite silly for my wife to be running around our house, trying to get off, when she has a husband who is more than willing to handle all of her needs."

I gasp, and his smile turns downright carnal. "Oh, Angel, did you think those vibrations were silent? You had me thinking the second floor was being invaded by an enthusiastic swarm of bees for a second there."

I feel my body heat with embarrassment. I can't believe he's known what I've been doing this whole time.

"Oh, none of that. No need to be embarrassed. I love the thought of you sprawled out on a bed, playing with yourself. The only problem is, I'd enjoy being the one to play with you much, much more."

I make a mewling sound as my hips cant, looking for friction that Nick won't provide yet. "I was also thinking about the medical results we got shortly after we married, the ones needed to add you as a beneficiary to my will and my top-tier life insurance. The same one that states in black and white that we're both in the clear. Oh, and that fancy new birth control you're taking." His hands drift, pulling up my tight skirt in the process. "So when you ask me what the hell I'm thinking, it's this: when I fuck you again, there will be no condom in sight. I will be filling up this tight little cunt with so much cum it will be dripping out of you every time you stand, walk, or bend. And just when you think I've had my fill of you, I'll fuck your face so thoroughly you won't even have the option to spit. You'll have to swallow every last drop of me. How you showed me you could that fateful night we met. The last time my cock's been touched by anyone besides me."

I don't hold back my moan this time, his dirty words making me wetter by the second.

I didn't miss the admission rolled into his filthy words. The ones that confess that he hasn't been with anyone since me. And for some godforsaken reason, I believe him.

Which is how I find myself pleading. "Nick, please."

His eyes meet mine, and he seems satisfied with what he sees. He hikes my skirt up until it gathers around my hips and pulls my panties off in a move that should have taken much more maneuvering.

I'm spread bare for the man who plagues all of my thoughts, especially my horny ones.

It doesn't even dawn on me that we're at our workplace, that someone might walk in on us at any moment, until he's dropping to his knees.

"Nick, shit. The door—"

"Is locked. As if I'd let anyone interrupt the meal I'm about to make out of my wife." He inhales deeply, making my body heat all the way down to my toes. "Fuck, I missed your scent. You smell so fucking good."

His tongue lashes out without mercy.

I lean back on the desk and arch into his sinful mouth. "Nick, oh my God," I try to whisper.

"Quiet, wife, or I'll have to find something to stuff your mouth with." His eyes are devious as his lips suck on my clit, almost sending me flying off the desk.

I know I'm not going to last very long. But the time might be cut in half when I realize that Nick's released his cock from his suit pants and is jerking himself off under my desk.

The sight is vulgar. Feral. And it makes me sink into the feeling of Nick's tongue toying with my clit.

A few seconds later, I come on a silent scream, releasing more of my essence into Nick's welcoming mouth, and he licks me clean.

I lean back farther on my elbows, my hands no longer able to support my orgasm-muddled body, when Nick stands with his cock in hand.

He seems even larger than I remembered, and the thought of him taking me bare has me licking my lips.

He keeps his eyes between my legs as he gives himself three more hard tugs, then aims his cum right onto my oversensitive pussy. Each shot lands firmly on my clit, sending me into an unexpected secondary orgasm.

Nick's hand covers my mouth when I started to cry out.

I didn't even realize I had made a sound.

My body gives out, forcing me to lie on the hard desk with my arms spread out. It's a miracle we didn't break anything.

He bends my knees and places my feet flat on the desk. "What a pretty little mess we've made, Angel." Nick's finger slides through my cum-covered pussy, swirling it around my clit until he takes his finger lower and pumps it into my soaked opening.

My mouth drops. He just put his cum inside me.

He watches my reaction intently, then repeats the motion once more, then twice. Before long, he's quietly filled me with his load.

When he seems satisfied, he puts away his still hard cock and zips himself up. He picks up my panties and slides them over my legs. When he's about to cover my drenched pussy, I stop him. "Where are your manners? A tissue would be nice." My voice sounds as if I've run a marathon.

He shakes his head once. "There's nothing gentlemanly about what I want to do to you right now. And if I didn't care about other people hearing you scream my name as you come, I wouldn't be dressing you right now." He leans over and lifts my ass with one hand while he shimmies my panties up with the other. "But you will have to endure the same torture as me, Angel. So you will walk around with my cum dripping from your pussy, and you will think of me every time you sit at your desk." He flattens his hand on my panties, making them stick to my body and I press into his warm touch. "And the next time you need to get off, you will come to me. Am I clear?"

I nod mindlessly as he smiles.

"Now that's a good wife."

CHAPTER THIRTY-SEVEN

LUISA

I NEED AN EMERGENCY girls' night out.

I sent out the SOS in the group chat, and to my relief, all my girls were ready to rally.

Now that's a good wife.

My knees have been wobbly ever since Nick left me in my office with the mess he made between my legs serving as a reminder of how dangerous his mouth can be.

I beat him home to take a much-needed shower. But I'd be lying if I said the sight of Nick's release on my body didn't send me diving for the showerhead for a quick assist.

Now it's right before nine p.m., and I know Nick is here, because I can hear him humming happily around the house. Most likely trying to lure me out of my hidey-hole to gloat about his sexual abilities.

And even though I want to fold like a cheap lawn chair, I promised myself I wouldn't give him the satisfaction.

Now that's a good wife.

I need to channel the woman I was the night we met. The one who had no issue taking charge and telling him exactly what I wanted instead of looking like a deer in headlights the moment I felt his lips where I needed him most.

I may be fighting a losing battle, but I'll be damned if I just roll over and give in to Nick because he willed me to.

I run my hands down my skin-tight black dress. It dips in the front, showing more than a hint of cleavage. It hugs my curves in all the right places before opening to a small slit above my knees. The dress looks much shorter paired with my sky-high silver heels. It's much more revealing than anything I'd usually wear, but tonight I'm not pulling any punches when it comes to taunting my husband.

He knows dirty talk is my weakness, and he expertly used it until I was spread across my desk in a heap of orgasmic bliss. Long forgotten were any of my reasons as to why having sex with him was dangerous.

But now he's awakened every sexual desire buried within me, and the petty part of me feels like it's only right for him to suffer a bit for breaking down my walls.

I tell myself that I put on the sheer red lingerie as a further way to stick it to him, but if I'm being honest, I hope to drive him wild enough to rip it off my body when I get home.

The sound of my heels on the main floor catches Delilah's attention. She lets out an excited bark before abandoning her dog bed in the living room.

Nick's back is to me as he sits on the couch, swirling the scotch around his glass. I can feel his smugness radiating off him from here. "Ah, has my dear wife finally come out of hiding? I swear I don't bite... unless you ask me very nicely—" He turns to face me, only to freeze on the spot.

I point at his face. "Your jaw, Lucifer. Might want to close it so all that drool doesn't make a mess of your expensive Persian rug."

He snaps his mouth closed and darts to his feet. He drops his glass on a side table haphazardly as he eats up the distance between us, a satisfied smile blooming on his face. "My, my, my. All this for me? Come on, give me a little spin." He lifts my hand above me, and I give him a little twirl.

"You like?" I ask innocently.

His eyes are too busy undressing me to notice the act I'm putting on, and it's going to make leaving him tonight that much sweeter.

"Yes, I like it very much. Where did you buy this dress? Doesn't matter. I want twelve of them." His hands reach for my waist, but I smack them away.

"Nuh-uh-uh. You're gonna have to keep your hands to yourself, Mr. Stonehaven. Because your wife is going out tonight."

His head jerks back. "Wait. You're *leaving*? Now? Dressed like that?" His voice raises slightly, almost frantic.

I fake pout. "Aw, what's wrong with how I'm dressed? I thought that you liked it." I cross my arms under my chest, purposely lifting my breasts in the process.

Nick's eyes steal a quick peek before they meet mine and narrow. "What are you playing at, Angel?"

I shrug. "Not a single thing. Going out with my girls tonight. I'm in need of a strong, hard cock...tail." I lick my lips and smile.

He releases a dry laugh as he points up and down at me. "Oh, I see. Is this supposed to be some kind of roleplay? Because I think all participants involved are supposed to know they're playing before you go and almost give a man a stroke by dressing like sin."

I lean down and give Delilah a nice pat, knowing damn well I'm exposing my lingerie in the process. I keep my eyes trained on him and see the moment he notices what lies beneath my dress. I swear the man stops breathing. "You be a good girl for daddy tonight." I bite my lip. "Okay, Delilah?"

The cute pup gives a happy yelp while her father seems on the brink of a nervous breakdown.

His hands go to the top of his head. "Wh-where are you ladies going? I'll drive you! Um, wait here and I'll get my—" A knock stops Nick from his frenzied movements.

I move closer to him. "Oh, did I forget to mention I hired a car service? It's the responsible thing to do since we never know how wild we'll get when we're out on the town." I place a chaste kiss on the corner of his lip and back away before he has the chance to grab a hold of me. "Whoops, I got some lipstick on you." I lick my thumb seductively, then smear the dark red lipstick further into his skin. "Oh man, you might want to take care of that yourself." I say as I take a step back and look pointedly at the bulge forming in his pants. "The lipstick, I mean."

I turn and make my way to the door, not wanting to keep my driver waiting any longer. Halfway there, I hear Nick's sinister laugh behind me.

"When you walk out that door, know that you've started a game you won't win. You really think you can out seduce me? I'll have you rethinking your decisions and begging me to stop making you come if you keep this up."

I don't consider that a hardship.

I simply shrug and peer over my shoulder as I open the front door. "I wouldn't be so sure if I were you. I seemed to have picked up a few new tricks. I guess that's what happens when you're married to the devil."

If only Nick could see me now.

Sitting in a booth with some of my best girlfriends, feasting on every appetizer on the menu, because our newly pregnant friend Amelia couldn't decide what she was craving.

"Guys, you don't have to stick to soda because of me. I'm totally fine with you all enjoying a drink. In fact, I feel guilty for holding you back," Amelia grouses.

"These are mocktails? Could've fooled me." Nikki, Amelia's very best friend, shrugs and winks at the mom-to-be.

Daisy blows out a big breath. "Trust me, Amelia. Last time I was at this place with you guys, I had the tequila hangover that will serve to keep me away from hard liquor for a very long time, so I welcome these fun mocktails."

We all laugh at the memory of Daisy having a few too many and being whisked away by Coach, who happened to be here and offered to take her home.

"Oh yeah. I totally remember that night." Isabella smirks. "That's the night Mateo and I finally... well, you know."

"Strikeout," we all say in unison before breaking out into laughter.

Isabella gave more than enough details after the fact, detailing how she and Mateo had the most explosive night together. They've been inseparable ever since.

She blushes. "Mateo would die if he knew how much I spilled to you guys." She looks around the table until her assessing eyes land on me. "Which is funny, because I don't think any of us have been debriefed about how you and Nick got together. How about you enlighten us?" She tilts her head while taking a sip of her drink. My cheeks start to flush.

"You guys know Nick is a private person. I would share more, but I have to put his boundaries and needs first. We're married but still a very new couple, and I don't want to rock the boat too much yet," I rush out, hoping the excuse lands true.

Isabella keeps her intense stare on me for a few more moments, but eventually, she deflates slightly. "Dammit. Why'd you have to drop the 'boundary' word in there? Now I have no choice but to be respectful!" She waves her hands in the air, and we all dissolve into giggles.

The waiter stops by and takes our third food order of the night right as my phone lights up. Again.

Because for the last hour, Nick has been blowing up my phone with texts and calls.

NICK:

Hi there. Checking in that you made it all right.

A shiver ran down my spine at that last message. He was getting to me, so I told him I was going to stop looking at my screen for the rest of the night so I wouldn't be rudely ignoring my friends. My phone has been doing the *Macarena* on the booth seat beside me all night, but I've held strong thus far.

When I lift my phone to check the time quickly, I notice that I have an email notification.

From Nick.

Our emails have continued, but since we now live together, they're mostly reserved for actual work conversations.

I don't let my finger hover over the unread message for long before I give in to temptation.

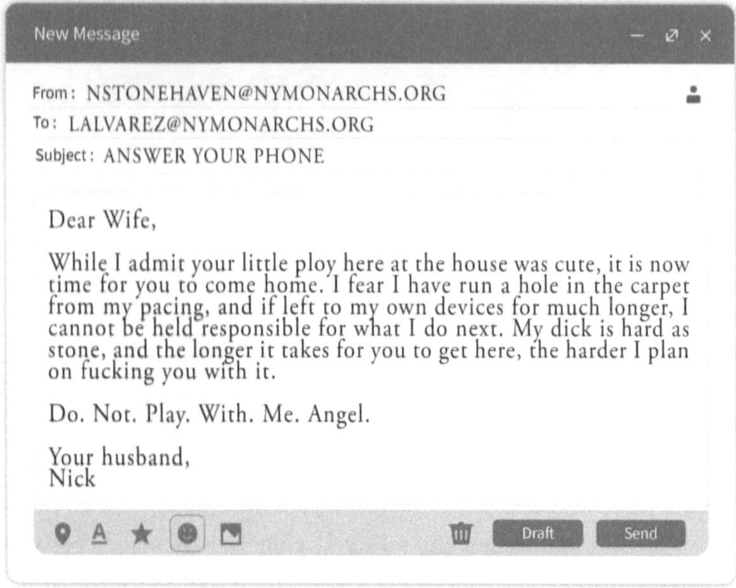

My panties dampen as I finish reading.

My skin suddenly feels too tight, my nipples too sensitive.

"Oh, I know that look. Did someone get a naughty text?" Isabella teases.

I clear my throat, trying to shake the feelings of arousal off, and flip my phone toward the girls. "Well, you wanted a little something from our personal life, so how about this?"

"I see the word dick! I'm covering my eyes until you're all done reading. And for the love of God, please don't read my brother's dirty text out loud," Daisy groans.

"It's not a text. It's an email. God, that's so hot, given that he's a businessman. Does he fuck you in his full suit in his office?" Amelia slaps a hand across her mouth. "Sorry, hormones. They sometimes get me super horny at a drop of a hat. Ignore me."

Isabella snatches the phone out of my hand, her eyes popping out of her head. "Holy fuck. You guys are so hot." She looks at me, then back at my phone when she starts to type.

"What are you doing?"

"Don't worry. I'll give you final approval. Just thought I'd up the ante. Pretty sure this'll get you a good spanking. At the very least, it'll earn some explosive orgasms."

"Lalala, I can still hear you!" Daisy yells.

We all send her apologetic looks as we laugh.

"Oh c'mon, Daisy. Let your sister-in-law live. I'm sure you're getting dicked down by the man who put that rock on your finger," Nikki says.

Isabella stops her typing to look at Daisy, and we both spot the moment her shield goes up and her public persona turns on. "Yeah, well, I guess I'm more private when it comes to that stuff. Or maybe I have to call my therapist and schedule a few extra sessions since I now know my brother likes to get kinky via emails." She forces a smile.

The other girls laugh, but Isabella and I share a secret look.

I've been meaning to have some alone time with Daisy to see if she wants to open up about her fiancé, but a part of me thinks that the situation might be more complicated than I'm privy to.

"Here. What do you think?" Isabella shoves my phone back in my hand and I read her response to my husband.

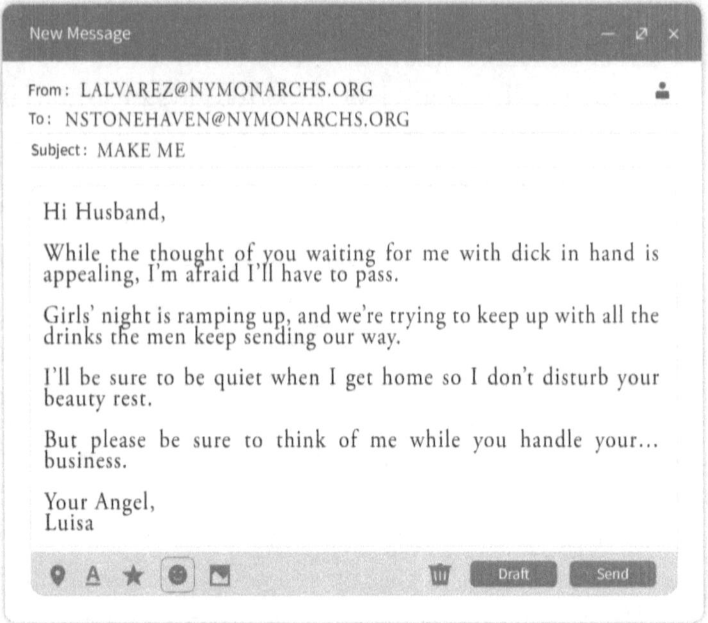

I release a hard laugh. "I couldn't."

"You could," Isa pushes.

I rock my head from side to side. "I shouldn't."

"Oh, but I think you should." She lifts my finger to hover over the Send button. I look at her expectantly, waiting for her to do it, when she shakes her head. "Oh no. This is your trigger to pull, girlfriend. Because once that man unleashes, you'll be the one on the receiving end of all he'll have planned for you. I don't want any three-a.m. calls, and I don't want to be cursed to kingdom come because you learned that your husband is into some freaky shit." She laughs, but my mind is lost in the endless possibilities of what Nick could be capable of when pushed to the brink.

And I like every single one of them.

So I hit Send.

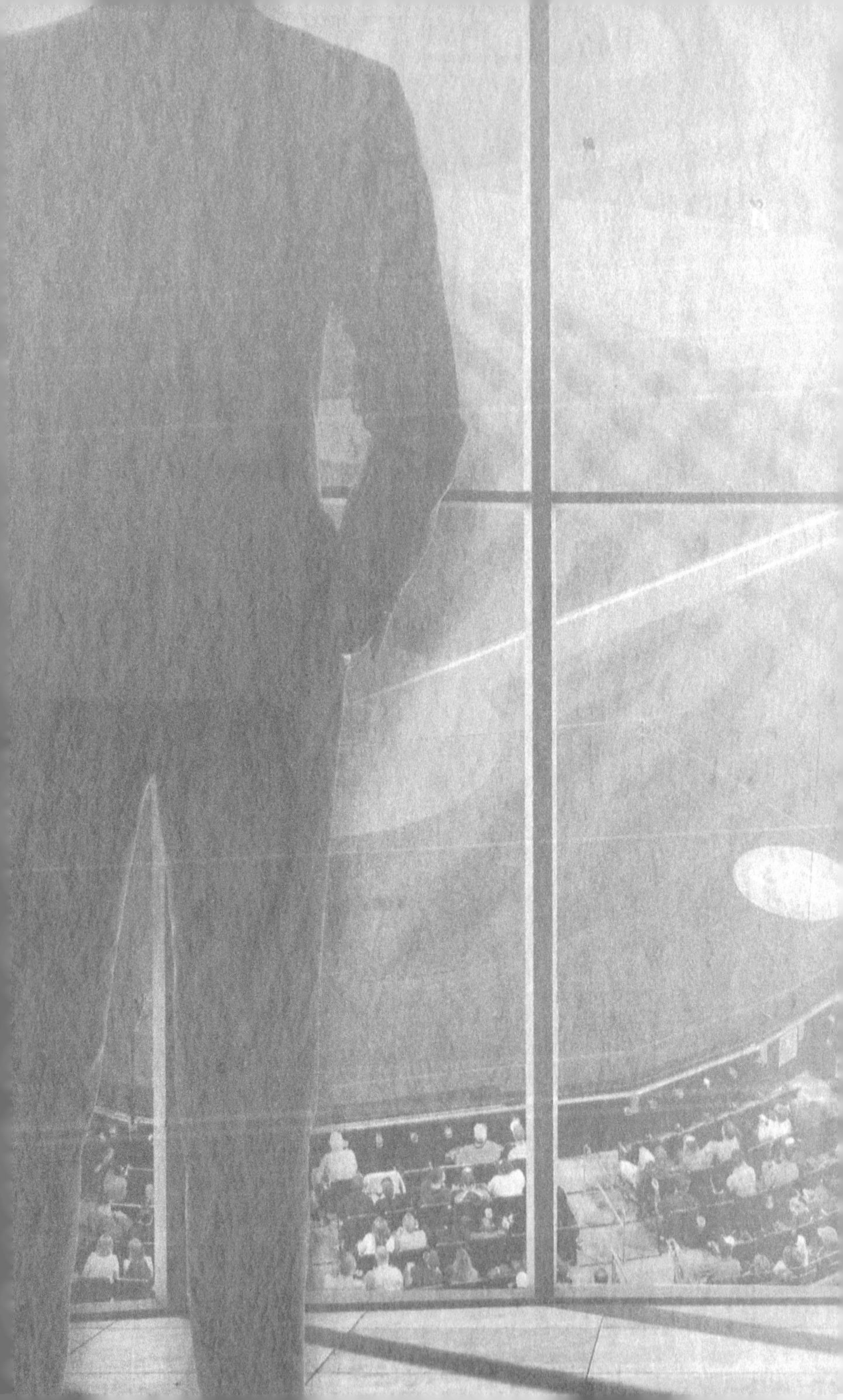

CHAPTER THIRTY-EIGHT

NICK

I WANT TO GO on a rampage.

Barge into that bar Luisa is at like I own the place.

Remove every man who has the audacity to look at my wife.

And... And...

A thought forms rapidly in my mind. I try to push down on the feral beast my wife has turned me into and force myself back into the mind of the businessman I am known to be. Quick and calculated.

I'm behind my desk in a flash, emailing my attorneys while on the phone with the person I need to negotiate with.

Thirty minutes.

A record time set for this kind of deal.

And a swift lesson for my wife.

CHAPTER THIRTY-NINE

LUISA

I'M HAVING THE BEST time with my girls.

Stuffing my face with cheese tortellini and breaded chicken. I tried my best to balance my meals earlier today so I could indulge in this goodness.

"Uh, is it closing time or something?" Isa asks.

I interrupt the torrid love affair I'm having with my pasta to see what she's referring to. Security escorting people out of the exclusive lounge.

"This place doesn't close until two a.m. And not everyone is leaving. Only the men," Daisy notes.

My eyes scan the room, jumping from person to person, noting how the wait staff place to-go containers in front of the male patrons as they wave them to the door with apologetic looks on their faces.

"That's weird. I wonder if something happened. Why else would they—"

No. This can't be...

"Excuse me, are you Mrs. Álvarez-Stonehaven?" a nervous man who introduced himself as the manager earlier in the night asks me.

I nod woodenly. "Um, y-yeah, that's me. Is everything okay?"

He lifts a cordless office phone and points it in my direction. "This is for you." He hands the phone to me, and I take it out of his shaky hand.

"Uh, hello?"

Silence greets me momentarily. I only hear the clink of ice hitting glass, followed by liquid being poured.

And then a voice.

"Ah, there she is. My beautiful wife."

Goosebumps rise on my skin. I suppress my surprise at hearing him on the other end of the line and instead growl into the phone. "Nick. What did you do?"

The women around me gasp, putting together the pieces of what's going on.

"Only what any respectable husband with deep pockets and limited sanity would do when his wife pushes him too far. I bought the bar and gave firm instructions to kick out all the men. Only security and the manager are allowed to stay since I suppose someone needs to run the establishment while the change of ownership is underway."

"You didn't," I say breathlessly.

"But I did." I can hear the grin in his voice. "It's actually in your name, so try not to trash the place. Consider it a gift for you and all the ladies, since tonight is now a girls' night in every sense of the word."

"Nick, this is ridiculous. I can't even—" I sigh, looking at the manager, who now won't look up from his shoes. "Did you threaten the manager?"

"Why would you ask such a thing?" His tone is riddled with delight.

"Because the poor guy won't make eye contact with me."

He groans loudly. "Can no one follow directions anymore? No, I didn't threaten. I simply implied the many unpleasant things that could happen to him if he dared to look at you anywhere below your neck. I am reasonable, after all," he huffs.

"Nick, that's a threat."

"Not according to my lawyers," he mumbles.

"Nick—"

"No, no, darling. I think this call has gone on long enough. Run off and continue to have a nice night with the ladies. I hear the tortellini and the mocktails are to die for."

I'm no longer feeling much pity for that manager.

"But just know, I'll be waiting for you once you get home. And I'm having quite the time planning how I'm going to have my way with your body."

"What? I'm, uh—"

"Nuh-uh-uh. You've made your bed, Angel. Now come home to your devil and lie in it."

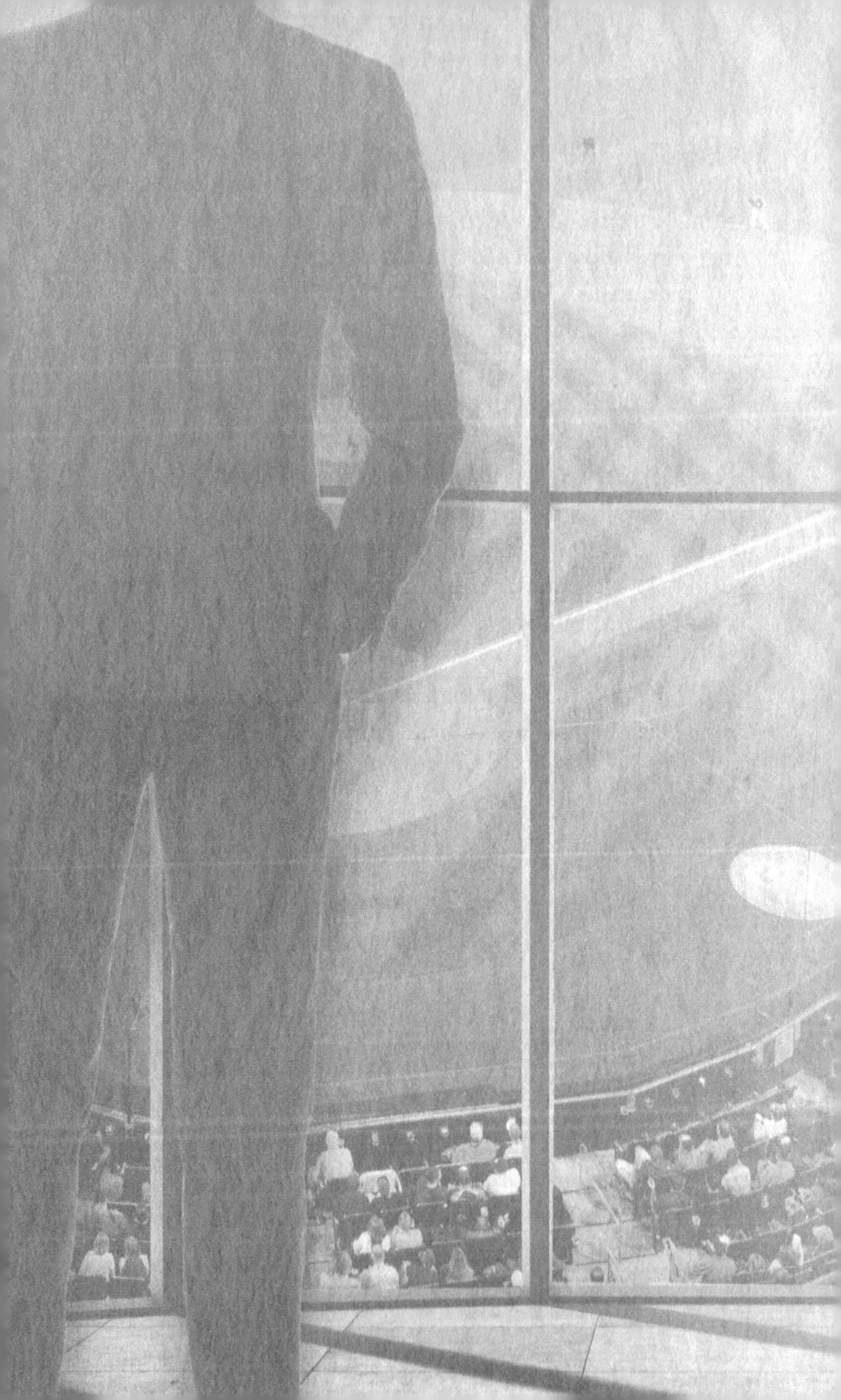

Chapter Forty

NICK

I LAY OUT EVERYTHING I'll need for tonight.

I'll admit, I enjoyed this little game Luisa and I played tonight. Only she has the ability to make me feel like I'm alive while simultaneously wanting to punish her for it.

I undressed down to my boxer briefs when I heard her enter the house a few minutes ago. I don't plan on keeping these on that much longer either.

I track the sound of her heels heading up the stairs until they're muffled by the bedroom carpet.

Our room is only lit up by the lamp on her nightstand, but I can see her dilated pupils and shallow breathing all the way from where I sit in the oversized chair by the bay windows.

"You rang?" She tries to seem aloof but fails miserably.

And while I love sparring with my wife, tonight, I don't plan on using many words.

I lean back, knowing my hard cock is barely restrained behind thin material, and beckon her over with the crook of two fingers.

Her brows raise, but she complies, like I knew she would.

She stops nearby but not close enough for me to touch her. Smart survival instincts. Except those became useless the moment she stepped back into this house tonight.

"What? Cat got your tongue? You seemed like you had much to say when you called me at the bar." She crosses her arms across her chest, trying to act as if she doesn't know she's already been caught in my web.

"Strip," I demand, my tone low and gravelly.

She sucks in a breath as she straightens. "What?"

I don't repeat myself. Instead I allow her to stand in heady silence as my eyes trail every inch of her body.

She bites her lower lip, and I clock it as the moment she knows it's time to get what she is due.

She reaches the zipper on the side of her dress and pulls it down. Then, one by one, she lowers each strap of her dress until it's pooled on the floor around her heeled feet.

I knew what she was wearing under her dress. The reminder alone was enough to send me running to spend ten million dollars on a bar that's probably worth half the price.

But as Luisa stands before me in a red, lacy see-through bra and matching thong, I know I'd pay billions to get her back in this room with me.

And while the sight is enticing, I'm afraid I don't have the patience to take my time and enjoy it thoroughly. What I have planned for Luisa requires her to be naked.

She hooks her thumbs over her thong and waits a moment, as if asking if I'm sure I want the sexy garment to be removed. I nod, and she slowly bends at the waist to remove them. Once they're off, she picks them up off the ground and flings them at my bare chest.

I release a humorless chuckle as I look pointedly at her sheer bra.

She unhooks it and holds onto the cups, keeping an air of mystery until the very last second, when she sends the bra flying my way as well.

She steps out of the dress, wearing only her silver heels. She makes no move to take them off, and I decide then and there that they will remain on her for the rest of the night.

I stand, closing the distance between us.

My thumb lifts and lightly traces a soft circle around her hardened nipple, giving it a slight tug before I lean in slightly and lift her into my arms, pulling a surprised squeak out of her before I toss her onto the bed.

"Spread," I command.

She hesitates, catching her breath, but then complies as she opens her legs and shows me exactly what I've been dying to see all night.

I place my hands on her knees and stretch her wide open obscenely so not a single inch of her is hidden from me.

Her pussy is bare, freshly shaven. And I grin, knowing she did that hoping we'd end up exactly like this tonight.

The more I stare, the more obvious it becomes how wet she is.

I can't resist. I swipe my thumb over her opening and firmly spread her juices across her clit. I don't linger. As soon as I hear her moan, I bring that thumb to my mouth and lick.

I force myself off the bed. I have a plan, and if I allow myself to get lost in Luisa, I won't be able to show her the naughty vision I had while she left me home alone tonight.

I leave her on the bed, spread open and waiting for me, as I grab what I need from the nightstand.

She didn't notice it when she walked in, and I'm looking forward to the element of surprise.

I climb back on the bed and put the U-shaped sex toy by her mouth.

"Suck."

Her eyes threaten to pop out of her head at my demand. But it doesn't stop her from doing as she's told.

She opens her mouth, and I push the toy in.

Of course I could have used her own arousal, but I like this sight much better.

She releases the toy with a pop, saliva strung along the toy and her lips.

"Spit."

She releases another moan before she spits on the toy, and I move away from her inviting mouth before my cock gets any ideas.

I move back down to her open legs and remove my underwear.

My hardened cock bobs between us, pointing directly at her wet pussy as precum leaks from my tip.

Patience, I repeat to myself for the millionth time.

I take the longer, thicker side of the toy and rub it up and down her slit.

"Safe word is 'sangria.' Repeat it to me and tell me you understand. If you want me to stop, use it, and this all ends."

I lift the toy from her entrance so she can decide whether she wants to give consent with a clear head.

"If you don't put that toy or cock inside me in the next five seconds, I can't be held responsible for the damage I inflict with my very pointy heels... Safe word is sangria, so move this show along," she pants.

My lips twitch as I resume playing with her and the toy.

"Sorry, wife, but this is how it's going to go. I'm controlling your orgasms with this fun little toy I picked up tonight. I spent the whole night cleaning it meticulously and coming up with what I want to do to you. I thought punishment would make the most sense, but after I tasted your pussy today, my cock wanted in on the action."

She groans. "Shut up and give it to me already."

"Sorry, no cock for you, dear." I insert the toy, pushing it in and out of her slowly until it's all the way inserted. "But don't worry; I will be having my fun." I make sure the top part of the toy is aligned perfectly with her clit before showing Luisa the small remote control in my hand. "And this will be my sidekick for the night. First, I'll start with this." I press a button, and the silicone vibrator inside her starts to give short thrusts, pushing up against her G-spot. Her mouth opens on a silent gasp, her eyes burning with desire. "Good so far, I hope?" I taunt.

Her hands fist the bedding as she nods.

I move above her body, planting kisses as I lead up to her breasts.

I bring a nipple to my lips and suck, circling my tongue around her hardened tip before I give it a quick nip and move to give her other breast the same attention.

She's writhing beneath me, and the sight of pleasure on her face makes me almost want to laugh, because this is nowhere near the extent of what I have planned for her tonight.

I continue to move up until my thighs straddle her chest and my cock is mere inches from her face.

She licks her lips, but I shake my head. She looks confused as I lift my cock to her lips and once more say, "Spit."

She does as she's told, spitting on me, but not before she runs the tip of her tongue over the head of my cock. I hiss as she swipes away a drop of precum.

"Good girl."

The words slip out of my mouth before I think it through, but the look of satisfaction on my Angel's face tells me that my wife has a praise kink.

I lean back down, inching my hardened length between her luscious breasts, and give her a carnal smile. "You see, while you were gone, all I could think about was you in that red little number you had on. And once I started thinking about getting you out of your lingerie, I couldn't get the thought of fucking your tits out of my head. Which is exactly what I plan to do."

I lift the small bottle of water-based lube I dropped on the bed earlier and drizzle a fair amount over her breasts and my cock. Once satisfied, I toss the bottle aside and start to massage her tits, warming the cool lubricant, circling and pinching her nipples as I go.

I give one test thrust and throw my head back on a groan. Fuck, this feels amazing.

She surprises me by smacking my wrists away and replacing my hands with her own. "Let me." She pushes her breasts together, creating a warm, tight channel for my dick.

I use my free hands to grab a pillow and prop her neck up so she can have a front-row seat to what she does to me.

"Always the gentleman, I see. And here I thought you were going to fuck my tits without any chivalry." She winks.

I pick up the remote from where I dropped it beside my knee and grin down at her. I turn up the level on her thrusts as I pick up my own. I allow myself to get lost in the feeling, our sounds of pleasure blending into one.

My finger hovers over a button I have yet to press. I keep my pace, fucking her as she meets my thrusts by bouncing her breasts up and down my shaft, jerking me off with her tits.

I speak between labored breaths. "Does that feel good for you, Angel? Having me fuck your tits while I control how that toy fucks you?"

A restrained cry escapes her throat. "God, yes. Please don't stop."

"Would it feel even better if I sucked on your clit?"

"Yes! But no! Don't move. I'm almost—"

"Oh, don't you worry. I'm not stopping anything, but this"—I wiggle the remote in my hand—"will assist me. Repeat your safe word for me."

"Sangria."

"Use it if you need to."

"I won't—ah, ohmygod. Fuck, fuck, fuck. Don't stop—"

I pick up the pace, imagining her pussy tightening around the toy that's currently thrusting into her wet pussy as it also sucks on her aroused clit. The thought almost has me coming on the spot, but I need her to get there first.

I press the suction button one more time, and it's as if a bomb has been detonated when she screams my name.

"Nick! Oh, fuck me, Nick. I'm coming."

She's bowing off the bed, her face contorted in orgasmic bliss as she continues to breathe my name like a prayer.

"Okay, okay. Turn off the toy. It's too much."

I quickly power the toy off, and her body melts into the bed as she struggles to catch a full breath. She catches sight of my cock poking out above her tits, and her smile turns devious.

I'm about to tease her about it when her words have me seeing stars. "Come for me, *husband*. Think you can get any in my mouth?" She opens wide and sticks out her tongue.

My hips punch forward. I feel myself coming before I can articulate it to my dirty wife.

The first rope of cum lands on her neck, followed by the second. I raise up on my knees, and the rest streak over her tongue, lips, and cheeks. The sight immediately burns into my memory.

She uses her fingers to daintily clean up her face as she licks her lips clean. She then sets her sights on my spent cock, moving to take me in her mouth. But I stop her with a hand on her shoulder.

Her brows furrow as she leans back against the pillow.

"You want an orgasm, you come to me. I'll clear my schedule and eat you out for hours on my desk. Buy you a new toy to test out when you need that feeling of your pussy being filled up." I swipe a bit of my release that she missed and slip it into her mouth. Then I grip my cock in my other hand and lift it closer to her face. "But this cock right here is off-limits until you come to your senses."

"What? What senses are you talking about? The ones you thoroughly fucked out of me? *Those* senses?"

I shake my head and force myself not to laugh. She's adorable, even when she's covered in my cum.

"The ones where you finally admit what we both know to be true. That we are more. More than this contract, more than the show we put on while we're in public, more than the fake marriage we pretend to be in. Because that's exactly what we've been doing—pretending it's not real, instead of the other way around."

Her chest rises and falls with each word she's taking in. "You know, for a guy who's trying to convince me that he doesn't want to give me his big dick, you sure are failing to make your point as you hover over my head with it. It seems to be taking on a second wind, like it's ready to go again."

"Luisa, I'm not joking with you."

"But didn't you say the next time you fucked me, you'd take me bare?" She reaches between her legs and pulls out the toy that brought her to the edge tonight. And for a moment I allow myself to scowl at it, knowing that it could have been me instead. "You made such a mess before. Wouldn't you like to see how your cum would look coming out of me?" She pushes her glistening tits together, reminding me of how easily they made me come a few moments ago.

I shake my head as I narrow my eyes at my wife. She knows exactly what she's doing to me. Avoidance, I expected from her. But sexual tactics are just plain cruel when I've done nothing but imagine sinking into her since the morning I woke up and realized she had slipped from my hotel room.

I'm not letting her run this time.

"If you want to fuck your husband, you can do so when you start acting like you intend on being his wife for the rest of your days."

Her mouth drops in shock as I move off the bed.

I was serious when I said I wasn't done with her yet.

"Now turn around and get on all fours so I can eat you out from behind. You can count the spanks. One for every text message you didn't respond to. Maybe then you'll learn your lesson."

But given the flush on her face and the smile of her lips, I know she won't.

Chapter Forty-One

LUISA

The November chill settles into my bones, but I don't dare take my eyes off the field.

Julian Vega, the first baseman from Miami who's playing for Team Dominican Republic, swings his bat, and the sound of the ball making contact is heard throughout the entire stadium. We all watch in awe as the ball is sent flying far into the stands, earning a grand slam and securing a win for the team.

"You're going to catch a cold, woman." A voice I would know anywhere comes up behind me. A large suit jacket is placed over my shoulders, enveloping me in a scent that is uniquely Nick.

"There are heaters in here," I grumble, though I still pull the jacket closer around me.

"Yes, but you're standing on the open side of the suite ledge, forcing me to come to your rescue. Being chivalrous is quite taxing when your wife refuses to wear a jacket. Now everyone can see my hard nipples through my dark shirt. I have no choice but to hold you close. You know, for decency and body heat purposes."

"Of course." I smile as his muscular arms wrap around me from behind.

"You smell good." He nuzzles my neck.

"I smell like you," I snicker.

"Not exactly. But if you'd let me drag you up to my office, I could rectify that."

The smile stays on my face as I shake my head. "You're incorrigible."

"What I am is in need of a fix, and my wife is my drug of choice."

He's kept true to his promise of keeping his dick away from me during our sexual encounters, and I really believe it must be some kind of sexual mental warfare. Because each day I find myself closer to giving in. Telling Nick that this, us, feels real. And, more terrifyingly, that I want to be his wife forever.

Wife.

That damn word Nick keeps throwing around as if it's permanent. And the jump my heart makes at the misguided hope that it could be.

I keep replaying the terms in my head. We stay married for a year, and then we quietly divorce.

Divorce.

I recoil at the thought of having to once again sign a document in which my true feelings aren't reflected.

I may have agreed to marry Nick under false pretenses, but those circumstances have since changed.

I have fallen for my husband.

I don't know if it happened during our mornings together, when we drink coffee, during evenings walks with Delilah, or midday visits to his office where he gives Marla a long lunch so he can eat me out on his desk.

Or maybe it happened while we handed out candy to trick-or-treaters. He bought my mother and aunts high-end

Hocus Pocus costumes, turning them into the real Sanderson sisters, something they have yet to shut up about.

He got devil horns and an angel halo for us. He wore the feathery halo all night, since he claimed it was only appropriate he dressed as something different on Halloween night.

Or maybe it happened on the nights I stayed up late, responding to his silly emails. Before this marriage even started.

Nick didn't marry me because he loved me. He did it so he could be in compliance with a will that's supposed to give him some mysterious asset. Something so important it was worth marrying a woman he never dated in order to secure.

Which makes me doubt what he's capable of doing once he has it and no longer needs me.

"Where'd you go?"

I blink repeatedly when I realize that Nick is standing before me, blocking my view of the celebrating players.

"Um, nowhere. Just thinking that I want that guy down there," I stammer.

Nick looks down at the field and back at me. "I'm hoping, for his sake, that you mean you want to sign him to the Monarchs."

I slap his chest playfully, but he keeps it in place.

"Talk to me, Luisa." I open my mouth, but he interrupts. "The truth. Please."

I have no idea what I was about to say, but he's right, because it would have been some kind of half truth.

His eyes soften as he seemingly holds his breath, and I can't find it in me to hide much longer.

"Nick." I drop my head to his chest, unable to look him in the eye.

"You're scaring me, Angel."

I huff. "Good. 'Cause I'm scared too."

His hands slip to the nape of my neck, his fingers tangling in my loose waves. "What are you scared of?" he asks slowly.

A part of me has a feeling he already knows.

"Nick," I whisper.

"Say it. Please." He kisses the top of my head.

I gather the courage to look up and almost lose my breath at the pleading look on his face. It gives me the final sense of security I need. "I—"

"Hey, am I still riding with you guys—oh shit, am I interrupting? Is this something newlyweds do? Are there not enough hours in a day for you two to keep it in your pants at work?" Daisy bemoans.

"Shit."

"Luisa, stay with me. What were you about to—"

"We're gonna be late. Mateo is gonna kill us if we ruin his surprise. I'm sure their engagement photographer doesn't want to capture us running into his apartment as he's down on one knee." I step out of his hold. "But I'm keeping your jacket. Come on, husband." I tug on his arm, but he's unmovable.

He tosses his keys at his sister. "Wait in the car, Daisy. We'll be right there."

She smiles mischievously. "If you're not down in five minutes, I'm driving myself. And I won't apologize for all the curbs I assault." She dashes out of the suite doorway.

"Nick, seriously. We have to go."

His lips flatten. "Fine." He releases a deep breath, then slides his hands over my cheeks. "But this conversation isn't over."

I release my own breath, the one caught in my chest. "I know."

He places a kiss on my forehead, and I pray the day never comes where these moments have turned into forgotten memories.

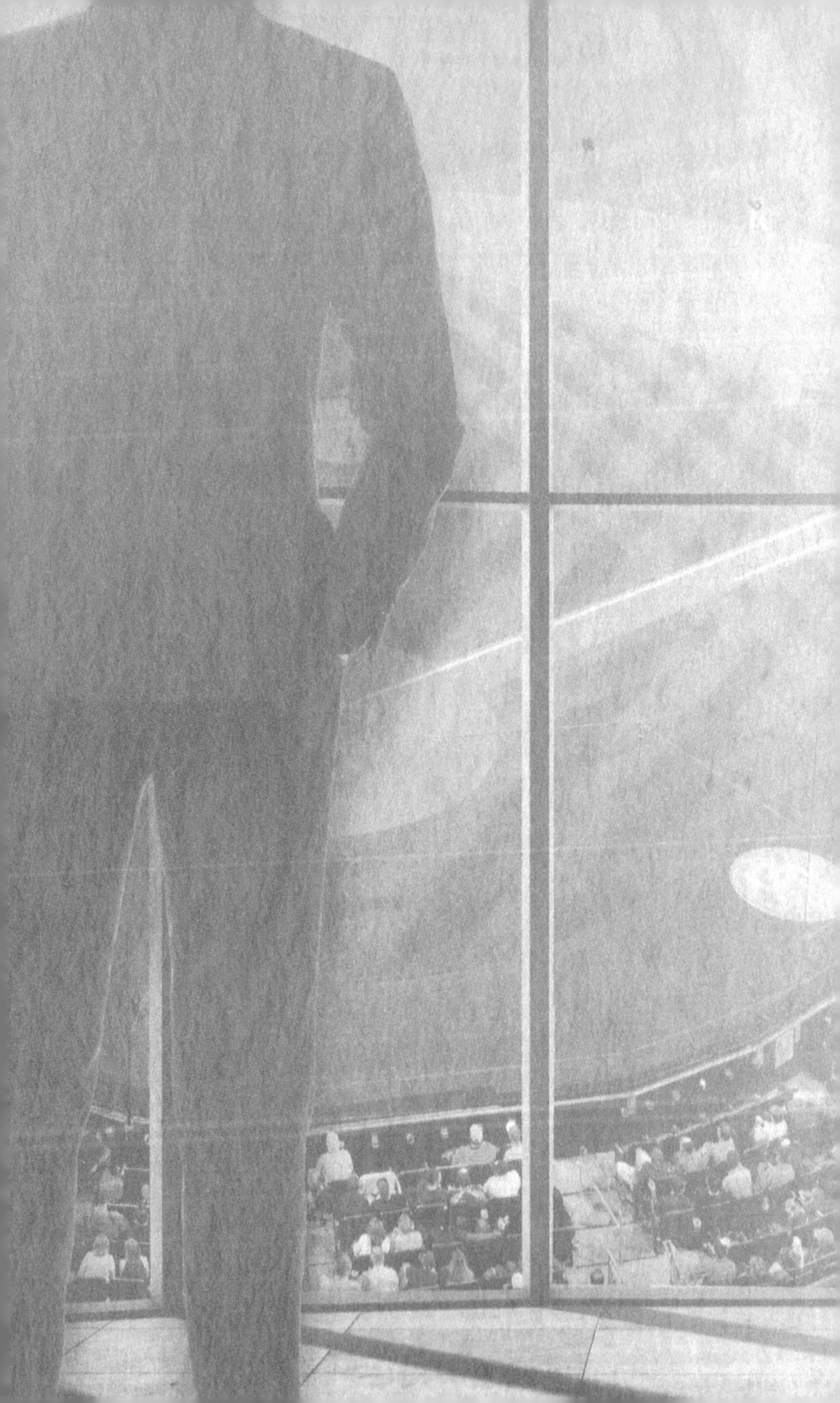

NICK

She's in love with me.

But I don't know what hurts more.

The fact that she won't tell me, or that she probably wishes she wasn't.

On the drive over to Mateo's house, I realize that it's the latter.

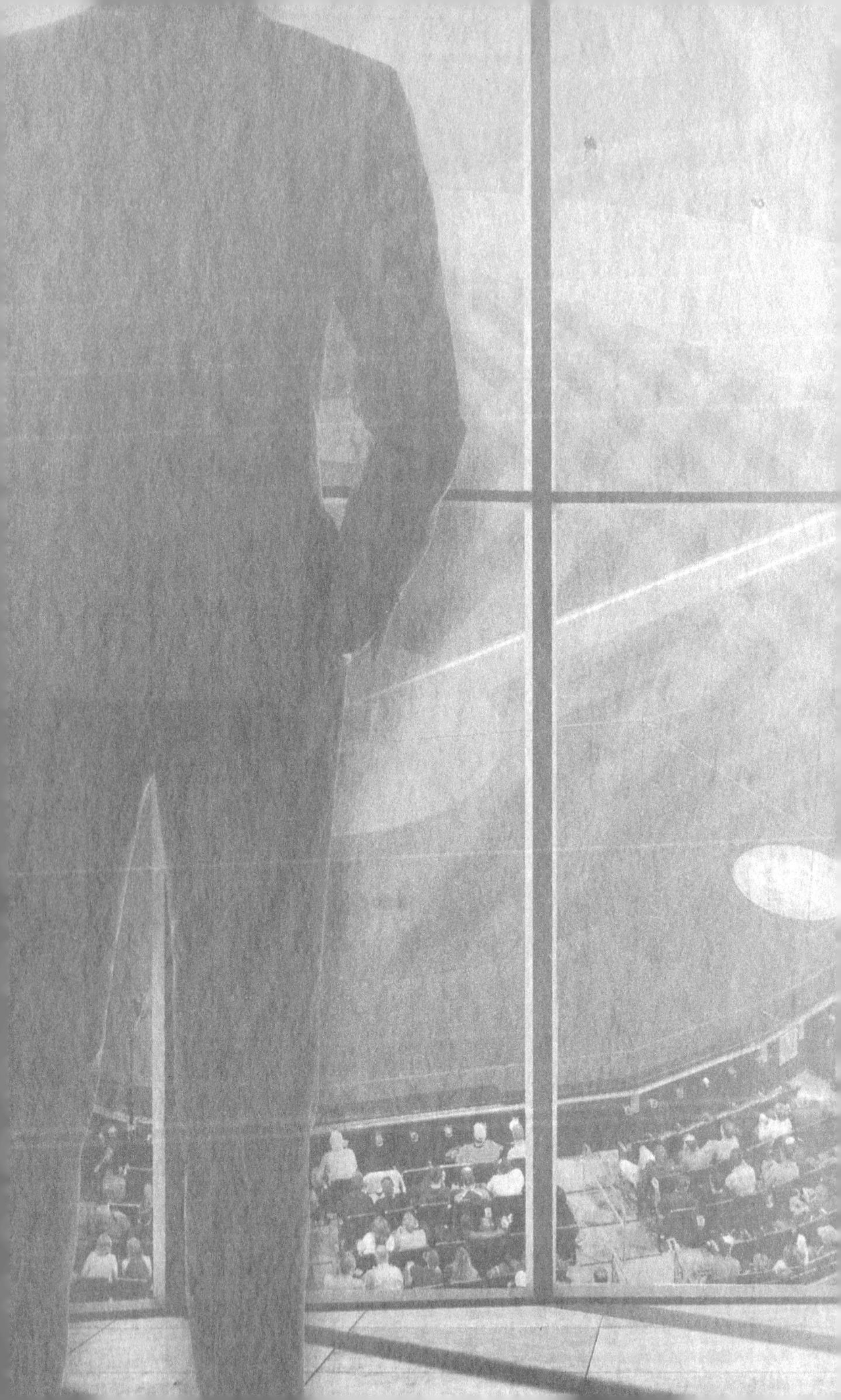

Chapter Forty-Three

NICK

Isabella said yes.

Obviously.

Mateo and his daughter set up the first floor of their apartment with white candles of all sizes, creating an aisle made of sprinkles that led to the kitchen. That was odd, but to each their own. In the kitchen, there were hundreds of bright yellow Post-Its stuck to the wall of windows that spelled out MARRY ME as tall as the starting pitcher himself.

On one Post-It, he wrote *cásate conmigo*. He left that one next to the impressive diamond ring.

As soon as the couple and Mateo's daughter were done wiping their tears, the rest of our group emerged from our hiding spots, sending poor Isabella into a crying fit.

Luisa softly wipes away her own tears as she listens to Isabella's retelling of the day up until the moment Mateo got down on one knee.

I never got down on one knee. Luisa never got to have a moment like this.

The thought slashes through me, and I force myself to take a deep breath.

Luisa catches my eye and makes her way toward me.

My arms open, and she slides into my hold so easily.

She looks up and smiles, my hand caressing her cheek. "These are my happy tears."

"I know." I bend down and kiss the spot I last saw a tear. "And I want to be the person who gives you all the happy tears." Her eyes widen, but I keep going. "And I want to be the person who's there when the sad ones come too."

"Nick." She gasps quietly, most likely trying not to draw attention to us during such an important time for the newly engaged couple.

I shake my head. This'll have to wait until another time.

I try to lift the mood, not wanting to have Luisa's head in a tailspin for the rest of the night. "Because I don't know if you've noticed, but I'm kind of partial to my wife. Although, that first night, I'm pretty sure those tears weren't happy or sad ones. Could you tell me again what you were doing that caused you to tear up at the same time you were having trouble keeping your saliva in your mou—"

Oomph.

Her elbow to my stomach hit a lot harder than I thought she could manage from this angle. Leave it to me to never underestimate my wife again.

Her eyes hold equal parts heat and indignation. "Really, Lucifer? Here? Now?" She goes to shove me away, but I spin her in my arms and tickle her neck with my short beard, then pepper kisses against her skin. "Okay, Okay. You win. Stop. You know I'm super ticklish right there." She wiggles her juicy ass against my front, and I release her before the little minx takes playing dirty any further.

"God, these two can't keep their hands to themselves for two seconds, I swear." Daisy rolls her eyes but doesn't hide her bright smile.

I know she's happy for us. I just wish I could feel the same about her relationship.

"Sorry, Daisy, but your brother and Luisa probably spend all day lighting their sheets on fire, so I guess you're going to have to get used to the PDA." Isabella beams as she looks between Luisa and me.

"Congratulations." I lean over and kiss Isabella on the cheek.

"Yeah, yeah. Send a card or something, but hands off." Mateo pulls Isa into his chest, and she places a giggling kiss under his jaw.

Coach Weston joins our circle. I'm surprised to see him here, simply because I've never seen the man anywhere besides the stadium grounds.

"Congrats, guys," he offers.

I jump at the chance to needle him a bit. "Oh, look, he speaks."

He grunts as he throws an unimpressed look my way. Daisy comes to his defense. "What are you talking about? Luke talks all the time."

Multiple eyeballs shift across the room, none communicating out loud what we all suspect.

"Bathroom?" Coach mutters.

"Down the hall, to your right," Mateo offers, and Coach moves swiftly in that direction.

Daisy looks at both couples standing before her. "What was that all about?"

My Angel seems to be the valiant one when she speaks. "It's nothing, really. I think the guys are busting his balls a bit. But..."

"What?"

"When it comes to Luke, aside from things that have to do with trades and contracts, well... He only really talks to you, Daisy." I pull Luisa into my arms, not liking having her standing a few steps away from me.

Daisy waves off the comment. "That's silly. I'm probably the only one who talks his ear off. Or maybe he talks to me because I'm the one stealing his lunch on most days, or it could be—"

"Hey, you don't need to justify it. It's fine, Daisy." Isabella places her hand on my sister's shoulder. "Even if he doesn't want to talk to us, that's okay. Means he feels comfortable around you. Or maybe he finds us all super annoying, which, in that case, would mean I question his state of mind, and we should kick him out of our home immediately," she teases.

I see Coach coming back our way and figure now is as good a time to invite everyone. "Hey, Luke, before you go, I wanted to let you know we're throwing a joint bachelor and bachelorette party. For Luisa and me, Mateo and Isa, and Daisy and Damien."

He keeps his face impassive, but I don't miss his clenched fist. "Pass."

Ah, yes. Man of many words, that one.

"Oh, you don't have to include me in the celebrations, guys." Daisy's cheeks blush slightly.

"Why not? You're a bride to be, and you have been engaged the longest. You deserve a night of fun," Luisa pushes.

Daisy smiles, but I know it's one of her fake ones, the one she reserves when she poses for pictures with our father. "Damien doesn't do that kind of stuff. He, um. Yeah. He won't be able to attend." The room goes silent, and she squirms. "But that doesn't mean I won't go! We'll have the best time. I can plan the night for the girls, and we can make it into a whole weekend, if you want. We can always get on Nick's jet and go somewhere. I know I'll be the odd woman out, but I don't mind, truly. I can bring board games, or, or..."

"I'm in," Luke answers, interrupting Daisy's rambling. When we all look at him in confusion, he shrugs. "I like board games."

"Right," I say, not bothering to hide the suspicion in my tone. "Board games. We'll be sure to have plenty of them for you, Coach."

He nods, then simply makes his way to the elevator to leave Mateo and Isa's penthouse without so much as a proper goodbye.

"Well, that's settled. Looks like we're having a party," Daisy squeals happily.

Luisa twists in my hold and catches my eye. She raises a brow, but keeps her smiling lips shut.

This is definitely going to be a part of our pillow talk tonight.

CHAPTER FORTY-FOUR

LUISA

"I'M NOT SICK."

I try to hold in my laugh and fail. "Nick, you've been blowing your nose all morning. And it looks like you're trying to compete in a Rudolph the Red-Nosed Reindeer competition."

"Am not." He harrumphs, running a hand over his shirtless chest.

"You need to take some cold medicine and get back in bed." I try to steer him out of the kitchen, but he won't budge.

"I am perfectly fine. It's probably allergies."

I narrowly escape the danger zone of his sudden sneeze attack.

"Okay, that's it. I'm staying home today. With my luck, you'll hit a counter while sneezing and I'll have to explain to detectives that my stubborn husband accidentally killed himself and that I swear I didn't do it for the life insurance policy."

He's shaking his head while blowing his nose. "Absolutely not. You have that call with Julian Vega and his agent. You've been preparing all week." He tosses the napkin into the trash, then straightens, suddenly seeming more alert. "You wouldn't call out of work if you were on death's doorstep, so why would you call out for me?" His brows raise subtly when I don't have an immediate answer.

This is how it's been for the past few weeks.

Nick doesn't outright say it, but I know what he's aiming for.

He wants me to admit my real feelings about him, about us.

And while we've continued to fool around every night in bed, he's kept true to his promise of not going any further until I'm ready to treat this marriage like the real deal. Not the arrangement we signed up for, but with boundaries so blurred, it's laughable to believe they were ever even there.

He's right, though. I wouldn't take a sick day for myself, even on the worst days of my PCOS struggles, yet I was ready to stay home and tend to him because he has a simple cold.

Because I know him. I remember him slipping me the details of how much of a baby he turns into when he gets a "man cold."

And I remember Daisy telling us a few months back, before Mateo and Isabella officially got together, that their mother died when Nick was eleven.

His late Dominican mother. The other fact that Daisy accidentally let slip on the night she had a little too much to drink. The night we now refer to as "strikeout," since Mateo came barreling into that bar to whisk Isa away and finally have his wicked way with her.

Nick has slowly slipped in details about his mom here and there, but I know that it's not an easy subject for him to broach, so I haven't pushed for more.

But now, as he stares down at me, his gaze a swirl of suspicion and hope, I wonder if I could actually do it.

Let myself be truly loved by this man. Put my heart in his hands and hope that he doesn't decide to toss it aside the second he gets his hands on his coveted asset, the same one he's yet to fill me in on.

Because even though I trust Nick's words and actions, I can't shake the knowledge of how our marriage came to be. The reason he kept his role as owner of the Monarchs this long, when he had no prior interest in baseball.

Some weird tug-of-war between him and his estranged father for this unnamed *thing* that is the reason for the ring on my finger.

How am I supposed to let myself fall when I don't know what's going to happen once the year is up and Nick has satisfied the terms of the will?

I'm no stranger to being loved by someone, only to have to question if they truly mean it. As a child, my mother would tell me she loved me but could barely make it out of bed most days to walk me to school.

There were times I believed that her depression was stronger than her love for me. Because, in my adolescent mind, I thought that maybe people loved you because they had to, not because they actually felt it.

The same distorted thoughts swirl in my mind now, making me worry that Nick thinks he's developed feelings for me because I'm his wife and his brain has convinced him he has to.

But my heart fights against that idea. I know the feelings I have, the ones I've worked tirelessly to keep below the surface. And if Nick feels a fraction of that for me, then maybe this thing between us can be real.

I have more questions than answers.

So I turn and leave Nick without another word and do what any responsible adult would do in this position.

I call my mom.

"Luisa, you're going to be late," Nick says grumpily as I slowly move through the living room.

The doorbell rings, and Nick takes out his phone to check the security cameras. "No need to check. I know who it is." I walk past the foyer quickly and open the door for my mother.

"Mija, you look so pretty dressed for work. I love when you wear a pink blazer. You pull it off so well." She gives me a big kiss on the cheek as I move around her to take off her coat. She takes me by surprise when she pulls me in for a tight hug. "And thank you for letting me help. I'm so glad I can do this for you. And for Nick." Her eyes beam with unshed happy tears.

This is my mom. The woman who never gave up on me, and, more importantly, never gave up on herself. As much as I told myself I was calling her to help Nick feel better while I'm at work, I know I also needed a reminder as to how far she's come.

She still has her moments, but for the most part, with a combination of therapy and medication, my mom has reclaimed her life and has spent every second I allow showing me how much she loves me.

I let out a slow breath, and the tension I've been holding in my body since my conversation with Nick in the kitchen slowly starts to dissipate.

The sounds of clanking pots and pans have me looking over her shoulder and smiling. Looks like she brought reinforcements.

"Ay Dios mío. Where is the patient?" Tía Marisol dramatically yells.

"I'm making sancocho for him but needed my caldero because I wasn't sure if your fancy pots would get the job done." Tía Gloria brushes past us without a second glance, rushing off to the kitchen to start chopping like a madwoman, I assume.

Nick's look of confusion is endearing. I'm sure his cold medicine–addled brain is trying to catch on to what's happening, so I move over to him and tug on his hand. "I'm going to work, but I called in the troops to help you feel better."

His eyes scan the main level of our home. One aunt in the kitchen creating beautiful chaos. Another in the living room, plugging in a humidifier that's older than me but surely trusted and true. And my mother unloading an oversized tote bag filled with wellness goodies.

"What's going on?" His voice sounds clogged with emotion.

I frame his face with my hands and see the longing written across his features. I place a soft kiss on his cheek and lean back. "We're taking care of you, Nick."

I swear his eyes glisten as he wraps me in a fierce hug, trapping the laughter in my chest. "Release me at once, you ogre. I don't want to get sick." I start to squirm when he rains down kisses along my neck.

"You kissed me first. And besides, we're married. My germs are your germs."

I finally wiggle free just as Tía Marisol comes barreling toward Nick. "Okay, time for the *vivaporu*."

"For the what now?" He panics.

I giggle. "Vicks VapoRub. Cures all. Oh, incoming…"

My aunt slathers a generous amount on Nick's chest, turning his eyes into saucers.

"Wife, help. I don't know what's happening here. Is she lubing me up?"

My giggles turn into unrestrained laughter.

"Ay, tranquilo. I'm being thorough. Got to get rid of this big, bad cold." She emphasizes the last three words by slapping his chest with both hands. "Toma, take the rest." She hands him the brand-new container. "Stick a bit up your nose."

"Is that what the instructions say to do? Because I don't think this should be going into any body parts."

She clicks her tongue. "Ay, you'll be fine. Let me know when you need me to reapply." She smiles as she walks off to the kitchen.

"No, I think I'll have it handled from here," he yells after her.

My poor husband seems so scared. Standing shirtless with a glistening chest, holding onto a small Vicks as he mouths, "Help me."

I wiggle my fingers at him before I close the door behind me. This should be fun.

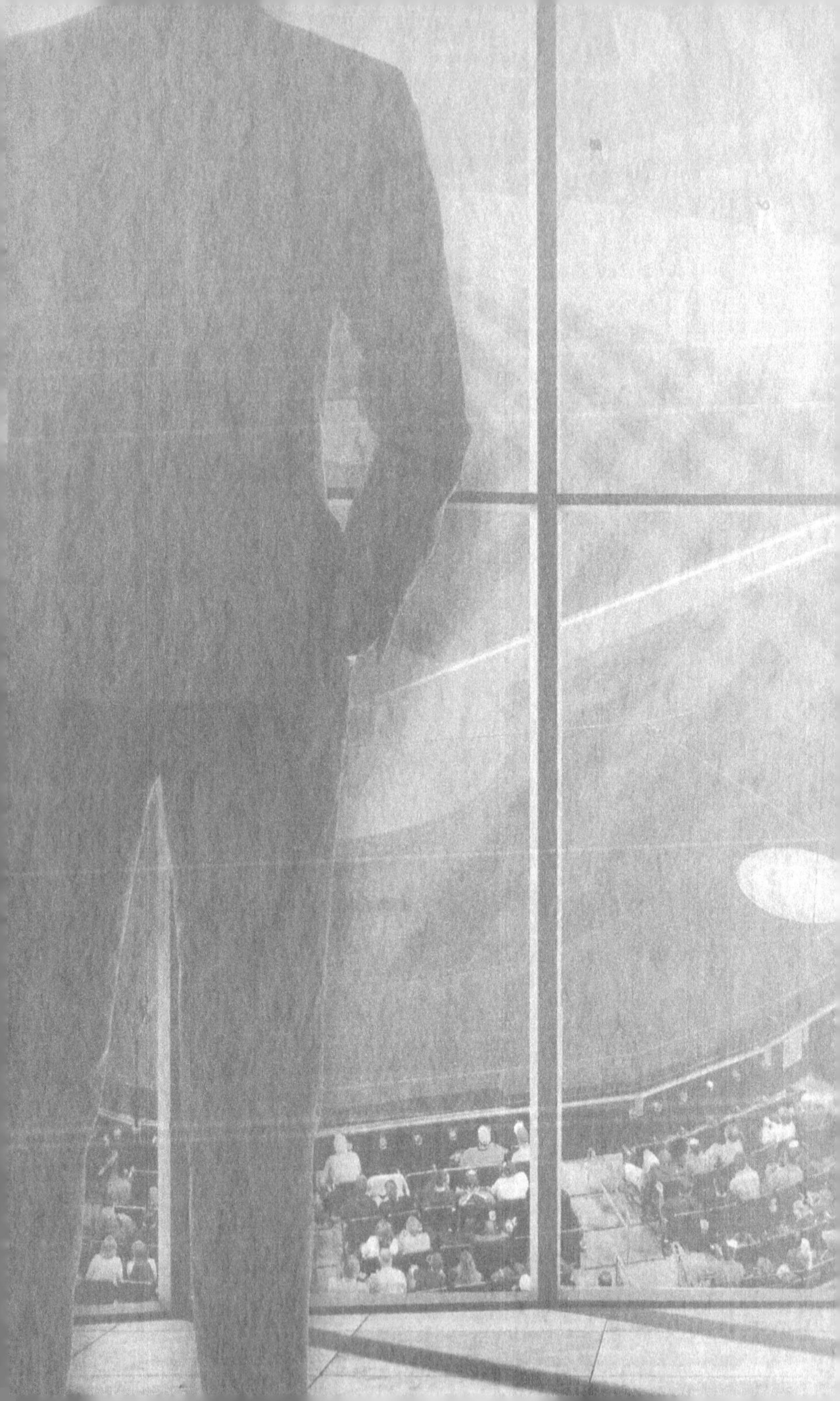

NICK

I'M ALLERGIC TO DUST.

And I made the mistake of opening a box in my office closet that holds old company files. I had forgotten how dusty they've gotten over the years. But by the time I found the file I was looking for, it was already too late.

The sneezing and watery eyes had taken over.

I knew if I took a simple antihistamine pill, I would be good as new within the hour.

It really was only allergies, but there's no chance in hell I'll stop my wife and her family from fussing over me.

In fact, I'm going to take great pleasure in it.

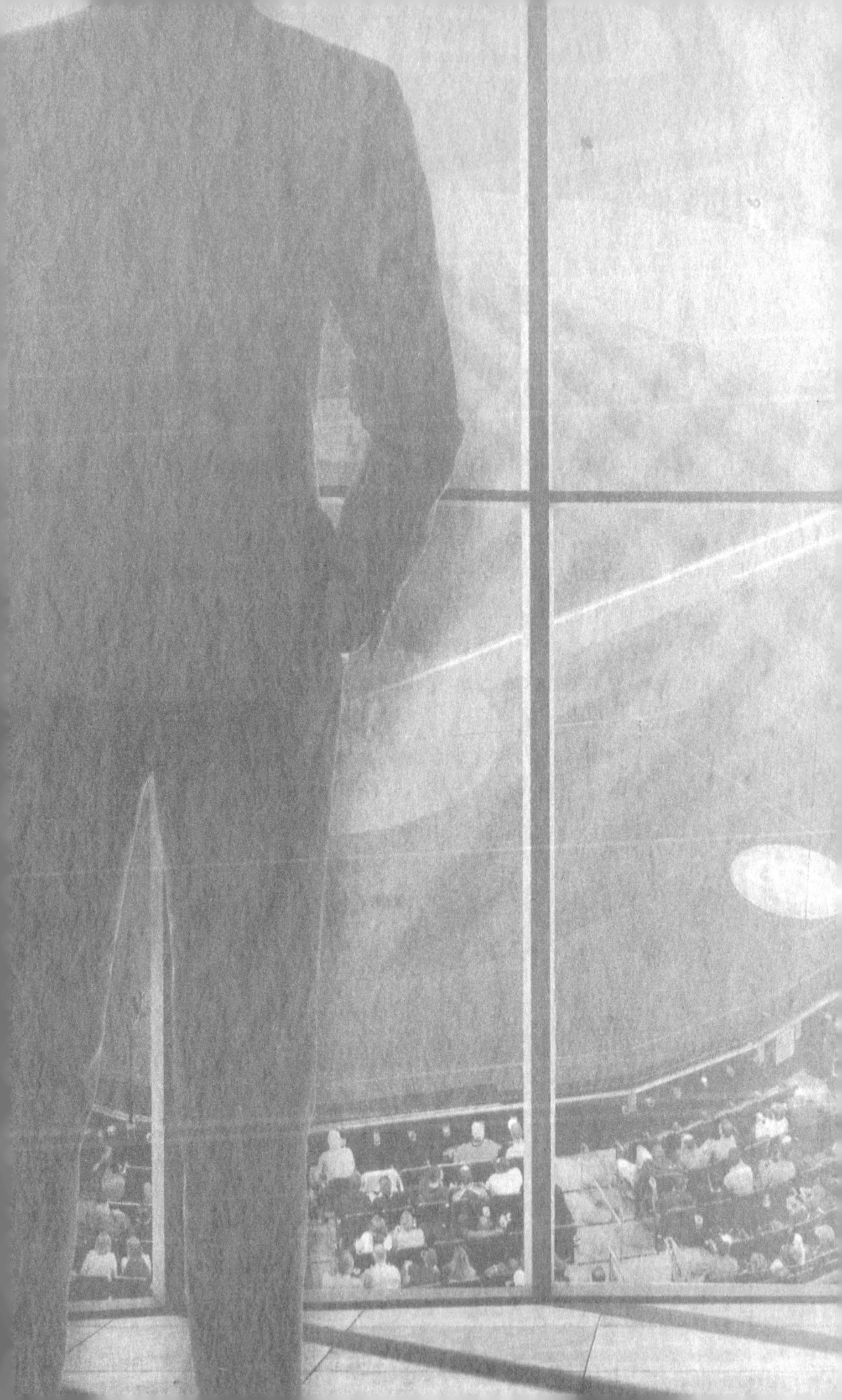

CHAPTER FORTY-SIX

NICK

I'M WOKEN BY THE faint feeling of lips on my forehead.

My arm instantly reaches out, because I'd know my wife's touch anywhere.

She yelps as I pull her down to our large, plush couch and spoon her aggressively. "Mmm, wifey's home." I tuck her laughing body impossibly close.

"I see someone is feeling better." I don't have to open my eyes to know she's smiling.

"I am. I love your family. Even your handsy aunt. They fixed me up. Made me feel better."

"You're talking like a toddler. How much cold medicine did they give you?"

"Haven't needed any. After my first nap, I felt much better. Good as new. Then they hit me with two servings of sancocho. By then, I swear I was fully cured. But once I told them I haven't had a home-cooked Dominican meal in almost two decades, they proceeded to make enough food for an army."

"And you ate it all?" she asks in astonishment.

I nod happily. "And I ate it all. Made me sleepy and my brain a little fuzzy in the best way possible. I haven't had a nap this nice in ages, much less two of them in one day."

She traces invisible doodles on my arm that's currently holding her flush against me. "Glad to hear it."

I blink my eyes open and lift my head slightly to look down at her. "Are you tired? It's been a long day. How did the meeting go?"

She sighs, and I don't miss how she sinks into my chest, hopefully seeking comfort. "It went well. I think we can snag Vega, especially since he used to play with Martinez and Torres. Said his current team is missing that camaraderie, and I know we have that in spades."

"Then what's the problem?"

"Did I say there was a problem?" She scratches my forearm lightly, and I almost forget to speak. It's nice to be touched by Luisa without an audience to prove our relationship to.

"No, you didn't. But I know my wife, and there's more to it."

She sighs again. "Just Richard being Richard. He scouted a player years ago that finally made it to the major leagues but is warming the benches in Colorado, and he wants me to sign him instead. Claims he'd be cheaper too since he's basically still a rookie." I take a deep breath, preparing to ask why the hell Richard's opinion even matters when she is the boss, when she continues. "But enough about work. Tell me what else happened while I was gone."

I would have continued to push, but when she places a tiny kiss on my bicep and nuzzles into it like it's a pillow, I relent. "Let's see." I think back on the day that had me feeling like a kid again. "I offered to help in the kitchen, and Tía Gloria threatened me with her spatula. Your mom made me drink an absurd amount of water, followed by two delicious lemon ginger teas. I've never needed to urinate as often as I did when she was done with me. Think she was really trying to flush the germs out of my body. But I'm sure they fled once they knew they were surrounded by lethal Dominican mothers."

"Oh yes, the teas are the best when you have a sore throat or when the dreary and cold, endless January rolls around."

"I'll keep that in mind." I kiss the back of her head. "We all ate here in the living room and watched one of Tía Marisol's telenovelas."

She scoffs. "Oh, yeah, right."

"You don't believe me?"

"All right, then tell me what happened on the show."

"Ricardo was caught cheating on Valentina. But he didn't know that Valentina had an evil twin named Carol, who was pretending to be her sister to get revenge on Valentina for not taking the rap for a crime she committed and therefore served five years in prison for. Christian's wife was kidnapped, and she was so distressed, she went into labor. Her first love, Carlos, put his feelings aside to help save Asusena. They got there in time to save her and deliver her baby, but the baby came out looking a tad darker than anticipated, and Christian is light-skinned. Do you know who does have dark features, though?"

She gasps. "Carlos?"

"Bingo."

Her body vibrates with silent laughter. "Oh my God. How many episodes did you watch?"

I shrugged. "One. I was dozing off by the time one of the grandmothers on the show revealed that she had a secret son who was now a local serial killer. Your family told me to rest while they packed up and prepared to leave. Guess I've been out since then."

"Seems like you had quite the adventure."

"I did." I pause. "Thank you, by the way."

"For what?"

"For taking care of me. Knowing exactly what I needed. For... making me feel like I had a mother again. Three, even. It made me miss my mom so much, while also feeling at peace, knowing that she'd be thrilled that I've somehow landed in the hands of such an incredible and loving family."

I can feel Luisa suck in a breath, and I fear she's stopped breathing.

"You can ask me about her, you know."

I feel her exhale. "You're a private person. And I don't want to pry. And... please promise you won't be mad at Daisy. This was totally an innocent slip, but she mentioned how your mother was Dominican. And I've always wondered why you've never mentioned it. And since you haven't, I figured you didn't want to talk about her."

"She did? That's... good. Really nice, actually. Daisy doesn't remember our mom, so it's nice to hear that she talks about her."

"She didn't say anything, really. She clamped up right after that tidbit slipped."

I hum. "My mother was my favorite person on the planet. For the longest time, it was just her and me. She was the person who helped me with my homework, took the tube with me to after-school activities, and took care of me when I was sick." I give her a gentle squeeze. "She was the smartest woman in every room she walked into. Put herself through law school while being a single parent, barely making enough money on the side to provide for the both of us. She tried to feed me well-balanced meals while hers consisted of instant noodles and anything that could be microwaved or came in a can. Little did she know that I secretly loved those cheap noodles and would have enjoyed eating them alongside her.

"She sacrificed every day of her life so she could become a barrister and provide a better life for us. Even though, at that age, I still thought we had a pretty decent life. I knew we were piss poor, but we were happy. Unfortunately, she had a blind spot in her brilliance, and that was my father."

I swear I feel her growl like a kitten beneath me, and I relish in her protectiveness. "I never knew he existed until my mother came home and told me she was pregnant with Daisy. That's also when I put together the fact that my father was rich. Came from old money. The kind that wouldn't acknowledge a child out of wedlock, much less to a dark-skinned Afro-Latina woman."

"What? All that time, he knew? And you guys—"

"Yes. He knew about me from the time my mother saw two pink lines on a pregnancy stick, and he never once made the effort to meet me or, at the bare minimum, make sure my mother and I could put food on the table. And it wouldn't have mattered if he had stayed gone. But somehow, he wormed his way back into my mother's heart and got her pregnant. This time, he promised to be involved and take a role in my life. Which was the first of the many lies my father would come to tell me over the years. He rarely showed his face after I met him. Forgetting to visit on my birthday or call for Christmas. I swear it was better when I thought he never existed, because then I wouldn't have to feel like he knew of me and still wanted nothing to do with me."

"Oh, Nick." Luisa turns over, facing me. "Your father is an imbecile and has no idea what he's missed out on."

"My mother... she was hit by a car that failed to stop at a red light while she was crossing a busy intersection. Here one moment and gone the next." I inhale deeply and slowly work to release it. "After she passed, things moved rather quickly. My father took us under his care, since the local news had caught on that he had two children who were left without a mother. A fact his second wife wasn't too fond of. The story spread widely among London society. He planned to send me to Connecticut for boarding school, and I begged him to send Daisy with me. I didn't want my baby sister, the last living, breathing piece of my mother, to be left in his callous hands. And he much too happily obliged, setting her up with a full-time nanny and enrolling her in the same boarding school as soon as she was able to walk."

Her fingers scratch lightly over my short beard. "I hate him. I wish I could come up with something more profound to match the feelings within me right now, but I think we can kick-start with hate."

I smooth the frown on her lips. "Don't give him the honor of having any feelings designated for him. He gets your indifference at best. And besides, life gave him a little taste of karma when his son became a self-made billionaire. I relied on some of those connections I made in boarding school, of course, and I'm not naïve enough to believe that having that leg up didn't help propel me. But I fostered those relationships and made people believe in me. And when it was time to find investors, my company had no shortage of them. Within five years of finishing grad school, I was running a billion-dollar media empire. While my father's generational family fortune of twenty million pounds was the cost of a small network I could buy on a slow day at work."

"Pfft. A measly twenty million. Get outta here," she says in an exaggerated New Yorker accent.

"Yes, yes, I know. Stupid money." I chuckle, but then feel her tense under me. "What is it, Luisa?" My eyes search her face for a clue.

She opens her mouth, as if waiting for the words to fall out. After a deep breath, her soft gaze meets mine. "Thank you. For sharing a bit of your mom with me. It makes me so happy to know that my family was able to provide a sense of comfort for you." She smiles weakly. "Even though I'm sure you like acting like a big baby."

"Luisa." I warn lightly, knowing she's beating around the bush.

She sighs. "Why are we married?" I jerk back, not expecting that question. "I mean, I know why… but I also don't. You said it was for something you lost and wanted to get back. That could be a diamond or a thoroughbred horse, and frankly, I don't think you'd go through all the trouble of owning a baseball team for either of those things when you can buy anything on the planet."

"Angel—"

She leans away from me and settles into a seated position on the couch. "I mean, sure, there is much to say about sentimental value. But was it really worth marrying me? I keep wondering, what could be so precious that you'd—"

"A house."

"A house?" Luisa deflates slightly, and I shake my head.

"The house my mother grew up in and the piece of land it sits on in the mountains of Jarabacoa."

Her eyes widen. "Oh, Nick."

My smile holds no warmth. "I was an idiot. My mother left that house in her will for Daisy and me, and I lost it on a bet with my father. He cheated, since he had insider information on the company we were competing to acquire. He knew he would be stealing another piece of my mother from me, and he did it with a smile on his face. I knew my father played dirty, knew he didn't have a noble bone in his body, and yet I still stooped to his level and engaged with him in this stupid bet, and for what? To prove what I already knew about us? That I'm a better man than he'll ever be, and when it comes to business, I'll always come out on top? Well, I guess I was wrong. A part of me will always be my father's son." I drop my head in my hands and feel the weight of my actions fall onto my shoulders.

"Hey, you stop that right now," Luisa scolds.

"Stop what?" I can't even bear looking at her now that I've admitted what I've done. But you bet your ass my head snaps up when I hear her next words.

"Don't you dare talk about my husband like that."

A heady mixture of shock and frustration fills my chest. "Careful, wife. For a second there, you almost had me believing you didn't think this marriage was fake. Or are we done lying and ready to call this what it is?"

"Nick." She struggles to take in a full breath. "We signed a contract. We're supposed to divorce in less than a year. You get your… your mother's house, and after that—" She places a hand on her stomach and steadies her breathing. She closes her eyes and asks, "And what happens when you get your house signed over to you? You no longer need to be married to me." Her eyes stare back with unshed tears. "What am I supposed to do, then?" she whispers.

I move in closer, my body vibrating with the need for her to hear me loud and clear. "Real, Luisa. This marriage is fucking real to me and has been for a very long time. And maybe I've been a little hypocritical, waiting for you to say the words that I'm so desperate to hear from you. But I'll remedy it right now." I grab my phone off the coffee table and pull up my email. I punch at my screen so strongly, I'm surprised my screen doesn't crack as I hit Send All.

Luisa's eyes dart between me and my phone. "What are you doing? What about the contract? You said it yourself that this was supposed to be a fair trade."

"Oh yeah? Well, fuck fair. And any little thing that comes between you and me."

Luisa's phone dings once with a notification. Then twice. She ignores it as she stares back at me.

I nod to her phone. "You might want to check that soon. It's only going to ring 133 more times."

"What are you talking about?" She finally reaches for her phone and freezes when she sees my name flashing across her screen, one incoming email after the other.

"I started talking to my therapist again after I left for London. After I realized I fucked up." Her mouth opens slightly at my admission. "When you wouldn't speak to me, I realized that running from my feelings had finally caught up to me. For a long time, I was fine bullshitting myself, but once I realized that my coping mechanism, my way to survive emotional distress affected you, I knew it was time to check back in with my doc and get my head screwed on straight. I'm sure she wasn't expecting I'd request multiple sessions a week via video conference." I manage a small smile at the look of shock on her face and the nonstop notifications I've caused.

"But the absence of you made for far too much free time in my head. I missed talking to you whenever I wanted, even if it was from behind the guise of my pestering emails. So... I wrote you anyway. Every day, multiple times a day, and left them in my drafts folder. If you asked me then, I wouldn't be able to tell you why I did it. But ask me now."

A tear runs down her cheek, but she doesn't move to swipe it away. Her eyes bore into mine as she finally dares to ask. "Why did you do it, Nick? Why did you write me every day?"

"Because I love you."

CHAPTER FORTY-SEVEN

LUISA

I suck in a shocked breath. "Nick."

"Have for a very long time, if I'm being honest." He nods to my phone, whose ringer seems like it's about to go on the fritz with the barrage of emails coming its way. "That man had no idea what this was, but knew he had lost something much too valuable to let go of."

My heart is beating faster than the notifications are coming in. The realization that Nick's feelings for me started long before we got married. Enough for him to seek help and work on himself. Not knowing that life would throw us this curveball and we'd end up married to one another.

Meaning he doesn't have this displaced feeling of loving me simply out of duty. Simply because I'm his wife.

Proving that I can trust his actions and words above the doubts that unjustly roam free in my mind.

I'm stunned by the revelation.

Of how his feelings seem to perfectly match my own.

But he must mistake my silence for rejection.

He places a soft kiss on my forehead and stays there as he speaks. "Read them. Please. There is no long, thought-out love declaration in any of them, but maybe if you look close enough, you can see what we were both too scared to admit.

That it has always been us. From the very beginning. From that first night in the bar. The night that changed our lives forever."

He stands, and I immediately miss the warmth and comfort only his closeness provides.

"Read them. I'll give you some space. I'll even sleep in the guest room if you need time to process it all. But please, just... read them." He leaves and makes his way up the stairs, only the sound of my phone and my breathing heard in the empty room.

I silence my phone and immediately open the first email.

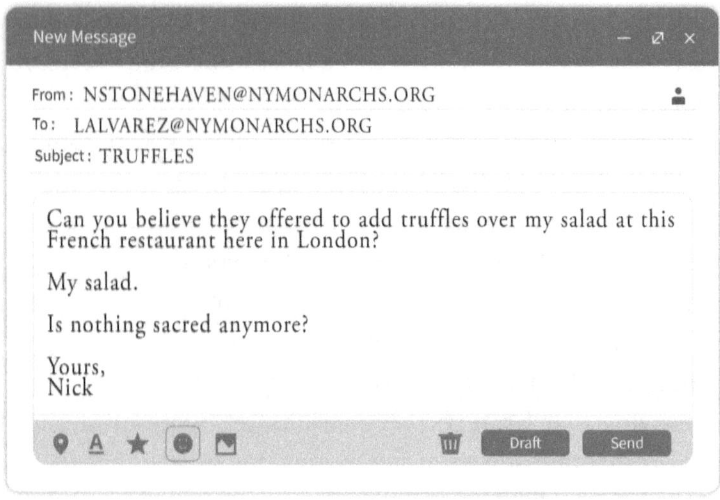

I don't blink as I swipe up to the next one.

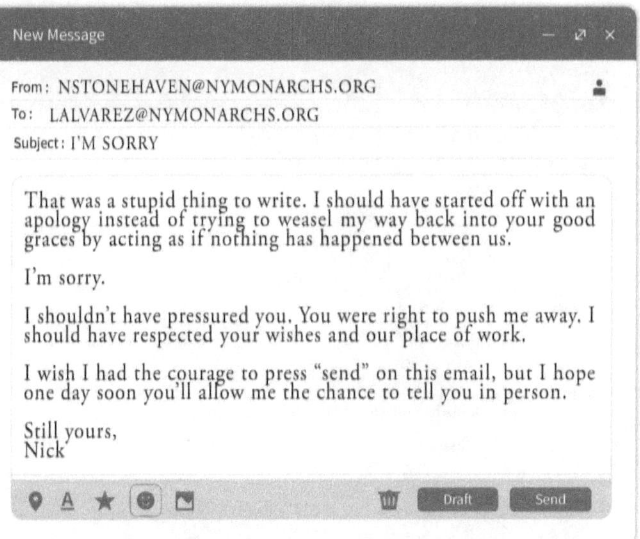

I move on to the next one.

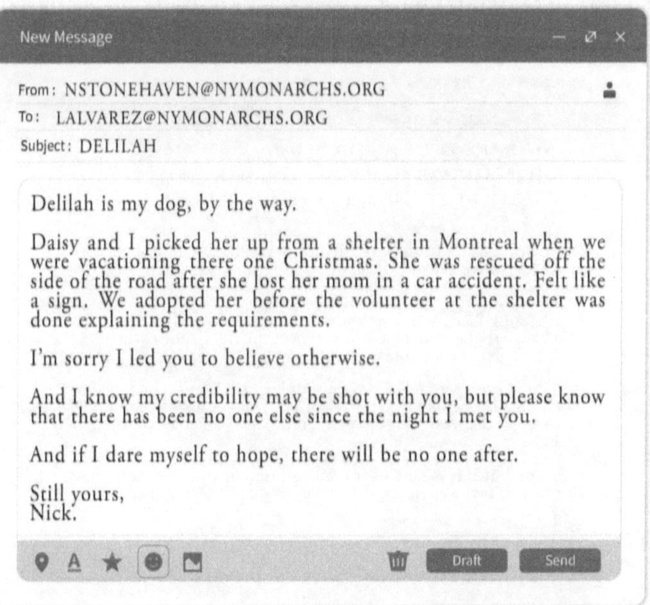

And the next one.

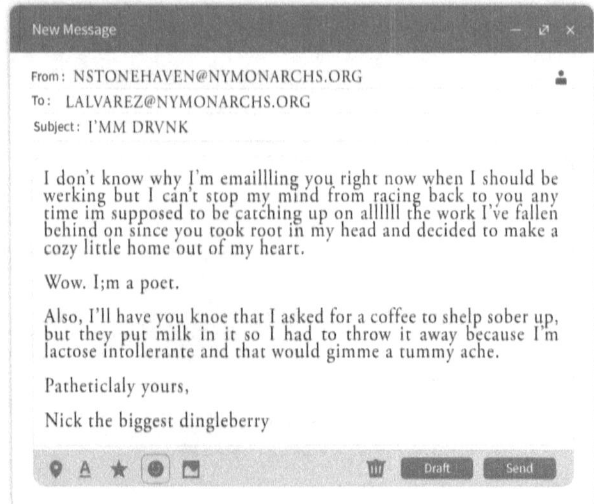

A hard laugh escapes from deep in my chest at the same time a tear hits my screen. I wipe it away, accidentally skipping a few dozen emails.

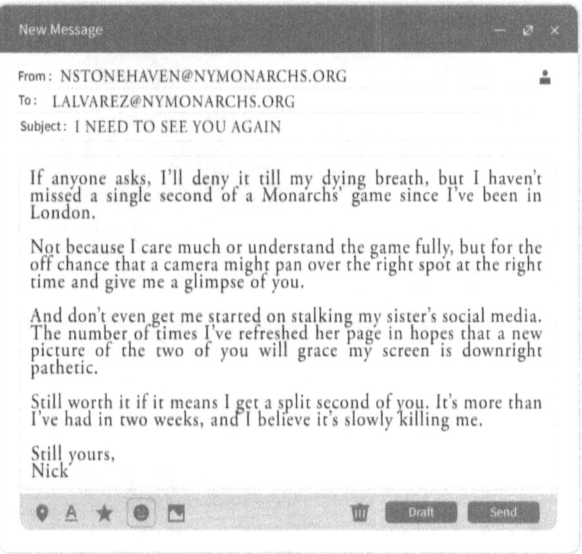

And the one right after.

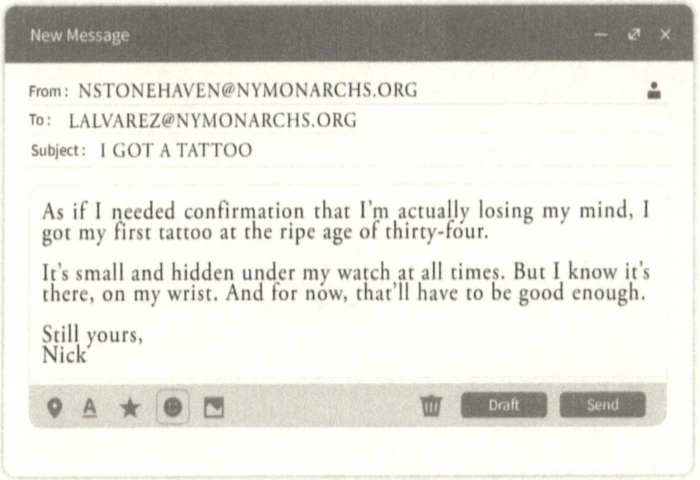

Nick is always wearing a fancy watch, only taking it off and placing it on his nightstand when he gets in bed. I make a note to take a peek as soon as I'm done reading these emails.

I promise myself I'll only read a few more. I'll be here all night if I read them all, and my heart is screaming at me to go find Nick.

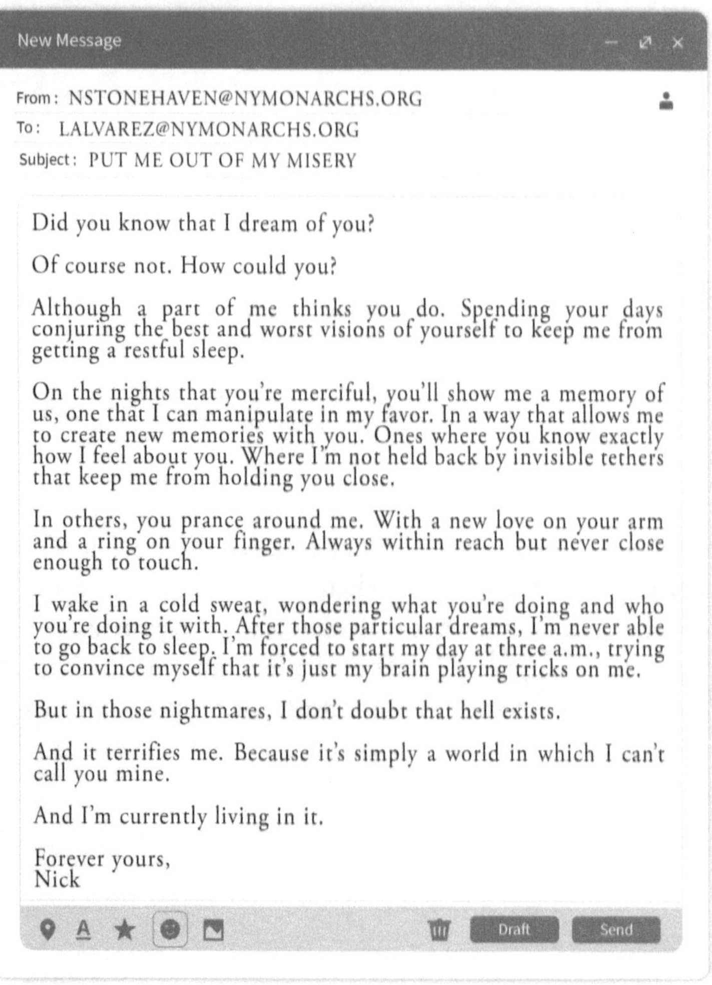

I cover my mouth to hold in the cry trapped in the back of my throat.

My mind tells me to stop, but my eyes skate past every word at my disposal.

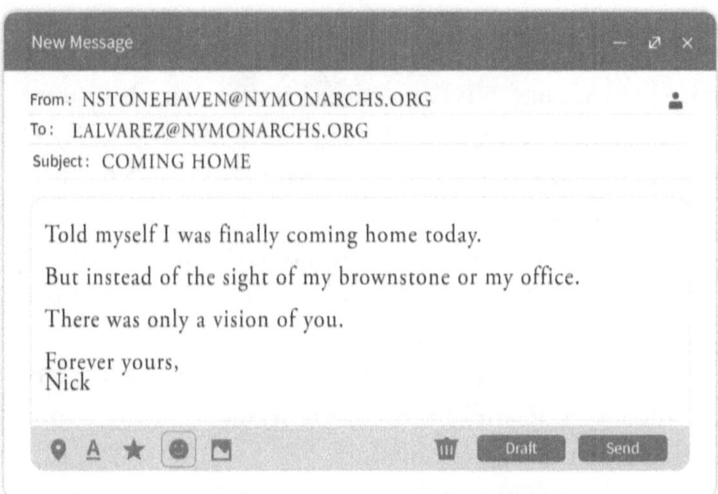

My fingers are trembling so badly I accidentally send the screen flying up and select an older email.

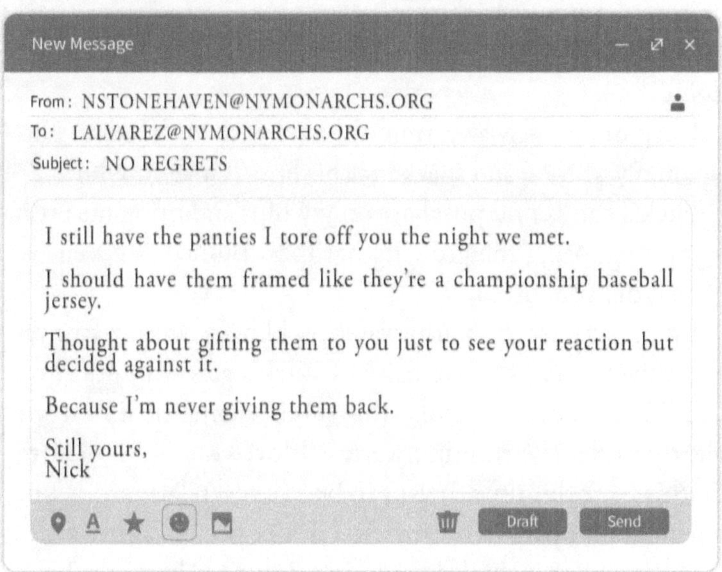

That absurd email was exactly what I needed to finally move from the couch and run up the stairs.

Delilah is hot on my heels, thinking we must be playing some kind of game, but I don't need her to see what her parents are about to do next, so I walk her to her dog bed in Nick's office and toss her a new toy from a stash I have hidden in here.

Once she's settled, I enter our bedroom and close the door behind me. I don't see Nick but can hear the shower running.

I'm pulling my blouse over my head as I make my way over to our bathroom.

Steam billows around Nick. His hands are braced on the tiled wall, his head bowed, the water from the rainfall showerhead sluicing over him.

The sound of my pants hitting the ground has him snapping his head up, his red-rimmed eyes boring into mine.

I peel out of my underwear and bra quickly and open the door to the expansive shower.

"Luisa," Nick starts, his voice gone hoarse. "What are you doing?"

I step under the water, frame his face with my hands as I lift up on my tiptoes, and speak into his lips. "I love you, Nick."

Nick's hands find purchase on my hips and bring me flush to him, ignoring the growing hardness pinned between us. "What did you just say?"

I blink against the warm water trickling down my face yet still shiver under the intensity of Nick's gaze. "I said I love you," I say more forcefully this time, hoping he'll hear me clearly under the running water. "I love you and I want to do this right this time. I want to be in a real relationship, one where I don't have to tell myself that I'm playing a role when, in reality, I don't think I could imagine a world where I was no longer your wife. Because I'm in love with you, and now you're stuck with me. So I hope you really meant it when you said—"

His lips crash onto mine, and I'm consumed by the ferocity of his kiss.

He backs me up against the slick tiled wall without leaving a sliver of space between us. My hands curl around the back of his neck as he angles us to deepen our kiss.

I moan into his lips when he lifts me higher, and my legs instinctively wrap around his hips.

His cock bumps my entrance, and we both gasp at the sensation.

His eyes meet mine, and a kaleidoscope of emotions reflects back at me.

Hope, relief, lust, and love.

I place a soft kiss on his neck, then whisper into his ear. "Please."

He leans back. "Please, what?"

I search his eyes, the same ones I hope to stare into for the rest of my life. "You really love me?"

His hands tighten on my hips. "This love... it fills my chest with worry. Worry that I won't have enough time to show you all the ways in which I can love you. Having to settle with this lifetime to love you deeply. Only hoping I will find you in the next and the one after that to prove my point." His forehead rests against mine. "I love you so much, it sometimes hurts to breathe. Knowing that you're walking around freely in this world with my heart firmly clasped in your hands while blissfully unaware of the power you hold over me. You've created a space in my heart that no longer knows how to survive without you. My love for you is firmly embedded in every fiber of my being. And I promise to make sure you feel it every day for the rest of our lives."

"Good," I whisper wobbly. "Then start now."

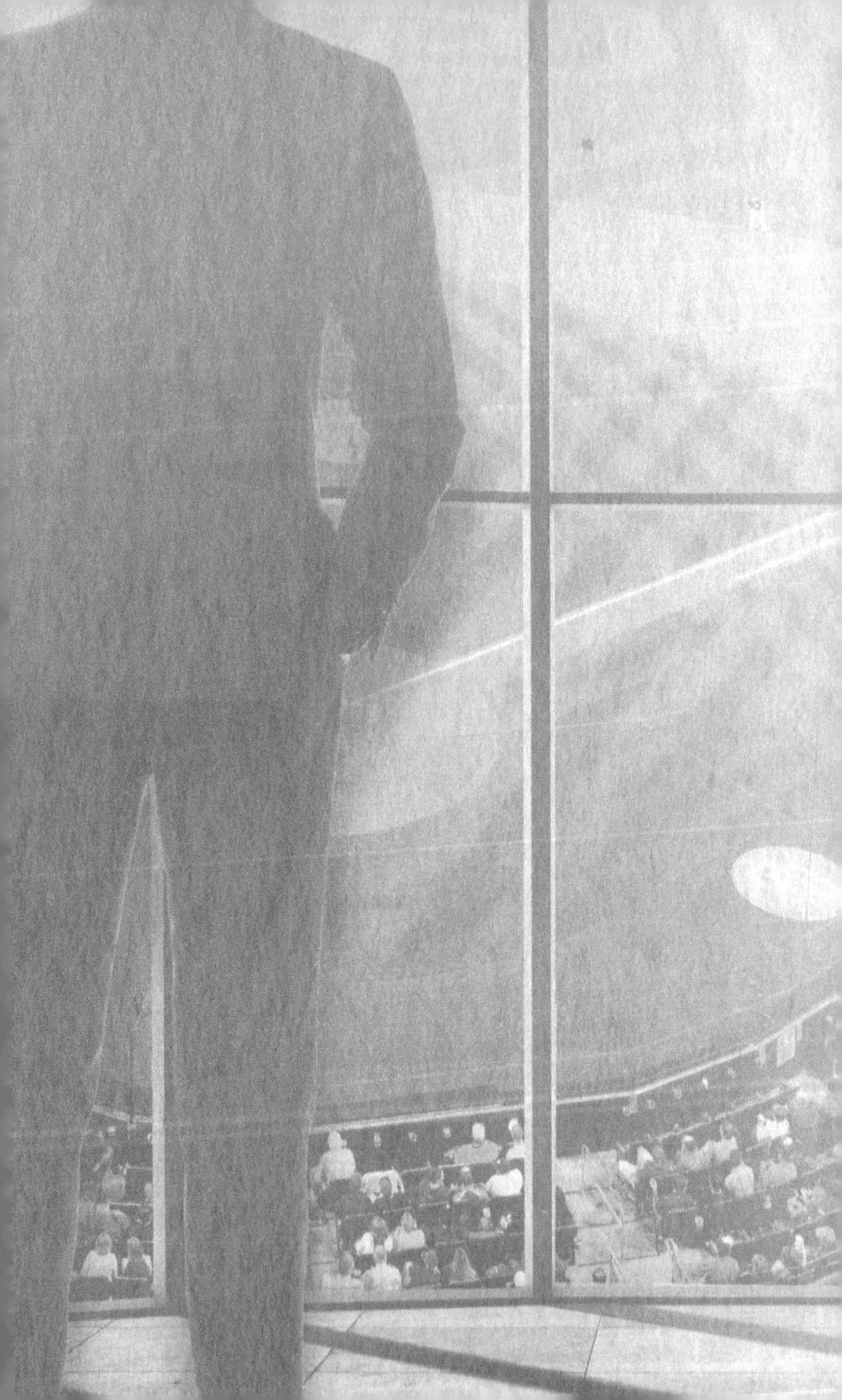

CHAPTER FORTY-EIGHT

NICK

EVEN WHILE DECLARING HER love for me, my wife knows how to drive me wild.

I bring her down slowly onto my hard cock.

But I stop when I see a flash of pain on her face.

"No, don't stop. Keep going, please. You're, well, you know."

I smirk. "No, wife. I don't know what you're referring to. Care to explain?"

She scrunches her face. "Not the time to gloat. You know that you're so bi—ah, oh my God, yes!" She screams as I drop her all the way down onto my cock, and I curse myself for thinking I wouldn't be just as affected by finally being buried in her tight pussy. Fucking bare, relishing her silky heat.

"Move. Baby, please," she pleads.

I lean her weight on the wall behind her and bracket my forearms beside her head as her arms keep a tight hold around my neck and I thrust into her.

She called me baby.

I go deeper.

She fucking loves me.

I take my right arm and hook her leg over it and pin it back against the wall, opening her up more and letting me hit that spot deep in her pussy that drove her wild the first time I fucked her.

"Yes, Nick. Right there. Oh God, this feels so good."

"Not Nick. Call me baby again." I grunt.

She smirks, looking far too pleased with herself as she bites her lower lip. I lean down to swipe her mouth open with my lips and nip her. "Just like that, baby. You know how to fuck me so good." She moans with her eyes closed as she shakes her head from side to side. "I'm so close. Please."

"Open your eyes, Angel. Look at me when you come."

Her eyes open, and her pussy flutters as she stares at my wrist next to her head.

I clench my teeth and keep my own release at bay as her mouth drops open and she whips her head toward me. "Nick, is that—"

"My tattoo. Was wondering when you were going to notice it."

"But it's. It's—"

"Your name, between two angel wings. In your handwriting, since I kept the note you left me at the hotel."

Her eyes start to water. "Nick." She gasps as her pussy begins to contract around me, and I know she's ready.

"Come for me, wife. Come for your husband. You've made your mark on my body. Time for me to do the same."

She screams my name as she comes, her vise-like grip on my cock triggering my release along with hers. I continue to slowly pump into her until our labored breaths begin to slow down.

I slowly drop her leg, wrapping it around my hip once more, but don't pull out of her yet.

"Nick. I don't know what to say." She looks back at the tattoo.

"Yes, you do." I cradle her face in my hands and kiss her gently.

She moves slightly and places a quick kiss to her tattooed name. "I love you."

My chest threatens to explode with happiness. "I know." She quirks a brow. "You got your hair wet just to tell me."

She laughs, and the motion has us both wincing.

I slide out of her, and she makes a small sound of protest.

"Are you sore? Was I too rough?" I ask as I scan her body for signs of discomfort.

She rolls her eyes. "You've kept me deprived of that kind of sex for far too long. Try to withhold from me one more time and see what happens."

I chuckle. "Is that a threat, my sweet little wife?"

She smiles, a real, adorable, unguarded smile, and I find myself doing the same. She untangles herself from my body and stands on unsteady legs. "Oh hush. And pass me the shampoo. Tomorrow was hair wash day anyway, so I was really only moving my schedule up."

I pour a generous amount of shampoo into my hands.

"Hey, watch it! That stuff's expensive."

I give her an unimpressed look. "I think I can swing it."

She mutters something about stupid billionaires, but I cut her off when I start massaging the shampoo into her scalp. "I'm sorry. What were you saying, Angel?"

"Nothing. You must be hearing things. It's that post-sex delirium getting to you."

I swat her ass, and she squeals.

After I rinse out her conditioner, I step out of the shower and hold up a towel for her. She wraps it around herself, then takes the second one offered for her hair.

"You know, you could have put a towel around that monster cock that's pointing my way before handing me mine."

I look down at my bobbing length and shrug. "My wife always comes first." I wink salaciously at her as she finishes towel drying her hair, only to toss it my way.

"My husband. The little exhibitionist." She pulls out a hair dryer. "Can you get us some water? I'm going to diffuse my hair before bed, don't want to catch that cold you had earlier." My smile widens, and Luisa catches my eye in the mirror. "Why are you looking at me like that?"

"I'll tell you later. After I tell you about my dust allergy."

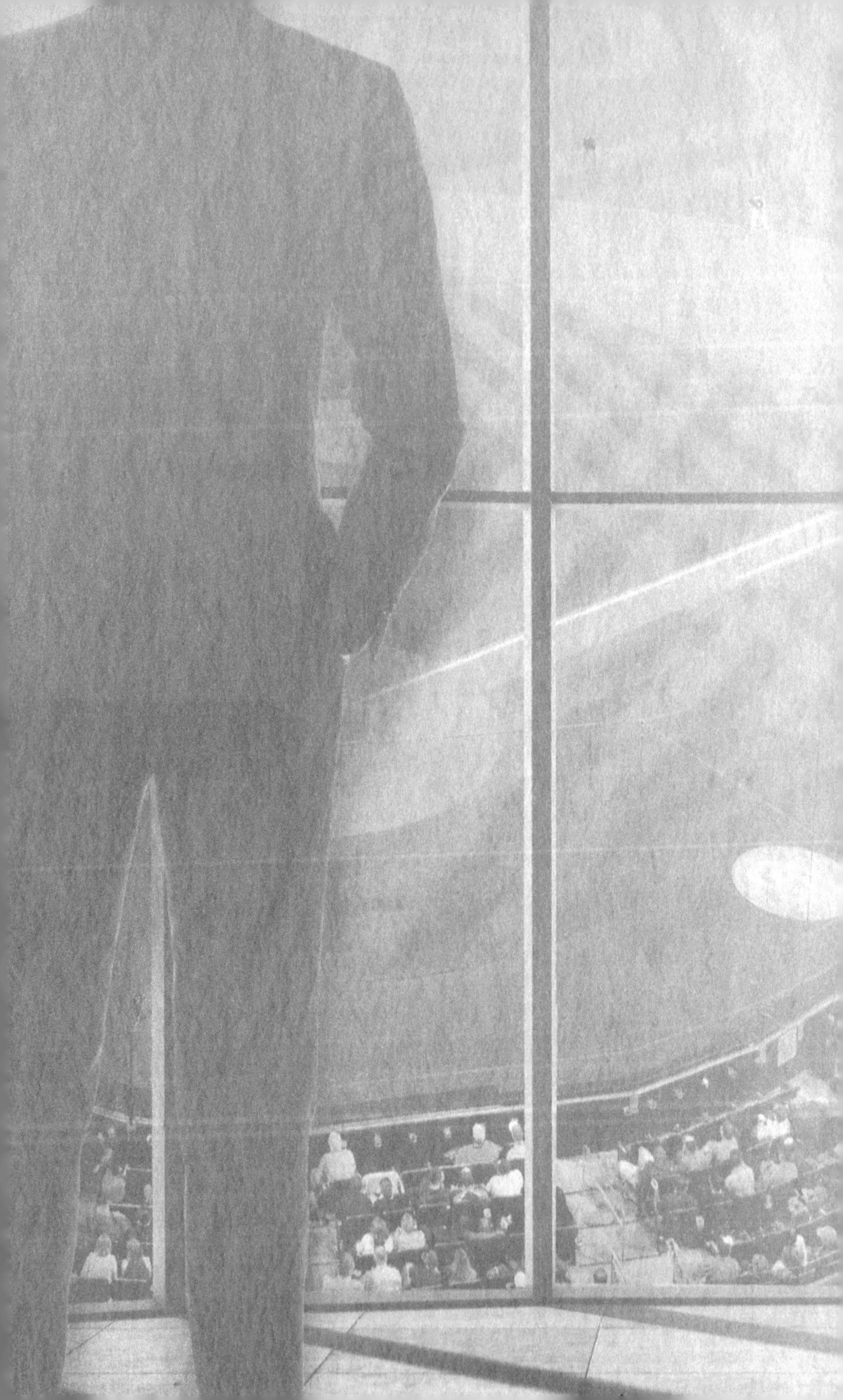

CHAPTER FORTY-NINE

NICK

Dominican Thanksgiving came and went in a blur.

I played dominoes with Luisa's dad and uncles and even managed to win a few times. I wooed the aunts by showing off the limited number of merengue moves I remembered from when I was a kid. And Daisy surprised us with an appearance after Damien was snowed in while working some nonexistent campaign trail out in Albany and couldn't join her for the small festivity she had planned for them. Luckily Luisa found out via the women's group chat and barged into the apartment Daisy shares with Damien and brought her over to our place with a weekend bag in tow.

It was nice to see my sister interact with my new family. I almost shed a tear when I saw her hang on to Clarissa for a few beats longer than usual when Luisa's mother pulled her in for a hug to greet her. Pretty sure I had to clear my throat when Clarissa only held her tighter.

We all laughed, and the women cried—happy tears, of course—and had possibly the best holiday of my life.

Now we're deep into dreary December, and I find myself staring at my wife as she moves around the kitchen.

She catches me staring and smiles. "I made coffee." She raises a mug in my direction and I meet her over by the counter.

I take the offered cup and fake pout. "No milk?"

She chuckles as she softly blows on the steaming liquid in her mug. "I can't believe you let me put milk in your coffee when you're lactose intolerant. And that I had to find out via a drunken email."

I take her cup from her hands and place both on the counter, then pull her into my arms. "The things we do for love, I suppose." I kiss her and enjoy the smile I feel on her lips as she kisses me back.

"Okay, Casanova. We only have a few minutes before we need to get out of here. We can't be late to our own bachelor and bachelorette parties, especially since we're the ones hosting."

"I thought this was supposed to be a joint event. Why Daisy decided to separate us for the first half of the day is beyond me," I grumble.

"It's a girls' brunch. She hardly thought she was excluding you boys from French toast and mimosas," she deadpans.

I burrow my face into her neck. "But this is different now. We are different now. I want to enjoy our very real parties to celebrate our very real marriage. I know we're doing it a bit backwards, but that seems to be the trend with our relationship, and I wouldn't change a single thing if it meant we ended up right here." I tighten my arms around her.

"I know, and that's very sweet of you." She pauses a bit too long for my woman, who has no problem stringing along sentences. Usually, ones that are much wittier and quicker than mine. "But let's just focus on hosting. Today should really be about Isabella, and even Daisy, who refuses to let us celebrate her. They're the real brides."

My head snaps up and my eyes flare. But she's quick to notice her mistake. "Luisa—"

"No, I know what you're going to say. I'm a real bride too. I'm just saying we're already married."

"Okay, fine. Then marry me again."

She chuckles, then stiffens in my arms at the look on my face. "You can't be serious."

"No, you're right about something there. You are a real wife, but you never got the opportunity to be a real bride. So let's plan it. You deserve to have those experiences. The wedding, the parties, the—you know, the whole shebang." I stop myself from saying a proposal. I have yet to figure that one out, and I don't want to tip her off in the slightest.

"Nick, I don't need all of that stuff. I'm happy. Truly."

She's on the second day of her period, so I know I'm playing dirty when I try to pull on her very sensitive heartstrings. "Don't you want your dad to walk you down the aisle? Go shopping for a dress with your mom? Have a weekend getaway with your girlfriends where you wear embarrassing tiaras and sashes and walk around with a cut-out picture of me?"

Her eyes immediately fill with tears and she points a threatening finger at my face. "I haven't called you the devil in a long time, but even Lucifer wouldn't go that low."

I smile as I place a gentle kiss on her forehead. "Pretty sure you were calling me a demon of some sort last week when I put that pink toy up your—" Her hand slaps over my mouth, but I pull it back down. "Say yes. Walk down an aisle to me, in front of our friends and family."

Delilah whines from somewhere behind the counter where I can't see her, and Luisa giggles.

"And our beautiful and definitely not needy pup." I shake my head. "What do you say? Will you marry this cheeky bastard for love this time?"

She smiles up at me, eyes twinkling with what I thought was love but what turns out to be mischief. "Nah, this time I'll marry you for your money." She taps my chest twice and slips out of my hold.

"Angel," I warn.

"Who knows. You could always try a third time for love. Maybe work on that winning personality of yours and lose a couple of abs so you seem more relatable."

"Wife." I take a step toward her.

"Oh no you don't." She grabs her purse from the counter and slides into her pumps. "No time for my 'sorry not sorry' blow jobs. Gotta go meet the girls!" She bolts to the door.

"Luisa."

She steps out the door but pokes her head back inside the house. "Yes, I'll marry you again, you big goof."

I grin as I pick up my long-forgotten coffee mug. "Good to hear that you've come to your senses." She blows me a kiss, but I raise a finger before she takes off. "Have fun at your brunch. We'll catch up with you later. But after, when we get back home, I'm going to need an in-depth presentation of your blow job categories. Please and thank you."

She winks. "As you wish."

Chapter Fifty

LUISA

It felt like a real bachelorette brunch.

After our conversation this morning about getting married again, I've allowed myself to lean into the festivities, donning the embarrassing sash and all.

It was too cold out to have Amelia bar hop with us, so we promised her we'd do another low-key event like a spa day so she could participate with us, and Nikki came down with the flu two days ago, so it's just my main girls with me. Isabella and Daisy.

Daisy did an incredible job mapping out the places we should hit up so we never had to walk more than two blocks at a time, and she handled all the reservations so we could roll into the good times.

After giving the restaurant a run for their money on bottomless mimosas, we ate family style, sharing multiple sweet and savory plates. The fact that it was a drag show brunch meant that I'll probably have no voice come tomorrow morning after the number of times I've yelled, "Yas, *Queen!*"

Even Daisy decided to let loose, participating in the show and waving dollar bills in the air. Knowing Daisy could be a bit of a lightweight, I made sure to make her table-side drinks myself, always giving her a full glass of orange juice with a splash of bubbly. I tried to be as covert as possible so she wouldn't notice and feel like I was trying to baby her, since I'm sure her brother does enough of that.

Now we're sitting in a private room at a quaint Spanish restaurant with views of the busy downtown sidewalk and a private exit, slowly sipping on cava, since we are old enough to know that it's not smart to switch up your alcohol once you're enjoying a nice buzz. Prevents you from having to be the big spoon to a porcelain toilet.

"Gosh, I know we ate less than an hour ago, but those queens had me dancing my ass off, and I think the patatas bravas are calling my name," Isabella says as her eyes scan the menu like it's her favorite romance novel.

"Oh yes, carb us up. I'm sure we're going to need it if we've got to rally before we meet up with the men. And let's order another pitcher of water. Hydration is key. Even if we spend the night peeing, it'll be worth it tomorrow when we're not hungover," I say as I pull out my phone to make an order that will go straight to the kitchen.

"What are you thinking, Daisy?" Isa asks.

Daisy nibbles on her thumbnail. "I don't know. That does sound good. And the gambas al ajillo here are the best in the city... but we already ate, and I have a dress fitting after the holidays, so I probably shouldn't."

Isabella and I scrunch our faces, but Isa speaks before I have the chance. "Okay, my understanding is that a dress fitting is for, I don't know, maybe to make the dress you like fits *you*?"

Daisy takes a small sip of her drink. "I know, but Damien's mother picked this dress that—"

"Wait, hold up." I put my hands up. "Your future mother-in-law picked out your wedding dress?"

Daisy stumbles over her words. "No, I mean, yeah. She said it was a classic silhouette. And it is very nice. But I doubt it's meant for someone who has my body type."

"Let me guess, someone with ass for days?" Isabella muses.

"Do you think my ass is that big?" Daisy worriedly places her hands on her hips.

"Wait, Daisy, are you being serious? You're drop-dead gorgeous. Women around the world would pay top dollar for an ass like yours. You're perfect. You look exactly like most of the women in my family." I pause as I gather the courage to say what I've been tiptoeing around. "Like a beautiful Dominican woman. Your hourglass figure was most likely passed down from your mother's side of the family. But I'm guessing not growing up around women of color might not have taught you from a young age how to love and appreciate every curve, bump, and stretch mark that adorns your body."

She's silent for so long that I think she might not respond to what I said, so I'm caught off guard when she does. "No one in Damien's family has my body type. Makes me feel like a sideshow every time I have to attend an important family dinner. And now that the wedding is in a few months, the comments on my body have ramped up. It started innocently enough. Things that most brides probably obsess over, trying to look perfect on their special day. But now it's become much more blatant. It feels like they're putting up with me at this point, like I'm some paid actor meant to stand in that day and do as I'm told. And Damien just sits back and lets it all happen, even when I—"

I internally curse the waiter who appears with our order. She's finally opening up, and I don't want her to run back and slip back into her shell.

"Daisy," I hedge, but she shakes her head.

"Sorry, must be all the bubbly getting to my head. I don't know what I'm saying. Was I really complaining about having an ass? Talk about being tone deaf when there are much more important things happening in the world. Ignore me. Tell me when you're planning on looking for dresses, Isa. I'm assuming Mateo wants to run down the aisle with you as soon as possible." She pours herself a full glass of water and brings it to her lips before I can wrap my head around her full one-eighty.

Isabella doesn't get a chance to answer, since the doors to the private room burst open, and Nick strides in with a big grin on his face, walking straight toward us.

"What are you guys doing here? We have at least two more hours of girl time before we're meeting at the theater," Daisy complains as her brother plants a kiss on the top of her head, then squeezes Isabella's shoulder in hello.

I lift my face, expecting a kiss, when I'm suddenly lifted. "What the hell?"

Nick takes my seat and promptly sits me sideways on his lap. "There, that's much better. Now greet me, wife. Plant one on me." His arms wrap around my waist, pulling me closer to him, and I throw my head back in laughter.

He takes full advantage and places quick kisses all over my neck.

"I think a dog with a full bladder has more patience than he does. As soon as we met up, he was ready to dash and crash your party. I'm surprised he allowed you guys to wrap up your brunch before hauling us over here," Mateo says as he grabs extra chairs for him and Luke.

"I don't know what you're moaning about, Martinez. The second I told you Isabella was only three blocks away, you had three hundred-dollar bills thrown on the table with your ass out of the chair."

"It's polite to leave a tip," he mutters as he takes a seat next to Isabella and places a sweet kiss on her lips.

"We ordered three coffees."

"Didn't know billionaires were so cheap," Mateo jabs.

"Easy there, Martinez. Before my husband goes and buys this place just to prove a point." My hands cradle the back of his neck as I lean down and give him what I thought would be a quick kiss but quickly turns into something much steamier.

"Children," Luke huffs.

"Guys, really. Get a room," Daisy complains.

"Wow, another meal with a show. I'm here for it," Isa cheers.

"It's our bachelor and bachelorette party. Let us live. Especially since we've decided to get married again. And all you losers are invited," Nick says between soft pecks, never once taking his eyes off my lips.

"Oh my gosh. There will be a wedding this time? You're really getting married again?" Daisy asks excitedly.

"Yeah. For real this time," I say before I have a chance to stop my kiss-drunk brain from spilling.

I pull back, eyes wide, only to meet Nick's amused ones.

"What do you mean for real this time?" Isabella asks.

"Shit," I whisper, panic stiffening me in Nick's arms.

He runs a warm hand up and down my back. "No use in lying now. Besides, you're marrying me for my money now, so we should be in the clear." I smack his chest as he chuckles. "It's okay, Angel. I trust them." He nods at the four sets of eyes that are trained on us, and I turn in Nick's arms to face them.

"So... funny story."

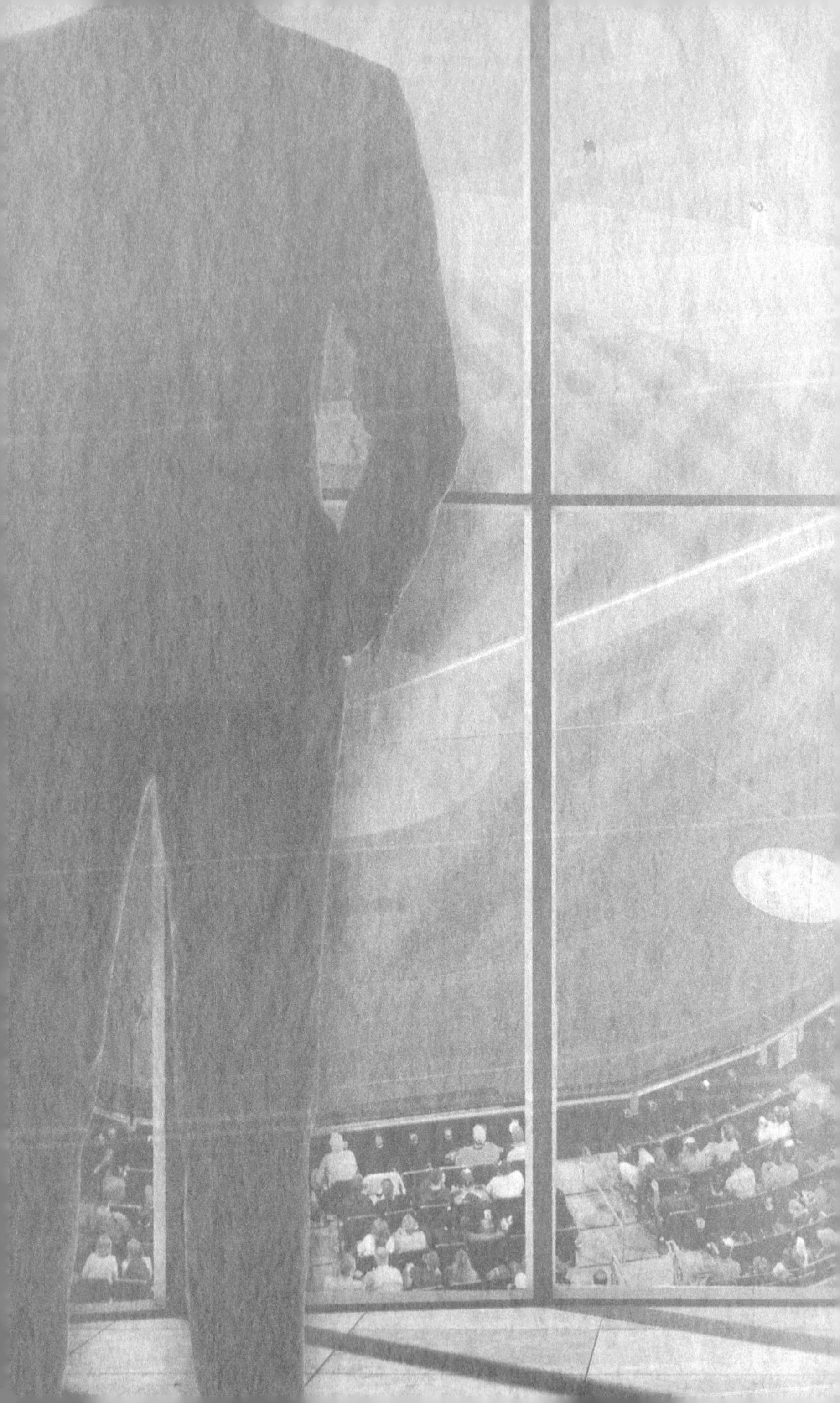

Chapter Fifty-One

NICK

"I knew it!" Isabella exclaims.

Mateo shakes his head.

Luisa and I told them everything. From how we first met to working together as adversaries—on Luisa's side since I was clearly smitten from day one—and getting married in my lawyer's office.

We left out the information about what my asset was, since I don't think this is the appropriate time to open that can of worms for Daisy. We also spared them the kinkier details, of course. My poor sister had to place her hands over her ears when she heard about the one-night stand.

I swear Mateo had to keep Isabella from climbing over the table as she hung onto every word of our story.

And if I'm not mistaken, I believe I saw a smirk on Luke's face.

But it was gone once Daisy's somber tone was unmistakable. "So, in the beginning, when you guys acted like you couldn't stand each other, you really weren't secretly dating?"

Luisa shakes her head. "No. We never dated before getting married. Actually, we went on our first date a few weeks ago after we said 'I love you' for the first time."

Isabella opens her mouth to ask another question, but Daisy speaks first. "You guys weren't in love when you were acting all moody, like you were seconds away from biting each other's heads off, right before getting married?"

"Well, that's debatable on my end, to be honest. I now know I loved her long before I married her, but I didn't know it at the time." I lift Luisa's left hand and place a kiss on her wedding ring. "But I'm sure Luisa was closer to planning her true crime interview outfit from prison than actually admitting her growing feelings for me."

My wife shrugs. "Very true."

Daisy deflates, her eyes scanning back and forth on the tablecloth, as if the world's answers are written on them.

"Everything okay, Daisy?" I ask, worried.

Her head snaps up. She scans our small crew while putting her fake smile back on display. "Yep. Just thought it was normal for couples to be a bit off before getting married. Only finding their footing later on like you guys did. But it seems like you guys were playing a completely different game from the one I pictured." She forces a laugh.

Luisa's fingers tap on the table a few times before she stops and straightens in my lap. "Daisy, you don't have to answer this if you don't want to. But..." She looks around the table, meeting everyone's eye before settling on my sister's. "Why are you marrying him?"

Daisy's eyes widen, but my focus is on the glass of water that's threatening to shatter in Luke's white-knuckle grasp.

He catches me staring and loosens his hold, but not before giving me a subtle shake of his head.

"Wh-what do you mean? Why does anyone get married? I mean, well, besides you guys." She fake chuckles as she pulls the neck of her sweater down an inch. "Because I love him, of course."

Luke stands abruptly.

"Where are you going?" Mateo asks.

"Quick walk."

"But you left your coat on your chair," Isa yells after him.

"Don't need it," he says as he steps into the frigid December air.

"What was that about?" Daisy asks.

"Oh boy," Isabella mumbles under her breath.

Now isn't the time to discuss what I suspect about Coach. Instead, I focus on my sister. Now that I truly know what it is to love someone and wanting to spend the rest of my life with that person, I can't imagine that she feels the same for Damien.

"Daisy, I'm your brother and I love you, but level with me, please. Is Dad pressuring you in any way to get married to Damien?"

"No," she says before I'm done asking the question. The look on my face must tell her not to bullshit me, and she raises her arms slightly. "He's, kind of... Well, you know Dad. He's been stressed the last couple of years with his business. And having contracts stateside, with the government, would help immensely. The fact that Damien and I were already dating seemed to please him. And he seemed so damn thrilled when Damien proposed, even if it was a bit sooner than I expected, and—"

"Daisy, do you hear yourself? Our sorry excuse for a father is absolutely manipulating you."

Luisa squeezes my thigh under the table, stopping me from saying something I would likely regret. I know my sister is a sensitive soul, and I'm not exactly delicate when it comes to trying to get my point across, but I can't stand for my sister to be a pawn in my father's mess.

"Daisy—"

"No, stop. I know what you think of me. What you all must think of me. That I'm some kind of idiot. Some weakling who can't make choices for herself. But you're wrong." Her eyes latch on to mine with a force I've never seen before. "And I'm sorry, brother, but you can't possibly understand where I'm coming from. You had a decade with our mother. Our sweet, caring, and beautiful mami. I never got that. I got a nameless rotation of nannies and a father I would see twice a year at most. I only have one parent left, and while I know he will never win any best dad awards, he's all I got."

My heart threatens to crack down the middle.

"Oh, Daisy," Luisa says softly, but Daisy shakes her head.

"Please don't. The last thing I need is your pity. I'm a poor little rich girl who has daddy issues. There is nothing original or extraordinary about me. My job was a handout from my brother. I live in my fiancé's apartment, which doubles as a storage unit for his accolades and is the place where he rests his head a handful of nights each month. My education, the one I'm not even using, was paid for by my absentee father.

"All I have that is truly mine are my choices. And dumb as they may seem to all of you, they are still mine. And if I'm making a huge mistake, well, I guess that's my mistake to own as well."

"Daisy—"

"We don't—"

"You shouldn't—"

The chill at my back signals that Luke has returned and heard every word she said.

"You don't love him, Daisy." Luke's harsh words silence us all.

Daisy crosses her arms in defiance, but the harsh tone of her voice has all but disappeared. "How would you know, Luke? You won't even RSVP for my wedding."

Luke walks back to our table, hands resting on the top of his vacant chair. "You really want me there, D?"

She juts her chin out and nods after a few beats.

The chair creaks under his hands. "Then I'll be there." He grabs his coat and tears out of the restaurant.

Daisy stares at her lap as we all share various looks of concern.

Looks like we won't be playing any board games tonight.

Chapter Fifty-Two

LUISA

Damien stood Daisy up for Christmas.

But after the explosive ending to our bachelor and bachelorette parties, we all seemed to act as if nothing had happened.

She's blended in so seamlessly into my family that a part of me feels like she's always been here with us.

Watching her and Nick go head-to-head in the kitchen, making my little cousins the judge of a blind taste test for the best Dominican dish, was the highlight of my day.

It was such a sweet holiday, my first with my husband and one that I will forever cherish.

But now we're in the new year, and I have less than two weeks until the trade deadline is up, and my reputation is on the line.

I'm trying to keep my cards close to the vest, because I don't want a leak deterring my plans for landing Julian Vega. He's on everyone's radar, and one wrong move could have me fumbling the biggest deal of the season.

Which is why I've purposely left Richard in the dark. I wouldn't put it past him to try and sabotage this deal for me, and that thought alone tells me everything I already know. Richard can't be trusted.

Nick was grumpy when I left him in bed this morning, sleepily mumbling "bad wife" as I kissed him goodbye.

But I wanted to get to work early and prepare for what I hoped would be the final meeting with Vega and his team. I plan on giving them a tour of the facilities and field while they're here. And I may have strongly suggested that Martinez and Torres, his former teammates and current Monarchs titans, be in the gym at the same time in hopes that a little reunion with his former mates might be the cherry on top to his eye-watering contract offer.

I'm done placing note pads on the conference table when I hear the door slam open behind me and whirl.

"What the hell, Nick? You scared the shit out of me."

But something isn't right. Nick has never set foot inside the executive offices without a freshly dry-cleaned suit. Now he stands before me in a white t-shirt that looks heavenly against his brown skin and a pair of workout pants and sneakers.

I should probably be more focused on the thunderous look on his face.

He quietly rounds the long oval table until he stands in front of me. His shoulders are laden with tension.

"Wife," he growls as he pulls something out of his pocket and brings it up to my face. "Care to explain why these are currently in my hand and not on your ring finger?" My shiny engagement ring and wedding band sparkle in the light from the floor-to-ceiling windows.

I go to grab them, but he pulls them out of reach, waiting for an explanation. "Calm down, caveman. I was so jittery this morning, running through my plan of action today, that I spilled coffee all over my sleeves. I had to take off my rings to rinse them and change my shirt. I must have forgotten to put them back on. Now hand them over."

He stares down at my open hand and flips it. Slowly, he slides my wedding band on, followed by my engagement ring. "You almost gave me a heart attack when I found them by the kitchen sink." He kisses my knuckles below the rings.

"Aw, thought I'd finally come to my senses?"

"Don't make me bend you over this table, Angel. Teach you a lesson and make you forget your nerves about your meeting. Two birds and whatnot."

I put my hand on his chest, and he allows me to push him back easily enough. "Don't even think about it, Lucifer."

"You know I love it when you call me that."

I roll my eyes and run a hand down my soft pink blouse. "I'd prefer not to look freshly fucked when I try to land this deal, thank you very much." I turn around and straighten the notepads and pens, trying to make sure nothing is out of place.

He sighs dramatically. "Fine, I'll be on my best behavior if I must." He wraps his arms around me from behind. "Have I told you lately how proud I am of you? Of how much you've managed to accomplish in such a short time while many in your same industry try and fail to knock you down?"

I bite down on a smile. "I swear, if you make me cry..."

He places a quick kiss on my cheek. "Wouldn't dream of it. But later tonight, I might be open to—"

"Knock, knock. I hope I'm not interrupting anything important. Or is this a personal meeting between husband and wife? Never quite sure what I might stumble into with you two." Richard's laugh is as fake as the knock-off Rolex on his wrist.

Nick stiffens behind me, most likely ready to strangle the man. He might need to get in line, because Richard's grace period with me has finally run out. "What are you doing here?"

His smile is condescending. "Now, kid, that is no way to talk to your work colleague, is it?" He chuckles.

"Hey, Dick. Can I call you Dick?" Nick starts.

"Only my golfing buddies call me—"

"Doesn't matter, but do me a favor." I can feel Nick's chest vibrating behind me as he speaks. "When speaking to my wife, you can drop the word 'kid.' I'll even give you some options to make it easier. You can call her Mrs. Álvarez-Stonehaven or boss. If not, you can call yourself fired," he thunders behind me.

Richard's cheeks turn bright red as he sets his sights on me. "He can't be serious. I know he's new to this world, but this is unacceptable." He looks between the two of us. "I'm afraid you've left me no choice. I've already thought about bringing up my concerns about you to the board, *boss*. And I'm sure they'll consider a vote of no confidence once I tell them you two are running around with no respect for this office. You've paraded your 'girl power' long enough. Now it's time to step aside and let the grown-ups get to work and whip this team into shape."

It feels like a punch to the gut.

My breath stalls, my lungs forgetting how to function for a few seconds before allowing me to suck in a deep breath.

I spent so much time making excuses for Richard. Letting things slide when I usually wouldn't. Convincing myself that if I made myself seem small and nonthreatening, he would leave me be and learn that I was here to stay.

But now I see that all that really did was make him comfortable enough to believe that he could mess with me.

It was my mistake to allow his behavior to go unchecked.

But it was his to fucking push me this far.

I place my hands on the conference table and lean over slightly, bringing me closer to him. "Tell me, Richard. What is it you're afraid of?"

He looks around the room, calling upon an invisible entity to appear and back him up. "Afraid? I have no idea what you're talking about, so you're going to have to enlighten me."

I look him up and down, dissecting the man before me as if he's the dirt under my shoe. "Is it having all your scouting options being passed over time and time again, only to be outshone by people less experienced than you in this industry?"

He scoffs. "Excuse—"

I shake my head. "No, maybe it's that you only propose players who are the offspring of those golfing buddies you mentioned, and you're worried I'm going to find out about all the other candidate files you've seemed to have lost or buried over the past year." I tsk, eyeing him up and down. "No, I'm sure it has more to do with your ego. That's what it all boils down to with men like you, unfortunately."

"I don't know what... who told you about that? I mean, wrongly accused me. Because if it was Mark or James, you can't believe a word they say. They—"

I straighten to my full height, my eyes pinning him to the spot. "No one told me anything. It was a lingering suspicion I've dismissed before, but something I'm sure the board would love to hear about."

"That's not—you can't prove—"

"It's a shame, really. We could have created something really great here with the Monarchs. But your prejudice about my age and gender far superseded any desire to actually work with me toward those goals."

"Oh, please. It was some light teasing at most. Can your generation not handle that?" I raise a knowing brow, and he notices his misstep. "Again, it's how I talk. No need to be so sensitive about it."

I reach back, and my hand latches on to Nick's thigh, holding him in place and preventing him from leaping over this table and showing Richard how sensitive he can make him feel in a split second.

I don't need my guard dog.

Especially since I'm about to do what I should have done long ago.

"Ah, yes. Why don't you use those amazing speaking skills when you drop your staff badge off at the security desk before you exit the building?"

"And why exactly would I do that?" he sputters.

I allow him to drown in the tense silence long enough to see the sweat bead around his hairline.

I thought he'd get the picture by now. But it looks like I'm going to have to spell it out for him.

"I expect your resignation on my desk by end of day. If not, I'm afraid I'll have to bring this all the way up to the commissioner's office. Luckily, Mr. Stonehaven was here as a witness, so the Monarchs' owner is already apprised of the situation. Now if that'll be all…" I plaster on the sweetest smile as I nod to the door. "Get fucked."

He takes a step back, and I swear I hear Nick faintly moaning behind me.

Richard doesn't spare us another moment. He darts out of the room, slamming the door behind him.

I release a tense breath and turn to find Nick's smoldering gaze on me.

Uh-oh. I know that look.

"Stonehaven."

"That was so fucking hot."

"Glad you thought so. Looks like I'm in the market for a new AGM."

"Do you have any idea how often I've thought about fucking you on this very table during a presentation? I'm sure I have a competence kink or something, because you running the show, getting shit done? God, it does things to me." His grin turns more feral. "Can you repeat that last bit you said one more time?"

I laugh as I wipe my face with my hands. "I said get fucked. I can't believe—"

He hums. "Ah, yes. My pleasure."

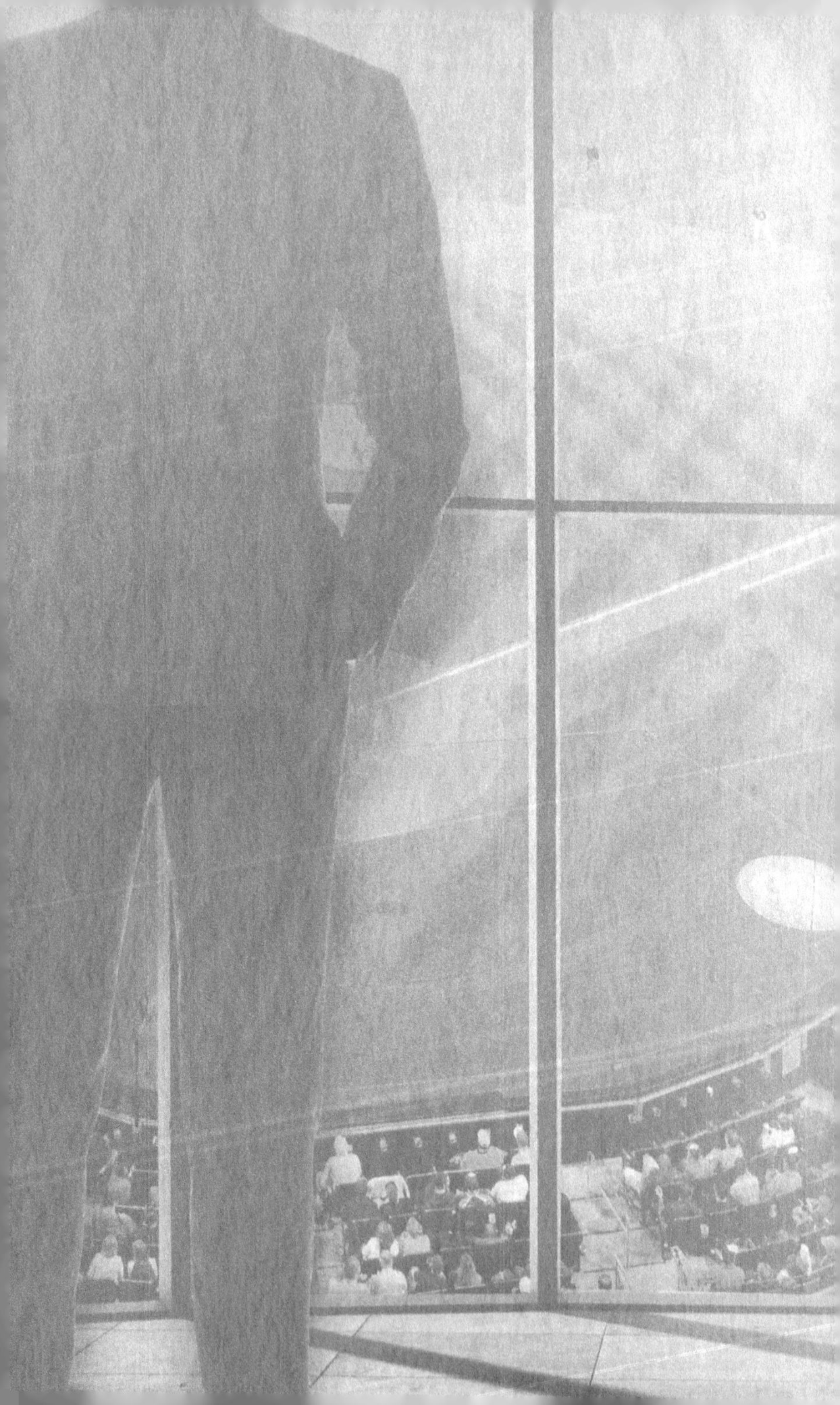

NICK

And get fucked, she did.

LUISA

"Did you buy the bodega on my parents' block?"

Nick shrugs as he moves us through the celebratory crowd.

"Your mom and aunts get their best chisme from there, and the current store owners were having trouble keeping the place afloat. So I bought it and gave it to them, rent free. Now they can focus on supplying your family with the best snacks and neighborhood gossip."

I place a kiss on his jaw. "You're a real softie, you know that?"

"Marrying my dream girl will do that to a guy. Especially when she's dressed like that." He looks down at the long emerald dress that hugs me in all the right places.

"Down, boy. We have to make our rounds and congratulate the players on Team Cuba for winning the series."

We're at the event space at Monarchs stadium, mingling with the who's who of New York society and retired baseball giants. Sometimes I forget that this is my job and find myself fangirling over players my father and I used to love to watch when I was a kid.

I remember the last time Nick and I attended a fancy event like this, before we actually admitted our feelings for one another. It's crazy to believe how much has changed since then.

For instance, my whole family is at this event, and I can see my dad and uncles taking a ridiculous number of selfies with a couple of hall-of-famers while my mother and aunts are over by the bar, indulging in baseball-themed cocktails.

I look around this room, and all I see is family. In the players, the staff, and the friends I've made along the way.

But when I look at Nick, I see my future.

For the first time, I dare to dream about the things I was once too scared of wanting.

The thought of little Nicks running around our home, causing havoc, brings a smile to my face.

I went to a specialist last week and decided to get real medical advice instead of doing internet searches and letting second-hand information from my extended family members send me spiraling.

Turns out, even though I do have PCOS, it doesn't mean that my ability to grow a family is off the table.

It seems as though I have absorbed every morsel of information about the terrible side effects of having this syndrome but have failed to recognize the possibilities that are still available to me.

After some rather up close and personal testing, my doctor saw that there is no medical reason I can't conceive. When we're ready, figuring out my ovulation cycle will be the priority, since my cycles can fall out of sync and make me irregular.

What was important for me to hear is that conception, whether spontaneous or through medical assistance, is not a sure thing for anyone.

I very well could have fertility issues down the line. There is no crystal ball to tell me what lies in the future. Our family building plans can look different when we decide to venture down that road.

I think back to Nick and Daisy's childhood and wish that they had landed with a loving family like mine when his mother passed. I love the idea of being a safe place for a child to land. And growing up as a first-generation immigrant has taught me that family is not only united by blood.

I have no idea what our parenting journey will look like, but I'm excited to allow myself to finally daydream about it.

For so long, I harped on feeling like my body had already failed before it even had the chance to try while also absorbing my mother's experience and expecting it to be my own.

I never realized how heavily that weighed on me until the burden was lifted.

"What are you thinking about that's got you looking at me like that? Not that I'm complaining." Nick pulls me into his arms and kisses me deeply.

"Food. Babies. You."

His eyes flash with heat. "Now, now, Angel. We've been getting plenty of practice. When do you want to stop taking your birth control pills? Because the thought of you carrying my child, filling you up with my—"

"Sangria."

His brows furrow. "You want a sangria?"

"Ugh, no. I'm using my safe word. Parents are in the vicinity. Keep your breeding kink to yourself until we're in the safety of our home, away from listening ears."

His smile turns devious. "We could always run downstairs to my office. We could use my shower to—"

I throw my hands in the air. "I give up. You're a lost cause."

He leans down and nips my ear. "All right, all right. I'll be on my best behavior."

"That's what I'm afraid of," I mutter.

The air seems to shift behind us, and Nick registers why a moment before my eyes land on the culprit.

"Oh look, the newlyweds are still glowing. Although I must say that I'm hurt that I have yet to be invited to any holiday dinners," George Stonehaven tuts.

"What are you doing here?" Nick all but roars.

"Settle down, son. Last I checked, you owned this godforsaken place. I would imagine you keep some semblance of decorum at your place of work." He raises a patronizing brow.

"Last I checked, you weren't invited."

"Ah, always so quick to make assumptions. Didn't you learn your lesson regarding getting all the facts before you make your final conclusion?" He shakes his head as he drops his hands into his pockets. "Or have you forgotten that I have a daughter who works here as well? My one child who still knows how to respect her father."

I don't know if it's the look he gives my husband or the mention of my friend—the one I now consider a sister—but before I know it, I see red. "That's rich, given that I have yet to see anything respectable about you, Paul."

"My name is George," he spits.

"What you are is forgettable. An inconsequential doodle in the margins of my husband's past. A pathetic excuse for a real man who knows how to step up and do what's right." I lean in closer, but Nick keeps a firm hand on my stomach, preventing me from potentially clawing George's eyes out like I want to.

"And if the latest stock reports are to be believed, the sole owner of a company that is dangerously close to going under. A man whose billionaire son has better things to do than dig him out of the financial ruin he's created. But again, I have better decorum than to gossip about these kinds of things." I smile smugly.

Nick has been keeping tabs on George since we ran into him at the first gala we attended. And he ramped up his search after Daisy alluded to her father influencing her to marry Damien. The same guy who made a surprise appearance tonight, only to whisk Daisy away before the party even started.

Nick only got the very in-depth report this afternoon while we were getting ready for the party, and he filled me in right before we arrived at the stadium.

Which is how I also found out the asshole isn't just visiting New York, he's living here. That's if his one-year lease in an overpriced midtown high-rise is any indication.

"H-how did you... that's not accurate. We're going through a..." He straightens, finding his composure. "That is quite frankly none of your business, and if I needed my son's help, I would simply ask for it, given that I'm sure I still have something he wants."

"I can take this one, Angel." Nick pats my hip.

I smile. This part is going to be fun.

"You still worrying about my mother's house in Jarabacoa?" Nick taunts.

His eyes dart between Nick and me. "You told her about that?"

"You know," Nick starts. "After so many marriages, you'd think you'd know that open communication is important in relationships," he mock scolds. "Of course I did. And soon enough, it'll be back to its rightful owners. Until then, you can make yourself scarce. Because you are not welcome here or in any other establishment in which my family sets foot in."

"Family? Really?" He scoffs.

"This guy bothering you, mijo?" My dad comes up beside Nick and pats him on the back while my uncles flank us.

They seemed to have appeared out of thin air the second Nick needed them.

I see Nick's eyes soften as he takes in the support of the men who have accepted him as one of their own.

"Nah, he was just leaving."

A heavy hand lands on George's shoulder, causing him to wince. "We got a problem here?" Luke asks. His face is impassive, but his bright blue eyes seem darker than usual. Ace Middlebrooks sidles up to George's other side, arms crossed. His imposing stature is on full display. The look on his face is nothing short of intimidating.

"I've had enough of this," George sputters while trying to shake off Coach's grip. "No one speaks to me this way. You may have found a way to get that old rickety house back, but I know you, Nicholas. Far better than you think I do. And I know that you have a weak spot, so it's best you play nice. Because you may not fall in line, but Daisy will," he sneers.

Coach taps his shoulder twice, forcing George to take a step forward.

"I do not need an escort. Who do you think you are?" George sneers, looking between Coach and Middlebrooks.

"Trash disposal." Luke guides George to the front doors, Ace two steps behind, and hands George off to security to take it from there.

The ambiance returns to normal once he is out of our line of sight.

Yet something tells me we haven't seen the last of Nick's dear old dad.

I knew Nick was still hung up on the less than pleasant interaction we had with his father.

I left him to stew in peace once we got home. I showered and got ready for bed, but after, he was still hidden away in his office.

It's funny how I don't recall making the decision to make instant noodles, but somehow I find myself in the kitchen, opening up the stash I bought for Nick the other day.

It might be cheap and overly processed, but it does the trick for cold nights like these.

I find him sitting behind his desk. He's removed his tie since I last saw him, and the top two buttons of his dress shirt are open, revealing his toned brown skin.

His eyes lift from staring at an invisible spot on the wall and track me as I enter his office.

I skip past the oversized chairs meant for visitors and walk around the desk to present my offering. "I come bearing gifts. This'll make you feel better." He wheels back his office chair, and I take a seat on the open space on his desk, placing a hot cup on each side of me. "One has the fake dried vegetables and the other one doesn't. Wasn't sure if you were feeling fancy," I joke.

He looks over at both offerings. "You like your noodles plain, don't you?"

"Duh, how can I enjoy the silky goodness if I have to worry about getting stray veggies in my teeth?" I nudge his knee with my bare foot.

"Then this is the one I like." He picks up the veggie one and chews on a large forkful of noodles. "Mmm, that's better than I remember." He looks up at me. "Thank you. For this." He lifts the cup in his hand. "And for tonight." He sighs as he looks down.

I clear my throat. "Wanna talk about it?"

"Not particularly." He places his half-empty cup on the desk.

I hum. "Avoidance. Sounds healthy."

He manages a small smile. "Don't worry. Remember, I'm back in therapy, so I'll probably save it for my next session."

"Am I going to get the CliffsNotes sent to my email again? Because that was my favorite."

He runs a large, calloused hand up my thigh.

"Nick, your dad is—"

"He's not my dad. Never was, and he never will be. Unlike your father, who stood up for me tonight."

Gosh, how could I forget? I was so hung up on ruffling George's feathers that I didn't consider how impactful my dad and uncles standing side by side with Nick would be to him.

"Did you hear the part where he called me mijo?" Nick's smile resembles that of a much younger man. Of a child who's been given the greatest gift.

"I did. And I'm pretty sure my uncles were ready to offer to bring in their peewee baseball players as backup during our showdown. That's how you know things were escalating."

"It's been a long time since I had a parental figure. At this age, I'm more used to a parent trying to tear me down than sticking up for me." His eyes lock on mine. "Made me realize that falling in love with you has made me whole. Filled in the dark spaces in my heart that I forgot were lacking affection. Every minute of every day, I discover more reasons why I'm the luckiest bastard alive, because, for some godforsaken reason, you've allowed me to orbit your light, and you love me as I am."

"Nick," I whisper.

"Being loved by you is nothing short of heavenly."

He stands then, hands sinking into my hair.

We're just a breath away from one another when his phone rings.

It's late. Who the hell is calling past midnight?

He must be thinking the same thing. It must be an emergency. I nudge him to check since his body seems to be struggling to release me.

"It's my attorney."

He answers the call and puts it on speaker.

"Hello, Nicholas. I know it's late. But it's still early evening here in London, and you told me to reach out immediately if I had any noteworthy updates in regard to your grandfather's will."

"Go on. I'm here with Luisa."

He squeezes my hand resting on his desk.

"Ah. perfect. Glad I caught you two together. It'll save me a phone call." I hear the ruffling of papers on the other end of the line. "Per your request, we've been combing through the will, having it dissected by multiple partners at the firm. And we found a loophole."

"What is it?"

"Your grandfather stated that you must be married for a year in order to obtain the property in the Dominican Republic. But what we never took into account was your mother's will."

"My mother's? She left the property to Daisy and me, and I gave it to my grandfather, so why would her will matter now?"

"Because she had more than one will, Nicholas."

"What?" Nick's voice rasps.

"She had another will drawn up in the Dominican Republic after Daisy was born. One that stated that her family home could never be owned by a Stonehaven, besides her children. And if you failed to take proper ownership within a year of turning eighteen, that property would automatically be granted to Daisy."

"Wait, hold on. I filed paperwork. The house—"

"The paperwork is invalid based on this new will. It was never eligible to belong to your grandfather, and at this point, even you. All this time, it's been registered in Daisy's name per the surrogate's court in the Dominican Republic. I'm sorry. There's nothing else I can do—"

"This is great news," Nick shouts. "No, not great. Fantastic. Daisy, she needs this. She was always the one who deserved the house. She has no memories of our mother besides photos and a few video clips. How soon can she get a copy of the deed? I want to plan a trip, have us all fly down together. We could... God, this is great. Did I say that already?" Nick looks between me and the phone repeatedly.

"You did," I say with a watery smile.

My soul soars for the man who has stolen my heart. It's as if I'm witnessing the emotional weight lifted off his shoulders right before my eyes. This agonizing ordeal is finally over, and I can't wait to be there to tell Daisy the good news.

The attorney chuckles good-naturedly over the line. "Glad to hear it. Guess that leaves one more thing for me to do for you."

Nick runs a hand through his hair, eyes brimming with happiness. "Oh yeah? What's that?"

"File for your divorce."

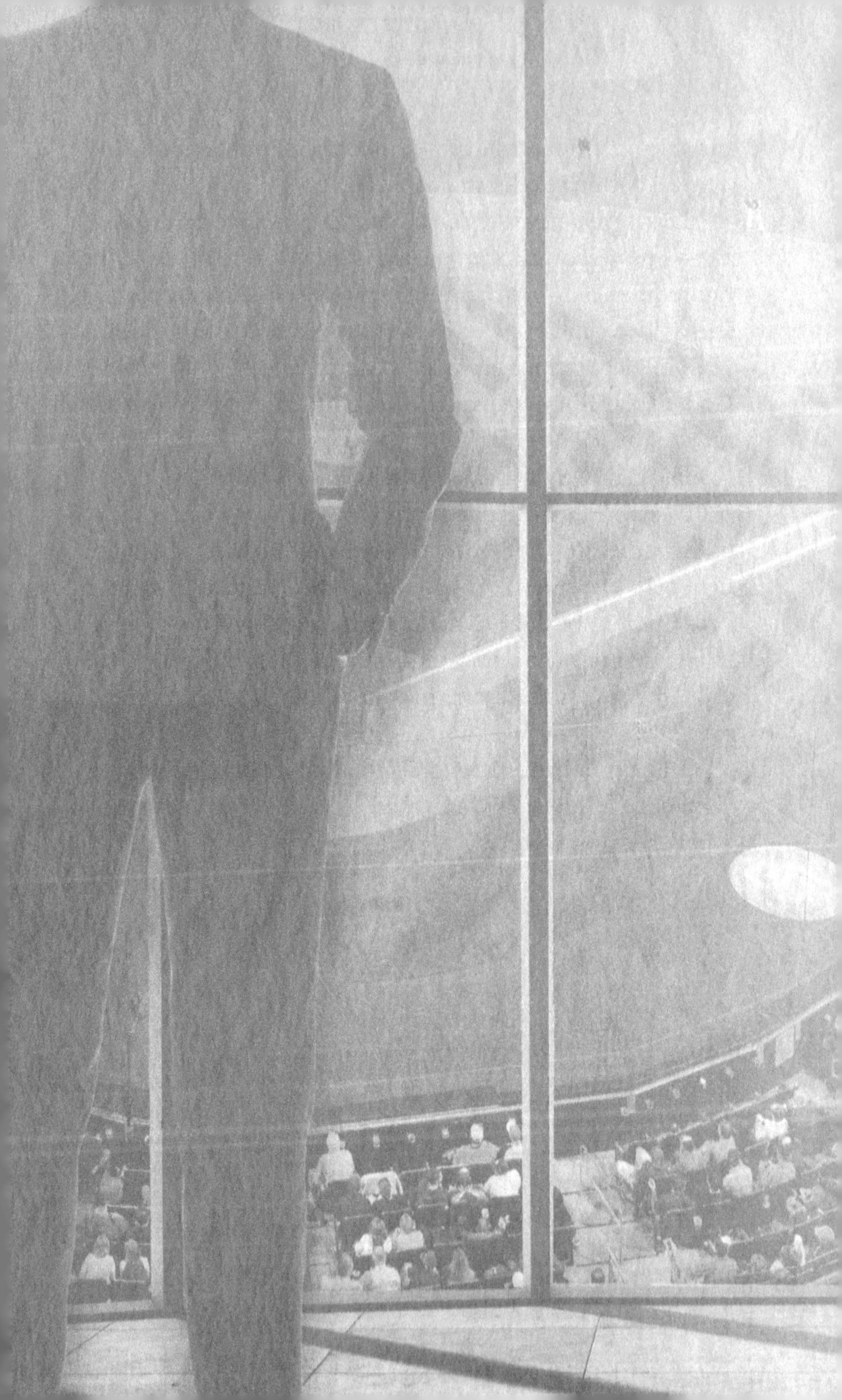

Chapter Fifty-Five

NICK

My Angel is a terrible liar.

And if I hear her say the words "I'm fine" one more time, I'm going to break something with my bare hands.

Divorce.

The second my attorney muttered those words, I swear I saw something in Luisa shatter.

Because she is still my wife and will forever remain that way.

After I not so politely told my attorney to shred any document that pertained to me getting a divorce and warned him to never bring the subject up to either of us again, Luisa gave me a smile that didn't quite reach her eyes and headed up to bed without another word.

I've pestered her all morning. She's seemed to somewhat recover from the shock of last night, but I can tell the conversation has shaken a bit of her confidence in our marriage, in us. And that's something I simply won't stand for.

If I have to spend the rest of my days convincing her that my love for her is eternal, I'll do so while on my knees and with a smile on my face.

Because she's worth every assurance. Every reminder. She's more than earned it, with every little bit of me that she's made for the better, merely by allowing me to be the man to stand by her side.

So I'll do whatever it takes to get that twinkle back in her eye. Even if I have to resort to extreme measures.

As I anticipated, Luisa makes an excuse to leave early for work.

I give her a goodbye kiss that would have been better suited for the bedroom, but knowing how easily I can put that dazed look on her face gives me way too much satisfaction.

The old version of me would probably be hung up on the fact that she's acting distant. But I know my wife. I know she needs a minute to digest that this whole ordeal is over.

And what's left is her and me.

Too bad a minute is all I'll give her.

Because I have plans for us today.

And it just so happens to involve an audience of seventy thousand baseball fans.

CHAPTER FIFTY-SIX

LUISA

YES, I'M FREAKING OUT.

I didn't realize how rattled I'd be by hearing the word "divorce."

But here I am, unwilling to put on my big girl panties because I'm spooked beyond belief.

For a split second, I worried about how Nick would respond to his attorney. And I hate myself for it.

I love Nick, and I know he loves me.

But it still happened. And the feeling was sickening.

I wish I could tell my brain that it's okay to be happy. To stop running.

But it's easier said than done. Especially when our marriage has been anything but typical.

So here I am, a few hours early to the Valentine's Day charity game we're hosting at Monarchs Stadium.

Daisy decided that we should host regular charity games throughout the season, since we had such an amazing turnout and generated so many donations for the cause.

Since it's Black History Month, we're hosting on behalf of multiple nonprofits that help aid and elevate Black voices in our community.

I was surprised to hear that Ace Middlebrooks, our third baseman, took quite the lead and helped introduce us to most of the charities we'll be raising money for today.

Though I should know better than to judge a book by its cover. Being married to Nick has more than driven that point home.

"You're here early." Isabella startles me from my running thoughts.

"I could say the same for you." I take in Isa's carefree smile. To think we became friends because she used to nanny for the man she will soon be calling her husband.

"I couldn't keep Anna home any longer. She said she wanted to see the stadium's retractable roof closed for the very first time. But I'm sure she was trying to get first dibs on the snacks in the family suite. I swear I don't know where her and her father pack away all that food." She laughs.

I hesitate a second too long to return the gesture, and Isa's eyes narrow. "What's up with you? You seem off. Are we mad at Nick? Did he leave the toilet seat up or something?"

I laugh for real this time.

I swear, girlfriends are heaven sent.

"No, everything's fine."

"Whoa, fine? Just tell me you hate me, why don't you," she deadpans.

"Okay, not fine. But it will be. Once I get out of my own way."

I give her a quick rundown of what happened last night.

"Hmm, I see. So you're not fine."

"I am—"

"No, you're an idiot. But it's okay. We've all been there."

"What—"

Isabella's phone rings in her hand, and the smirk on her face puts me on high alert.

"Mr. Stonehaven, to what do I owe the pleasure?" She smiles like the Cheshire cat.

"Put it on speaker," I mouth. She rolls her eyes but does it anyway.

"Hi, Isabella. I'm calling to see if you've seen Luisa. I've been calling but haven't been able to reach her."

The slight worry in his voice makes me kick myself for leaving my phone on my desk when I came down to the suite level.

"Don't worry, boss man. I have our little *Angel* right here with me." The way she says Angel has my mind flying back to the night I showed her Nick's dirty email, the one where he called me by his second-favorite nickname—wife being the first.

I can't see him, but I swear I can picture his whole demeanor changing. "Is that so?" he says, sounding a little too pleased with himself for my liking. "Then do me a favor, Isa. Can you make sure Luisa is in the stands behind the home team dugout before the game starts and not the suites?"

"Sounds like you have something interesting planned. I'm in."

"Traitor," I mouth to Isa, and she muffles a giggle.

"Oh, and one more thing, if I may. Tell my wife I love her."

"Aw, of course I will—"

"And that she's going to pay for every second she allowed herself to doubt us. I'm going to take real pleasure in reminding her that she and I are a forever kind of deal."

"Oh. Yeah. Uh, I'll..." Isa sputters.

"I know I'm on speaker." I can hear the smirk on his face. "See you on the field, Angel."

My jaw drops. "Field? Nick, what are you—"

"And bring a pen. You've got a new contract to sign."

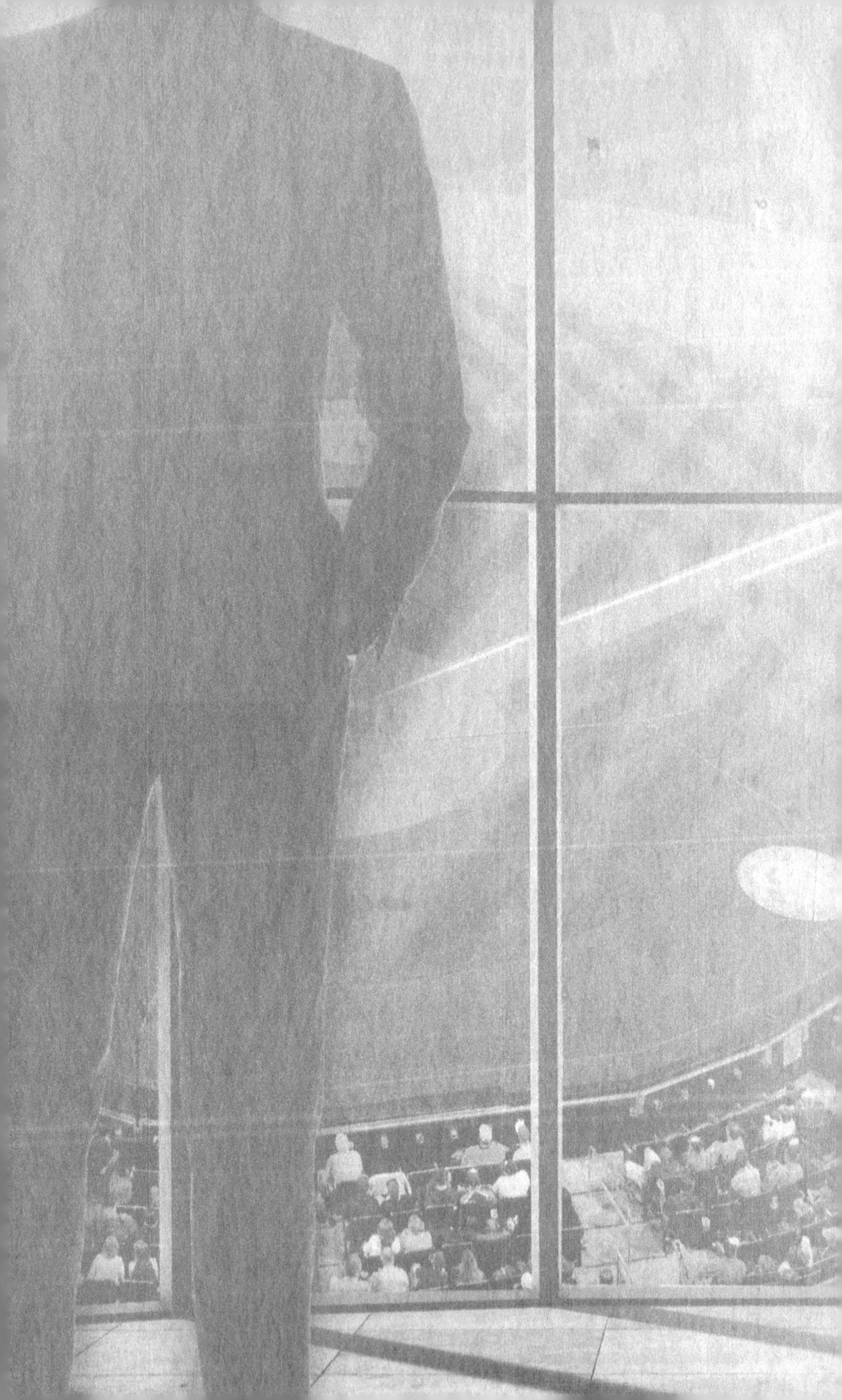

CHAPTER FIFTY-SEVEN

NICK

It's too late to back out now.

I probably could have done this from the comfort of our home.

But when her insecurities are loud, it's my duty to make my love for her even louder.

"You're all mic'd up. You sure you want to do this? You don't even give out interviews, and this is for sure going to go viral," Daisy says as she does a final mic check.

"I'm sure. You need to run through the plan again?"

She rolls her eyes playfully. "I think I've got it. You've only made me recite it to you ten thousand times."

I'm happy that our relationship hasn't taken a hit since the joint bachelor parties, but I'm still holding out hope that I can convince her to stop her train wreck of a wedding from happening next month.

"All right. Then off I go. Wish me luck," I say as I exit the dugout and step onto the Monarchs' field.

I keep my head down, staying focused on the task at hand and not the confused sounds of the thousands of baseball-loving fans in the stands.

I make it to the pitcher's mound and finally allow myself to take in the sight.

I'm struck by an unexpected onslaught of emotion as I look around me.

This place is a thing of beauty. Filled to the brim with joy from New Yorkers who make this place feel like home.

The place that brought a new sense of purpose to my life.

The place that, more importantly, led me to my wife.

I take a deep breath as I lift my mic and smile as I greet the awaiting crowd.

"Good afternoon, everyone, and welcome to Monarchs Stadium. It is my honor to have you all here today. I am proud of this organization and the good we provide by hosting these charity games here in the heart of the city. And I am happy to announce that I will be matching the final total of donations we raise tonight."

That earns me an enthusiastic round of applause. I hope the crowd can keep that energy as I spill my heart out on the field.

"I'm sorry. Where are my manners? I have yet to introduce myself to you. Some of you may already know who I am, but I want to take this opportunity to make this official."

I look down at my watch and smile. "Two hours ago, I submitted paperwork to have my name legally changed. So I'd like to *re*introduce myself, I suppose. My name is Nicholas León Álvarez-Stonehaven. I'm hyphenating." I wink at the crowd as they cheer. "It's only fair, since my wife has taken my name and heart as well. And if I'm being honest, being an Álvarez is one of the greatest honors I'll ever have in this life." I smile to myself.

"Speaking of the love of my life." I shield my eyes from the bright lights with the hand not holding the microphone. "I believe you may have heard of her. She's only the most impressive woman in the sports industry. But then again, I am her husband, so I may be biased. Ah, there she is."

I see my sister not so gently pushing Luisa onto the field. My wife's rosy cheeks are visible all the way from here. It's only going to get worse for her stage fright, I fear.

She smiles and waves as she makes her way toward me.

Her heels keep digging into the field, so she stops halfway into her journey and chucks them behind her, causing the crowd to burst into laughter.

"Lucifer," she warns, careful not to move her lips due to the many camera angles pointed our way. But I don't miss the barely restrained tears—hopefully her reaction to hearing my new last name.

I pull her in for a live TV-appropriate kiss, then whisper in her ear. "Fancy seeing you here."

She manages to chuckle, but her body remains tense. She's probably wondering why I've dragged her all the way out here, so I move it along.

"Some of you may have heard that my beautiful wife and I eloped last fall. I promise you, there's a good story there, but I'll keep that between Luisa and me." I sneakily pinch her ass, and her face continues to turn a pretty shade of pink.

"And while I wouldn't change a single part of our story, I do find that I need to remedy something immediately."

I take a step back and, while keeping her hand in mine, drop down to one knee.

The noise level is deafening, but I only have eyes for my woman.

"Nick. Wh-what..."

"You should have had this the first time, but I'm doing it now. And don't worry: this time I got your dad's permission." I point to the dugout. "Everyone, wave to Dad, Javier Álvarez."

The crowd cheers as Javier takes a step out of the dugout, decked out in full Monarchs' gear as he waves to the crowd, recording the whole thing on his phone while in selfie mode.

"Luisa." I bring the attention back to the most important person in the stadium—and in my life. "I have loved you since long before my mind could even reconcile the fact. It's stubbornness only rivals your own. I vowed to be your husband months ago, but today, I'm negotiating for more."

"Of course you would negotiate at a time like this!" she yells, and a small chuckle escapes from her lips.

"I want to update our terms." I clear my throat. "I want a full life with you, Luisa. One where we drink Dominican hot chocolate on cold winter nights. Spend weekends watching mind-numbing reality TV and outdated romantic comedies—"

"Careful. You were doing well there for a moment," she fake scolds.

I smile. "Days where I fight with our dog over who gets to cuddle you the most, nights with family and friends dancing around our kitchen and forgoing the dining table to eat in front of the TV." I look over at the crowd. "To watch a Monarchs game, of course." The cheers ramp up again, and I can already see a few weeping ladies slapping their husbands on the arm as they point in our direction.

"But most importantly, I'm asking for forever and a day. This lifetime and the next. Way past the moment we're dearly departed. Because my body may have finite time here on this earth, but my soul seeks nothing less than eternity with yours."

A tear streaks down her face as she smiles.

"Marry me, Luisa. Again. Because marrying you is the greatest thing I've ever done, and I'll do it as many times as you allow me to." I lean forward and kiss her ring-clad hand. "So what do you say, Angel? Ready to dance with the devil for the rest of your days?" I manage a small smirk, even though my heart is racing inside my chest.

She starts nodding her head before she speaks. "Yes! I'll marry you a hundred times more, as long as you don't propose to me in front of a million people ever again!" She laughs as she throws herself at me.

I catch her easily and pick her up.

"You're certifiably insane, but I love you, so I'm not so sure what that says about me." She laughs into my neck.

I pull back and place a soft kiss on each cheek, where her tears stream down her face. "Oh, c'mon, love. You know there's no crying in baseball."

My laugh gets caught when she leans in to kiss me. The flashing lights don't hold a candle to the dizzying feeling of having Luisa in my arms.

I lift the mic once more as I pat my jacket pockets repeatedly and tsk loudly. "Seems like I've forgotten something important."

I whistle, and a fuzzy ball of fur bounds our way.

"Delilah." Luisa gasps as our beautiful pup hops onto her hind legs to greet us. "What is that?"

I take the rolled-up piece of paper from Delilah's mouth. "Such a good girl. Say hi, Delilah." She preens under the crowd's whoops, and I swear I hear Luisa grumble something about how she's just like her father.

"I didn't get you another ring. I know we're quite partial to this one, but I believe I've thought of something that could symbolize our love a bit better. Though I'll warn you now: it comes bearing a bit of work... like your marriage to me."

"Oh God, not another contract."

I hand it to her. "Open it."

Her eyes scan the top of the document, and she freezes. I turn off the mic pack behind my back so no one can hear us. "It's yours, Luisa. If you want the partnership, it's there. Hell, if you want the whole thing, I'll give it to you. But I figured since you already have your plate full with being—"

"Yes! Yes, I want it. I want to do this with you. Together." She kisses me deeply, and I couldn't give a damn about who's watching as I pull her in closer.

Delilah happily yelps beside me, and I recognize it's time to wrap this up and give the field back to the professionals before my overexcited pup desecrates it.

"Can I make it official?" I wiggle the microphone between us, and she buries her head in my shoulder. "Go on, showman. But remind me to never invite you to karaoke night with the girls. You seem to get power hungry with a mic in your hand."

I turn the microphone back on and test it quickly before announcing, "It is my greatest pleasure to announce the newest co-owner of the New York Monarchs, Luisa Álvarez-Stonehaven." She smiles as she shakes her head. "Oh, she's also the majority owner, possessing 51 percent."

Luisa gasps. "Nick!"

I smile mischievously at my wife as I muffle the mic behind my back. "Have you learned nothing, wife? Always remember to read the contract thoroughly. Never know who or what you'll get stuck with." I wink. "Now let's hurry along. I have plans to sleep with my new boss tonight. Can't wait to see what all the fuss is about."

LUISA

It's my wedding day.

For real this time.

And I'm spending it in the beautiful mountains of the Dominican Republic.

My family and I have made so many trips down here to enjoy the sun, sea, and sand, but we've never ventured up this way.

But now that Daisy is the sole owner of this quaint little house nestled on the cliffside of Jarabacoa, we get to enjoy moments like this for the rest of our lives.

And I would like for it to start immediately, since my betrothed has gone full traditionalist on me and had us sleeping in different rooms last night, stating that I was to experience every aspect a typical bride on her wedding day would.

But there is nothing typical about flying your entire wedding party and guests on your husband's plane.

Excuse me, our plane.

And I'm sure not every groom rents out an entire floor of a nearby hotel so guests can mingle and not worry about a place to stay, since Nick's mother's former home is a three bedroom.

But none of those silly facts matter now.

Because I'm about to be a wife. Again. But I swear this time feels different, so bear with me.

You see, this time I'm wearing a white dress. It's flowy and comfortable and it even has pockets, which is the holy grail for dresses.

My hair is down in loose waves, and since we're getting married in the lush backyard, surrounded by greenery, we've decided to forgo the shoes and just do the damn thing barefoot.

I check my natural-looking makeup one last time in the mirror and hear a smacking noise behind me as I spot Nick barreling through with his hands covering his eyes.

"Ouch, that hurt. Who decided to put a wall there? I swear this place isn't up to code. We probably should have done a run-through before we flew everyone out here. But there's nothing we can do about it now. Let's hope I don't have a massive goose egg in our wedding photos."

"Nick..." I try my hardest to hold in my laugh. "Are you... nervous?"

"What? Me? Nervous? Psh, nonsense. I could marry you in my sleep... in fact, I'm pretty sure I have. We were in Vegas, and you decided—"

"Husband, come here," I coo softly.

He looks hesitant. "But—but I'm not supposed to see the bride yet. And I'm following all these rules, though most of them feel quite archaic, if you ask me. But it's just... today is a big day. And you're the person I talk to when I need to work through the good, bad, and mundane. Who else am I going to tell that I caught Mateo and Isabella fooling around behind the old chicken coop? Or that Daisy keeps nagging Luke to reapply sunscreen, even though we're canopied in the shade. Of course he did as she asked, which is another thing I want to talk to you about."

Okay, I guess the man has clearly suffered enough separation anxiety if he came over moments before I'm due to walk down the aisle to give me some last-minute chisme. I move into him, and his arms wrap around me instinctively, his eyes still steeled shut.

"I swear I'm not looking." He nuzzles my neck. "Hmm, you smell nice. I didn't see any rules about kissing. So I'm going to kiss you here." He kisses my neck before moving up to my cheek. "And here." Then down to my lips. "And right here."

I kiss him back, and I feel the anxiety drain out of him.

When we separate, I nudge his chin with my nose. "Want to hear about a more modern wedding tradition?"

"I'm scared to ask, but go on."

I rest my chin on his chest as I stare up at him. "It's called a first look. Where the groom gets to see the bride before the wedding so they can have their initial reactions to themselves before officially meeting up at the altar. This is mostly done to get the wedding photos out of the way, so people can go straight into the reception afterward."

"And... do you want me to call over the photographer now?" he hedges.

"No, I want this moment just for us. It can be our little secret, like the start to our marriage was."

"You sure?" he asks, already smiling.

I step out of his grasp and hold out my arms. "Yes, I'm sure. So open your eyes already and compliment me, please."

He laughs as he slowly blinks his eyes open. He goes silent as soon as his eyes land on me. "My God, Luisa. You truly are an angel," he says reverently, running his hand across his scruff.

"Yeah, I guess you clean up pretty well too." I'm taken aback by the sudden wobble in my voice.

My heart threatens to beat out of my chest as Nick takes me in. The sight we must make. A bride twirling around in her billowing dress for her husband, who's donning a cream linen suit, his pants cuffed at the ankles.

He's on me before I even notice him move. Our lips meet in that familiar dance that is uniquely ours.

I speak into his lips. "You ready to get married and start the rest of our lives together?"

He sighs as his watery gaze meets mine. "Forever and a day. This lifetime and the next, remember?"

He intertwines our fingers and tugs me out the door, but not before throwing a wink and a salacious smile my way.

"C'mon, now. It's showtime, wife."

NICK

Daisy's Wedding Day

"I can't believe she's actually going through with it."

Luisa settles into my side as we watch the hundreds of guests enter the ornate church.

"I really thought we could talk her out of it, but it seems like there's no changing her mind," Isabella says solemnly.

"You doing okay? Looks like you're planning on committing a felony or two today." Mateo nods my way.

"Trust me, you don't know the half of it. I have my jet on standby in case I lose my mind and decide kidnapping isn't such a bad idea."

"And to think that she wasn't even allowed to have bridesmaids. What kind of fucked-up family is she marrying into? I hate the thought of her getting ready by herself. No girlfriends around her as she prepares for the biggest day of her life." My wife sulks.

Mateo checks his phone. "Still no response from Coach. Do we think he'll actually come to this?"

Luisa and Isabella share a look.

"Doubt it," they say in unison.

I'm not an idiot. Luke's reaction to my sister's upcoming nuptials has raised more than a few eyebrows among the group.

The only person who may be truly clueless is my sister.

But I haven't exactly had a moment to fester in the frustration those thoughts bring, because my mind's been elsewhere, like how illegal it would be to pull the fire alarm in an eighteenth-century church.

The answer: very.

"I called her earlier, but I couldn't hear much over the hairdryer and someone shouting orders. No doubt her future monster-in-law," Isa complains.

As if it weren't bad enough that my dear old dad was pulling the strings on this relationship, it seems like my sister has managed to find the only person who could give my father's scheming a run for his money. Damien's mother.

My gut churns.

This can't be Daisy's life.

My mother would be livid. She would stomp up those church steps and threaten anyone who dared to stand in the way of her and her baby girl.

God, I wish she were still here today. She would know exactly what to do.

Mateo's eye catches on something. "I'm pretty sure I just saw Coach's truck drive by."

"Really? Maybe he can talk some sense into Daisy. Those two sometimes seem to have a language of their own. I mean, how else could anyone get Coach to spare them five minutes? The man rarely talks to anyone else," Isa exclaims.

"Oh, he'll dig up a few choice words for us anytime we need a swift kick in the ass mid-game, trust me," Mateo muses.

I feel guilty. A few weeks ago, I married the love of my life, again, before our loved ones. Danced the night away barefoot until we could no longer stand on our feet. I enjoyed island life for a blissful week, creating experiences none of us will ever forget.

And my sister gets... this.

A venue that seems more suitable for a funeral than a wedding.

Even the skies have taken protest, breaking our week-long streak of sunny spring days and instead offering up the gloomiest sky known to man.

"It's probably going to rain. And I'm sure we're the last ones to enter the church. Which isn't great, since we're the only people among the hoard of social climbers here to represent Daisy's side of the family. And yes, I'm not including your dad in that roundup," Luisa harrumphs.

"You won't hear any complaints from me," I grumble.

My phone buzzes in my dress pants, and I use the interruption as an excuse to delay the inevitable.

I'm shocked when I see a text from Luke.

Confusion overwhelms me when I read what it says.

LUKE:

> INCOMING. BRACE FOR CHAOS. CALL YOU IN 15 TO DEBRIEF.

I lift my phone and show it to the group. "I'm not close with the man, so can someone tell me if he moonlights as a spy? Or am I missing something else altogether?"

The women read the text in half a second. Must be a talent they've developed thanks to all the romance novels they read.

Their gasps take me by surprise.

So much so that I turn my phone around to reread the text, scrolling up and down to see if I missed something.

Their heads are now on a swivel, surveying the area as if they know something I don't.

"Care to clue us in on what's got you checking the area for snipers?" I ask, exasperated.

"Mateo, is that Coach's truck?" Isa points at a vehicle at the corner of our block, turning our way.

"Yeah, it is. But I wonder why he's heading in the opposite direction of the valet."

The side windows are tinted. I'm sure those aren't street legal, but it's not the time for me to play boy scout.

The driver's side window rolls down, and a grinning Luke comes into view. The sight alone has me taking a step back. I don't think I've seen that man smile in the year that I've known him.

And, honestly, it seems like he's a bit out of practice, because it's looking quite feral from where I stand.

I lift my phone and point at it, hoping he can provide some damn context.

But he simply salutes us as he rolls by.

The women screech, jumping up and down in each other's arms.

I'm ready to demand they tell me what the hell they're yapping about at a time like this when I realize Coach has tossed a white veil through the open window.

That motherfucker.

I chuckle to myself. I'll deal with him later.

But for now, I allow myself to smile as I look up at the sky. The clouds part for the first time all day, and the sun breaks through, shining down on us.

"Would you look at that? Looks like a lovely day for a runaway bride."

Just Married

DAISY

I CAN'T BREATHE IN this damn dress.

I tried telling Vivian in so many ways that I thought it was too tight.

But my future mother-in-law never listens.

And I never stand my ground.

Maybe I just need some air. I'm sure I'd be able to breathe better if I left this stuffy room that reeks of hairspray and burned split ends. Not sure if my hair will ever return to its natural curl after today's ordeal.

I push open the door that leads to the back of the church parking lot and leave it propped open so I don't get locked out.

I don't know why I was expecting a cool, calming spring breeze when I'm in the middle of downtown, where all I can feel is the heat from the building's air conditioning unit and all I can hear are the sirens of a nearby ambulance.

If I don't get a full breath in soon, they might have to circle back and pick me up.

I start pacing but stop when I realize my pointy shoes are giving me blisters. Because of course they are. I look back into the room where my comfy Converses are calling my name.

But I don't think it would be deemed appropriate for me to get married in my scuffed-up Chucks.

A startled laugh escapes me at the thought, and before I know it, I'm bent over with my hands on my knees, laughing uncontrollably.

How the flying fuck did I get here?

The laughter subsides as silent tears run down my face. I need to reel it in before it ruins my makeup, but I can't find the strength in me to care.

Gosh, I really need to catch my breath. I'm starting to feel lightheaded, and I don't need a fainting spell on top of the mess I've made.

A wailing noise brings my attention back to the parking lot. Only then do I realize it's coming from me.

I cover my mouth with my hands. The last thing I need is the paparazzi to get a shot of me having a full-blown meltdown ten minutes before I walk down the aisle.

My father and Damien would never let me hear the end of it.

I close my eyes and knock my head back against the brick wall a few times.

I can't do this. I never should have let this go on this long.

I've had a healthy dose of doubts leading up to today, but last night, something broke inside me. Specifically when Damien and my father cornered me at our rehearsal dinner and told me that I would be quitting my job with the New York Monarchs effective immediately.

Now that I was to become Mrs. Fischer, the wife of a New York senator with clear goals of becoming the next president of the United States.

They didn't ask. They informed me.

If they'd asked for anything else, I would have done it. I always have.

But the Monarchs are my family. The one place I feel truly at home. With people who love me unconditionally.

And I can't leave them. I won't. But I don't know what to do. The clock hangs over my head, and I'm running out of time.

I hear fast footsteps headed my way, and my eyes fly open. With my luck, I might get mugged before meeting my groom.

For a second I consider it might be a great excuse to postpone the wedding.

My thoughts snap back to the present as I realize that it's Luke. He's here, and he's closing the distance between us.

"Y-you came. You actually made it." I hiccup.

"What's wrong? Did he do something to you?" His eyes scan my body, looking for the source of my distress.

"I'm okay. Just taking a little walk around the block. Apparently it's my wedding day. Can you believe that?" My smile must look deranged.

"Daisy, girl. Talk to me. What do you need?" His warm, calloused hands squeeze my bare upper arms, and I sigh deeply.

I can breathe again.

"If only it were that easy, Luke."

"Try me. I'm going to ask you one more time, Daisy. What. Do. You. Need?" he asks through gritted teeth.

I force my breathing to match his as the silence surrounds us.

No longer can I make out the sounds of honking yellow cabs or pedestrians rushing their way back to work after lunch.

It's just me and Luke. And the answer to his question.

"I don't want to marry him," I say on an exhale.

"You don't want to marry him?" he parrots back to me.

I manage to shake my head.

He steps back, releasing his hold on me. His warmth is gone, and the tightness in my chest returns.

He runs his hands over his unruly beard and slowly starts to nod. "All right."

"What do you mean, all right? Everything is far from all right. I have five minutes to get my ass out there." I start to panic again.

He steps closer. "I'm going to make this real simple for you, Daisy." He cradles my face in his hands, his glacial blue eyes searing deep into my soul. "You're not getting married today."

"I'm not?" He shakes his head. "But—but what do I do now? There are over three hundred people waiting in the church. And I don't know if Nick can alert the media and tell them that I've fallen ill or have my father postpone—"

"Do you have any of your belongings in that room?" He nods at the propped door as he gently wipes away my tears.

"Uh... um, yeah. My phone and my weekend bag." I start stepping side to side, my feet now killing me.

Luke looks down at the pointy witch heels poking out from under my dress. "Okay, here's the plan. You're going to gather your things, ditch those heels, and slip into the Chucks I'm sure you sneaked in here. I'll text your brother to prepare for what's about to go down. Then we're going to walk out, nice and calm, and you're going to sit your ass in my truck. Because you, Daisy, are not getting married today."

He smiles widely, and it's a sucker punch to the gut. I've never seen him smile like this, and now I'm glad I haven't, because it's downright devastating.

I shake the absurd thought from my head and try to grasp at what Luke is so clearly trying to communicate with me, but my oxygen-deprived brain is having trouble catching up.

"Okay, so toss the shoes and grab my phone and bag."

I nod, the pieces slowly coming into focus.

"I'm not getting married today." I smile my first real smile in what feels like forever.

"You're not getting married today." His smile now matches mine.

I go to move but stop to turn back to Luke. "Wait, and what are you going to do?"

He grins as he nods at the black truck in the mostly empty parking lot.

"Daisy girl, isn't it obvious? I'll be the one driving the getaway car."

THE END

HOME RUNNER
COMING EARLY 2026

ACKNOWLEDGMENTS

Fair Trade was such a fun ride. It's insane that I enjoyed writing it so much while being in the throes of postpartum.

I must sound like a broken record at this point, but none of my books would be possible without the love and support of my husband, Hugh. Thank you for being my favorite coffee supplier and the best dad to our two little kiddos. We are so lucky to forever call you ours.

Melissa, thank you for taking care of my baby girl. I still chuckle at the sight of me sitting in my room trying to hit word counts while you're a few feet away, trying to wrangle my six-month-old daughter into taking her naps. You are the real hero in this story, and I'm so grateful for your help.

My beta and sensitivity readers have truly become some of my favorite people on the planet. A major thank you to Carla, Esther, Andrea, Lela, Callista, Maria, Brenda, Ayushi, Laura, and Logan for taking this story and making it the best version it could be. I live for our unhinged google doc commentary.

A special thanks to my PA Anlly, who has been such an integral part of the release process for this book. My Dominican queen, thank you so much for everything you have done for me and this project. You made the months leading up to this release so much fun, and I can't wait to see what we come up with next.

My editor Beth, who makes sure I sound like I've had a full eight hours of sleep every night (I've forgotten what uninterrupted sleep is). Thank you for making this the best book it can be while also teaching me ways to become a better writer. And Nyla, for proofreading and making sure this book is ready to be placed in my readers hands. Your friendship and support is something I cherish dearly.

I never thought I would be thanking a former professional baseball player, but here we are! Juan Samuel, thank you for taking the time to talk to me and giving me a behind-the-scenes look into the baseball world. Your nuggets of wisdom will carry on through the rest of the Monarchs series (although forgive me for the artistic liberties I will undoubtedly take).

My friends deserve gold medals for the amount of mayhem I unleash on our group chats. Eternally thankful for Salma, Taylor, Hannah BY, E, Marie, Ruby, Becs, Chip, Elena, and Hannah G. Whether it's author related or simply being a listening ear, I appreciate you all for holding my hand along the way.

To my readers: I honestly don't know what I have done in this life to deserve you, but I will continue writing stories where we can all feel seen and loved. It's the bare minimum, since it's how you make me feel. Until next time!

www.ingramcontent.com/pod-product-compliance
Lightning Source LLC
Chambersburg PA
CBHW030335010826
48973CB00004B/1007